JAKK'S JOURNEY

JAKK'S JOURNEY

Thomas W. Sulcer

Photo and image credits

Artwork/image-collages including cover and diagrams and spaceships and planets by Thomas Wright Sulcer using Sumoware software. Images within collages credits: people/faces/models via Shutterstock; public domain images from Wikimedia Commons include NASA, United States Fish and Wildlife Service (Ramos Keith/Steve Hillebrand/John and Karen Hollingsworth), the United States Department of Energy, Lissa Haggblom, Anna Frodesiak, Fae, Carley, Cutis J, Bob Gries, Stephoccitan, Bain News Service, JPL/California Institute of Technology, ESA and G. Bacon (STScI), Banjoman1, FaizanAhmad21, Melissa M. Escobar, Matt Reeves, Szaaman, Lover of fashion, The Heart Truth. Photo image within collage by Carol Conger Miller used with permission.

For further information, contact the author at tomsulcer @ outlook.com.

Acknowledgments

The author wishes to thank Gary Nissenbaum for his excellent story analysis and constructive criticism which guided development and characterization and which led to substantive improvements. Thanks in addition for insightful comments and suggestions by Carolyn Johnson, Karyn Marshall, Susan Nanney, Andy Roth, Dave Sulcer, and others. Thanks to Geoff Smith of Bibliocrunch for his astute sentence-by-sentence editing, and to the CreateSpace team for interior formatting.

Table of Contents

1

You Don't Know Jakk

Jakk stood. The waiting room outside the principal's office looked like it did on his last visit, with pear-shaped secretaries squinting at screens, the occasional ring of a phone, keyboards clicking, a sharp-tongued plant pointing to the ceiling from its cylinder of dirt. High school was like a ceiling blocking the wild expanse of blue, an education mill to prepare kids for college and not, say, morph them into quasi-aliens. He missed summertime, when he could skinny-dip in a neighbor's pool late at night, but now, in autumn, it was fist-hard chairs, eight hours a day in the factory.

"Have a seat," said the principal.

Jakk continued to stand. He looked down at the beefy biomass, the frames of his glasses indented into the sides of his face where facial fat was unable to protrude. The irritating "have a seat" voice had the same nasal sound that blared on the schoolwide intercom about bake sales, parking pickup rules, the "zero tolerance toward violence policy," a seemingly never-ending message that had caused Jakk to whinny and stomp his foot, provoking a few others to follow suit. But the intercom was only the first of a long list of frustrations and it was only ninth grade. Four years of this?

"High school has rules and procedures," said the principal.

A no whinnying rule? Jakk stomped like a horse counting out an arithmetic problem.

"Got it. You're a horse. In high school, you must learn how to be a human," said the principal.

The principal had a relaxed manner, almost friendly, like they were guys in the locker room talking about, say, the best way to toothpick spinach from teeth, but his smiling veneer must have masked some anger since Jakk found himself exiting school. Three days of mandatory leave. He was not even allowed to get his books. He was proud he stuck to his equine strategy although he sensed the bovine principal had one-upped him. This was not supposed to happen. Every cartoon show insisted that any half-witted kid could outfox any adult. *Learn how to be a human.* How would reading *The Sun Also Rises*, written by an alcoholic who loved bullfights and committed suicide, help Jakk learn how to be a human? As he trudged home, he looked through open classroom windows at students crumpled over desks, fluorescent lighting drizzling like antiseptic rain to wash away the bacteria of thought. If his classmates slurped nonsense, Jakk was a real thinker, a drinker from the trough of truth, the master of his fate. But the arena for action was the school and he had been exiled from it, so he felt semi-ridiculous. School had been getting less fun ever since kindergarten with its crayons and freeze tag, a bait-and-switch to suck kids deeper into the drudgery of school.

Jakk paused at the dreaded cemetery. Why hurry home? He went in. It was hillier than he expected. The class divide continued even here, with the rich dead "living" in fancy marble mausoleums. He sat on the grass, soft and moist in the mid-morning sun. A fly buzzed by. Flies were death's undertakers, laying eggs in decaying flesh, sitting on stones nearby and rubbing their hands together in gleeful satisfaction. Had that fly been born from a dead human, part of his or her biomass escaping death by buzzing about?

He thought about the dead. They had lived, breathed, sat through school, worked, stumbled, died, then were dumped into the grave. None wiggled free, not one prophet or sage or president, no warriors, no school principals, no students. All dead. Sure made the notion of *learning how to be a human* seem pointless—if being human was about living, everybody ultimately failed the test. He imagined writing a Sage app to resurrect images of Buddha and Zoroaster and Confucius and Jesus, sitting around the

Friendly-Doodly ice cream hangout while a user hurled questions at them like Pokémon balls. Say, fellas, is there an afterlife? If so, here's twenty dollars, text me the directions. But they would stare back with mint jubilee in their beards. Jakk liked life but the idea of existence made no sense. Why would a creator make creatures with a fierce will to keep living, only to doom them to die? Life seemed like a mean joke.

Jakk felt gravity nudging him lightly into the grass. It felt like he was wrestling with a styrofoam dummy but he did not take gravity lightly. It was a scary force, double-teaming with death, since the two bullies pushed the formerly living people into their graves and kept them there. Gravity. Grave-ity. Was the only escape skyward? He looked up. The blue sky seemed immense with possibility. Leaves rustled overhead. If there were no answers on Earth, maybe there was an answer in space? In his peripheral vision, he saw a grey clump getting bigger, falling fast—thump! It bounced six feet off the ground, startling Jakk to his feet, bounced again, then rolled to a stop. The squirrel must be dead, but it moved, shook vigorously for ten seconds, and hopped to the nearest tree as if nothing happened. Gravity and death had tried to double team the squirrel, but it defied both by rolling itself into a ball and bouncing.

Jakk walked past Sheela's veritable hacienda, terracotta roof tiles exuding so much Spanishness you'd expect to see caballeros whooping as they galloped back from a rodeo. Her street was a proper street. Houses were spaced properly and looked manicured by a talented stylist. In contrast, Jakk's street was cluttered with houses pressed up against each other, garbage cans in driveways, and neighbors with attitudes fierce enough to set off smoke detectors. A neighbor's storm door sounded like a dog bark when it closed, which set off a chain reaction of dogs barking which his father thought was fun: "barking gives them exercise." It was how canines ranted. Jakk could get students to rant simply by pointing to something and saying "what's with that?"

How things changed. Sheela had been his fifth-grade playmate, competing to jump the highest on her bouncy bed, playing with medieval army men with her dollhouse as the castle. Once they turned her entire second floor into a set-piece battle with warriors with names like "Kloog the Magnificent," "Battlebucket," and "Holy Zowie the Third," until she said she heard her mother's car. His impromptu repurposing of a blanket as a trawling net enabled them to quickly sweep the warriors under the bed—doll death by blanket supernova—just in time for it to have looked like they had been studying all along when her Mom peeked in her room. Another game was "Mount the Horsie"—stallion Jakk on hands and knees and Knight Sheela straddling his back thundered into her sister's room to terrify the stuffed animals. Another time she *really* mounted him—grabbed his waist and started pelvic thrusting and said "I'm the stallion and we're making ponies so whinny with delight," then complained that she was having trouble finding Jakk's vagina. "You need a horsie penis," he said, and when she grabbed a bedside flashlight and turned it on, they convulsed in laughter like cucumber slices tumbling in a salad.

Sheela had the perfect mom. How he wished he had a mother like that! She often served him and Sheela grilled cheese sandwiches in between brush strokes of an oil painting of Wilbur (her horse, which Jakk secretly renamed "Photon Fury"); now the smell of oil paints drying made Jakk hungry. She made him feel like he was a duke vacationing at their country estate. Playdates were always at Sheela's since he was embarrassed by his handyman father—a suspected but never-proven perv and a Mr. Mom who insisted on playing peek-a-boo with other mom's babies despite repeated glares. Jakk expected any day to return to his house surrounded by police leading his father away in handcuffs. To think such a creature had raised him: it was a painful thought that child abuse might have happened to him as a baby, or worse, that he himself had child-abuse DNA lurking inside him. His workaholic mother, half-Indian and half-Chinese, was rarely home. His father once remarked with a smile that "she got her diploma and it was backseat for Buddha ever since."

Playdates with Sheela ceased … by sixth grade, maybe? She took up horseback riding, an expensive pastime that Jakk's family could not afford. A few years later, she blossomed over a summer, like magic, boom, it was unreal, to become more beautiful than her mother. Sheela became *Sheela*, as if an italic wind blew the letters in her name sideways like palm trees beside the ocean, while the letters in his name stayed boring, and perhaps shrunk slightly? She became a top student, winning honors and friends to become the unofficial princess of the grade. When she walked down the hall, it was an event. Her friends were like roadies for her one-woman rock band. Guys stopped to watch her float past like an Egyptian queen being rowed up the Nile. Even teachers admired her. In contrast, Jakk morphed from a promising student into a blotchy-faced boy destined for a bright future as a handyman's helper. Would Jakk one day drive a minivan clanking with greasy tools on missions to unclog toilets or insulate attics or chase raccoons from underneath porches for dubious money and zero respect? People avoided eye contact with him. He became a quasi-invisible sloucher loping through halls and eating lunch with other untouchables—that is, before the suspension.

Jakk walked past rich-kid houses in the affluent part of town, with shrubberies trimmed as if by a skilled Italian barber. A dog on a porch growled at him, backed up by a lawn sprinkler that went *tick tick tick tick tick* like a blind sentry spraying water bullets. Dogs didn't seem to bark at other kids. Could their snooty snouts smell a lack of money? He paused to look at the house. Would he ever own a house one day, complete with a sexy wife? If so, he would measure time not in days but in "fucknights," counting one unit of time for each night of sex. He would look lovingly at his lucky wife and tell her "we've only been married for 755 fucknights but I feel like every fucknight is our first."

The dog kept growling while he was trying to enjoy his romantic musings. Jakk bent low, growled back, and to his surprise, the dog charged fast at him across the lawn, fangs bared. Jakk picked up a stick, held it firmly between both hands, and the dog lunged hard at it, chomping, allowing Jakk to simply swivel the crazed animal into a bush. No more barking. Problem solved. *Lucky for you I found that stick, otherwise you'd be a dead pit bull.*

Jakk's plan was to linger at the library until school let out. He saw his reflection in the library door: almost six feet tall, green T-shirt frayed yet clean except for a line of dog drool, blue jeans, brown hair a bit over-grown, sad eyes looking back. He felt halfway invisible like his reflection. He opened the door slowly. Inside there were cheerful moms with clingy kids, a homeless alcoholic with a fading tattoo of a motorcycle, job seek-ers trawling Internet job boards, a village idiot with glasses hunched over like a professor deep in thought. He pulled out a chair at a table and sat, thinking.

Overhead fans whirred like a jetliner in flight: *suck-hush, suck-hush.* High school *sucked* yet he had to *hush up* about how it sucked. How could he complain that it was a "giant waste of time"? Courses slogged along like a tired army. By reading ahead and using the Internet, he had finished most of the entire high school math and science curriculum by last August. Art and English and history and social studies were boring. That the school would treat its best student so callously after his reasonable complaint about the principal's obnoxious misuse of the intercom—it wasn't fair. Screw high school. Why should he play along—to get into college? What if college was more of the same?

Toys had been fun, but in the past few years his best toys—his train set, his Lego robot warrior that he programmed to attack dolls, his exploding volcano, his Erector Set—had grown boring, eclipsed by the new toy that had to stay zipped in his pants when class was in session. He could not whip it out to play with it during social studies. Worse, his toy required other toys owned by girls to work properly. How could he ask a girl if his toy and her toy could have a playdate? Worse still, he felt guilty whenever his eyes spied thighs or did a swan dive down a cleavage. In a word, high school was torture.

He sensed he didn't know what his life was about. He felt a hunger to have everything now—but what, and how could he get it? His swirl of con-fusion seemed to drift off and be sponged up by books. A librarian offered him a sandwich. She had probably heard that he'd been suspended. He was careful not to get crumbs on the carpet in the lounge while he ate the toasted bread, creamy cheese, turkey, mayonnaise, and soggy lettuce. He felt better.

He explored the library. He could live here. A sign read ENJOY COLLEGE WITHOUT TUITION AND TESTS AND GRADES—YOU CAN EVEN FALL ASLEEP IN CLASS! An entire section of college-level DVD courses on the raid-and-trade Vikings and weren't they cool, early civilizations with chariot wars, nanotechnology, Roman military technology, how to build a computer. Scientists could spray on gold only an atom thick. Cool! The library was a school without teachers! It offered learning with nobody telling him what to learn or at what speed. He didn't have to read literature, flowery and useless and silent on the important stuff like how to change a tire or program a computer or get a woman to have sex. The library wouldn't make him read Hemingway or write about how wonderful citizenship was or endure criticism from a principal about his choice of animal identity. He could study what he wanted to.

This radical thought felt oddly comfortable. As he weighed things, the idea jelled into a feisty determination. He resolved to himself, firmly and indelibly, like signing his own constitution—the constitution according to Jakk—that from now on he would be in charge of his own education. He graduated from his high school at that moment.

The problem was logistics. How could he ditch school, be free like Huck Finn, and move into the library? He was fourteen. Parents and schools had to be handled. He had no money. He didn't even have a beat-up old car or a license to drive it. If he got a job, it wouldn't pay much. He needed food and shelter, and he didn't want to scrounge or beg or have to fend off weird crazed types in a slum or shiver in a hallway of a condemned building like a starving poet.

So what could he do? He could keep getting suspended by annoying the school authorities but that wouldn't last, they could make his life difficult, possibly transfer him to an even weirder school. Fighting them head-on was not smart; rather, what he needed to do, he came to see, was to appear to conform by doing the minimal amount of work to satisfy expectations. If he appeared to be struggling with his courses, the rule-enforcer types might leave him alone. His body had to be in school during his 8 A.M. to 3 P.M. shift at the boredom factory, but how could his mind be elsewhere?

Fate intervened when he happened along a tablet computer. Perhaps a kid forgot it on the shelf? His first instinct was to bring it to the lost-and-found drawer. He hesitated; in his hands was exactly the right tool to bring the library to school. If he sat in the back row in class and kept his mouth shut, he could learn via the tablet. He rummaged through a trashcan and found a grocery bag to conceal it. When he got home, he spray-painted his tablet computer grey after taping over the screen. He wrote a Java program to hide the display, so with the push of a button, his secret world was replaced by an image of a motorcycle.

The next day, Jakk intercepted the school's letter in the mailbox, forged a signature, and mailed it back. Then he headed for the library. Suspension ended and he went back to school, walked the same halls with the same slouch, but he felt like a secret alien. He was on a radical frequency, a Jakk-wavelength, oscillating like a photon, part wave and part particle. He had two sides: his real inner self studying what he wanted at a gallop, and his outer robot self, pretending to be an average student, ambling like an old mare. If anybody looked closely, they might have seen a feisty glimmer in his eyes, but nobody did.

He went through the motions of being a student. He sat in the back row of every class. He could get away with feigning studiousness while reading his tablet and listening for the call of his name or a too-quiet silence. Once when he looked up, everybody was looking at him, so he shrugged and the boring class resumed itself. He studied meaty subjects like computer programming and particle physics and ignored non-issues like sexism. When he overheard a teacher saying how English needed a gender-neutral pronoun in addition to "he" and "she," well, what about the word "it"? Problem solved. Jakk had no interest in poetry or music except for piano. Afterschool theater seemed egotistical and frivolous. *Be an actor?* Why pretend to be somebody else? He handled the increasingly rare teacher intrusions with a quizzical look and shrug, with a jigger of nervousness to foment almost touchable public embarrassment. It worked. They left him alone.

He did enough to earn Cs and Ds by occasionally peering up from his tablet, inhaling a factoid or two from a whiteboard, and turning in five-minute homework assignments. He borrowed audio CDs and DVDs from the library, digitized the files, then studied them on his tablet computer in class, sometimes with an earplug he hid with a lock of his hair. Twice his tablet was confiscated but he said it was needed for notes and he got it back. The school's supposedly high standards proved to be a facade. High school was not about real learning but conformity—daycare for teenagers—and it would not insist on him learning anything. Holding back a slow student another year meant wasting $10,000, so it promoted mediocrity to the next grade. There was a consonance of sorts, a poorly cloaked deal: the school wanted him out, he wanted out, and they were duct-taped together for the sake of appearance like a bad marriage. He was promoted to tenth grade.

When his grades fell from straight As to slink near the bottom, spiced with written complaints from his teachers, his mother insisted that his father read him the riot act. Instead Jakk found himself as a handyman's assistant examining a dripping pipe.

"You dream about becoming a handyman like me," said his father.

Jakk studied the old man's eyes for sarcasm. Handywork was what a man did after failing at being a criminal.

"You need a college education to fix that there pipe," said his father.

"It is a pipe," said Jakk.

"Which is part of a system: plumbing, electricity, and boards—all interacting. What if fixing this here pipe means we gotta move this here electric outlet? You gots to know people because they write the checks, so study anthropology, get the grades, and go to college."

"To fix a pipe?"

"Absolutely! Most important, in college, study women."

"Women are a different species. They're aliens."

"Women are like your computers, you know, things going in and things coming out. What happens inside? Nobody knows, but you gotta study them."

His father's pep talk degenerated from there but had no effect on his lackluster grades. Jakk managed shrinks with blank stares and shrugs, and limited funds soon ended these visits. He knew what he was doing and he stuck to his agenda. He studied computer architecture and physics and military history, nothing showing up on his report card of course, but he gave himself straight As on the report card he only cared about. While his classmates studied citizenship, Jakk studied war. He played computer simulations to refight the battles of Hannibal, and when computer and online human opponents proved inadequate, he wrote programs to simulate tougher opponents. He distilled strategy to geometry—bombs exploded like a sphere; bullets flew in an almost straight line while bending like an inverted second-degree function; battles were lines trying to become circles. He loved astronomy and space, black and boundless, a highway with no speed limit signs, no potholes, no fast food restaurants, no friction, and a need for speed because everything cool was light years away.

It was around this time, early in tenth grade, that an overall objective began to emerge, beautiful in its simplicity, yet so profound he was tempted to buy himself a trophy. Learning how to be a human was about *staying alive*. The main job of being a human? *Not dying.* All humans before him had failed the test. *They did not know how to be human since they wanted to stay alive but failed*—so why should Jakk heed their paltry advice? He would focus his magnificent brain for this grand purpose. He ruled out studying medicine—true, scientists were making progress in prolonging life but not in stemming aging. He researched the question heavily and it became clear that *if* there were ways to stay alive, these methods were not on the Earth. That was where everybody died. So his focus shifted to leaving it. What held him down was gravity, unseen and mysterious but real, so he focused on understanding it. Nobody understood it. There were intricate theories but no real answers. Working through particle physics, he came upon string theory—powerful math with sexy implications. Solve it, and he could figure out gravity, exit the Earth, and search for eternal life.

$$\mathcal{L}_{\beta\nu} \quad \overline{\psi}_{-c}\omega_\alpha Z^{z\alpha} \quad \frac{i}{4}(s_-)_{a\alpha}\partial_-\psi^b_-\overline{\omega}^\alpha Z^\alpha_b \quad \frac{i}{16}(s_-)^\alpha_a(s_-)^a_\gamma\omega_\alpha \overset{\leftrightarrow}{\partial}_-\overline{\omega}^\gamma \quad \frac{i}{32}\overline{\psi}_-\overset{\leftrightarrow}{\partial}_-\psi_-\omega\overline{\omega}$$

$$\frac{i}{8}\partial_-(s_-)_{a\alpha}\psi^b_-\overline{\omega}^\alpha Z^a_b \quad \frac{1}{8}\gamma[(s_-)_{a\alpha}\psi^a_-\partial_-\overline{\omega}^\alpha \quad (s_-)^{\rho\alpha}\overline{\psi}_{-\alpha}\partial_-\omega_\alpha] \quad \frac{i}{4}(s_-)^\alpha_a\partial_-$$

Equation 5 of 17

$$+ \mathcal{E}_{\mu\alpha}\left(K_{\nu\beta}K^{\alpha\beta} - 3K^\alpha_\sigma K^\sigma_\nu + \frac{1}{2}KK^\alpha_\nu\right) + \Lambda_5 + 2K^2)\mathcal{E}_{\mu\nu} - K_{\mu\sigma}K_{\nu\beta}\mathcal{E}^{\alpha\beta} - 4K^{\alpha\beta}R_{\mu\nu\gamma\alpha}K^\gamma_\beta$$

$$+ KK^{\alpha\beta})R_{\mu\alpha\nu\beta} - \frac{1}{6}\Lambda_5 R_{\mu\nu} + 2K_{\mu\beta}K^\beta_\sigma K^\sigma_\alpha K^\alpha_\nu - \frac{13}{2}K_{\mu\beta}\mathcal{E}^\beta_\alpha K^\alpha_\nu + (R - 3K^\alpha_\sigma K^\sigma_\mu)\mathcal{E}_{\nu\alpha}$$

$$V_F = \lambda^2 \frac{e^K}{\det K_i{}^j}\left[\left\{(1+f_+)(1+f_-)\right\} - 2\left\{\left[1 + \frac{|S|^2}{M_{Pl}^2}\left(1 + f'_+\frac{|\phi_+|^2}{M_{Pl}^2} + f'_-\frac{|\phi_-|^2}{M_{Pl}^2}\right)\right]\right\}\right]\frac{|\phi_+\phi_- S|^2}{M_{Pl}^2}$$

String theory was a tough puzzle but math came easily to Jakk. He was adept at computers and he could access powerful Internet databases. He spent months focused on pinors, vectors, supersymmetry transforms, photons, gluons, and gluinos, and the more he worked at it, the more he wondered *how did those little wigglers vibrate?* They were snippets of string so incredibly tiny that no microscope could ever see them. It was all about vibrations. It was like looking at the raised eyebrow of a female and trying to guess which of her hundred billion neurons were firing. There were bigger pieces: 18 quarks—6 flavors with 3 colors each—and 6 leptons—making 24 fermions. *Why were some electrons, called muons, 200 times heavier than regular electrons? Did they not exercise?* There were too many constants, such as the speed of light and the mass of an electron. If Jakk could figure out the string's basic shape, then how it danced with other shapes would become clear.

Since there were so many particles, weird spins, orbits and charges, he simplified the puzzle by associating each particle with one of Sheela's body parts. Her ankles were positrons; her inner thighs were electrons and selectrons (left and right); breasts were bosons (positively charged if tilted outward); her vagina was hopefully not a black hole; her clitoris was the Start Button possibly leading to the Big Bang; and these associations helped him visualize the puzzle pieces of string theory. Her body parts energized him like matter in motion, the puzzle of the universe all there, several hundred parts, sometimes vibrating, spinning, teasing him with muffled exuberance. He thought about it often, how the body parts interrelated, what vibrated what, like if her elbows, spinning one way, could change her ankle's trajectory, that sort of thing. In this manner, he could channel his sexual frustration into a worthy intellectual goal. Jakk was attracted physically to the feminine shape but he had no clue what women were about, no clue whatsoever, and no matter what his dad had said, Jakk doubted that they offered Women 101 in college. Women were painfully mysterious jumbles of emotion and irrationality. If a woman was only a consumer product that arrived in a box with styrofoam and shrink wrap, then at least there might be a manual inside explaining what did what, which buttons to press and in what order, a warranty card, and especially a frequently asked questions section.

Puzzling out string theory via Sheela's body parts kept him perplexed for months, working through the math, having his computers in the lower bunk crunch through the night while he tried to sleep in the bed above it. It often ended in a frenzied bout of masturbation with a squirt of gravity-defying liftoff that hit the ceiling and dribbled down like a sad puppy from the glowing fluorescent sticky-stars. Still, the solution eluded him. He put every variable into a computer program in seventeen simultaneous equations—spinning and charging and revolving—so when it worked, the equations would balance and the program would not hang, but the program always hung. It was frustrating.

In November his 98-year-old piano teacher died. Her death had been expected for such a long time and had not happened, so people had come to believe she was immortal. It was Jakk who came upon her slumped body by her piano. Miss Derrickson, an African American civil rights activist, had taught kids, their kid's kids, and their kid's kid's kids. She loved God, was a good person, had probably never broken even one of the Ten Commandments. She gave turkey sandwiches to the homeless. The community loved her. But none of her deeds saved her. Jakk held her wrist, felt her cold skin, lifted her carefully up on the piano bench, and leaned her against the keys. Gravity had slammed her under the piano but paramedics would not find her there on the floor. He kissed her on the cheek, said "Bye, Miss Derrickson," phoned 911, pointed his middle finger at the ceiling and said "I hate you, God." Just in case God existed. What did it mean? It meant no piano lesson next week.

Science Olympiad

Can YOU program a computer
to mimic a real live breathing human?

CONTEST RULES: Four students per team. Program computer to have conversation (1) read typed sentence (2) reply with typed sentence (3) repeat. RESTRICTIONS: Humans and computers limited to 5000 word dictionary. NO: why questions, conditional or subjunctive tense, past tense, abbreviations, misspellings, hardware modifications, Internet connections, if-then sentences, contractions. Conversations have to be about the subject of dating. Five players (4 human, 1 computer) behind a wall. Is the other player a human or computer? Team with most correct guesses advances to the finals.

NEW JERSEY is....
not just a parking lot
between Philadelphia &
New York, much more
than smokestacks along
the turnpike, remember
it is YOUR state so
please love it like it loves
you!

Competition to be held at Rutgers University

In January, still tenth grade, he was offered a spot on the Science Olympiad team—odd because of his mediocre grades. He would have declined except Sheela was captain. This year's contest was to program a computer to pass the Turing Test—to successfully mimic a human. Could team members ferret out the opposing team's computer in five minutes by typing back and forth? At the afterschool meeting, Sheela gave orders like a CEO: two other students would research questions while Jakk would program the computer and when the two protested, she said "sorry, we're going to win." That was that. Meeting adjourned. She must have remembered he loved computers. And was an excellent choice: he knew Java and AIML and fuzzy logic and intelligent agent modules. Maybe she saw him lugging a computer from the dump?

Next day the computer arrived. Jakk took it home and opened the cover: a 64-bit processor, solid-state hard drive, and RAM galore. It was a powerful machine. He decluttered the hard drive by removing ads and memory hogs such as the Sidebar and drop shadows. To save space, he converted each of the contest's 5,000 allowed words into a two-bit UTF-8 code. He found a database of real-world conversations and downloaded paired sentences.

He wrote the main program in a month. An incoming string of typed text would be forwarded to two controllers. The first would parse the string grammatically using logic—for example, "Are you friendly and generous?" would parse to "Are you friendly?" *and* "Are you generous?" The second would search for similar paired sentences—for example, if the string "Is [name] friendly?" was typically followed by sentences like "[Name] is snarky when hungry," then it would offer that reply, substituting in a name. A master controller would remember what was said and check for inconsistencies.

Diagram of Jakk's computer program

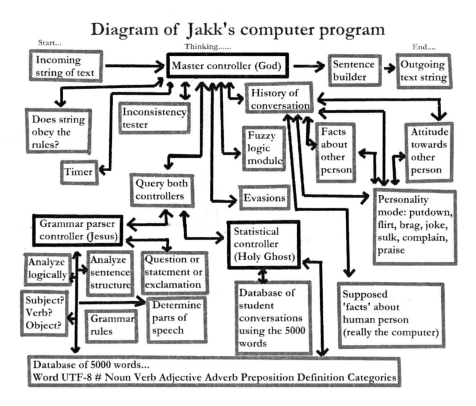

Jakk was proud of his design. It was an improvement over typical chatterbots as it used fuzzy logic with truth values between 0 (false) and 1 (true), which allowed for guesses. It could go into show-off mode, flirt mode, putdown mode, brag mode, snark mode, complain mode—ideal for New Jersey—so its character could appear consistent. It took another month to debug it, test and retest it. Finally, he took it to school.

"Do you have a tattoo?" Sheela typed.

Yes. Who are you? replied Jakk's program.

"Sheila," she typed, as she had to use a spelling from the list of 5,000 approved words.

Hello, Sheila.

"What is your tattoo?"

You naked on my motorcycle.

The program deduced Sheila was female so it bounced into flirt-mode. Jakk gave the computer a male personality since most contestants would be male. "Naked on my motorcycle" was figured out statistically; some guy must have made a similar comment somewhere on the Internet. Sheela told Jakk that he'd done a good job. He smiled. He felt like a hero.

The Science Olympiad was at the state university, Rutgers, in a large auditorium with a temporary divider, so each team had a side. The five team members (four humans, one computer) had consoles connected to the unseen opposing team; only the judges knew who was connected to the computer. Forty-seven teams were whittled down to eleven by lunchtime, since most computers did not work, and several teams were disqualified when judges decided the students were deliberately trying to mimic computers. Jakk's team advanced to the final match, which displayed the typed conversations on a large screen. Students and parents and a few reporters watched Jakk's computer joust with an unseen human opponent.

"Are men the dominant sex?" typed the opposing human.

What is your name?

"Morgan."

Men are the dominant sex.

"Please clarify."

Women cannot program computers.

The reaction from the crowd was scattered chuckles, a few hoots, and a subdued boo. Morgan's "please clarify" was a clever way around the restriction against "why" questions. And Morgan turned out to be a woman—Jakk's computer must have assumed Morgan was a man—and she correctly guessed that she was indeed interacting with a computer. Further, Jakk guessed wrong—his opponent was a human, not a computer. So Sheela's team came in second. It was heartbreaking to watch Sheela sit while smug Morgan waved her cheap trophy and blabbed "No student today could be that sexist" to reporters. Jakk had programmed for months. What did he get? Blame.

On the bus ride home, he sat alone and watched the turnpike's industrial landscape in the night, smokestacks with red lights blinking to ward off low-flying planes. Did Sheela think that Jakk believed that women couldn't program computers? Well, so what if he did kind of think that? He had to pull stuff from the Internet quickly and if sexist stuff got sucked in by accident, that wasn't his fault. Second place in the state, wasn't that impressive enough? He was proud of his accomplishment, dammit.

They went back to being strangers, avoiding eye contact in hallways. A reporter picked up the sexist angle and feminist bloggers kept the dumb incident alive. Then came an editorial in the *Star-Ledger* about sexism in the computer industry that, among other things, accused high schools of reinforcing sexism, and mentioned Sheela's high school by name, with a link to a YouTube video that replayed the conversation between the Jakk-box and smug Morgan that practically went viral. True, when his English teacher had spent a week on sexism the previous semester, Jakk had been reworking his equations and hadn't paid attention. And Jakk hadn't paid attention a few weeks ago to the teacher's cutesy lesson about why spelling matters: Jakk looked up to see the second chart held by the smiling teacher that said *The boy helped his Uncle jack off a horse.* Lower-case j. The class thought this was funny. Jakk thought it was stupid. Masturbation as a topic was so repressed in school that the only way it could be handled, so to speak, was to joke about horses being jacked off, an animal that didn't have to sit in boring classrooms with genitals covered by blue jeans. Horse sex was simply lifting a tail and doing it right there on the trail. Stallions didn't have to buy roses or sing songs or ask mares how their day went. Horse sex was simple: clasp the female around the waist and get to it. It was why humans could ride horses—horses felt the clasping when being saddled up, which made them relax like they were being fucked, so humans could mount them. See, Jakk didn't need history teachers or biology teachers; he could figure this stuff out on his own. *Why weren't women more like horses?* When a few knuckleheads looked at Jakk, hoping he might whinny, he shrugged and returned to his tablet.

In April, it happened. He had a breakthrough. Sheela helped, although she didn't know it, so she was no longer in his personal doghouse. Girls were playing volleyball while boys watched from the sidelines, waiting for their turn. Volleyball was boring but he liked watching women tumble about with legs splayed in exciting vulnerability. Sheela dove for the ball and her body in mid-flight—ankles near earlobes—one hand outstretched with the other rotated backward—airborne thighs—the image stuck in his brain, stopping him, and then he saw it—six leptons, six quarks, plus two-thirds, minus one-third, their respective antimatter particles aligned. That was it! The position! So close to her elbows but not too close, in that Goldilocks state, spinning so everything jibed. Could it be the solution to gravity? He ran home without signing out and plugged in Sheela's splayed ankle and knee data points with one inner thigh in the 2 P.M. position as he remembered. His computer didn't hang! Amazing. He triple-checked the logic. It clicked. So simple! Sheela's past injustices were more than repaid by her volleyball dive, even if he did not get a long enough glimpse of her underpants.

In time the thrill of discovery gave way to the cold calculus of reality. Sooner or later others would make the same discovery. It was only math. Mathematicians watched volleyball too. If he published it, he would get credit but not much money. And what if he was wrong? He decided not to reveal his discovery but test it instead. If he built a spaceship that traveled faster than light, he could explore the galaxy, or monetize his invention and buy a mansion twenty times bigger than Sheela's. He could become a rich asshole!

He took over the garage on the pretext of doing a science experiment for school. It was a basic two-engine design: the first would cancel Earth's gravity and the second would grab the moon's, so there was no need for rocket fuel. He could traverse space by grabbing gravity from distant stars and stop by grabbing gravity behind him. The idea of recycling so much energy would make his father's environmentalist Unitarian friends' nipples erect. He experimented with plastic and metal tubing, reversing wires, pulsing electrons in double-alternating circuits. He worked in afternoons, not evenings, in case neighbors became curious about random glows from the garage, wearing goggles and an anti-dust respirator. Once a spark caught on sawdust and as he was peeing out the flames, his father burst in and said "A space creature with his own fire extinguisher!" and joined in the firefighting effort, their streams crossing like swords until the dynamic duo blackened the embers.

A few months later his first gravajakk was on his workbench, made from a car tire rim, empty inside with a bottom and two layers of reciprocating tubes encircling it, hooked up to 48 D-cell batteries. He flipped the toggle switch, shook baby powder inside the gravajakk, and the grains hovered, suspended, and slowly fell to the bottom! Earth's gravity was flummoxed! The hammer fell slowly from his hand and landed on the concrete with a soft thud. It worked! His brain flared with a neural-intellectual orgasm, a convulsion of happiness. He was the first human to figure out gravity! He did it all by himself! He imagined parades in his honor. Maybe the planet Uranus would be renamed Jakk—that would stop the jokes! Since he could patent the gravajakk but not the solution to string theory, he reckoned he should fly faster than light to clinch his fame, and until then, he would keep his discovery secret.

During eleventh grade, he began building a spaceship from parts scavenged at the dump. The vehicle grew sporadically from the shell of an old Honda Odyssey minivan. He removed the windshield and seat, built a place to stand with a bubble top for his head, found air tanks and a heater.

He hinged the garage roof to open like tipping one's hat sideways. His father drove him to a dump near the airport where he found a discarded pressure gauge and altimeter.

Senior year, at lunch, he hung out with a nerdy out-group who loved video games and techie talk.

"In *Huck Finn*, the most frequent character is the letter 'e,'" said one.

"No it is the space character—everywhere, pushing words apart, free and invisible," said Jakk.

Jakk spoke in a newscaster monotone like a scientist describing a past experiment to colleagues. It gave his lunchmates a false sense that they knew him. They hung together, the four of them—or was it seven, he never bothered to count—but they didn't do things outside of school as a group. They got top grades in math and science (except Jakk) but flopped in the coolness department. They debated whether isolating the Higgs boson would bring faster-than-light video phoning. They found sports boring. They seldom talked about sex, although the subject of building a robot that could give blowjobs came up several times. As time went by, Jakk started to tolerate these guys. Even though they knew his grades were lackluster, they considered him their intellectual peer.

2

Hit the Road, Jakk

The day of his experiment was like most others, though he walked to school with a slight bounce in his step, glided through halls like a windsurfer, and eagerly went over checklists on his tablet. April 1 would have a full moon with gravity ripe for the grabbing.

While waiting for history to begin, however, he sensed something was amiss. There was a slight giggle. Classmates glanced at him with caution. Sheela sat with legs crossed, her blonde hair hanging like a curtain of death, staring at him like she could see through him but she did not like what she saw. Their eyes met for a few dangerous seconds. What was going on? She gazed at him like a cat gazes at a helpless bird on the grass. He broke off first. As he pretended to read his tablet, he felt her eyes upon him as if she was checking out his body in the same way a man visually breathes in the body of a woman. His thighs felt warm. He heard rushing air. She was blowing up a balloon, the long slow whoosh, breath, whoosh, breath, and a pink balloon grew in size until it was practically bursting, a cylindrical clown-style one like at kids' parties to be twisted into giveaway toys. She held it in one hand, angled it upward like an erection while looking at Jakk, then relaxed her grip and air rushed out, the balloon deflated, flopped earthward. She sat there, smiling, holding it while the class snickered. Jakk also laughed nervously. He was irked at himself for laughing, even though he was surely the butt of her mysterious joke. His psyche was in panic mode, red lights flashing danger, but luckily the teacher began the lesson.

Why would his former playmate and the school's unofficial princess-valedictorian focus her perplexing demonstration on him? He had done nothing wrong. He was not in her social circle. He thought of her like argon, a noble gas that did not combine easily with other elements, with a fixed number of electron friends orbiting and Jakk was not one of them. Was there a miscommunication? Maybe Sheela was simply degenerating into a typical suburban female whose blood bubbled with sarcasm. Could she somehow have known about his upcoming space voyage and the balloon was a comment he was not going to lift off? Was it a comment about his sexual inadequacy? That did not make sense either, since there was nothing sexual between them other than Jakk, like every other guy in school, loved looking at her body. Still, it was nice to get even negative attention from such a beautiful woman, as if he mattered. But so what—in a few months, after graduation, she would be out of his life.

At three in the morning his alarm clock beeped and he crept past his parents' room, walked downstairs, closed the driveway door gently, and opened the garage door. His minivan spaceship seemed to smile with possibility. He stood in the captain's stand and smiled, enjoying the moment. He went through his checklist: batteries, food, winter coat, extra socks, air tanks, heater, gravajakk, munchies, tablet computer, camera. It was simply a test drive; he would return soon with photos from space and be Earth's most eligible bachelor, famous and rich and young. He pushed the garage roof open with a pole to reveal a welcoming night sky. He flipped on the gravajakk and its coils shone with fluorescent wonder, alternating greens and blues neutralizing Earth's gravity. He pushed the pole through a hole in the floor and his *Jakk Jalopy* rose slowly over the garage and hovered; he poled the roof shut.

It was a beautiful night with a slight breeze and an April chill. He pointed his second gravajakk at the moon and felt the tug of its gravity. He floated up like a hot air balloon. He saw his neighbor's houses, the Unitarian church, Sheela's house, the grand hotel, the dark cemetery, the high school. He put on his winter coat as he rose faster and faster. He looked for military planes checking out the unexplained blip on their radar, but he did not see any, and now he was already higher than they could fly. Earth's spherical shape became clearer. Stars became brighter. He imagined Earth as a giant mother, opening her arms, releasing him, unloving him, as if he had figured out how to slip through the emotional bonds of her love and float away to some unknown place. In response, he held out his hands as if to tell the Earth that he still loved her warmth and oxygen and water and trees and humans and rocks and clouds, that his departure did not mark a break in this love. He tossed a pink tennis ball, caught it, tossed it again, and as he got higher, it did not come down as quickly as before. Gravity's grip was loosening. He put a scuba regulator into his mouth to breathe. Once he was high enough, he turned off the gravajakk and hovered. He was like any object in the universe—a comet or floating rock or planet or star and he felt infinitely small. Space extended in every direction, on and on, and its immensity thrilled and scared him.

It was time to test the speed limit. While the most powerful sources of gravity were the sun or Jupiter or Saturn, they were too close to allow room to accelerate quickly enough without risking a collision, so he focused his gravajakk on Betelgeuse, a red supergiant some six quadrillion kilometers away. Since it was so far away, its gravity was so weak that it took a long time before he felt even the slightest tug, but slowly, gradually, he inched forward, picking up speed, with Earth slowly shrinking as space grew darker. He saw Saturn with its rings off to the right, and soon he passed the solar system. Stars began to come at him like snowball specks hurled to the side. He was hauling. Stars were beginning to look like bent lines. He expected his jalopy to rattle or shake but it seemed eerily still.

The sky turned completely gray and the stars disappeared. What happened? He was moving faster than light! He did it. Humans were not doomed to be stuck in their light cones for eternity. Great! He accelerated to several times the speed of light so when he stopped and turned around, he could record his position with his camera to prove faster-than-light speeds were possible. He turned off the gravajakk, pivoted it backward, but could not grab gravity behind him since everything was gray. He could not locate the sun behind him.

He realized the enormity of his mistake.

He could not stop. He stopped accelerating but still he was probably moving at warp nine. He tried focusing the gravajakk directly behind him to guess where the sun was. It did not work. The pink tennis ball was in his face so he hurled it out the window to watch it disappear into the gray. He became frantic, pointing the gravajakk everywhere, hoping to God that Betelgeuse had exploded so there would be no star to crash into, praying to Jesus to rescue him even though he did not believe in Jesus, flipping switches, putting his arm out the window to try to grab air to slow down but there was no air. There was a thud, the air bag whomped open while his standbelt grabbed him, another thud, then things went blank.

Jakk slowly opened his eyes. He was alone in a room, white and bright, one with *no doors*. Was this heaven? Maybe he had been wrong about an afterlife. He regretted giving God the middle finger. He felt alive. Maybe he was immortal? He stood slowly. His *Jakk Jalopy* was gone. There was Earthlike gravity. The rectangular room had large windows—was that how he got inside? His clothes were changed; he wore a sleeveless muscle shirt attached to a mini-skirt, leaving his private area open from below. Maybe he would have to master the feminine art of crossing legs to prevent mental photography by prying eyes? There were no buttons or zippers and the outfit felt smooth like an egg yolk without being slimy. His shoes were made of the same stuff. There was not much else in the room except a mattress and pillow and blanket.

He walked to a large window. He saw a city by the sea, vehicles gliding on air, sidewalks with strange creatures as well as humanlike beings like himself, and weird skyscrapers, some of them floating, rectangular and oval shapes of blended purples and oranges—some resembled Christmas tree ornaments, bulging in odd places like overdressed ladies emerging from SUVs at a country club. Unlike Earth, the horizon curved upward. He pushed on the window, gently, and it opened! He felt a breeze, balmy and summery. The building was next to the coast, with waves glimmering in sunlight, yet there were no smells of ocean. Maybe he was too high up?

He noticed that he was not breathing. Why not? He breathed in and out to assure himself that breathing was possible. Was he dreaming?

When hours went by and nothing happened, he decided he was either a prisoner or was waiting to appear before a heavenly judge, and a slow panic started to sink in. He found he could sink his fingers into the flat wall material about an inch deep, and use the fingerholds to climb the walls and parts of the ceiling, although digging through the wall proved impossible. His fingerholds disappeared and the wall kept reverting to its flat shape. Leaning out the window, he discovered that the building's exterior was unfortunately not made of the same climbable material.

Across the street, there was a video of himself on a giant display—he jumped and the image of him jumped. Why was he on television? Curiously, his acne was gone. He felt his smooth face. He tried summoning creatures on the street below but nobody paid attention. He was too scared to cry. Would he spend eternity in this room? He regretted not sharing his discovery before he left Earth. Everybody there would continue to think that Jakk didn't know jack. He would never monetize his gravajakk contraption, read about himself being the first human to break the light barrier, or drive by school in a $300,000 sports car and not offer Sheela a ride. His mind threatened to hang in an infinite loop of horror. Fear was like a nasty virus inside his mind's operating system. He imagined borrowing a cell phone to call his father for a ride—"You're on Betelgeuse, son? Oh, I'll be there in fifteen minutes." He wanted to roll himself in a ball of disbelief. He scrambled to prepare arguments about why God shouldn't cast him into Hell, despite not believing in God not long after he stopped believing in Santa. He never murdered, never did drugs … okay, maybe he should have returned that tablet but he had been planning to do so one day. He found fear to be freeing: since death was imminent, he had nothing to lose by fighting the fear, fighting death, like a boxer going down swinging.

If he was a captive, then his captors were highly advanced technologically since they could stop his spaceship and keep him alive. How did they do that? Their vehicles flew without evident propellers so they could manipulate gravity just like Jakk. Since there were diverse creatures with multiple limbs, convoluted heads, squiggling ways of walking, some like octopi with tank treads, plus human-looking creatures, it was probably a tolerant world. But why imprison him and not the other humans? If they wanted to kill him, they would have; if they wanted to free him, they would have done that too. Perhaps they were trying to figure him out. Were they afraid of him? He must be interesting since he was on television. Had he traveled across the galaxy to become a zoo animal for curious eyes? He tried using his arms to spell the word "friendly." He tried blowing kisses from the likely direction of the unseen camera. He shouted that this was against the Geneva Convention. He felt foolish, helpless, and angry. He was a good guy. He didn't mean any harm. The sun did not sink into the horizon but dimmed so the shadows of buildings and people simply became grayer. Street activity lessened, night set in. He slept.

He awoke in sunlight. There was a white cube on the floor, knee-high, *and a fellow prisoner*, human-sized, wrapped in gray, face bandaged, with *humanlike toes* sticking out. Jakk said "hello." It did not respond. He walked over and touched it gently on what was possibly the shoulder. It flinched but said nothing, so Jakk walked over to the window and stared out at the cityscape. Why would prisoners be given a scenic view? He hadn't eaten but he wasn't hungry—why not? He said hello again to the fellow prisoner, who stood up, began walking with arms outstretched like a blind person, bumped into the cube, put forth hands—human-looking hands with five fingers; Jakk counted twice—felt the box for ten seconds, and ambled over to the wall. Jakk touched the box too. Nothing happened.

If he was on television, what could he do to attract attention, earn himself some sympathy, or even a rescue? He regretted spurning school musicals. He faced the window, untangled his hair with his fingers, and sang:

Who are you, you Hugubuian Hugubus?
Why do you make me sing for clues?
My name is Jakk
I shall not attack
I am not an animal for your zoos!

Jakk thought he heard a slight giggle. Did his fellow prisoner understand him? He cautiously walked over to the creature, ready to jump back if necessary, and slowly removed the bandage from its face. It was a human-sized face with a mouth *but no nose and no eyes and no eyebrows*, like a desert of sand with a bump where a nose might have been, smooth skin from the hairline to mouth, a genetic deformity.

"Who are you?" asked Jakk.

"Who are you?" It was a woman's voice.

"You're human! You speak English! I am Jakk."

Jakk learned she was not human but Andronian, born on an asteroid in the orbit of Sirius, grew up on Canopus, and they were indeed prisoners. It was odd speaking to a person whose face consisted of only a mouth. He did not know where to look. But although it was somewhat unsettling having a talking biomass as a fellow inmate, it was much better than being alone. She could speak and understand English because of the translation cube. They were on a planet orbiting Betelgeuse. When she would not reveal her name, he decided to call her Reena.

"Who are Hugubuians?" Reena asked.

"My name for our captors," he said.

"Why are you here?"

"The Hugubuians think I did something wrong?"

"What did you do?"

"I don't know."

"Where are you from?"

"Earth."

"Where is that?"

He did not know how to answer this question.

"Why did you come to Betelgeuse?" she asked.

"To be the first human to fly faster than light."

"Travel by yourself?"

Why was Reena asking him questions? Was she a spy to report on him? An eyeless spy did not make sense. He found out they blinded her. Would Jakk be blinded next? He looked out the window to savor the view in case it was the last thing he ever saw.

He wondered if she could read his brain. He stared at her and thought *Reena would you like the honor of having sex with me?* She noticed a lull in the conversation.

"What are you thinking?" Reena asked.

"I was wondering if you had any brothers or sisters."

"One of each."

"Oh."

Experiment finished. She could not read his mind.

"What will happen to us?" he asked.

"We will be hurled by trebuchet into Betelgeuse."

"But why—what did I do? I have rights. I am a U.S. citizen. *I am from New Jersey!*"

"You did something wrong because you are here."

"No hope?"

"Nope."

If the aliens wanted to kill them, then why were they still alive? He studied the view again. He observed what was not there: no trebuchet, no baby strollers, no creatures with uniforms, no clocks, no garbage cans, no boats, and no giant balloons to hop on. If Reena was right about imminent enhurlment, he had to act. If he jumped out the window, he would splat on the sidewalk and gravity would get him that way. He couldn't dig through the wall. Could he rework his clothes to resemble a guard's? Unlikely, since he didn't know what they looked like. Could he play dead and overpower orderlies carting him away? He doubted that would work. He inventoried resources: clothes and mattress and pillow and blanket and shoes. That was it. Then he thought: *Reena's mind* was a resource.

"Suppose we lowered ourselves one story. Could we break into windows below us?" he asked.

"There are probably guards on every floor."

"Could we lower ourselves to street level?"

"Yes, but there are guards there too."

"How can we lower ourselves?"

"A blanket fiber."

Jakk tucked his blanket between them to shield it from unseen cameras. He tried tugging at an edge. He finally dislodged a single thread, pulled, and it kept coming out. He tried to break it. It was incredibly strong.

"Will it support our weight?" he asked.

"Yes."

"This is our escape."

"They will get us on the street."

Jakk casually walked to the window, looked down, and estimated twelve stories by comparing it with the building across the street. He lowered the thread one story, pulled it back, and counted how many times that length wrapped from his palm to his elbow. There was a flagpole jutting from the building. In window reflections, he counted six stories down to the flagpole. He remembered how sneakers were sometimes suspended on wires above the intersections of his hometown. If he could wrap the thread around the flagpole, then he could pendulum seaward, Robin-Hood-style, possibly. He tied a shoe to the fiber, tugged it firmly to make sure it held, pulled out the fiber into a circle and looped a handhold with the rest of the attached blanket, and made release knots to lessen the jerk when the fiber tightened. He rehearsed the risky jump in his mind. If the timing was wrong, if a gust of wind threw him off, if the fiber broke, if the flagpole broke, if the knot came undone, if he released at the wrong time—then he would die. It was easy to think logically through this new "string theory," but the prospect of actually acting on it was terrifying. He sensed he lacked the nerve. And could he trust Reena? If he told her his plan and she didn't want to swing with him, then she might be a spy, but that was a good thing, since it meant the aliens were trying to understand him and might not execute him after they realized he was a good creature. So he told her his plan.

"I will swing first," he said, as if it was a done deal. There was a long pause.

"No, we swing together," she said.

So she wasn't a spy and they were slated for execution. Neurotransmitter molecules of horror tried to reclog his synapses; he took a deep breath and tried to relax. A key would be getting sufficient arc on the swing, so he would have to jump hard to the right, fall close to the pavement, swing out left, and release at a 45 degree angle to be thrown into the sea.

"Please bring me with you," she said.

Did he have to bring her along? She doubled their weight and her blindness might slow him down. But she had told him about the strength of the thread in his blanket and warned him that he was going to be executed. She knew some things about this place. In the short term, he was better off alone; in the long term, he was better off with her. He sighed.

"I'll hold the loop, and you hold on to me," he said. "If we hold it together, we might not release at the same instant."

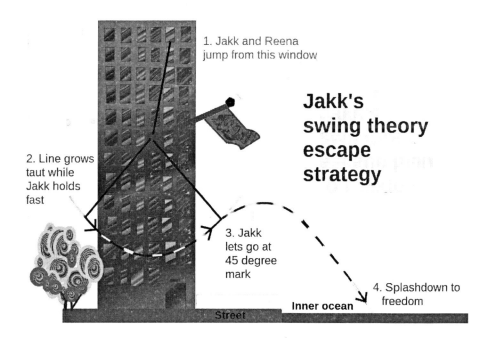

1. Jakk and Reena jump from this window

Jakk's swing theory escape strategy

2. Line grows taut while Jakk holds fast

3. Jakk lets go at 45 degree mark

4. Splashdown to freedom

Inner ocean

Street

Despite lacking eyes, she somehow seemed to brighten, and he thought how sweet it was whispering his plans to this human-bodied creature, how he loved watching her lips move and feeling her breath on his ear, being close to her.

"When we hit the sea, we must swim underwater, very far, away from pursuing watercraft, until we reach the other side," she said.

They waited until nightfall. He lowered the shoe out the window to flagpole height, swung it to the right, lowered it slightly, swung it to the left until it wrapped around the flagpole a few times. He yanked hard on the line—real hard, almost wishing that it would break, but it held. He made a hand-holder of ten loops past the release-knots. He put both hands in the loops and squeezed hard and balanced on the window ledge. She followed his voice to the ledge, climbed up, put her arms around his back, and swung her legs around his hips. He was scared. *This is as close as I'll ever get to making love to a woman before I die*, he thought. He wondered how hard that first initial jolt would be at about four stories high. Fear focused him. He and she were a united bundle of life, a desperate couple at a dangerous dance, bungee jumping on their first date to the death. It was time.

"Ready?" he whispered.

"Yes."

He lifted her to the right, balanced on the ledge, held the loops taut, then let himself tilt to the right as if he was beginning to fall, waited for the angle to be right, then jumped with all of his strength while holding the loops with all his strength. Would his hands be strong enough? They accelerated like bungee jumpers, his stomach crept to his throat, they twisted slightly and were pulled to the left as the ground approached fast. He felt the *click click click* as the knotted releases gave as planned, slowing their descent, and he raised up his thighs to secure her further, and then the loops yanked hard, and he held on, barely, straining with all his might, swooping low to the ground, perhaps ten feet over the sidewalk. He guessed when they'd reached the 45-degree angle happened (since his view was sideways), and let go, the two of them free-falling seaward, feet first. She squeezed him tight. He wrapped his arms around her.

It felt like plowing into a snowbank. His butt and elbows hurt. Water was everywhere, in his nose, refreshing until he worried about drowning, but then he remembered that he did not have to breathe, and he relaxed. He tested his arms and legs—they weren't broken.

He tried to look around in the dark water. He felt which way the bubbles went to determine which way was up. Where was she? He swam deeper, looked up, saw a silhouette in the fading light, swam to her. Was she hurt? They took turns putting their hands on each other's faces, nodding *I am okay.* Were there sharks or barracuda or jellyfish to contend with? He should have asked earlier. He resisted an instinct to swim to the surface. He put her hand on his waist, and together they became an ungainly sea creature. Jakk swam turtle-like, reaching and pulling, trying to find a consistent motion while remaining together, her hand holding his waist. He wondered what it might be like to make love to her. He swam down, down where it was so dark that if they separated, they would not find each other again. The sea floor felt smooth like the bottom of his town's swimming pool. They swam for several hours until the sea became a lighter blue. They were in a few feet of water. He stopped, touched her face, put her hand to the surface, brought it back down. She put his hand on her face and nodded yes. Carefully he stuck his head above the surface, scanned the horizon like a submarine periscope, then motioned her to the surface.

"I see a shoreline, empty beach, in the sea far off a moving light," he whispered.

"Searchers," she whispered back.

"What should we do?"

"Find a spaceship. We have to get off this planet."

Barefoot, Jakk led her to the shore, up the beach, dripping in the warm night. She began feeling around the middle of his garment. What was she doing? He heard a click, a hiss, felt warmth over his body, and within seconds he was dry. Just like that. She dried herself similarly. They walked up a slight hill and in a clearing there was a road with several unattended vehicles. He described several.

"A dune buggy can do sublight speed," Reena said quietly.

"We have no keys," said Jakk.

"Flip it over."

Jakk tugged on the side and to his surprise the hovering vehicle flipped over, exposing the engine, which Reena probed with her hands. Soon it lit up and began humming. Jakk flipped it back. The buggy had only one long seat, no steering wheel, a confusing dashboard, no roof, and no rollbar. It looked like a souped-up motorcycle. *This was a spaceship?* Jakk sat on it; Reena climbed behind him, her thighs warm against his. There were two pedals.

"How do I drive it?" he said.

"Right pedal is forward, left pedal is reverse," she said.

"How do I steer it?"

"Tug the round sphere. Hug the land."

He could drive it forward, loop backward, go in any direction. He did a 360-degree roll. The vehicle apparently had its own gravity, as Jakk and Reena were not pulled toward the ground when upside down. He made for the mountains, avoiding lights from nearby dwellings, until he found a clearing in a forest and parked. She felt the compartments and handed him what looked like digital binoculars. He looked around. It was starting to become light.

"The main gate will be closed. Roads will be watched," Reena said.

"Why does the horizon curve upwards?" he asked.

"We are inside a hollow sphere which contains cities and lifebeings and water."

"So where is the outside?"

"Beneath us."

Unlike Earth, Hugubu had rim gravity which pulled things to the shell. That was weird. Things inside the shell were held to the shell by gravity; things outside the shell were similarly held, so there was no risk of falling to its empty center.

"What powers the sun lamp?" Jakk wondered.

"Betelgeuse," said Reena.

"Ah."

In another compartment, he found what looked like a pistol with an LED display. He pointed it at a tree; the target glowed yellow. He described this to Reena.

"Great! We can blast through the main gate!" she said.

"You mean kill them?" he asked.

"They will kill us."

"My high school has a zero tolerance policy."

Jakk didn't know where that thought had bubbled up from. He had never thought much about right and wrong but resented that the issue had been thrust upon him. His main concern was survival. Maybe Reena was a husband-murdering terrorist who would kill him once she no longer needed him to escape. Maybe the aliens erased her face to prevent her from wiping out an entire village. He stowed the gun in the compartment. Still, she *felt* friendly. He wanted to swap out the murdering thoughts in her head in the same way his handyman father would swap out a broken toilet out of a bathroom: loosen the base nuts, lift the cracked porcelain, empty the soiled water to a bucket (easy does it!), clean up, attach a new one—now who will have the honor of the first poop?

His mind was wandering. His brain nagged him with repeated hints about how pleasant a quick nap could be. That was how you get caught. The beach where they had landed was swarming with searchlights, about twenty minutes behind them.

"How much ground is between us and outer space?" he asked.

"A few meters."

"Can we break through by hammering or ramming or blasting?"

"Probably not."

"Was the shell hollowed out from rock?"

"No, it was assembled."

"Then there must be holes created when it was built. I'll look for molding."

It was how French carpenters hid the space between wall and ceiling. His father had taught him that. Jakk gazed at the irregular hillside. He noticed several flat sections between two smooth mounds, as if to hide a joint between two sections of mountain. They drove there. When he yanked at the foliage, it came up in a clump, revealing a large circular doorway. He tried to turn the twelve foot wheel-handle but it wouldn't budge. She felt the wheel with her hands and clicked something. He turned it and it opened. Wow: beneath him was dark space with stars blinking in the distance. He felt a breeze.

"Will the buggy fit?" she said.

"Yes. Is there a tracking device on the buggy?" he asked.

He flipped the buggy again. She rummaged through the engine with her hands and removed a metallic blinking box, and handed it to him, and he hurled it down the mountain. He put one foot in, then his whole body, then climbed down to the outside, stood up, inverted. So cool! Bidirectional gravity held him to the rim, upside down. The planet's outer surface looked barren like a craterless moon. His eyes adjusted to the darkness of space. He looked back inside the hollow planet at her standing upside down and he savored a glimpse of her lovely legs.

"Space is warm!" he said.

"Betelgeuse is a warm star," she said.

He climbed back, drove the buggy through the opening and parked outside under the stars, pulled back the foliage plug and closed the round door. They sped away from the planet. They were not being followed. He had an urge to just point the buggy toward Earth, but at sublight speeds, it would take them more than 650 years to get there. She suggested he look for a bluish asteroid with red flecks, fly to it, and hide out at a planet under Orkannian control where Hugubuians could not arrest them.

After a few hours of flying toward the asteroid, Jakk saw a rectangular-shaped planet like a giant shoebox. Jakk circled it several times. It appeared to be uninhabited. It had transparent sides and an entrance hole on the side. He saw winding paths through trees, a river, a mountain with a pool on top, clouds, a sandy beach with waves, a mini-ocean that extended to a transparent wall. The planet was lit by a downward-facing sun lamp that hung from the planet's ceiling, dimming in the twilight. He drove through the opening, dodged a cloud, felt air against his skin, and landed on dunes above a beach. He remembered a kid in third grade describing his vacation to Hawaii during show-and-tell. This was better, much better. He felt like he was in a magazine advertisement for a Caribbean resort, minus the hotel and sunburned tourists.

"I will name this planet 'Mergetroid.' Will we get in trouble with the Orkannians?" Jakk asked.

"Probably not," said Reena.

"Who are the Orkannians?"

"Creatures three meters tall, stubborn and fierce."

Orkannians, she said, were fine provided you obeyed their rules. The entrance at the side of the boxlike planet was the only way in or out. It would be easy to be trapped inside, but she said not to worry.

"We are alive and free!" she said, lifting her arms and sporting a wide grin.

It *was* a powerfully good feeling. Jakk had saved their lives. His eyes inhaled her curvaceous body, her hips and lips, her sexy shoulders, her butt curved playfully on the sand. He resolved to become an authority on her bodily shape in case there was a pop quiz. Best things about a blind girl-friend: she couldn't catch him ogling her *and* she depended on him. But the light was dimming. He yawned and slept beside her on the sand.

He awoke slowly, felt the warmth from the planet's lamp and heard the soft crush of waves breaking like someone snoring. His head was moving slightly up and down on Reena's midsection, resting beneath her breasts. She had somehow changed into a flower-patterned bikini. Maybe she found one with her hands in the buggy? He imagined her thighs were smooth hillsides to explore. He sat up and stared at her midsection. She lacked a bellybutton. When his eyes moved to her bikini-held breasts, he studied their shape like an artist might study a nude model. What lovely structures. He yearned to talk to her breasts as if they were giant eyes. He gazed up to her face, and to his surprise, *he saw two eyes looking back at him.* He fell back onto his elbows.

"Who are you?" he said.

"Reena."

"You have eyes! And eyebrows! And a nose! I thought they melted your face."

"It grew back."

Reena's sea-green eyes were enhanced by bushy but defined eyebrows. How had they simply grown back? Those eyes had just watched him ogling her body and he felt a wave of guilt crash through. He felt reduced from hero to pervert. She should have *told* him she had eyes instead of letting him ogle her. Still, it was amazing how she morphed from a blind basket case to a supermodel.

"I was checking for signs of sunburn," he said.

"You are thorough."

He grinned. Reena was a real woman who knew what to say, unlike snotty balloon-blowing Sheela. Reena had feminine smarts, a knowingness, a timeless grace in her eyes. Looking into her eyes recharged his soul like a cell phone. If her beauty confused his brain, it energized his hands, which danced around not knowing where to park themselves. Then he had a thought: when she had been blind, she was dependent on him; sighted, she could be dangerous. Where was the gun?

"It's great your face grew back," he said. "So … have you been here before?"

"I heard about it. It is impossible to get hurt here."

Reena ran to the water and dove in like a porpoise. She emerged dripping, her body lithe and graceful. He felt like they were Adam and Eve tasked with repopulating a fresh planet. They walked along the beach and found a boat similar to a canoe. He paddled while she sat facing him. She pointed toward a *waterrise:* a river emerging from the sea, which flowed upward. As the canoe approached the cliffside, the front end raised up and the entire canoe climbed vertically, carried upward by the river. Gravity worked sideways at this stretch, holding them and the canoe against the vertically flowing river. Cool! At the crest, the canoe tilted horizontally again, gravity returned to normal, and they followed the turquoise blue stream as it meandered through green forests.

Soon they were at a small pool at the mountaintop. It was the highest point inside the box planet. The stream apparently flowed down a giant pipe and returned to the sea. They could see for kilometers in every direction—hillsides, the meandering stream, waves crashing in the distance. Their mini-world was surrounded by a transparent wall where the world simply ended, deep space on the other side. From here, the gigantic Betelgeuse looked smaller than Earth's sun.

"Want to see something cool?" she asked.

Reena jumped off the mountain, soaring with her arms like wings, catching an updraft and looping back around toward him. "Come on!" she shouted.

It looked dangerous but fun. Jakk paused, took a deep breath, raised his arms, felt the lift, and jumped. His arms became like wings. They hang-glided through warm air currents, explored mountainsides and valleys, flew near the planetary edge over a misty valley, feeling as light as butterflies. They splashed into a blue lagoon midway between mountains and sea. Underwater, in clear swirling currents, he saw plants swaying in the ebb and flow like samba dancers. As they swam, he watched her legs open and close like flower petals in time-lapse photography. They climbed out and walked past tall grasses.

Sure beats high school, and Reena sure beats Sheela, he thought. He was so glad that he'd left Earth. Eden was not a garden but a planet, a harmony of colors and a soft sky. They peered inside a cottage with only one bed, his penis informed his brain. He felt ecstatic. The stress of captivity was gone. He felt as if he could breathe in the feeling of forever, the happiness of eternal moments, the sensations of sun and sky and sand and water. He might lose his virginity before he was thirty.

But as he followed her back to the lagoon, questions kept announcing themselves like party crashers. Why were there no mosquitoes? No fish or birds? Why were the trees so neatly spaced? How did they both fly? How did her face grow back? Why wasn't he hungry despite not having eaten for days? If Hugubuians were so advanced, how could the two of them escape so easily? Why wasn't she scared? Why had they melted her face? How had she angered them? His restless mind risked undoing his snake-less Eden. Were the only ones with a chance for happiness those persons who could stop themselves from asking questions?

"Why did you leave your planet?" she asked. Her foot made a question mark in the sand.

"To get away from weird women blowing balloons?"

"You were not part of an expedition?"

"Just myself."

"Why travel alone?"

"Easier."

"What do you want?"

What a perfect question. A supermodel on a paradise planet—could he construct a sentence without the word "hump" in it? But he had to appear to have worthy ideas.

"To be youthful forever? I found no answers on Earth—only humans deceiving themselves, believing in religious fantasies with afterlives and ghosts and celebrity worship until they died. If there are answers, they have to be somewhere else in the universe."

She studied him closely as he spoke. He learned she was 307 Earth-years old (the conversion was approximate: Betelgeusian time was measured in asteroid swing-bys, and absolute day-length varied depending on their distance from the giant star.) What had she been doing during all that time? It was somewhat unsettling. He wanted to know how she stayed young but he didn't want to bring up the subject of death. That would dampen their date. She explained how life's necessities were condensed into a simple powerful pill for oxygen, temperature regulation, water, and energy. An "everything pill," Jakk thought. It explained why he felt no hunger, no thirst, no chills. She fetched one from the space buggy. He held one. It was small but extremely dense. When he put one in his mouth, it dissolved with a warm fizz and made a whistling sound through his teeth.

"Did you explore Earth thoroughly?" she asked.

"No, but most of my planet isn't much different from New Jersey."

She asked him about religion on Earth. He said that some humans believed that if you're good, you go to a balmy all-you-can-eat cafeteria where you never get fat, or a fiery furnace if you're bad. That there was a human who lived two thousand years ago, a human who could bring the dead to life by touching them, who was supposedly tortured to death because his dad was God, which Jakk saw as proof that humans were mentally challenged.

"You flew faster than light," she said. "You are not mentally challenged."

She saw him like he saw her: a puzzle, equations with unknown variables. She was the first person to try to really understand him. She was making greater progress than his parents, the rule-bound school, sarcastic Sheela, even Miss Derrickson. That a discussion with a like-minded being might derail a chance for future sex was starting to become less important, and what was increasingly surprising was that he was enjoying a conversation with a female. His mind wanted to hump her mind. *So this is what love is*, he thought.

"Suppose you're the only intelligent human," she said.

"Well I don't know, but okay, let's start our flowchart with that premise."

"You arose miraculously from Earth's primordial soup."

"I showered regularly, sometimes with shampoo."

"But since you are only one type of human—male—why not bring along a female?"

He was tempted to say something corny like "because I wanted to meet you" or "because I haven't met the right woman yet," but even though there was some truth in both statements, his growing respect for her intellect dissuaded him from dodging her question with a light comment or flirtation. It was surprising that, many trillions of miles from home, he had found a female mind he could talk to without rolling his eyes.

And so he thought about why. He loved being free—free all by himself—free without commitments or rules or chores or hall passes or deadlines, or having to buy flowers, or having to remember anniversaries or birthdays, or remembering not to put shoes on the coffee table, or lighting farts for fun, or not restraining burps even if it was going to sound like a motorcycle engine revving, or not having to play any of the repetitive, ceremonial games that men and women play. He wanted to do what he wanted. Period. If he told her this truth, would she see him as immature and not have sex with him?

Truth is, it was complicated. He found himself fascinated by her eyes, each a fountain of delight, but as hard as he tried to keep eye contact, he found himself overwhelmed by her body. His brain shrunk and moved south to his penis bulging beneath the fabric. It began to give orders to his brain, dictating what words would come out of his mouth, reluctant to weigh the morality of fibbing or to think through consequences. The headline in Jakk's newspaper—the only story—was the incredible nearness of her thighs. He was not as afraid of female tubing as he once had feared, such was his desire. His second brain dictated words to his mouth:

"Many women wanted to come with me."

Just like that. He lied. Reena would never know about Sheela's balloon humiliation. The idea of securing a long-term friendship seemed less important than having sex with her. Words didn't have to be true so long as they achieved results.

"You run from love," she said.

It was girlish talk like in *Splashable* magazine but he didn't feel a need to unpack her meaning. The hum and lilt of her murmurings was like being massaged by words. What the words meant was less important.

They walked through beach grass to the hut with a thatched roof, cobalt blue door, and yellow windows. Inside was one large room, floating furniture, two comfy chairs, a table, and a king-sized bed behind multi-colored beads. Against a wall, he saw what looked like a harmonium with five keys on each side. A ragganalian, she said. She stood behind him and moved his hands gently to show him how to adjust the pitch and beat and octave. Tones emerged like creeping vines with a newfound wanderlust. He loved the sensation of her soft breasts on his back. He let go of the instrument, turned to face her, put his hands gently on her head and kissed her mouth. She pulled back, startled.

"What are you doing? Are you cleaning my mouth?"

They looked at each other in mutual puzzlement. Oral hygiene? He'd assumed that kissing was one of those behaviors every creature understood without having to explain, customary throughout the Milky Way, like smiling. He looked outside. The sundim was like an Earthly sunset except purple with green and blue streaks. The clouds looked like a kid added food coloring to mashed potatoes and pounded away. The soft greens and blues played across her skin. She lit a candle by blowing on it, causing a wiggly light to add a creamy glow to her smooth skin, shadows emerging like sand dunes. He wanted sex but he did not know how to begin. He sat beside her, smiled, tried the kiss maneuver again. This time she did not flinch. He focused on her midsection. His hands groped her body, touching, exploring.

"Did you lose something?" she asked.

"I am looking for something."

"You are exploring my body?"

He pressed a button and his clothes swooshed off and folded themselves on a shelf. He kissed between her breasts, behind her earlobes, and above her knees. She seemed puzzled yet excited. He swooshed off her clothes. He lay on top, gently exploring, but he was having trouble finding his destination. She giggled. He kept probing but not finding the opening. Where was it? Minutes elapsed. No respectable guy in a movie ever looked for where to insert it. *Guys never ask for directions when motoring through an unfamiliar county.* The idea of the vagina scared him. It was too scary to look at. If he had his druthers, he could go through life without ever having to look at one.

"We are alone. We need others," she said.

"No, we really don't."

Visual inspection became necessary. He mustered courage and looked between her legs. Only skin. No hair. No vagina. Not even a crease. It explained his difficulty. While he felt a slight relief in not having to see a real vagina in the flesh, his frustration with the lack of one was immense. She lifted her body for a fuller examination. Even mannequins had a crease where the plastic halves were glued together, which he once felt with his fingers at a department store. He kept looking, behind her buttocks, on her back, an armpit, to satisfy himself he exhausted all possibilities. The initial surprise gave way to a resigned frustration. She said that scientists removed these unsightly structures generations ago.

"I am flattered you wanted to reproduce with me," she said.

Since they did not eat, there was no need to poop, explaining her lack of an anus. In her world, community approval was required, since new beings affected everybody. Lovers needed a permit like one for deer hunting.

"So you have no vagina and men have no penis?" he asked.

"I can make a vagina if I want," she said.

Slowly her wonderful horizontal smile morphed into a vertical vagina complete with pubic hair. "Like this," she said, moving her now-vertical lips. He backed away, startled, and stared. A talking vagina. He should have guessed. No doubt about it: they were different species. It was awkward. Her mouth reverted back. So weird: an alien with face-morphing powers. *I saw a vagina and lived.*

"How do you have sex?" he said.

She explained that sex required clergy to facilitate coupling. This only happened publicly to discourage infidelity and prevent overpopulation. He was proud not to have puked on her breasts. He felt like an anthropologist struggling to understand a freshly discovered tribe. They cuddled on the bed and slept.

He awoke to sunlight bathing the room like liquid honey. He whooshed his clothes on. He heard noise outside. She looked at him. The door burst open and soldiers swarmed in, cold and faceless. He froze.

They'd been found.

Back to jail.

He would die.

She would die.

3

Hijakked

"Do not hurt the creature," Reena commanded the soldiers as they encircled Jakk.

So Reena was one of them, a Hugubuian spy investigating him—*the creature*. Soldiers slapped two black bands around Jakk's wrists with no visible cord between them—alien handcuffs. The soldiers had humanlike faces. They weren't the Orkannians, who are three meters tall—unless Reena was lying about that too. Their left arms were an orange suction hose similar to an elephant trunk, and their right ended with a black hammerlike device. Jakk imagined they could suction him close and hammer away. Their purple and blue–striped warsuits were loaded with compartments, and their movements were smooth and coordinated, like synchronized swimmers. They wore a thin wire band around their heads, probably a communications device. He saw no guns to grab.

No wonder escape had been so easy. Authorities must have known where they were at every moment. He felt used. But why had Reena risked her life swinging from a thread?

An argument erupted between a creature Jakk dubbed Three-Eyes Two-Noses and a human-looking creature he named Max the Mad Scientist. Their language sounded like an audio clip played at high speed. Max looked like a high school senior with several Ivy acceptances in his pocket.

Jakk's wrists were pulled by an unseen force that escorted him inside a colorful warship with fins and guns to a small cell with a video screen, bed, mirror, closet, and window. The handcuffs came off. He looked out at the black of space as his beautiful rectangular play-planet receded from view.

Reena entered the room.

"Why all the tricks?" Jakk asked.

"My assignment," Reena said.

"I'm a high school student! I've never done anything wrong. Why would they kill me?"

"Speeding? Smuggling?"

"I never went through customs!"

"We found tiny creatures in your digestive tract."

"Bacteria are in every living creature."

"We have no bacteria and we do not want any."

Max the Mad Scientist entered.

"The prisoner did not kill despite a chance to and deserves a hearing," Reena said.

"Where are you from?" Max asked Jakk.

Jakk said nothing. If aliens didn't like bacteria, they wouldn't like Earth.

"Is your world self-contained?"

Jakk didn't understand what that meant so again he said nothing. Reena and Max left. From his window, he saw a smaller spaceship fly away. Earth. Hugubu. Mergetroid. He was beginning to hate creatures his size and love small critters such as bacteria since they weren't pointing guns at him, imprisoning him, deceiving him, giving him detention, or blowing up balloons in class to mock him. He worried for the billions of bacteria in his gut since he hadn't eaten anything in days—his microscopic friends had been silently starving while he romped on Mergetroid with the traitoress. He tried pushing on the empty space where a door might have been but was restrained by an invisible force. The cell had a closet. He could fit inside it if necessary.

He heard a klaxon. Footsteps pounded in the hallway outside his cell. He figured the ship was under attack but almost certainly not from an Earthling space cavalry bent on rescuing him. He wished it was his handyman father hurling two-by-fours and socket wrenches at his captors. He regretted not leaving a note before leaving Earth. Perhaps he might escape execution if his captors were captured? The ship heaved and Jakk was knocked sideways. Bright orange and green flashes reflected on the walls. Gas clouds entered the ship and Jakk heard soldiers inside firing.

He retreated to his closet, cringing as he heard his captors squawking to each other. Through a crack in the closet door he saw a Hugubuian soldier slumped in his cell. New noises emerged like badly tuned trumpets with squeaky rats inside. Then mostly silence.

He guessed the invaders killed the Hugubuians. He was relieved that his captors were dead but would the invaders kill him too? He heard a *click click* sound and a strange wheezing that he assumed came from the attackers, so he named them the Sprockneesh. If the Sprocks found him, what would they do? He looked like a Hugubu. If they found him he would almost certainly be killed.

Jakk opened the closet slightly and looked at the dead soldier on the floor. He found a tablet in a compartment and quietly took it back into his closet. He whispered "English language." It worked! Computer menus in English. He leafed through menus about warsuits, close range attacks, atomic pistols, pulse phasers, and how to transfer outfits. He pushed a button to switch clothing with the dead soldier, whose naked body was smoldering and burned as if struck by lightning. He rubbed burned flesh on his face, dragged the soldier to the closet, then played dead on the floor, but the noise must have attracted attention. Several Sprocks entered. One kicked him but he remained motionless. They went away.

From the floor, with one eye slightly open, he studied his enemies gathered outside the open door. Five human-sized creatures who looked like beat-up zombies who had caught fire and were extinguished by kitty litter. In his weapons kit there was a hand grenade: push a button, throw it, and it would laser anything living except the hurler, like a porcupine emitting killer beams, but he would have to throw it in the right spot. He was scared to act but even more scared not to. He rehearsed the throwing sequence. He pushed the button and tossed it, turned away, and the room lit up with a phosphorescent pink. He heard sizzling sounds. The ship smelled like ammonia steaks on a grill. He stood up and walked into the hallway. Dead Sprocks smoldered motionless. There was an additional odor of heated cheese, like when his father wrapped up pizza slices in tin foil then heated it with his blowtorch.

Jakk was alive!

He briefly searched the ship to make sure that everyone else was dead. Reena the Traitoress must have left earlier on the other ship. He switched to an unburned warsuit from a storage area. He was now the ship's captain but he had no idea what to do. In the command screen, he saw four ships creeping up—scattered pink and black and edgy—different from the Hugubu design so he figured they must be Sprock warships. He scanned a panel for weapons, pushed buttons, and turned dials. "Fly me to Earth now," he shouted. Nothing happened.

Jakk figured the ship's weapons hadn't worked before so he had to try something different. He found a pistol with atomic bullets, climbed into a smoking hole in the ship's hull, leaned out into space, and aimed at the four ships, fired until his gun clicked empty, clambered back into the battered warship, and studied the screen. Nothing seemed to change as the seconds passed. Had he missed?

Then the screen lit like fireworks, silent explosions of vivid yellow-orange festooning the blackness of space. Several expanding bubbles slowly headed toward him. He said "survive atomic blast" to his tablet, which responded by suggesting that he head for the anti-shock chamber down the corridor. He ran to it and closed the hatch and the chamber filled with blue-green foam.

There was total silence.

He felt a violent shake.

Then there was darkness everywhere.

The foam was gone; so was his spaceship. Stars circled at high speeds, circling and circling, and he figured he was hurtling end over end in deep space. He tried to barf but nothing came out. He tried to think but the spinning made that difficult. There was neither friction to slow him nor gravity to anchor him in one spot. He would spin in place forever. He fumbled for the controls on his spacesuit—one played music, another turned on a light—finally he found one that released air, so he found the nozzle, adjusted it, used the air to stop himself from spinning.

There he was.

Alone.

In deep space.

Spacesick but alive.

When the nausea wore off, he looked at the velvety blackness of space, the stars, Betelgeuse burning red in the distance. He felt an incredible yet disturbing feeling of peace now that there were no creatures to outwit or kill, no jails or classrooms to break out of, no spaceships closing in, no handcuffs, no females to trick him or mock him with balloons. His everything pills from the warsuit could keep him alive for weeks. He was free like Huck Finn. He was his own gravity.

What was there to do?

There was nothing to do except exist, think about existing, and try to survive. He thought life was worth living and how it was fun exploring new places. A great big grin burst across his face. He was no longer a prisoner! Still, he knew he couldn't hover forever like a space idiot—or rather, he would hover forever like a space idiot, a dead one, if he didn't do something. He was free but not safe.

During much of his life, he had been alone in his own fine mind, floating in it like he was now, but there had always been the chance of being with people—either to get away from, annoy, ignore, outfox, or ogle—but there were other people. Floating through the void, there was no such choice. He was in solitary confinement of a sort, but was space a jailer or an enabler? He wondered where he was. He was here. That was all that mattered, and he thought the whole idea of location was dubious since it meant being somewhere in relation to somewhere else. He wondered what he was doing. *I am existing, I am living, what does it look like I'm doing?* But it wasn't that simple. To keep existing, he needed other things, other creatures, a floor to stand on and yes, he needed gravity, air to breathe after his pills ran out, even his fashion magazines with beautiful models in ridiculously over-styled poses. Such was his predicament: he needed things, but things tended to cause problems. He wanted Reena without her treachery, high school without sarcastic Sheela, Earth without killer gravity yet with enough gravity to keep his stuff from floating into space. He sensed his thinking was off, somehow. He remembered his principal's comment that he did not know how to be a human.

Boredom tried to set in, but survival occupied his mind.

Systematically he explored the spacesuit's controls and compartments. It had a mini-library with information about this alien world and its technology. He found gadgets: a hammer, stethoscope, rope, and other stuff. It was better than Batman's utility belt. Finally a virtual transparent screen appeared in front of him. He moved the pointer with his eyes. Blinking made it click. How cool was that!

He watched a video about how his spacesuit worked. Gauges measuring vibrations, heat, movement, photons, and radiation popped in and out. He detected heat energy from a particular spot behind him. He air-nozzled himself in that direction. It was not a star. He squinted at it, magnifying the view several thousand times. It was a perfectly spherical shape. He clicked on it, and text scrolled by. He was looking at a mini-planet inhabited by creatures called the Immortals who lived forever inside a shield of great tensile strength to keep out dust and protect them from Betelgeuse's bow shock. It was a floating space hotel. It had about the same gravity as the moon despite its much smaller size.

Eternal life. This was something he earnestly sought. Could they make him immortal too? Good luck and fate brought him to the exact spot in the incredibly vast galaxy. Thank you Hugubuians and Sprocks!

He nozzled himself toward his newfound heaven. The shape got bigger. As he approached the planet, he pointed the nozzle to slow himself down just as a message flashed that he was out of air. He landed softly on his feet. He set a flashlight on the surface and it didn't float away. He gently jumped and landed slowly like a bouncing moon astronaut. Luckily there was gravity, otherwise he would have bounced into space and floated away forever.

He hopped around the sphere, circling it several times, but there was no entrance. How did the Immortals get in and out? Where was the welcome mat? It was closed up tighter than high school for latecomers. It was like his prison cell back on Hugubu: did these creatures not believe in something called *doors*? He imagined happy creatures inside, lounging in a garden, making profound conversation beside a waterfall, striking poses like magazine celebrities. He found an all-purpose tool, clicked it into a hammer, and banged on the sphere's surface. It didn't make a dent. He was about to strike harder when the surface turned into an image of a scary-angry green face with an ice-cream cone–shaped head.

"Do not bang on our shield. Leave now," said the head.

The shield returned to its black-grey color.

"I want to be immortal. Can I live with you?" asked Jakk.

Silence.

"I am a human. I need help or I will die. Please help me," said Jakk.

More silence. He pleaded with the blank screen. He would do whatever was needed. If they would not let him join them, could they teach him how to become immortal? Could they help him survive until he was rescued? Could he borrow a spaceship? He banged again to no avail.

He knelt and thought while trying to keep panic from settling in. He tried to think logically. Why wouldn't they help him? If these creatures figured out the secret of eternal life, wouldn't they want to share their secret? Maybe the Immortals were inside but imprisoned by the scary creature?

Slowly, surely, reluctantly, he came around to the horrid realization that they would let him die. They were heartless and mean and selfish beings, not teachers or role-models worthy of emulation but *enemies*. Alive forever, they were opposed to more life, particularly his life. Why? It was like an exclusive society which stopped admitting members, a country club, a fancy-pants college that would prefer not to have a handyman's son, and his heart hardened against them—hardened like the shell that encased them.

How did the Immortals stay alive inside their shell? All beings needed energy. From where? Any initial fuel would have been used up ages ago; therefore, the energy source must come from outside, probably photons from Betelgeuse. So he walked to where Betelgeuse was directly overhead and looked down. Was he standing on photovoltaic cells? Possibly, because the sphere rotated at the same pace as its orbit, so this side was probably always facing Betelgeuse. How did the sphere defend itself against occasional nuisances such as himself, other than the shield? What if an invader blocked the flow of photons? The sphere didn't have an internal weapon such as a laser to repel invaders, or they would have used it on him already. But there must be guards inside. Jakk blinked through the databases in his warsuit. If he could create a distraction that caused a guard to come outside, he could slip in while the Immortal was distracted.

He put his ear to the solar panel surface, tapped with the hammer, and listened with the stethoscope. He did this for different places on the sphere. On the opposite side, there was a slight change in sound, so maybe there was an entrance there? He figured if he spray-painted the panels facing Betelgeuse, a guard would probably emerge from the secret entrance to kill him, so he needed something to distract the guard yet signal Jakk that the door was open. So he left a screwdriver spinning on the sphere's right side, between the hypothetical door and the solar panels. He figured it would spin until its batteries ran down or it was turned off or shot by the guard. Then he spray painted a few solar panels, scrambled quickly to an in-between location on the sphere's left side, and listened with his stethoscope.

It didn't take long.

The screwdriver stopped.

Jakk ran to the bottom and saw light from an opened doorway, jumped in quickly, and pressed several buttons to close the door behind him just in time to prevent a spindly multilegged robot, similar to a praying mantis, from reentering. His ruse had worked!

Jakk's eyes adjusted to the dim light. The place stunk like sweated-up gym outfits and foot odor. The reek made his eyes water. It made his town's dump smell like an arboretum. He followed a hallway to the inner core. In cubicles against the walls, he saw extremely fat sleeping shapes, but a few roused the others until the entire community was aware of him.

"Who are you?" one blared in a raspy voice.

He was about to say his name, but figured they might have friends who would extract revenge.

"I am ... Eternal Life," Jakk lied.

"What are you doing here? You are trespassing! Leave," said an Immortal.

"Don't you creatures bathe?"

The place seemed like a prison with perennially lethargic inmates. He looked around for someone preparing to attack him; apparently they lacked weapons. He felt an urge to offer a finger-wagging sermon, like a Unitarian minister upset with people who didn't recycle enough.

"I need to borrow a spaceship," he said.

His request was met with derision, laughter, shaking of heads, and calls to leave. He had no close-range weapon but they did not know that, so he brandished his index finger as if it were a gun, and they became silent.

"Where is a spaceship?" he demanded.

One pointed to a closet. He kicked through a locked door and saw a small vehicle with a crane on the back. It was like a tow truck for outer space. He climbed in, studied the controls, backed into a shelf, knocked over weird paints that mixed into fluorescent shapes, and flew it to the empty center of the large room. He spun a few times to practice how to operate it. Several extra-fat Immortals slithered over to block his exit.

"Please get out of my way," he insisted, but they didn't move.

If he killed them with the tow truck's laser, their fat corpses would block Jakk inside. But they refused to budge, even when he brandished his finger again. He maneuvered the vehicle until he found a large panel with wires. An electrical box? He drove into it, sparks flew, and the ceiling lights went out. He turned on the tow vehicle's headlights and returned to the center of the room. The Immortals cried, complained they would die without energy, and swore vengeance.

"Silence," Jakk said, brandishing his finger.

At a loss for what to do, he browsed through his databases again. He learned they were several hundred thousand Earth-years old, give or take. They slowed their bodily processes to exist with minimal energy consumption. Most had no regular heartbeats. No parasites or bacteria could sicken them. They slept almost constantly, occasionally replenishing what little energy they spent with starlight from Betelgeuse. Since learning required energy, they did not learn or even think much. There was no shower.

"Help other living creatures when they ask. You left me to die," said Jakk.

One Immortal argued that they left Eternal Life alone, so Eternal Life should leave them alone. Fair was fair. It was wrong for Eternal Life to need something, wrong for Eternal Life to expect others to provide that something, and wrong to hurt them if they failed to provide it: wrong, wrong, wrong! Eternal Life was a needy creature who vandalized solar panels, trespassed, vandalized their power box, stole their tow truck, and was leaving them to die. Jakk said that if they had simply helped him, none of this would have happened in the first place.

The Immortals blocking his exit slithered sideways like slugs, staining the floor. He drove to the door, pushed the exit button and zipped outdoors to the free clean smell of space. He saw the mantis-guard robot trying to clean off the spray paint. He put distance behind him and gloried in the warm starlit sky. His radio picked up a distress call.

"Who did this to you?" asked a voice, identified as an Orkannian commander.

"Eternal Life did this to us," said the crying Immortal.

The commander sounded puzzled but dispatched a rescue ship that would arrive in three days. Then the Orkannians would learn what really happened and would hunt him down. Swaths of identity clung to him—images, recordings, spray paint, the tow truck—and he had to either scrub off traces of identity or put serious distance between him and them. Problem was, the tow truck was powerful yet slow, limited to sublight speed. They would catch him soon unless he skedaddled on a faster ship. He flew until he found a cosmic parking spot: no painted lines on asphalt, no sign saying pay the meter or we will tow your ass. Unlike in New Jersey, he could open the door without worrying about denting another vehicle. He took an everything pill, which hissed life into his mouth. He savored the silence of space.

His encounter with the Immortals was the opposite of what he had expected, seriously disturbing, and while the goal of staying alive seemed worthy, it added a huge question mark to his general idea of wanting to live forever. Had he done anything wrong? Their argument about wanting to be left alone had a logic to it, but he needed to live. What had happened was not his fault, still he felt guilty, somehow.

Wherever he went, he seemed to make enemies. An Earthling woman was upset with him because the computer he'd programmed made a sexist remark. Hugubuians were upset because he was smuggling bacteria. Sprocks were surely upset that he blew up their ships. Immortals were upset that he vandalized their sphere. Orkannians would be upset that they had to hunt him down. It wasn't his fault—or was it? He didn't feel like it was his fault. He was a good person but stuff kept happening to him. He felt out of step on the escalator of life. He hungered for a place where he could peacefully coexist with other beings, to learn and live and grow, to find a better and longer life, maybe even live forever, but he found himself galloping like an outlaw across space prairies and seeking a canyon hideout. He was a space pirate, an outlaw on the run—and he had to keep running, but he was growing weary of the whole business and he knew, from watching movies, that sooner or later they would close in on him.

He wanted to keep seeing himself as being the master of his own fate, but this was an increasingly difficult notion to maintain. Why was he unwelcome everywhere he went? Was it bad luck? How could he grab control of the steering wheel of his life? He turned the triangular steering control of the tow truck and spun around, watching the stars circle overhead, then stopped again.

Harder still was trying to understand why bad stuff kept happening to him. Was there a God somewhere, angered by Jakk's atheism, testing him, playing with him, washing him in a cosmic dishwasher? He imagined God as a fat Mafia don, twirled mustache, smoking a cigar but not getting mouth cancer because He was God, teasing Jakk by showing him only parts of things, revealing string theory but confusing him with the Immortals, teasing him with glimpses of Sheela's thighs yet confusing him with her sarcastic behavior. How could his episode with Reena be anything but proof that there was a sadistic jokester toying with him? But the joke seemed as cruel as the rusty blade of a knife: why create creatures hungry for life, only to have them die? Worse, why create a universe in which some creatures, in order to keep living, had to cause other creatures to suffer?

He wondered where to go. His spacesuit suggested two possible hideouts: a Trash Planet—a planet-sized garbage dump devoid of creatures, and an Art Planet—a haven for freaky types. Each moon-sized planet had Earth-like gravity and was a day away. The Art Planet was like a high-rent village with tough zoning laws, and was visited by Hugubuians and Orkannians. While there were increased chances of being captured, he might find passage to a safer galaxy if he could disguise himself. Entrance to the Art Planet would be difficult, but who would want to go to the Trash Planet?

Trash planet

The tiny speck on the horizon grew larger. It was mostly gray, no clouds, no lights, no hotels. He flew in low, made several passes, marveled at kilometer-high piles of clean junk. There were no discarded spaceships. The tow truck was hot—easily tracked—so he couldn't keep it much longer. He parked near a giant mound of discarded machinery. That there was no dust or oil or accumulated crud on surfaces suggested a Hugubuian influence. He marveled at the changing styles. Discarded crap on the bottom had serrated edges in swirl patterns while higher up junk seemed sleeker. It looked like a gradual mass extinction of machines, an archaeologist's dream of discarded droids and robots. He stared sadly at the face of a discarded six-legged robot, his three

LEDish eyes looking into Jakk's, and wondered what it might say if it were still working. Probably something like "Avoid my fate, Jakk, and stay alive forever."

So with no discarded spaceships to fix—if he could have figured out how to do that—it was time to check out the Art Planet. Sometimes artists worked with trash. Perhaps he could stow away on an artist's spaceship as garbage? He brought up the screen on his helmet and asked for a location where artists scavenged through fresh trash and zipped his tow truck over to it. After an hour, a spacecraft descended with lights blazing, with periodic flashes as if pictures were being taken. Jakk programmed the tow truck to fly itself back to the Immortals' planet. He hid in a pile of trash until a mechanical arm lowered to grab some junk, and then jumped into what was scooped up. He was a stowaway!

Art planet

After a few hours, the Art Planet came into view. There were steep purple and blue mountains rising vertically like giant hair brushes, smudgy in spots as if daubed with oil paint, highlighting winding shadow-strewn valleys. It was an Earthlike outward-facing planet, not a giant shell like Hugubu. Jakk didn't see any roads except one by a small town near a lake. In the distance, a mechanical volcano rhythmic pulsed plastic ribbons skyward that waved like party streamers: was it an art exhibit?

When the spacecraft landed, he clambered out quickly before the artist inspected his haul. There were piles of junk everywhere. From behind a vat of phosphorescent yellow paint, he saw a creature emerge from the spacecraft. He looked like a blue-green octopus with a large head, one eye, and multi-jointed arms instead of tentacles. That was an artist? How could it have depth perception with only one eye? One-Eye swirled over so he played dead like one more piece of junk. Jakk was picked up by the powerful creature, trembled like a mouse about to be eaten, and looked at the creature eyes-to-eye. One-Eye's eye was a liquid globe with pulsating red veins and strange shapes floating in there. Jakk heard scratchy sounds like an ancient modem trying to connect.

"Who are you?" One-Eye asked.

Jakk figured an artist wouldn't be fond of war, and Jakk was wearing a soldier's uniform. Jakk said he was a Hugubuian soldier trying to desert and begged One-Eye not to turn him in. One-Eye's tone turned menacing.

"Who are you *really*?" asked One-Eye, raising his giant eyebrow.

Jakk had to tell the truth. He explained his imprisonment, the Sprock battle, his visit with the Immortals and his need to evade the Orkannians. One-Eye smiled, let him down gently, and said he was an outcast too, a failed genetic experiment who left his home planet to escape public ridicule. He dabbled in robotic-sex collages and sculptures in which nanobots rearranged molecules based on emotions. One-Eye had been building a following until the Sprock menace cut off most of his customers. He figured Jakk had perhaps a week before Orkannians arrived with warrants and weapons.

The Art Planet, he explained, was built a thousand years ago by Hugubuian engineers as a penal colony, but over time artists moved in, often as a tax evasion strategy, until it became a hangout for freaky types. Five hundred years ago it became self-governing. Every week an intergalactic bus would bring art buyers, and Main Street would become an outdoor street festival. That bus was the only sensible way off the planet. After it returned to Hugubu, it went intergalactic, making numerous stops in the Andromeda Galaxy, so Jakk should not get off at Hugubu. Problem: bus tickets required gold coins, which Jakk would have to earn like everybody else—by creating art. There were no summer-type jobs in food service since there were no restaurants, no janitors since there was no dirt, no staff coordinators since scheduling was handled by robots. One small problem: Jakk knew nothing about art. He regretted ignoring it in high school.

One-Eye's workshop was packed with weird stuff from several galaxies. He pointed Jakk to a discarded musical instrument from Alpha-Cygni. Jakk pressed a button and a beam shown on his hand, so when he moved his fingers, it played. There were vats filled with screw-like pieces, long metal strings that followed your hand like a magnet, sandy globs that giggled, a table with endlessly spinning dials, a spiral rotating like a wayward lepton. Liquids swirled in diverse shapes and patterns inside a vertical cylinder with gravity-surrounds, mixing, and then separating again. Jakk had thought art was old paintings and sculptures. How could he make anything so clever?

One-Eye said great art was stuff that you never got tired of, tempted you to keep learning the more you experienced it, revealed truth subtly, indirectly, transported you to a higher understanding. It *emerges*, he said. Art has structural integrity—a center straddling unity and diversity that teases you, engages your spirit like a beautiful princess with dance in her eyes or like teenaged boys stealing a dune buggy.

"Art is sex on Friday when it's deeply into Tuesday," said One-Eye. "It can make you feel immortal for a split second, like the stillness of holding your breath when a goddess floats past. It is pouring your soul's flashlight on your fears."

"Oh," said Jakk.

"What do you know?" asked One-Eye.

"Computers?"

The conversation continued, but after hurling weird idea upon weird idea, they agreed Jakk should build a cityscape that responded to sound.

If it heard talking, buildings would pop up and dance; if it heard banging sounds, they would keel over. One-Eye helped him with materials and motors while Jakk programmed it with the help of a recycled droid.

What was cool was how quickly his creation was built. He coded with a Hugubu programming language variant, amazingly easy-to-learn yet logical and powerful. Much of the coding was done by giving the computer spoken commands, like "if you hear a clapping sound, shake the buildings horizontally but not so much that they fall down." The computer took it from there, and even had its own self-learning module. He admired Hugubu technology. If only he had had this language back at school, he could have built a non-sexist computer for Sheela's contest in a fraction of the time. The guts-level programming had been done thousands of years ago, and what Jakk was using, essentially, was like a powerful object-oriented C++, written for somebody who knew nothing about programming. If he said *shhh*, the buildings would be quiet, and might even shush him back! If he said "go to sleep," the buildings would lie down with canopies flapping when the buildings snored. If he commanded "buildings fuck," they would hump like chimpanzees on cocaine. One building that floated a few inches over the ground he called the "Pavilion de la Jakk." The idea of humping—midsection pelvic thrusting—was so startling that One-Eye borrowed the idea for his Dancing Flames exhibit.

"Is it art?" asked Jakk.

"How should I know?" said One-Eye.

"What is art?"

"Crap that sells."

One-Eye said "put in a water-rise," remembering Jakk's encounter on Mergetroid, and the computer took it from there, installing a water-rise flowing from a coin-throw pond to the top of a skyscraper. There were glitches: since there were an odd number of buildings, the hump command sometimes caused a threesome that sent the water-rise splashing droplets off the table. One-Eye's Dancing Flames exhibit featured blowtorch-like figurines that burned each other in new patterns, and at one point, One-Eye's smock got scorched. Jakk was having so much fun he almost forgot how precarious his situation was.

One-Eye dressed Jakk with a beret, mustache and beard, and paint smock, and said he should call himself *Jacques Jacques.* If his image was picked up by cameras, he might find himself awaiting enhurlment from an Orkannian trebuchet.

Jacques Jacques and One-Eye brought their creations to the art fair. It felt like a county fair minus hay and livestock and was jammed with weird displays and funny-looking aliens, misfits and creatures pretending to be misfits because they thought it was cool. It was as if San Francisco's Haight-Ashbury gay community had a masquerade with a robotic theme.

When the space bus arrived, the atmosphere shifted from country to city. It seemed like the street itself was injected with adrenaline. One-Eye said that *she* was here. She was a favorite among artists, a fancy lady from a star-system known for its orgiastic partying who always bought something—even when it didn't fit on the bus. Extra-huge artworks could be shipped by the alien equivalent of ocean freighters. Sometimes extra-large creations were simply hurled by gravitational forces to Hugubu, where a shipping agent would catch the art and have a tugboat-like droid maneuver it to the buyer's garden. No problem for Jakk's cityscape: it would fit easily on board. What he needed was a buyer with gold.

There was a mechanical problem at first. The buildings didn't rise off the table for the first few shoppers. Since the exhibit did not hear the sounds, the erections did not schwing as hoped, so buyers shuffled past, confused. An adjustment to a sound sensor fixed things—architectural Viagra—sprouting buildings with perhaps a bit more oomph than needed such that they wiggled with frenzy like in an earthquake. One-Eye winked at Jakk.

Jakk sensed an impending silence, a hushed feeling, like a sunny day got sunnier, as activity slowed, creatures quieted, and everybody stared at a female human-looking creature with a lit-up gown. She ambled with a boy in tow, her naked breasts wobbling like playful poodles. She was shapely like a toned swimmer, fleshy like a summer sigh, with Cleopatra eyes. She walked with panache, like she was being filmed, knew it, liked it, expected the attention as if it was natural, and made the attention seem natural and fluid. If she had magic, her boy did not; he was a pokey creature out of step with his famous mom. Wherever she walked, she transformed creatures into her servants, ready to satisfy her tiniest implied need as if it were a royal edict. She sucked psychic energy from those in her presence. She was art in motion. On males, her beauty was like a stupidity virus that invaded their brains, making them stutter; women blathered about nonsense, desperate to become her friend, hoping that her beauty might rub off on them and transform them into schwingmeisters of the first rank. Jakk felt unworthy. No way she would ever buy his sophomoric diorama. She stood in front of him, looked at it for a few seconds, saw the buildings rising and falling based on nearby sounds, put her hand to her chin.

"Worthless," she said, looking right at Jakk.

He was speechless. His brain seized like an unoiled engine. Would he be spotted? He felt like he was on television with the whole galaxy watching. His mind started to hang in an infinite loop. Her boy clapped his hands. The buildings bowed. The boy laughed. "Buildings wobble because it's windy!" the boy said. Lobby awnings flapped like flags and buildings swayed like daisies, which brought more chuckles from the boy. The experimentation went on until, unbelievably, against all odds, a reluctant sale was made, with Jacques Jacques finding gold coins in his hand. He might survive because of the little clapping motherfucker. He shared the twelve coins with One-Eye, keeping five to take him to Hugubu and then to Andromeda.

One-Eye said his buyer was a cosmic movie star who attended "It parties" where celebrities cavorted before hungry cameras. One-Eye said movie stars were creatures that everybody felt like they had fucked. Moviegoers sometimes literally climaxed during the film's climax, even creatures hundreds of years old. When the movie star was having her on-screen orgasm (simulated or real: tabloids speculated endlessly on spectral analysis of her facial grimaces), moviegoers climaxed simultaneously with help from sex droids called physiotherapists. The practice was declared therapeutic by respected medical associations. Indeed, regular orgasms ranked right up there with laughter as a life-prolonging activity. Maybe that was why Hugubuians seemed to stay young for so many centuries. In pop culture, associations between movie stars and orgasms built up to the extent that seeing a movie star in public could sometimes prompt zealous fans to orgasm right on the spot. It was viewed as a polite way to greet a celebrity as well as a way to relive a movie in one's mind. "Like getting a free movie," said One-Eye. Jakk nodded but insisted that he would never be that moved by a movie.

Jakk had spare time before the bus left so he checked out other exhibitions. There was a booth with zombielike creatures, arrayed in a figure eight, playing peek-a-boo with each other. Next door was a trebuchet: for a gold coin, you could have yourself hurled across a field into a hillside of rubbery teeth. The idea was to experience public execution from a criminal's viewpoint without, of course, dying.

But it was the exhibit next door that caused him to freeze and smolder like dry ice. There was a movie on a giant screen of Jakk killing the Sprocks. He couldn't believe it. That was him! There. Blasting the Sprocks. What did it mean? He was an action hero. The screen cut to him arriving on Hugubu, lying unconscious, getting an enema to remove his bacteria, lasers zapping his acne, a medic feeding him an everything pill, Reena, his save-me save-me dance to the cameras, swinging out—sheesh, his butt was only ten feet off the ground; he knew it had been close—splashdown, the underwater swim, stealing the dune buggy, telling Reena not to kill or vandalize, canoeing on Mergetroid, the frustrating non-penetrating sexual encounter—they *had* to show that? where were the cameras?—then blasting the Sprocks before the whole thing started over again. There was nothing about him surviving so he guessed the Hugubus probably thought he was dead? If so, good. But why would they release this footage?

Then he had a thought: maybe the artist had rigged it so each viewer saw himself or herself as the hero of the movie. It was an easy hypothesis to test. He asked a bystander with a droopy green garment like a weeping willow what he was watching.

"A suicidal creature almost hurls himself into Betelgeuse at horrendous speeds, is captured, escapes, tries to screw a senator's daughter without assistance—" the bystander convulsed with laughter—"without assistance, is taken prisoner again and then—can you believe it—blasts the Sprocks who kill his captors. He zorks the Sprock commander, destroys several Sprock war boats, interrupts the entire attack."

Jakk tried to act nonchalant. Was he famous? Infamous? Still a criminal? Would killing the Sprocks lower his chance of execution? He didn't know how to take this in, so he would continue to be cautious. He strolled to the next exhibit but this time he saw something so unbelievable he felt like supercooled dry ice with frozen leptons.

It was impossible. There it was. He was stunned. There she was, in front of his eyes, in a three-dimensional holoscopic projection, dancing and singing—Sheela. Balloon-blowing sarcastic Sheela—his former playdate Sheela—what was she doing here trillions of light-years from home? Was he dreaming? She was wearing a buzzing iridescent outfit unlike anything on Earth. Plus she had a mole on her face that she'd never had before. There was no way that girl could chase him across the galaxy. Impossible. Right? Maybe there were parallel universes, and he'd stumbled into one, and there was a Hugubu female who happened to look like Sheela. It couldn't be an accident that the Jakk tape loop was next to the Sheela tape loop.

Was this a trap? Someone was using images to bring him out like they lured Robin Hood into a public place. Jakk looked around. He tried to gauge whether anybody was looking at him but they were all absorbed by the movie. He quickly walked away, paid his gold coins, and boarded the bus.

The space bus was not a beautiful vehicle. It looked like a flying stomach with eyes, surrounded by glass, with a trunk to hold engines and communications gear. It looked like a beaver dick. He never saw a beaver dick, but one would definitely look like this space bus. It was a zero-gravity model—no up or down—with strap-handles for standing passengers like a subway car, efficiently allowing passengers to enter or exit from any direction. It would have been cool to drop a tennis ball inside it, just to try to guess where it might bounce. He wondered if anyone got motion sickness, then remembered they didn't eat food. There were chairs in every direction, so you could sit upside down next to an alien right side up, check the insides of their ears or visually explore other orifices—if they had any—and converse with the weirdness of seeing a face with the mouth above the eyes. Would this make weird aliens look even weirder, or finally look normal?

A benefit of not having separate floors was being able to see in practically any direction. He found a seat looking at stars. The bus's gravity held him upside down, close to an exit, where he could leave quickly if necessary.

What he had seen was real. But what *had* he seen, exactly? Could it be that Sheela had built a spaceship and followed him to Hugubu, was caught and executed, and the Hugubuian authorities had made this tape before killing her as a way to capture him, their remaining bacteria-smuggling Earthling? No, unless she had read his computer, learned his plans, built her own spaceship, and her balloon had meant that her spaceship would also blast off to Betelgeuse? But he had been careful with his computer, with virus protections and firewalls, plus the intensive design parts were not connected to the Internet, so no virus could slip in and no information could slip out. Maybe Hugubuians had read his mind while he was unconscious and extracted her image from his dreaming brain, but why would they do that? What about the mole on her face? Nothing made sense. Nada. In short, there was no acceptable explanation for his personal Twilight Zone, unless he would give up rationality totally and admit there was a God, and he was almost 100% sure there was no such thing. He realized he was a baffled creature being Sheela-ed but he could only console himself with the realization that even if he did not know, he *knew* that he did not know, and many creatures were clueless but did not know that they were clueless. At present, however, his only working theory was that he was being *relentlessly tracked across the galaxy by a vengeful human female.*

Customers boarded with their purchases. Several had balls circling above their heads like an angel's halo while making a low whirr sound. Jakk thought they were cool to look at but somebody snickered that they were gaudy. The movie star and her boy sat next to Jakk's skyscraper diorama, which attracted many children on the bus who played a game of "give it the most absurd command." Astonishingly, the creation kept learning tricks Jakk could never have dreamed up. He was proud of his artwork! One kid yelled *put out the fire!* A vertical skyscraper morphed into a fire engine with red lights flashing and drove itself around looking for flames until it squirted the boy in the face! The entire bus erupted in laughter.

In the commotion Jakk didn't notice the woman who sat next to him, although he began to sense a coconut fragrance. He tried to look at her with his peripheral vision while avoiding eye contact. He glimpsed her reflection in the window—it was Reena—Reena the traitoress, the false confidant, the senator's daughter, co-star of the movie *Jakk Jacks the Sprocks.* What were the chances she sat next to him accidentally? Were there not millions of creatures on the planet Hugubu? Why couldn't women simply let him alone? He imagined himself as an Immortal and she hovered outside his shell, spray painting his panels and threatening to blow his box. How could it have been that she ventured to the Art Planet? She was in the movie with him—maybe that was why? There were open seats left; she could have sat elsewhere. He guessed she knew it was him, and his heart sunk with the probability that his cover was blown, that he would soon be back in prison and be executed by trebuchet. But what could he do? He could jump off the bus and try to escape into the crowd; if she followed, he might overpower her since he saw no guards, but then he would be arrested by Orkannians in a few days. Perhaps he could commandeer a space buggy but it would have to have warp drive.

He hid his face in his hands as the bus lifted off. He tried to avoid being recognized but he felt her beauty and warmth. It was torture having her so close yet being unable to talk with her. There was a spark of hope—he remembered she advocated for him back on the warship. He supposed she had an answer to the Sheela riddle. He wished he could read her brain.

He felt a slight thump on his thigh. Caught. It was her hand with a piece of paper and a pen. He hesitated, took the message, and opened it tight to his body like a poker player examining his cards. The message said: *Jakk, run no more. Live on Hugubu for as long as you like.* He sighed. Why the subterfuge and scribbled messages? *Why are we scribbling like this?* he wrote. She wrote something then handed the message back to him. *When they learn you're alive you'll be mobbed as a hero.*

It made sense. Sprocks killed Hugubuians; Jakk killed Sprocks; Sprocks were the bad guys and therefore Jakk was a good guy. QED. So what if his actions were merely in self-defense? Luckily he killed, nay, zorked the Sprock commander. Bonus points. His smuggling might be forgiven. He scribbled *Will I be executed?* She wrote *No, you are safe.*

He looked at her. She looked at him. She looked happy. He leaned over and gave her a long slow deep kiss. He didn't care whether anybody saw. He didn't care what shape her mouth might contort into. Screw customs. Screw the universe. He would have screwed her face if only there was a private bathroom or a large umbrella nearby, but instead he quietly asked her about the Sheela-show, but she deflected his questions and said that Max would explain. She said Max was their friend, a trustworthy cutting-edge computer scientist. Jakk was beginning to appreciate the value of friends. It was amazing how his prospects flipped from space criminal on the run to forgiven war hero with one message scrawled on a piece of paper.

The bus slowed to maneuver through a battlefield. Jakk saw dead Hugubu soldiers floating, dead Sprocks, hunks of blast-deformed metal, still-spinning glass shields, a swirling console with lights blinking. It was an avant-garde highway vehicle pileup except there was no friction to stop the spinning slabs. One burned Sprock spun slowly, eerily, floating in a cloud of its own yellow blood, and when it slowly turned, its wide-open eyes, steely and frozen, seemed to look directly into Jakk's before it slowly spun around again. Reena said that the cleanup was postponed because of continued danger.

Soon the planet Hugubu appeared, its outer surface like the Moon's, desolate with occasional meteor craters. The bus headed toward an opening like a lit-up volcano that was hollow inside, and passed turrets and a checkpoint as it entered the innersphere.

Inside the planetary shell, everything went from dark to light, lit by a giant lamp redirecting photons from Betelgeuse. Jakk's eyes adjusted to the tropical terrain as the craft oriented itself with its bottom facing the inside surface, flying over the sea where he and Reena had swam to escape. It was like Earth except the horizon tilted upward like a welcoming smile; the upper sky was not blue but a greenish brown from the opposite side of the innersphere. The city came into view: floating skyscrapers, vehicles moving continuously without stoplights. He saw the building where he had been imprisoned. The bus eased into a central area surrounded by a purplish weaving structure that resembled a spray-painted sandcastle supported by one thin leg; another resembled a waterfall of flowers. The buildings were asymmetric, each with its own unique color scheme. He saw floating art and LED-lit sculptures hovering in place. Theatregoers watched an outdoor performance by hovering around a floating stage. When the space bus stopped, there were no buh-byes from stewardesses with manufactured smiles, just a disturbing message that the bus was not traveling on to Andromeda as scheduled. Why not? Jakk felt uneasy. He didn't like having to trust Reena.

"When you greet Max, offer your right hand and he'll shake it," Reena said.

"Why?" Jakk asked.

"He knows Earthling greetings."

"If I don't, he'll greet me by fondling my crotch?"

"Our customary greeting."

Jakk and Reena ambled with departing passengers through a crowd. There was Max wearing standard Hugubu drabwear which looked like a giant paper towel combined with a muscle shirt. No police. No soldiers with guns. That was reassuring. Jakk tensed as Max's hand reached out and gently groped his crotch as he said "Welcome." No crunch. It was a pleasant sensation. Jakk did the same to Max's smooth, junkless mannequin crotch, and thought *hey buddy, too bad a space turtle munched your package.*

"Like a city tour?" Max asked.

"Sure," Jakk said.

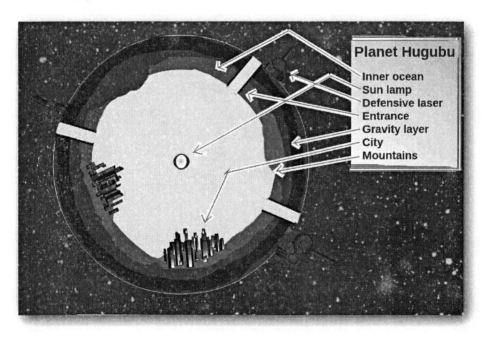

Jakk and Reena and Max walked underneath floating buildings and sculptures. There was an outdoor movie made not from light projected on a screen, but from red, yellow, and blue water squirted from tubes and controlled by gravafixers, resulting in drippy images; Max said these movies were possible only when it wasn't windy. A people-mover sucked commuters in a clear tube from the suburbs, commuters reading without any apparent train around them. There were no vehicles, pollution, nor horns blaring but smooth movement and a harmony to public life. The society used anti-gravity technology like Romans used concrete: it was everywhere, floating buildings, hovering escalators. It cut down on noise. The city had a creamy quality, smooth like squished bananas without the fragrance. Jakk kept glancing over his shoulder for a squad of soldiers stomping toward him, but nobody bothered him.

An uneasy silence overcame them, as if nobody knew what to say without giving offense. Jakk wanted to know why a top Hugubu scientist was escorting him around. Had they sent a spacecraft to Earth to retrieve Sheela and was she waiting in the city somewhere with a basket of flowers that included a note asking for Jakk's forgiveness for her balloon mockery? Why were there no flies or mosquitoes or birds or any creatures? Could he shower? Were cameras following them as they strolled? Did they have hotels? If so, how would he pay? He understood diddly squat, understood that he understood diddly squat, and this awareness bothered him. He thought about the word *understood*, that understanding was based on standing under, knowing from below, a knowledge held together by gravity, and he wondered whether this thought was profound. It was not. Jakk knew jack. That was a profound thought, he thought, and he mentally saluted his intelligence while sneaking a look at Reena's swan-shapely legs. Should he cloak his cluelessness from his newfound friends so they wouldn't look down on him, or worse, unceremoniously dump him? He might once again find himself in a doorless room facing execution. Could he trust them? With no clear enemy to battle or task to solve, his apparent freedom was unsettling.

Unusual creatures were everywhere: a many-headed hydra-being that slithered with octopuslike legs; a six-legged giant ant, probably a robot; a blob on wheels with poodlelike fur; a mostly-human looking street musician with purple hair waving her hands to play a camera-controlled instrument. Maybe a third of creatures looked human? It seemed like tolerance ruled. Two bloblike creatures conversed in what looked like sign language with hands emerging from their heads. Two others with foreheads blinking walked hand in hand like lovers. Jakk listened while Max spoke about historic sites, like where the Treaty of the Five Hands was signed with the Orkannians, or where metallurgists designed the so-called eyeschotaboo foldings that enabled spacecraft to withstand faster-than-light collisions with dust particles, and it was the basis for space noodle technology with an expanding nerf-like chemical—it was how they had slowed Jakk's speeding minivan and saved his life. They walked by the spot where Max had been awarded the Krokzeen Prize—like the Nobel Prize—for inventing a number system based on flipped quarks—like upgrading Roman numerals to Arabic numbers, it sounded like. Jakk wondered whether there was a plaque with Max's photo, like an employee of the month gets at a fast food restaurant.

They walked by a large window with a male Hugubuian floating horizontally about four feet off the ground in a room with lights, a few technicians, and what looked like a giant machine surrounding most of the room with billions of tiny needles sparkling. The patient was naked with no underarm or pubic hair, no penis, mannequin-like.

"What's going on in there?" Jakk asked.

"Body repair," Max said. "Takes ten minutes. We visit annually. It's painless."

To Jakk's astonishment, the naked Hugubuian became ten times larger, expanding symmetrically in all directions, and Jakk could see inside the enlarged body. The cells were the same size but now they were separated from each other by air. Max said that each cell was controlled by a separate gravawand; that was what the tiny needles did. Hugubu bodies were different from humans: there were multiple hearts in each body that could be controlled during the operation; brain tissue was scattered throughout the body and could hibernate at will; bones could shift from extra-strong to soft like jelly by manual control; muscles were thinner and stronger.

Technically, a Hugubuian was not an individual but a *dividual*—a lifebeing who could be divided into parts, although the parts could not be separated for long periods of time. When the repair technician began to walk inside the blown-up creature, cells moved out of the way in advance, creating a workspace. The technician replaced one organ with another. He used a medical tricorder to check the patient's circulatory and nervous systems. He smiled and waved to Max and Reena, walked back out of the expanded body, pressed a button, and the body collapsed back to its original shape. To Jakk's amazement, the patient woke up, smiled, and walked away. Max explained that periodic cell repair enabled longer lives, since problem cells or dysfunctional organs could be swapped out. Cancer happened occasionally but it was easy to treat since the offending cells were easily spotted and removed one by one. Could they do that to Jakk? Max shook his head; it required thousands of years of genetic adaptation before they could engineer cells to be detachable.

Max led them by a stream. "Why are we going this way?" Reena asked.

"Quickest way to the theater," Max said.

They passed a grassy field with mounds of gold piled in designated squares. Robots whirred, taking coins from piles and adding them to others. It was a bank.

"Where are the walls, vaults, guards? Anybody could steal it," Jakk asked.

"Yes but they would be caught," Max said.

Max stopped close to a huge pile of gold with his name on it. Jakk saw Reena's smaller pile nearby. It was weird how something so valuable could lay in a pile on the grass. Of the thousands of piles, Max's was one of the tallest. He was one of the richest Hugubuians. With open-air banking, Max said, everybody saw who had what so theft and bribery were impossible. There was an empty square with Jakk's name on it. He was the poorest creature in the whole field.

"Why did you people imprison me, then pretend to let me escape?" Jakk asked.

Max and Reena paused, as if debating how to answer.

"We apologize. We suspected you were a Sprock spy," Max said.

"I'm a high school student!" Jakk said.

"We know."

"From Earth! From New Jersey!"

"We know."

Before Jakk had arrived, a space bus had gone missing and they'd lost communication with a distant colony, so there was a predisposition for suspicion. The smuggled bacteria did not endear him to authorities either. Jakk figured that Reena had convinced Max that he was good, but there was something odd in the extreme switch from suspected bacteria smuggler to innocent high school student—why didn't Max grill him further?

"Sprocks killed your guards," Max said. "Why not side with them?"

"I figured they'd kill me since I looked like you," said Jakk.

Jakk recounted his adventures in space up to the Art Planet. "I sent back their tow truck," he said.

"Orkannians can be stubborn," Max said.

"My father can try to arrange a deal," Reena said.

Max shook his head and said that the Orkannians would execute him if they caught him but he was somewhat protected from capture by Hugubu law. He would have to pay damages; until then, they had to guard against Orkannians swooping in to kidnap him. But how could he raise the money?

"I could sell more art," Jakk said.

Max and Reena laughed heartily. Jakk was beginning to warm to them. They were his kind of aliens. He never felt this way about anybody else before. There was mutual respect, a curiosity, like they could open doors for each other. Why would this happen so far away from home? Friendship was a bond like love, a living thing in its own right, requiring feeding like a spirited puppy, needing commitment, a shared pulling among three stars, not unlike gravity. Would it limit or enhance his freedom?

"Why was my classmate Sheela dancing in the Art Planet video?" Jakk asked.

Max beamed with delight, almost in tears.

"Decades of code writing, almost losing funding several times, and it finally worked! It's wonderful to hear you say it was your classmate. So how can I explain it? When something radically new comes from simple things, it is *emergence*, like when two hydrogen atoms and one oxygen atom makes a water molecule. Suppose you work backward and undo the emergence. That is how my God program works."

4

Jakk in the Box

Traffic stopped. Everywhere foreheads blinked. Now what? It was a citizens' meeting. About twenty creatures, a mix of humanish and freaky types, gathered in a circle. Other circles formed nearby. It was democracy in real time: citizens exchanged information with each other and with government. When Max spoke, everybody listened.

Jakk learned that a blockade by the Sprocks—the Sprock Block—was beginning to form but might take months to finish. While Hugubu was protected by a Betelgeuse-powered laser, the planetary encirclement was beyond laser range, in effect making Hugubu into a besieged castle with no travel in or out, not even to tropical Mergetroid or the Trash Planet or Art Planet. This did not seem to unnerve the Hugubuians, so Jakk didn't think much about it either, except it made it less likely that Orkannians would hunt him down. Apparently Jakk caught the last space bus in to Hugubu—good—but he was stuck on the planet for the foreseeable future—not good. Citizens voted to ration supplies and run defense drills. Then they disbanded. A citizen spotted Jakk.

"It's him! From the video!"

A crowd surrounded Jakk as Reena and Max looked on.

"It's you!" said an octopus creature, smiling.

"It's me," said Jakk.

"You did it!" said a blob.

"I did it," said Jakk, although he wasn't exactly sure what he'd done.

The idea of celebrity came like a sudden pleasure rush to his brain. The universe finally figured out he was cool, a being of import, someone who possessed a certain *je ne sais quoi*. He could bask in the attention. He could be worshipped. One humanlike guy approached and asked if Jakk would pose for a quick video with his teenaged daughter—"I'm going to lift her skirt," he said, "and you act shocked that she has no vagina." Jakk ran to Reena and Max as the mob followed.

"Max, do something!" Reena said.

Max touched his forehead and lights blinked on the headset over his ear.

"Jakk, you have Celebrity Status 25. Citizens must not approach you, initiate conversation, or block your comings and goings, but if you talk to them, your protection ends and they can pal around with you like they've known you your whole life. Got it?"

It was a decent change, but not great. Everybody looked at him with puppy dog eyes, seeming to want his magic spark to enliven their dull lives with a brief and painless shock. Jakk wondered why he got only Status 25. Shouldn't the war hero, savior of Hugubu, get Status 1?

As they walked through the longing crowd, Max and Reena explained that Hugubuians emerged from a primordial chemical soup similar to Earth's but from a warmer water-based planet in the Andromeda Galaxy. They quickly became the dominant species. It only took them a half-billion years compared to four billion for humans to evolve. They managed against great odds not to destroy themselves and excelled in medical technology. When they learned to soak starlight directly into their skin thirty thousand years ago, they no longer needed other creatures.

"You wiped out all other species?" asked Jakk, amazed and shocked.

"We did not kill them. We abandoned them," said Max.

"You abandoned the whales?"

"We did not have whales. We had sea cows."

"You abandoned the sea cows?"

"Sea cows munched plankton, blew air out their blow-hole, and went moo."

"That was heartless."

"Humans are nicer? You grow cows on farms, kill them, then eat their insides."

Arguing with Mad Max the scientist was proving difficult. How did Max know so much about Earth? Probably his goddamn God program. Jakk wanted to impress Reena with his debating prowess and was beginning to regret skipping forensics and history and environmental science in high school. He didn't like to think of himself as an animal-murderer and plant-murderer, but in this debate, he found himself scrounging like a bottom feeder for arguments to support his position.

"The cow would never have lived but we gave it life," said Jakk.

"So you are God? You create creatures, get hungry, then eat them," said Max.

"But you abandoned all creatures!"

Max explained how it became a major nuisance to keep boring animals alive, animals that didn't create philosophy, think, or better themselves. They just ate other animals, loped around, pooped, scratched, and mated to make more boring animals. Bacteria were a particular menace, requiring vigilance by the immune system and DNA to encode defenses against it; this took up valuable genetic real estate, so there was less space for cool stuff such as regeneration of lost limbs or multiple hearts or tissue detachability. So they left these creatures on their home planet long ago; when a scout ship returned, they found their former planet devoid of life. What happened to the abandoned creatures? The mystery was never solved.

Reena watched Jakk and Max spar. Why was she silent? Jakk knew that the key to victory was often simply to persuade sidelined third parties to enter on your side. She could pick the winner with a smile. Maybe she thought Max was right but wanted Jakk to save face? Maybe she was trying to encourage a budding friendship between Jakk and Max? Finally, she spoke.

"Earth has amazing colors. Their clothes are bedazzling," Reena said.

It bothered Jakk that he didn't know how they knew so much about him and his world, but he could see how Reena might be impressed with human fashion. Hugubu women wore outfits that seldom changed, the same-old throwwear, tight-fitting and functional, excellent for carrying tablets without pockets—gadgets simply adhered to the chest, possibly by gravity or magnetism. Reena wore the standard Hugubu garb revealing her sexy legs but she would have looked fetching wearing a T-shirt or towel or giant leaf.

"Earthling clothes are frivolous, not functional," Max said.

"Humans call it fashion," Reena said.

"Reena is right," Jakk said, although he secretly agreed with Max that fashion was a waste of time.

"Humans shave sheep, dye the shaved wool, then wear it—yuck!" Max said.

Jakk and Reena smiled at each other. Max couldn't win: it was two against one. Was that it? Reena changed the topic to find a way for Jakk to win an argument with his know-it-all opponent. She was a sensitive lifebeing. Jakk found himself feeling sympathetic for Max who, despite his impressive scientific acumen, was flailing in the wooing department. Maybe the contest was not who could win the argument but who could win Reena's affection, so he tried a reversal, similar to a move he had seen at high school wrestling matches.

"Maybe it was right to abandon the lesser creatures," Jakk said. He didn't really believe that, he just threw it out to see what would happen. "Flu isn't fun. I like swimming in your sea without whale poop or sharks or barnacles. Your ocean is as safe as a swimming pool! Screw the whales and sea cows. Your cities are clean. And I love my zit-free face."

Max put his hand to his ear. "Excuse me, Sprock stuff. Jakk, let's explore my program later, okay?"

Max departed, and Jakk found himself alone with a hot Hugubu senator's daughter—like being on a date without having to risk rejection! It was fun simply walking down the avenue with her. He found himself gesturing for the sake of gesturing, keeping his hands moving since he didn't know where to park them. He felt like singing her a song so stupid that it wasn't stupid. Onlookers tagged five meters behind them. While it was great being alone with Reena on a sandy beach, it felt sexy to parade in public, a status thing, a few more pumps of air into his ego balloon to be walking in public with a female whom almost all other males wanted.

"Can I take you to a restaurant?" Jakk asked.

"We do not have restaurants," Reena said.

"Your apartment?"

"Nobody has an apartment. We have dormitorios."

"How can we speak privately?"

"What must be kept secret from the community?"

Dating Reena was proving difficult. Hugubu seemed like Earth. She seemed human. But he didn't understand Hugubuian romance. He felt naked, forced to conform to an unknown code, afraid to act lest he upset some rule he didn't know. If he tried to have sex with her, it might become another interplanetary joke-video. Sex was weird enough in private, but in public? Further, he was not sure exactly what he wanted with Reena. He didn't feel comfortable with the idea of humping her face since her eyes would be watching his balls swing back and forth. There were no public bathrooms, no beach cabanas or other semi-private spaces. Could he shower?

"Let me smell you," she said.

She sniffed all around his body. He liked this.

"You are not smelly. There is no dirt in our world," she said, "no bacteria."

She suggested a swim, so they walked to the lake while curious fans trailed them, annoying Jakk, but he would have to remove his clothes or they would shock him. (Reena had explained this to him; they had given him a special suit in prison, as the sea was his one possible escape route.) He looked around. The tailgaters looked away when he looked at them. He knew that unseen cameras were filming him. It was like being in an intergalactic real-time Facebook.

His desire to swim overcame his nervousness about being naked. He whooshed off his Hugubuian garb and plunged into the surf. Reena joined him with her mannequin-y crotch and bouncy boobs. It was great. He shook his head underwater. He ran his hands through his hair as if he was shampooing. He felt cleaner even if Reena was right about the planet being dirt free. He cavorted underwater like a frisky otter.

When he returned to the surface, the onlookers were still watching from the beach.

"Remember, don't talk to them," said Reena.

"They are rude," he said. He'd had enough. "Please leave us alone," he said to them.

That was a mistake. Almost instantly the small crowd morphed into a huge gathering. Creatures came out of nowhere. News trucks hovered. News boats steamed in close. It was an instant press conference and he was naked. Creatures removed clothes and swam out. Reporters jostled for every tidbit of information. Questions came fast and furious.

"Jakk, are you and Reena a couple?" asked a reporter with a wobbly chin.

"Will you speed faster than light into any other stars?" asked another with no nose.

"Did you kill Sprocks by sperming them with your penis?" asked another.

"Why do you call Hugubuians 'Hugubuians'?"

"Are you applying for citizenship?"

"How did you survive deep space?"

"Can children learn how to milk a cow by squeezing your penis?"

"Who do you want to play you in your upcoming movie?"

"Are bacteria crawling out your butt right now?"

Jakk looked at Reena, who started laughing. That was not helpful. The crowd began to laugh as well. There was no reason for anybody to laugh; it was simply nervous laughter, contagious like a yawn.

There was no point striving for privacy so Jakk walked back up the beach and gave the galaxy a good look at his naked floppy self, which he hoped would behave itself. Reena stood by him. So much curiosity was intermingled with scant facts. His strategy was to reveal everything until they got so bored that they would leave him alone.

"Careful—I sperm creatures if they get too close," he said with detached seriousness.

A few scattered, but most stayed, smiling. They got the joke. The words "public relations" came to mind. He was meeting a whole species for the first time. He had better watch his humor. While irked about his loss of privacy, he could not alienate aliens, so to speak, who had not intruded upon his privacy. They were out there watching him on a screen. It was a wonderful opportunity for him to define himself, and perhaps it might lead to income to pay for damages to the Immortals' sphere?

A swath of the lake opened to reveal a long-haired goddess wearing a golden robe. Somehow, a force pushed water away from her so she wasn't wet like everybody else. A Hugubu talk show host?

"Welcome, Jakk," she said with a studied casualness.

"Thank you," said Jakk, sounding like a plastic politician.

"Would you like to tell your story to the galaxy?"

Jakk looked at Reena, who shrugged as if to say "get it over with." He told them about how he was a top high school student, his spaceship's inability to brake, the dastardly Sprock attack, and being exploded straight to the Art Planet. He skipped over his encounter with the Immortals.

"What do you seek?" she asked, looking sincere.

Jakk was not sure how to answer this. He knew he wanted to be immortal like a god, buff without the sweat of weight machines or exercise regimens, tan and grinning, drink in hand, but in his present situation, he was being treated like a celebrity-god, almost, so he felt less of a need for the eternal stuff. A request like "may I have a stable of supermodels please" might provoke a backlash, just like his sexist computer's "women can not program computers" comment did back in high school, but maybe he should heed biblical advice such as "ask and ye shall receive?" If he asketh, he might receiveth. Maybe if he toned down his harem request with a humorous comment like "I would like beautiful buxom babes with bulging bosomy breasts" and said it like it was a joke, then they might admire his capacity for creating poems-on-the-fly with wit. If he said "I would like a few good friends," it might sound corny, and he was starting to feel a bond with Reena and Max. He needed gold but he did not really "seek" it. He would like to be even more famous, but he could not say that, lest it undermine his growing celebrity, which was becoming like a game for him. He wanted fun but could he say that?

"Great video games! Sleek spaceships! Immortality if there's a button for that," he said.

The crowd's upbeat feeling deflated slightly. He was different from them. They had much longer life spans, but the problem of death seemed to bother them too. Did they pity his short life span? He thought about what they had in common: creature-hood, a love of life, a hunger to stay alive, a love of zany ideas, a quiet and desperate sadness that their lives would linger but not last. Like him, they were stuck in the crucible of mortality, the unavoidable life-death deal, hoping for escape via a trap door.

"Will you prong Reena tonight?" asked a reporter.

"Have you figured out the right orifice?" asked another.

"Do humans dream of electric sheep?"

"If you and Reena have kids—if you find the right orifice—will you raise them as Hugubuians or Earthlings, and could I have a follow up?"

Jakk smiled, tried to act natural, clicked on his clothing, and walked to Reena. She pushed a button to dry him off, held his hand, waved "thank you," and reinvoked celebrity privacy. Again creatures kept their distance, magically, as if the event never happened. Light dimmed in the late afternoon.

"Is that what press conferences are like here?" asked Jakk.

"No, this one was unusual. What are electric sheep?" asked Reena.

"Sheep are Earthling animals that provide wool and go *baa* and are not electric."

"Have you ever dreamed of electric sheep?"

"There is an Earthling book entitled *Do Androids Dream of Electric Sheep.*"

"How would reporters have known about such a book?"

"Max's God program?"

Reena laughed. It was delightful watching her laugh. She tried to suppress her laughter, which backfired, causing her to laugh even more.

"Do you get it?" she said between bouts of laughter.

"Of course I get it," he lied.

"Max researched Earth with his God program and fed them obnoxious questions," she said.

"Reporters don't usually ask such obnoxious questions?"

"Exactly. They would not have known about electric sheep. Max is a prankster!"

"The press conference was a joke?"

"Yes, much of it. 'Did you kill Sprocks by sperming them?' What a wit."

"It was not funny."

"It was funny."

"It was *not* funny."

"It *was* funny," and she started laughing again, which felt like sandpaper on his ego.

"The public thinks my penis is a weapon."

"Well, is it?" she laughed. "It pointed at me. Did you think I was a Sprock?"

Her laughter resumed with suppressed intensity. This was still not amusing. He was a visitor, unfamiliar with their customs, a battle-tested hero who deserved medals, not derision. First visit, imprisonment, second visit, pranked. It was not fair. He was not in control of his fate or his image. Being the butt of a joke smarted. It stung worse than sitting on a scissors.

What motivated Max? Reena—it was about Reena, was it not? Max was courting her, trying to impress her with his smarts, showing off to a 307-year old beauty who looked like a teenager by using Jakk as a toy for their mutual amusement. Jakk had killed Sprocks when trained soldiers failed. He had war prowess—prowess, he liked that word. He wasn't sure whether he was in love with Reena, but the rivalry with Max had whetted his appetite, and he found himself wanting to win Reena if only to stick it to Max. *All is fair in love and war.*

"Is this conversation only between you and me, or is it public?" Jakk asked.

"Both. It is recorded by authorities but inaccessible to the public," she said.

"Can Max eavesdrop on us now or later?"

"No."

"Why do authorities eavesdrop?"

She explained that it prevented violence. There were practically no murders, no crime, no terrorism. Children could roam the planet unattended, though murders occasionally happened when a spurned lover went ballistic. For example, one unfortunate hydra-headed celebrity was jettisoned by an enraged partner into Betelgeuse, and his frantic cries for forgiveness, sent minutes before his cells boiled, became a comedy routine. But such incidents were rare since all criminals were caught. There were no locks on Hugubu, no safes, no passwords, no security guards. They could leave gold in piles in a field. Where were the few criminals jailed?

"With the Immortals," Reena said.

"There were murderers in there?"

Reena nodded. Jakk had never thought of immortality as a punishment, but he held fast to the idea that immortality was a good thing, that the Immortals simply went about it the wrong way. He figured that any creature with a brain would know that dying is bad and therefore living forever is good. It was a no-brainer.

"I would like to be a Greek god—forever youthful, sexy, and happy," Jakk said.

"I would never marry a Greek god," Reena said.

His first thought was that Reena considered herself unworthy of marrying somebody with Jakk's theoretical prowess, but then he figured he should probably ask her to clarify what she meant, as there might be something more to it. She was older by a few hundred years, after all. Maybe if she became a Greek goddess too, she might feel herself worthy to be in photographs with him? Important factoid: her answer suggested that it was possible for them to marry, and that was good.

"Being immortal is like writing a school essay but there is no deadline," Reena said.

"Great! You have more time."

"*If* you ever finish it."

Reena's idea of Immortal Jakk was a creature who could sleep all day, watch a sunset, fly to cool galaxies, read a newspaper, do something or do nothing, that somehow this was being "disconnected" from real life, whatever that was, and she wasn't taking into account that she could be immortal as well. Together, they could cavort through strange galaxies like bar hoppers or stealthy late-night skinny dippers, hopping over fenced-in swimming pools, bursting in on wild parties.

"Jakk, if you were immortal, nobody could teach you anything. Nobody would mean anything to you. You would be *everywhere yet nowhere*. You wouldn't have to wrestle with the question of whether you love me. How could I love you if you could cavort with a harem of supermodels without consequence?"

He rummaged mentally through his past utterances—had he ever mentioned a harem of supermodels? He had not. Maybe Reena guessed this was how all males thought? The good news was that a harem of supermodels was on the bargaining table. He figured his future wife Reena would give him Saturdays off, or possibly every other weekend, to visit the harem to bolster his sexual prowess, and she would allow such excursions since she would benefit from his increased experience by herself enjoying better orgasms. It was common sense. But he decided to keep this to himself and focus on the core argument: death bad, life good, me Tarzan, you Jane, we swing vine, dodge death, defy gravity, leap to lake of life.

"I am good, motivated, a seeker of knowledge, not a slacker," he said.

"You are good because you are under life's deadline, constrained by the threat of death to learn and work and grow and live."

"I'll try being immortal for ten thousand years and then submit my conduct to a review."

"You would become obnoxious."

"I promise that I wouldn't."

"You are obnoxious even now."

Reena seemed to be winning the argument. How could he still be right? If she was right, he would have to rethink his worldview, to disassemble his skyscraper of correct knowledge, remove a pillar while trying to keep his building pointed at the truth. Reena must be wrong. It must be simpler: he liked life, life was good, why not have more? There had to be something wrong with her argument except he could not spot what the flaw was. Perhaps being "obnoxious," whatever that meant, wasn't all that bad. Maybe she was right in general but he was the one exception: he could be immortal since he wouldn't become obnoxious. He would promise to be nice. He would sign a promissory note to that effect. He would even fly around in a cape with skin-tight leggings, stopping bank robbers and rescuing kittens in trees, if required by the immortality contract. He didn't like losing an argument to a woman, particularly one he wanted to somehow fuck. He wanted her to respect him, since her respect was probably necessary for her to enjoy their lovemaking, and how could she do that after she trounced him in debate? He was trying to safeguard her future pleasure. She smiled at him, looking supermodelish cute, but he was not ready to concede.

"Do you want to die?" Jakk asked.

"No," Reena said.

"So you want to be immortal."

Jakk put his fist under his chin. That was how philosophers looked pensive. Maybe it would help him think up a better argument? A thought emerged. It felt philosophical. He could use the word *crux*. It sounded powerful, right up there with *vortex*.

"Here is the crux of the matter: if we are born immortal, we are rude jerks, but if we are born mortal, we can learn to be nice. Since you and I were born mortal, we have learned to be nice, so now we can safely convert to being immortals. Problem solved."

She smiled to reveal that she acknowledged and admired his problem-solving acumen. He had figured out string theory so he could easily decipher the less gnarly problem of immortality. She had wonderful breasts. He wanted to alternate kissing each one, cuddle them like sleepy puppies, enjoy each for eternity; they wouldn't begin to bore him for several thousand years at least. He felt obligated to reinflate her ego after she had been out-debated by the master, so he would throw her a bone. It was his way of caring. He prided himself on that.

"If we were on my high school debate team, I would want you on my side. You almost convinced me that immortality was bad!"

They strolled hand in hand in the twilight. The hand-in-hand business was what females wanted; he had read it in *Splashable* magazine. A giant screen displayed his earlier interview with the reporters. He sensed a pressure for him to keep dating Reena since it could help Hugubu and Earth foster an interplanetary friendship at some future time. Reporters got the story right. They didn't fall for the sperm-weapon theory or the electric sheep. They must have compared notes, checked references, and figured that Max had toyed with them. Still, Jakk wanted revenge.

"Tell me about Max," Jakk said.

"Super smart. Top scientist. Eligible bachelor. 310 Earth-years old."

"He played a prank on us. We need to return the favor."

"Max saved your life—his God program proved you were not a Sprock."

Great. Jakk's rival also saved his life. Why was life complicated? What would he do now? He still wanted to nail Max with a good prank—how about by nailing Reena?

Jakk yawned, and Reena took him to a dormitorio with giant SHHH! signs floating outside. Inside were creatures suspended in mid-air, sleeping, turning slowly, wrapped in thin blankets in a building without a roof, not needed since it neither rained nor snowed. He remembered he didn't need a toothbrush.

"Not an apartment but a togetherment," Reena said.

"A groupment?" said Jakk.

"Goodnightment. Lift your arms."

He did so and floated up two stories. A blanket wrapped around him and a pillow floated to his head. He looked up at the tiny lights of cities above him, on the upper rim of the innersphere—they looked like stars. He forgot to kiss her goodnight. What if somebody bumped a switch accidentally and he plunged to the ground? What if there was a power failure? Pillows were not needed but they gave him one as a gesture to help him feel like he was back on Earth. His worries were overpowered by thinking about her body, the space bus, his cityscape, her breasts, Reena with Sheela's hair, like waterfalls of sunny gold cascading down her shoulders. It was his best sleep since cuddling with Reena on Mergetroid.

Next morning he awoke with a smile. If he had to be stuck on an alien planet, Hugubu was the place. It was like the summer camp his family could never afford to send him to, with so much to see and do that serious thoughts about immortality, metaphysics, and right and wrong seemed to float away like bubbles. He remembered the joy of visually drinking in a summer morning back in Jersey when he was ten, the wide-open leaves and the buzz of insects, the momentary pleasure of sniffing the rose bush that climbed his porch. He felt a similar joy now on Hugubu, enjoying the enchanting lure of new things to see and new creatures to meet, except without the insects or fragrance of roses. An everything pill felt heavy in his hand; when he put it in his mouth, it popped like hundreds of tiny explosions, pleasant and invigorating, as water and energy and air and heat molecules untangled themselves slowly, efficiently, like a controlled nuclear reaction. He did not have to swallow it. The pill freed him from the fuss of eating, showering, cleaning clothes, using deodorant or doing other Earthling nuisance chores. If the Hugubu way was liberating, it could feel too clean, like plastic wrap or a fake Christmas tree.

Some days Reena journeyed with him, or Max, and their presence was convenient since he did not have to pay for entrance fees or transportation. Other times he was on his own, followed by a security robot in case Orkannian agents swooped in. Max and Reena took him to the creature museum, to Aragonne Rock near Hugubu University for hang-gliding, to an airborne music festival, to a park with interactive fake plants with singing leaves and syncopated shrubberies. Jakk wanted his own personal gold pile so he could venture beyond the places Max and Reena liked, such as the interactive war games which he was curious about.

There was the annoying problem of how to pay for the damages to the Immortals' sphere. Being a celebrity did not automatically mean big bucks. He couldn't charge for autographs according to Hugubu law. He lacked rights to the movie remake *Hero Human Helps Hugubu* nor could he get royalties from the JakkAction toy. He couldn't even afford a lawyer to ban release of a six-inch model of himself that sprouted a boner when squeezed and was packaged with a similarly sized model of Reena as a two-for-one playset. His persona was achieving immortality in images and plastic but the images were jumbled and confused. He was like a brand released before the product was ready, an operating system still loaded with bugs. His image floated off of him to be distorted into odd shapes by creatures with dubious agendas. How had this happened?

But Max didn't mind his penio-centric (the paparazzi's term for Jakk) human friend. Together, they explored the drippy caves that had been created by one of Max's student's architectural algorithms. It didn't seem to bother Max when a passersby saw Jakk and began humping air like an escaped convict doing an imaginary chicken. Others wanted Jakk to sign the mindless JakkAction bonering toy, apparently unaware that Jakk was earning nothing from the purchase. The persona of Jakk as a penio-obsessed creature overly impressed with his own organ got blown out of proportion. It was not fair. He was a joke-celebrity, like a Sarah Palin, sexy yet stupid, respected for his Sprock battle but better known as a public source of amusement. When he tried to rein in his celebrity, it galloped madly like an Andalusian war horse spooked by a firecracker. He struggled to control his image like a typist whose hand positions were off, so the text of his life emerged as a jumble.

The "Human Museum" idea was floated as a win-win: a vehicle to help Jakk repay the Orkannians, plus indirectly paint Jakk as deserving of better media treatment. Public curiosity about these newly discovered creatures called humans was tremendous: how did they live? what did they wear? what they were like? Max loaned seed money and several banks loaned the rest, but the project had to jell quickly to recoup the start-up costs. Developmental stages were skipped. When highly paid museum consultants pressed for better answers to questions such as "If humans are smart enough to build space rockets, why do they continue to believe in religion?" and "Why are there chairs?" and "Why do humans sometimes have mirrors above their beds?" time-pressed Jakk knew that truth had to wait behind marketing. He believed the short-term need for gold trumped any long term need for authenticity. So when his high-priced consultants suggested answers after watching Jakk hesitate to answer their questions, Jakk found himself saying "Sure, that's what humans do." How would anybody know? Earth was far away. There could be no fact-checking; Jakk was the only human. Maybe Max and Reena knew more about humans than the others, such as about Jakk not being besieged by swarms of leaf-clad females back on Earth begging "Please, Jakk, can I hop on your spaceship?" but they were in his camp financially and needed the museum to be a machine cranking out gold. The museum was built in a few hours, exhibits whipped together, and staff hired.

On opening day there were throngs of ticket buyers. Jakk smiled as he watched gold coins pile up in the ticket-taker's window. His money troubles were over. Visitors explored the Jakk-wing to watch recreated videos in vivid color on the walls: one video showed Jakk winning debates with his contemporaries Einstein and Newton about gravity, another with him shooing off adoring supermodels with hairspray as they struggled to clamber aboard his spaceship, another with Jakk critiquing the war strategies of Napoleon and Caesar and Hannibal and Sun Tzu and Alexander the Great, another with Jakk declining an invitation to be appointed president of the United Nations by saying he could do more to help the whales by using his extensive computer programming skills to optimize mating strategies. There was the life-sized Jakk (really a robot) perfecting his war skills in a video-game parlor while he ate pizza. A photo gallery showed Jakk figuring out *The Theory of Everything* by playing volleyball, having the solution come to him right before he made a super spike. Visitors flocked to exhibits that showed igloos, log cabins, Pueblo caves, penthouses with reflecting pools like the one where Jakk lived, and McMansions. A few listened to a holographic model of Jakk's father as a naked handyman, wearing only a tool belt, singing and dancing in a widescreen mini-movie. The first num-ber was "Lefty Loosie Righty Tighty," whipped together in five minutes, based on his father's enlightening of Jakk about how to open and close heating valves; the model moved his hands as if he was dialing breasts. A second song went like this:

Woman! I've watched you walkie walk walk
Woman! You've watched me gawkie gawk gawk
Woman! Enough of your talkie talk talk
The time is now! Woman! (pause to thrust hips) *To spackle and caulk!*

Outside, Reena and Max and Jakk watched visitors entering and exiting.

"Something is wrong," Reena said.

"Look at the crowds!" Jakk said.

"The exiting faces seem less happy than the entering ones."

"Maybe they're exhausted from the fun."

"Jakk, you need to ask them how they liked the museum."

Jakk didn't want to ask them for their opinion—the Human Museum was extraordinary, unique, and enchanting, and what good would come from querying a few diffident guests? He didn't want to trigger a bad vibe or encourage criticism. He wanted to keep the upbeat feeling of celebri-tyhood. This was his day and he wanted to revel in it, but Reena insisted, so he met with a few exiting visitors, although many didn't seem inter-ested in talking to him. One customer wanted her money back. What was going on? Another irate visitor used words like "inauthentic" and "boring."

This negativity proved acidic. Jakk stomped off, embarrassed. He had worked hard. It wasn't fair that pea-brained creatures didn't appreciate his excellence. So much was riding on this. He ran and ran.

He stopped and looked around. He was alone for the first time since he'd returned to Hugubu. In the distance, he saw waves on the ocean. Something didn't feel right. There was an eerie stillness, a too-quiet feel-ing. He turned and saw a creature with a large net he recognized from photos as an Orkannian. He started to run back but was swept up and lifted off the ground. But then he felt something wrap around him and pull him back. It was Max. How did he get there so quickly? Max wrapped around Jakk, his body flexible like plastic, and said calmly in his contorted state that the kidnapping of Jakk would be treated as a war crime. They were gently lowered to the ground and the net came off. The Orkannian stood resolute in metallic stubbornness, a wiry robotic-looking giant three meters tall, glowering over them.

"The vandal Jakk has not repaid for his destruction," the Orkannian said.

"I will pay for half," Max said and began writing on a tablet.

The Orkannian agreed but insisted on full payment by the end of the week, then flew off without a spaceship. Jakk looked at Max and Reena. He felt like a loser, unworthy of being anyone's friend, hatching bad investments and leaving others with the bill, then requiring rescue after running off like a little kid. He thanked them for saving his life but he found it difficult looking either of them in the eye.

"We have to make the Human Museum work," Max said.

Jakk was discouraged but Max insisted it could be done, so the three friends brainstormed. By law, the museum could not prohibit cameras—visitors could share what they saw by posting it, so why would any future visitor pay the entrance fee? They could watch Jakk's string theory discovery for free, and even that wasn't such a big deal; Hugubuian elementary school students mastered it in second grade. Since visitors did not drink or dine, there was no opportunity to sell pricey sodas and hot dogs and drinking mugs saying I VISITED JAKK'S HUMAN MUSEUM AND YOU DID NOT. The exhibits were boring. Max thought visitors needed an authentic human experience, something available nowhere else. Reena agreed. They needed fresh material. What was unique about being human?

What the triumvirate designed seemed radical. Since there were deadlines, several wings were built in less than a day. Walls could be sprayed together, floors lasered together in a minute, and utilities slapped in by robots.

The first exhibit, dubbed "Jakk's Journey," gave a visitor the experience of being digested by a giant human. They could walk in, get gobbled by rubbery teeth, and swallowed down a slippery corridor by waves of contracting muscles to a jiggly stomach (a sudsy hot tub) while listening to Reena's voice explain human digestion. Then they were shunted through the digestive tract to be slathered in brown paste and pooped out whole. They could shower and repeat as many times as they liked.

The second exhibit was an educational exploration of human reproduction. Visitors would strap-on sexual organs made of self-lubricating plastic, with working models of penises and vaginas that expanded and contracted based on moaning sounds, letting partners take turns being on top, doing it horsie-style, side saddle, with or without assistance from farm implements, and of course having their "human encounter" filmed to show friends and relatives. They could choose the "Roman method" with children watching or the "modern method" behind beaded curtains on a waterbed. A side wing allowed visitors to experience the joy of birth. They would strap themselves into a gurney, spread their legs, give birth to the next visitor in line, and so on.

The third exhibit explored human religion. A visitor could experience being Moses turning sticks into snakes and parting the Red Sea (a large tidal pool), Siddhartha walking barefoot around a makeshift Indus Valley and then reincarnating into a smiling beaver (an outfit with plastic teeth was whooshed on), Jesus walking on water before being crucified then lifted up by gravawand technology to heaven, Zeus hurling lightning bolts at other visitors who would get a mild electric shock, and Joseph Smith having sexual liaisons with numerous plain-faced women.

The fourth exhibit allowed visitors to enjoy the experience of human thought while enjoying mind-altering substances. A neuroscientist in Max's university wrote code to alter the minds of visitors so they could experience having a human mind intoxicated by alcohol, marijuana, or heroin, or experience what it felt like to be dizzy, have vertigo or sleeplessness, even schizophrenia during an orgasm. Visitors simply wore the appropriate mind helmet in a room with a springy floor and walls. For an extra fee, the visitor could watch a split-screen video of themselves toppling about with weird facial expressions during their altered state.

What miffed Jakk was that Max and Reena created the best ideas. What did Jakk do? Not much. This was different from his Science Olympiad stint when he *was* the team.

The revamped Human Museum was a crowd pleaser. Lines were so long they had to combine wings: creatures would enter through the giant vagina then be pooped out through the giant anus, right by the gift shop, which featured an improved and patented JakkAction bonering toy with Verita-Sperming™ action. Strong ticket sales permitted a second bank loan and enabled Max to pay off the Orkannians. Jakk had pocket money for minor excursions without security escorts if he wanted.

He was learning how to handle being a celebrity. Max was busy with science and Reena with a fashion project so he didn't get to see them much during these days, but he found he could explore in his free time. Jakk found himself on a talk show paired against a bespectacled balding critic.

"Your penio-centric museum is fake!" the critic said.

"It's an authentic experience," Jakk protested. "I am an authentic human, and humans are big admirers of the penis. We name strips of land that jut into the sea *peninsulas*. Knights joust with penie-like poles; missiles, bullets, swords, and spears are shaped like penises. Women love shampoos. Why? They come in six-inch cylindrical bottles that squirt lotion when squeezed and resemble penises. Married women insert a penis-like hyphen between their father's last name and their husband's. Why? To remind everybody of their nightly pronging."

"Your hormones distort your judgment. You are sex-addled," said the critic.

Jakk wrinkled his nose. If there was a slight emphasis on human sexuality at his museum, it was the right amount, and he suspected his critic was unconsciously jealous of Jakk's authentic sexual organ. He felt pity for creatures who could only fuck head-to-head, eyes watching the banging up close, inches away, eyebrows slamming into eyebrows. Wouldn't Hugubuian lovers get headaches? He wondered whether kissing was possible between thrusts. With a shrug, he just walked off stage. He could ignore critics because his museum was attracting crowds and was paying for itself. It was popular, therefore it was a success, so screw the critics.

Jakk liked being a celebrity, although the novelty of crotch-grab hellos from long lines of well-wishers began to fade. He explored. It was easy to go practically anywhere on the planet. He learned to drive air and sea vehicles. He so excelled as a ribbon-cutter that he bought a shiny titanium-oxide pair with the letter J engraved on the handle. He rode with firefighters to extinguish a towering skyscraper blaze—a drama-less affair because creatures could jump out with their gravawands; robots wrapped the building with flame-resistant plastic then sucked the smoky air into space, so it was mostly a matter of cleaning. He was guest of honor in a parade along the city's main avenue with flags waving, cheers, and kisses blown from bystanders. He evoked curiosity: what he liked (space dodge ball), how he talked ("awesome" entered their language overnight), his favorite gesture (a shrug and a smile), even his random opinions muttered on inane talk shows were requoted as truth:

- Sex with a willing droid clears your sinuses like a flash flood
- The most fun thing ever is to be in a stadium where everybody does the wave
- Someday I may be older but until then I remain floating in my teenaged guyness
- A clue to what sound your female will make when orgasming is in her name; so Katie will go *eee*, Deepu will go *ooo*, and Reena will go *uuh*

His utterances came to be called Jakkanisms, akin to Confucius's analects, and were packaged into bestselling books. One abridged version was sold as party favors; another was used in a point-of-purchase merchandising display to help sell space buggies; another adorned dormitory walls. The sayings begat weird discussions—such as what happens when a woman named Deepu goes *eeeee* upon climaxing—is she having an out-of-body experience or had she changed her name? When questioned whether Earthling women's names truly determined their climax moans, Jakk grew indignant and cited double-blind experiments from a leading Danish university. When a call-in viewer said his wife Lalalaleepee climaxed with an *ooo*, Jakk assured the caller that his wife was faking it.

The lack of a cultural intersection offered huge leeway for creative interpretation since many in the viewing public had no idea what a flash flood was—even Jakk's closest experience was when his parent's basement flooded after a freeze popped a copper pipe. He could get away with being outrageous. He was nudged in that direction continually. He saw his role as a purveyor of mindless absurdity. It sold tickets. It kept him in the news. If he was a joke-celebrity, so what, he was a rich joke-celebrity. He was talked about and sought after. He even bought himself a JakkAction toy which reverted to its original shape after a friendly squeeze.

He was one of Hugubu's most eligible bachelors. He got marriage offers from females he never met. One sent a 3-D hologram of herself naked and smiling. Another bragged about having multiple vaginas. A purplish one had jiggly structures sloping like volcano dribble. One sent a video of five children crawling over her naked self as she held a sign that read JAKK LET'S MAKE FIVE MORE. There were females who wrote poems to him about the sex they insisted that they'd had with him. Another promised a free penis tattoo that frowned when it was limp and smiled when it was erect; it would further his celebrity, she argued in a 12-page missive. He wondered whether the news media exaggerated his discomfort with Reena's mouth-vagina, perhaps to encourage wacky females to engage in even wackier stunts, such as undergoing surgery, or prancing in public with life-sized Jakk robots, or claiming that a four-legged jellified chihuahua with umpteen snouts was Jakk's baby, and could he please pay for child support? Betting on which type of female name Jakk liked best was big business. The tabloid media loved it. He was money in the bank.

Could Jakk father a child? The scientific consensus agreed that it was possible for Jakk to have offspring with most lifebeings if doctors first equalized the number of chromosomes, which required a supposedly pain-less testicular operation using a tool shaped disturbingly like hedge clip-pers. He was on their version of *The Dating Game*; luckily he wasn't chosen, or he would have had to endure a weekend with a hairy female with a face like a Saint Bernard on steroids.

Celebrity was practically a form of immortality, right? It was what he had wanted, was it not? His exploits would outlive him, he supposed, as undying images, retold tales, maybe a floating monument. Other times, however, his fame seemed more like a hollow statue for him to squeeze into, a hat to wear so he could play himself, or an outrageous caricature of his real self. Celebrity-Jakk would sell tickets to keep the real Jakk swim-ming in gold.

Sitting by himself in a park, he pondered. Wind seemed to nudge the shadows in the late afternoon, gray versions of trees on the clean grass, artificial trees that didn't have to struggle for sunlight or water or carbon dioxide. If he felt unsatisfied by his celebrity self, he was unsatisfied with his real self too. What was life all about? He felt like a donut suspended in a pleasure vat, not fully happy but happy enough to spin slowly in hot bubbly fat.

It was the problem of freedom: what does one *do* with it? When he was imprisoned, it focused his mind on escape, but what should he do now that he could go anywhere within Hugubu? He remembered the freedom of floating in space, how wonderful it was, the total privacy, but then he thought that he didn't understand freedom at all. Mark Twain was wrong. If freedom wasn't floating on a raft in the Mississippi, what was it? Did he need privacy to experience full freedom? He was tired of having to act nor-mal when anything he might do could appear in the tabloids seconds later. He altered the dynamic of every room he entered. Even walking along a street, his presence often affected the mood of passersby like a magnet disturbing a gravitational field. An awkward hush would fall over the crea-tures as they tried to appear nonchalant but really were chalant.

The only private place in an extremely public world was in his own brain. There he could romp in his own weirdness, but still there were problems: if a funny thought betrayed itself with a smile, would a hidden camera pick it up? His celebrity built on itself in a positive feedback loop, increasing his sense of self-importance and decreasing his respect for others. Creatures weighing his every word as if he was an Earthling prophet made them begin to seem frivolous and boring. They soaked up even his dumbest ideas—how snakes humped ("imagine the letter S next to a backwards S"); whether curly hair should be wrapped in a bun; whether fake blue-green plants were sexier than fake yellow-green ones. He felt compelled to smile constantly, to feign interest in the everyday. It was easy at first when he was excited by pretty much everything, like Lindbergh freshly landed in Paris, but smiling became a chore. How could he complain? He would look like a jerk if he appeared ungrateful. They longed to be him. They thought he had a magic they lacked. He longed for a private place, where he didn't have to worry that sprouting a rod while hovering asleep in the dormitorio would cause him to awake to a swarm of reporters asking whether Sprocks were nearby.

The next day he went kitesurfing with Reena in her white Earthling bikini. She said she designed it herself, though he couldn't understand why she had to have a picture of a human vagina, complete with pubic hair, on the bottom piece. If she was trying to entice him, it was having the opposite effect, but he was reluctant to insult her fashion sense.

Since the inner ocean was spherical, it was possible to circumnavigate it by riding a single wave generated by an underwater machine—if one could stay in that sweet spot between valley and crest. After floundering for a half hour, he became adept at staying on the board. He felt as if wind and waves were part of him. Reena remarked how Jakk seemed to learn the sport effortlessly. She had taken years to master it. He enjoyed the physicality, surf without salt spray, imagining Reena being made love to by a powerful wave tossing her in its tender hands.

In a remote spot, they came upon burned metallic structures, twisted, still sizzling in the water. These were the remains of Hugubu warships. They paused to look, bobbing in the swells. He thought about how clean war seemed on a video screen, blinking green blobs attacking blinking red ones, and the blasted hulks reminded him of the scariness of real war, its liquid ferocity. It could have been his fate on that Hugubu warship.

Back in the city, Reena persuaded authorities to build a house for Jakk with curtains and no cameras, a reading lamp and king-sized bed and a roof. It would be his private realm. Getting permission was difficult since Jakk was a foreigner, but Reena used her political connections. The Jakk Shack, as it came to be known, was a one-room bungalow, built by a robot that welded glue-polymer synthetic molecules with a spray gun. Then the roof was hosed on, and the shack was finished in ten minutes. It was permanent, according to a green-faced construction official with clipboard and pulsating earlobes, and might someday become a tourism site. Jakk thanked Reena, walked inside, and locked the door, relieved to be out of the public eye.

Next day there was a knock knock knock.

5

Jumping Jakk Flash

"*Sportliche Klassik*," Reena said.

"What are you doing?" Jakk asked.

Reena's beaded Persian princess outfit with see-through sashes and a veil reminded him of Jasmine from *Aladdin*. She held the fashion magazine *Splashable*, possibly retrieved from the wreckage of his mini-van spaceship. She asked his opinion about the black Stevie Nicks–type outfit, the tigress apparel, the smoking 50s look, the faded flower cardigan, even a raincoat of fake grass, and Jakk said they were interesting. What was the plan? Earthling fashion for Hugubuian women? There was something odd when humanlike females wore dresses to hide nonexistent genitalia. It was like a freshly arrived immigrant who forgot to say the word "the."

"Like this outfit?" Reena asked.

"You are divinely gorgeous in it."

"Am I beautiful like Earthling women?"

"You're a knockout, a schwingmeister, a launcher of ships."

"Do I look fat in this?"

Sheesh, just like Earthling women. Why do women think they look fat? He was tempted to say that she looked like a fat woman who had just eaten ten other fat women.

"You're a ten," said Jakk.

"Be in my fashion show?"

"Yes." He had no choice. He owed her, big time.

Jakk liked Hugubu throwwear clothing, drab but functional, with electronic controls, sensors, easy-dry, climate control, stain-proof, and no buttons or zippers! How cool was that? Back on Earth, where "menswear" was a one-word sentence describing how real men reacted to the idea of fashion for men, throwwear might appeal to style-unconscious handymen, plumbers, electricians, bowling alley attendants, and lumberjacks.

But why was fashion the "in thing"? For almost all of their long lives, Hugubuians didn't fuss about dating or marriage or reproduction or sex. Such was Jakk's theory, as he had said on a talk show to scattered applause. Hugubuians had better stuff to do. Females didn't need makeup, high heels going *clack clack clack*, expensive hair appointments, or perfumes. Genetic alterations nixed a need for bikini waxes, but maybe there remained an unconscious hunger for flair and frills and flowers—fashion genes that scientists had failed to scissor off? Now, with the Sprock menace, time for mating was running out, and fashion was a prelude to a giant planet-wide orgy, Jakk had said on a talk show again to mild applause. He described himself as a sociologist, and he urged the audience to applaud for him once more since he was bringing sex to the entire planet.

Had he caused a vast Columbian-style culture transfer by bringing that magazine to Hugubu? In 1492, the Old World and the New World swapped diseases and ideas and memes and people, like lovers swapping spit. Could his journey be having a similar effect? If the Earth-Hugubu transfer had started, there was no going back. To hell with blowback from females averse to feeling like they had to spend on fashion. The swing factor was males—they stopped, stared, caused traffic tie-ups—and females noticed, got competitive, and it was downhill in a rolling rush.

Reena's *Keeping Abreast of Fashion* extravaganza generated media buzz, free publicity, and demand for tickets. Excitement was enhanced by a curious pop song about how the Earthling fashion Moses (Jakk) brought the tablet (*Splashable* magazine) down from the mountain (Earth). Jakk was lucky enough to snag a front-row seat. The gala opened at a freshly built

Greek-style (though roofless, of course) building with pillars and statues and lights and a red carpet, and it featured seats on either side of a long runway with hovering lights. Glitter machines were primed and ready. They could launch balloons without worrying about polluting the ocean and endangering sea life. Max sat between Jakk and Reena. Something about Reena was different, but what?

"Your God program is a giant camera pointed at Earth," Jakk said.

Max smiled.

"You sent a probe to Earth to steal Earthling fashion know-how," Jakk said.

"I'd love to show you but I'm corralled with Sprock business," Max said.

Yeah, right. You're not too busy to play practical jokes or court Reena from a distance. Mark my silent thoughts, Max. You will be pronged by a retaliatory Jakk-prank.

Five dancers in glittering outfits strutted forward on the runway and waited. Reena handed Jakk a baton.

"Choreograph them, Jakk," Reena said as a song came on.

Jakk held out his hands to say "what" and the dancers all moved in the direction of the baton. So he got up and started moving the baton. To his amazement, they followed his every move with perfect synchronization, circling, turning, jumping, even when their backs were turned, so communication must have been wireless. It was one more example of how everything on the planet, from building buildings to fashion shows, happened at light speed. The song ended to applause; he bowed and handed the baton back to Reena. Runway modeling got underway.

Naked models swam the breaststroke in a pool behind the stage, climbed stairs dripping, paused briefly under a giant blow dryer that whooshed as sexy outfits flew on and wrapped themselves without zippers or buttons. Then the usual promenade began with eyes facing forward to a center spot where the model would pause, turn back, and then forward to audience *oohs* and *ahhhhs* while Reena did her sales spiel. How did Reena know so much about Earthling fashion? The model would be gravawanded backward to a rear waiting area and the next model would swim out. Only one model was visible at a time, an improvement over Earthling fashion fests. Outfits were borderline Earthlingish glitzed with Hugubu high-tech: flashing LEDs, gravity-lifted skirts, circling overhead lights. A fetching concoction was an overhead "rain cloud" that held tiny raindrops around the body. A screen behind the stage showed the model in real time from a different angle. Another outfit alternated displaying a tropical beach and a wrapball tourney, changing back with each step. One model did a three-second mini-dance wriggle to show body hug and fit. Twins mimed losing their car keys, bent over, oh where can they be, to show the wrinkle-free fabric grip, while Reena explained what car keys were.

Coolest of all were detachable breasts. Since, by custom, Hugubuian females showed their nipples like African women in *National Geographic*, the Earthling habit of partly hiding breasts was intriguing to the audience, making males forget that they were familiar with nipples, so when they couldn't see them, they got excited again for no reason. One model removed a fetching cashmere sweater to show how both breasts could not only become erect (technical term: "breastrections"), but could clap like hands. The next model had three breasts in front and three in back, bouncing as she strutted in high heels. A svelte Nubianlike beauty had one large breast with a face that read EARTH-STYLE NYLON FIBERS IN SEVENTEEN COLORS! The next model had breasts that themselves had breasts—seriously wobbly—which drew groans. The twins showed how to detach their breasts, tossing them to each other like circus performers juggling, and the breasts would magically reattach themselves while the garment rewrapped itself clockwise. Then two breasts sang in harmony: "My knees may think, my eyelids may blink, but my breasts are talking to you, my breasts are talking to you …" Jakk heard the audience laugh, saw himself on camera open-mouthed, and waved. They loved to try to shock Jakk and marvel at his reaction.

Reena got on the runway. "Now the men!" she announced.

This caused understandable consternation in the audience. No right-thinking Hugubuian would ever think of males as needing fashion. A critic would later describe this part of the show as triply random-radical. A parade of penisless male models pranced, then emerged from wetness to reveal sculpted figures in black suits, robes, evening wear, turtlenecks, sexwear—for their combination public-private marriage, explained Reena. Jakk felt sad for their mannequined midsections like, guys, please, have your geneticist grow you a real wiggler. Sure enough, the next model sported a fake wiggler as a decoration. An outfit like a bare chest elicited applause until it started to grow chest hair that cycled among psychedelic colors—a subdued boo from the audience. Suits and ties were out, but the hot items were floating hats, detachable nipple covers, and an African safari jacket with pockets to hold tablets.

Reena gestured for Jakk to model. He walked to the pool entrance where his clothes flew off. He swam naked and climbed the stairs. Staying in the public fancy required him to act outrageous—*I am simply doing my job*, he told himself. The warmth from the blow dryer felt awesome. Then a garment wrapped itself around him. On the screen, he could see it was a macho Spanish-style serape thing with flames on the sides. It didn't feel like cotton—a tad crunchy yet pleasant. He strutted to the center circle, spun, grinned, did a quick impromptu dance to applause. Reena removed one of her breasts and threw it at him! What an honor! Or "off her." He caught it, kissed it to wild audience applause, and tossed it back. He was whooshed to the rear where his regular outfit was rewrapped around him. He had accomplished something! He felt like he belonged to the inner clique. Max modeled next but something was odd about his outfit: it was traditional Hugubuian garb? Forgot to change? Wardrobe malfunction? So why was Reena clapping? *Too bad she didn't toss you a breast*, Jakk thought. *You're not keeping abreast in our competition to woo Reena.*

Last to model was Reena, who moved like a goddess in sequins flowing like an ocean wave. She looked at Jakk and Max, twirled and smiled, thanked everybody for the fun. Jakk was thankful for having a Bollywood starlet with verve and smarts for his friend.

Max leaned to Jakk. "Tomorrow I'll show you the God program," he said with a wink.

Reena and Jakk walked alone to the Jakk Shack and stood at his door. He felt awkward. He liked her. Should he make a move? Her body confused him. It would take time for him to adjust. They stood in awkward indecision. She kissed him on the cheek and walked away with a light smile. He watched her walk away. His mind dried up like a desert sea, revealing skeletons of regrets and second guesses among the shipwrecks of bungled dating moves. Should he have kissed her on the lips? Should he have invited her in? Should he have tried to have sex with her and, if so, how? Neither Earthling nor Hugubuian women came with instructions. He realized he knew little about dating or mating etiquette or romance. He liked Reena, but did he love her? He wasn't sure. What was love, anyway?

He sighed and went inside, and thought about Reena's first dress, what she wore before the one she modeled in, why it bothered him … *that* was what Sheela wore when she blew the balloon! Wasn't it? Was his mind playing tricks on him? Same ruffly pattern. Same buttons. How could two females, one on each side of the galaxy, wear the same dress? He lay awake puzzling about this for hours before he finally fell asleep.

Max's office at Hugubu University was in a tower overlooking a manicured meadow with treelike shapes, buildings hovering, and creatures ambling with heads in devices. It was as if the creature-weirdness quotient was in full bloom. The elevator whizzed by many floors that apparently housed a huge computer. Hadn't they learned about miniaturization technology? The door swooshed open on a huge office with wide windows and a panoramic view of the valley.

"Welcome!" Max beamed from his console. They crotch-grabbed hello.

"Nice office," Jakk said.

A secretary beeped but Max asked for no further interruptions please. "How can I get anything done with this Sprock business?" he complained.

"What's the problem?"

"They're nuisances. Check this out."

Max hit a button and Sheela appeared on the screen. Earth Sheela, blowing up the balloon. Max paused the video. Her mole was gone. It was the same dress Reena wore at the gala. The viewing angle was from where Jakk had sat. It could not have come from a giant camera. How did Max do this? Did the God program read Jakk's mind? It was disturbing and amazing at the same time.

"What was that about?" asked Max.

Jakk was too stunned to answer.

"What does it mean when a woman blows a balloon?" asked Max. "Was it a tease? Did she like you? Was it mocking behavior?"

"She was probably mocking me."

"Is she your Helen of Troy who launched your boat to Betelgeuse?"

Jakk tried to think. Even if Max had pointed a giant camera at Earth, why would he have done so before Jakk arrived? And the scene was from *inside* the high school so there was no way for the camera to have recorded it. Had Max plucked this memory from Jakk's brain and restored it in full breathing color? But the scene was so vivid—he doubted he could remember the position of the other students in the class that day, the colors of their shirts, what pens they were using, but this information was all there and seemed right. Even more disturbing was how Max's computer focused on this highly troublesome moment in his life. The aliens seemed to know more about Jakk than Jakk.

"How did you do that?" Jakk asked.

"You provided the data."

"I did not."

"Was that Sheela?"

"Yes."

"Did that happen?"

"Yes."

Max beamed with such delight, it looked like he'd won the Nobel Prize and experienced orgasm and childbirth all together in one fevered rush. He was like butter, so close to melting into the floor with happiness, trying hard to maintain a professional demeanor.

Max said Earth had quadrillions of variables, but it was a closed system and their numbers were finite, with a fixed number of molecules and a steady flow of photons from the sun. Hugubu technology evolved over thirty thousand years to make computer chips that were extremely compact, powerful, and crunched data at light speed, and could be built into huge supercomputers that could hold a galaxy's worth of data. It used subatomic particles for ones and zeros. Advances in mathematics helped; for example, a number was represented by an n-dimensional matrix to expedite processing.

"But how does the God program work?" Jakk wondered.

"Suppose a visitor emerges from a given direction. We know the exact path the craft traveled, at what speed, exactly when it whomped into our space speed bumps. We extract information about the visitor's weight, height, appearance, cell structure, DNA, organ systems, until we know exactly how many blood cells there are, how many molecules, the exact heart rate—everything in incredible detail. We study the spacecraft's dimensions, contents, materials, shape, logic, engines, and databases. The result is that the computer knows everything about you at a specific point in time."

"So?"

"Here's my question: can it figure out what happened a nanosecond earlier?"

"No."

Max smiled. "But the present emerged from the past. It didn't whoosh out of nowhere. So the computer guesses what happened one nanosecond before."

"Suppose it guessed wrong."

"Then there would be an inconsistency. It keeps guessing until it is consistent."

"That would require a powerful computer."

"We have a powerful computer."

Jakk looked at Max. Was this a giant joke? One more embarrassing video for the media?

"Let's take a simpler example. Consider yourself. You arrived at 9:18 A.M. I know how fast you walk, the elevator speed, the elevator wait time, so I can tell you when you left your house with great accuracy."

"What if I stopped to watch a space bus float past?" Jakk asked.

"Suppose I knew there was no space bus."

"Fair enough."

"The computer figures out the exact world one nanosecond before you arrived. Now we have a new baseline time. We simply repeat the process for the nanosecond before that, and before that, until it retraces your trip, your planet, everything. There is only one solution to explain how you got here."

"It might figure my trip trajectory, given the speed and path."

"Yes."

"But how could it guess what Sheela did that afternoon?"

"Remember, it has information from Earthling databases such as Wikipedia, your biology, your *Splashable* magazine. It knows your planet is almost perfectly round, with a specific gravity, surrounded by air, suitable for a being such as yourself, with a slightly elliptical orbit about a medium-sized solo star. It knows your exact age, what you were wearing, what you eat, what type of social world you come from, your language, knows what bacteria lived inside you and on your skin, their DNA, everything. In short, the program figures out you and your world and every creature in it *as if it was God!*"

Jakk had a hard time taking this in. "It figured out Sheela? What she looked like? What she said?"

"Yes. If she had looked differently, the initial starting-point data would be different. You may have taken along a different fashion magazine, for example, or something else would be different."

"I can't believe this."

"Proof is staring you in the face."

"Can it map thoughts?"

"No, but it can map every neuron—its exact location, length, and electrical state in perfect detail, every neurotransmitter molecule in every synapse, in all bodies, at every point in time in history."

"It didn't know what I was thinking when I arrived."

"Right," Max said, "but it mapped every neuron in your brain."

"Why couldn't the computer guess I was friendly?"

"We guessed after studying your past, which took time."

"What's in your computer now?"

"The entire 4.5 billion–year history of Earth."

"Impossible."

"Look at the screen! Every data point, creature, molecule, and relationship."

"Impossible!"

"It knows exactly which clouds were above your town two million years ago."

Jakk was impressed. Or was it another prank? If so, it was an amazing one. His skepticism ebbed but he wanted more proof.

Max said that the Heisenberg Uncertainty Principle washed out at the subatomic level, which greatly simplified processing, since the computer didn't have to map quarks or leptons or other subatomic particles. Asteroid impacts added a wrinkle but could be controlled statistically by before-and-after analyses. How old was the sun? It guessed 4.57472049392838888 billion years old. Earth? 4.55471042938470 billion. Max added data points from Hugubuian astronomy—which knew about most asteroids—to improve accuracy. Still, the computer required as much energy to do the processing as from a thousand nuclear explosions—497 kergums—but that was free from Betelgeuse. The massively parallel computer worked by writing programs that wrote programs, and so on for thousands of levels. And code never bottlenecked since it wrote its own debuggers. It crunched nonstop for ten days. Max stopped it when it worked backward to the creation of the Earth.

"It goofed. Sheela had a mole in the Art Planet movie," Jakk said.

"It was still crunching when that movie was made. I morphed Sheela's body onto a samba dancer's moves," Max said.

The program boosted efficiency by replacing variables with constants when it could. For example, if a particular gene remained unchanged for millions of years, it used a constant. It did logic checks to ensure accuracy. It compared historical texts against archeological evidence to spot errors and resolve discrepancies.

"Could we check out Helen of Troy?" Jakk asked.

Max typed and dates appeared onscreen. Earth at four billion years ago was a waterless cauldron, then came water turning blue the sea and sky, plants came along, then dinosaurs. Max moved the virtual camera over northwest Turkey. Closing in, Troy was built, abandoned, built, abandoned, repeatedly over hundreds of years, until they found one iteration with a sustained war. The time? 1207 BCE. Max panned into the city walls and looked until they found Helen of Troy. She was short and missing a tooth, with others slightly crooked. Ancient dentists were essentially handymen with alcohol and pliers.

"*That* face launched a thousand ships? Sheela would launch ten thousand," Jakk said.

"And Reena would launch twenty thousand," Max said, smiling.

Jakk goofed. He should have said Reena. So that was it. Max's strategy to win Reena was devious—use Jakk's infatuation with Sheela to undermine his shot at Reena. Reena was real and near while Sheela was unreal and far. Would Max tell Reena what Jakk had said? Truth was, both females were equally beautiful according to Jakk's personal standards, which involved similarity to supermodels modeling underwear. He could write a subroutine to calculate beauty quotients based on facial symmetry, eye color, hair softness, and both females would score around 9.8 on a 0-to-10 scale. Sheela was pretty on the outside but spoiled on the inside, while Reena was primed for mating and bored with stuck-up scientists like Max, which tipped the scales in Reena's favor.

"Reena would launch fifty thousand," Jakk said.

"Reena could start World War Seven," Max said.

"Reena could stop a supernova."

"Reena *is* a supernova."

The ridiculousness was too much. They keeled over laughing. Jakk found himself liking his rival while knowing full well that Reena was fated to love Jakk.

"Was there a Trojan horse?" Jakk asked.

"Query the database."

No, Trojans were never horse-shaped, appeared above an image of a condom. Jakk retyped, specified, and saw the famed Trojan horse—not a towering contraption but a wooden donkey-shaped structure only ten feet tall that only held one Greek soldier. Evidently the Trojan horse myth grew bonerlike over successive retellings until it was a huge wooden fucker carrying forty hoplites.

"A condom is supposed to protect against invading sperm?" Max asked.

Jakk nodded.

"So why call it a Trojan? The real Trojan horse contained invading sperm."

Jakk was primed to spew an explanation but Max's forehead blinked.

"Sprock business?" Jakk asked.

"Yes, but feel free to explore the database," Max said as he started to walk away.

No doubt about it, Jakk liked the guy. Max was growing on him. But a disturbing image of Max and Reena trying to have sex came to mind. How could it happen? He pitied two sad aliens trying to fuck head-to-head although it would make a cool video for science class. Why were there so few photos of Hugubuians mating? Perhaps they mixed sperm and egg in a tube. Jakk would save Reena, give her a humping by a real man with a real penis. She would get jakked by Jakk.

Jakk studied this incredible program. Historians would no longer have to guess about the past. How cool was that! He could watch imperious Caesar being murdered. What did he really want to know?

Was Cleopatra a fox like Elizabeth Taylor? No, she had runny make-up and worn down teeth since sand sometimes got into Egyptian bread. Turns out there was a Jesus who died on the cross: a painful image, no nails in the feet, but three nails, two in the right hand and one in the left, blood dripping like tears. Why are humans so mean to other humans? Jesus' body was put in a cave and blocked by a boulder. Jakk focused the computer camera on the entrance for several days and nights. There were no Roman guards: why would soldiers guard the grave of a poor religious activist? When the boulder was rolled away, there was no body inside the cave. Had Jesus escaped death? Jakk moved the virtual camera inside and rewound the camera, and watched how diggers from a neighboring cave made a hole, removed the body, covered the hole, and buried the body outside Jerusalem. No life after death. It was a magic act, a sleight-of-body. The kicker: Jesus had a secret twin brother who poked holes in his hands and walked from town to town showing the holes, pretending to be the resurrected Jesus. So a two-thousand-year-old religion was based on a magic trick. Jakk was sad nevertheless because he secretly held out hope that there was a God, a Jesus, an afterlife like an all night Jersey diner where you could eat truckloads of juicy hamburgers without worrying about cholesterol.

Real history was fascinating and boring and cool and saddening. He replayed Roman wars, taking a high angle over battlefields, speeding them up to watch battles unfurl in fast-motion. It was time-lapse historiography with toy soldiers: accounts of how Hannibal outflanked the Romans at Cannae were mostly correct; Caesar's double encirclement of Vercingetorix at Alesia was much more of an uneven fight numerically than Caesar had reported in his book. No wonder why the major monotheistic religions emerged where three big continents intersected; it was where most of the fighting happened. Belief in one powerful God gave warriors a battlefield edge by dampening doubts. Roman parents really did fuck while children and servants were in the same room, like sex was a chore akin to washing dishes. *What are mommy and daddy doing? Making your baby brother or sister.* Such details were omitted in books like *Little House on the Prairie.* The Battle of Trafalgar was cool. So was watching Japanese carriers explode and sink at the Battle of Midway. It was not cool watching sailors get munched by sharks.

Jakk got a wide-angle view of history, a deep picture of patterns and trends. He saw its value. It was where he came from. He regretted not studying it in high school. What struck him was how so many humans died in so many wars—animals too: elephants plunging down precipices in the Alps, horses blasted to shreds by cannonfire—and for what? So some goddamned general could march in a parade? These were his ancestors, behaving badly, trying to climb out of their primeval soup with misguided efforts. It was not until 1700 that people began exploiting machines and fossil fuels instead of slaves and serfs. Things improved but still there were wars. Colonization. Nationalism. Genocide. Oswald assassinated Kennedy, a one-person job. Reena would probably not be impressed with Jakk or his species. Maybe she had perused it earlier—why else would she have known so much about Earth?

He backtracked through Max's earlier queries. First query: *What is Sheela's DNA?* It produced a super long string of A, C, G, T. Why ask that? Next query: *Is Jakk a Sprock agent?* No, like duh, Sprocks were not on Earth. Next: *Is Jakk a good person?* He was good. Jakk smiled. Next: *Is Sheela a good person?* Yes; why ask that?

It took a while before Jakk trained the God program on his upbringing. Had his handyman father abused him as a baby? He paused. Did he really need to know this? He loved his father, but face it, the guy was weird, he filed his fingernails against flat concrete surfaces when walking through town. He reluctantly queried the computer. Surprise: not a pervert. Relief! His father spent much time teaching Jakk all kinds of things, such as making a cat's cradle, mobiles, marionettes for a puppet show, a toy horse out of plumbing pipe. They built a model train from scratch out of discarded soda cans and wire. His father told him why he should express his feelings to himself. The computer showed three-year old Jakk in a sandbox.

"Place the golf ball on the gravity machine!" Jakk's father said.

Young Jakk put the ball on top of a cone-shaped triangular sand pyramid and it rolled down the spiral pathway, curved around the hill, almost jumped the track, wobbled into the cave through the middle and came out the other side: the other kids were ecstatic! A mom stood behind Jakk's dad, peering intently with a frown, but his father sensed her unease and confronted her.

"Play makes kids smart," he said. "They learn engineering."

But the anxious mom dragged her boy away despite the child's protests.

"Jakk, you will be smarter than that kid," Jakk's father whispered and winked.

His father had a relaxed sense of knowingness, no fear, a mastery of the social situation that defied the prejudice of tiny-minded moms. He had a presence. Also at the playground was Sheela having her dolls play beach volleyball. Sheela's mom watched Jakk's father's parenting, liked what she saw, and called to set up playdates.

Querying the God program, Jakk learned his family was astute financially. This was another surprise. Why didn't he know this? His parents never talked much about money other than to not spend it. They were not pauper lowlifes like he thought. His parents saved his mom's steady income consistently, bought stocks and real estate, owned four multifamily dwellings, didn't overcharge tenants, and fixed things promptly. "Every time wet hands reach for a paper towel, paper executives dance with delight," his father said once. Years of rolling up tubes of toothpaste to squeeze out the last dribble, short showers, replacing dryer sheets with a sock sprayed with white vinegar, drying jeans on radiators, shopping at garage sales— "saving cents makes sense," his parents used to preach. It was why, in early December, the family bundled up in winter coats, barreled into the minivan, whizzed along Highway 24 with all windows down, singing. His father called it *Believing in de-leafing*; it saved money by not having to vacuum out all the dead leaves that had accumulated after numerous trips to the dump. To Jakk, a wet paper towel drying in the kitchen was one more embarrassment keeping him from asking classmates over; to his parents, it was money unspent to be invested. Jakk's joke about his father's wallet, having a steep ratio of receipts to cash, was technically correct but missed the point. Each summer the guy grew hundreds of tomatoes in garbage cans alongside the house irrigated by a drip hose. The guy kept taking college courses—free from the library on CDs and DVDs, of course—on finance, stocks, investments, spreadsheets, psychology, pretty much everything. He knew stuff. Like Jakk at school, his father hid in plain sight. When his mother was laid off, they got by.

The extent to which Jakk's family avoided Country Club memberships, fancy vacations, designer clothes, parties, expensive cars, and dining out was out of sync with the community. When Jakk's father mingled with the other moms after school, many subjects were uncomfortable: a jaunt to Nantucket, prep schools, two weeks in Rome. The bond between Jakk and Sheela's families was a tenuous aberration that did not last. If Jakk's family was essentially alienated in its own town, the affluent families had different problems: alcoholism, infidelity, boredom, stoned teenagers, video game addictions, shopaholism. One mom was afraid to come out of her house. Another had a weird fetish for gargoyles. One mom made her kids manicure her nails and rub her back, effectively turning a tweenaged daughter into a salon worker. Why? She knew that in a few years she wouldn't be able to get her daughter to do anything so she was *collecting it forward*.

Another surprise: Sheela's parents were in trouble financially. Her dad had been fired but pretended to go to work. It reminded Jakk when he pretended to go to school during his suspension. Sheela's mom struggled as an art store owner, her older sister went to an expensive college, their heavily mortgaged house was ripe for foreclosure. Another surprise: Sheela's mom and dad bragged to each other about their affairs with other lovers. Why? Procreating done, they wanted variety. Bad surprise: Sheela's mom had breast cancer. Left one. She didn't know. Ouch. Great surprise: Sheela had a snippet of video of Jakk naked in the school shower. How did she get that?

6

The Jakk Addict

The God program camera followed Sheela home after the fateful balloon day. She ate a chocolate chip cookie, went upstairs, removed clothes, showered. She was skilled at lathering. Suds cascaded down her back, rounded her hips, massaged her like liquid hands. Each breast weighed about 0.95 pounds. How many hairs on her head? 125,439.

Sheela toweled off, put on her bathrobe, and walked to her bedroom. On her wall was a poster-sized photo of Jakk—Jakk riding a motorcycle—Jakk with no acne. She must have photoshopped away his pimples. Every afternoon she saw him on her poster looking handsome, so handsome that if he was gay, he might consider doing himself. How did she combine his image with a motorcycle? The simulation's virtual camera was in a corner of her room but she turned to face it square on—*it seemed like she looked right at him across the galaxy*—of course she couldn't see him, but he was startled. Her gaze lasted a few seconds. Then she took a magazine and swatted at the ceiling. It was a spider in the corner. He caught his breath. He rewound, paused when she looked at him, and said "hello."

Sheela's diary revealed her focus on an idealized Jakk who was unwilling to approach her. She did much behind-the-scenes maneuvering to shunt away rival approaches for the science competition, which was why the group adopted Jakk's program so quickly. She was why he was chosen for the team in the first place. She guessed correctly he was the one who slipped in the schoolwide intercom announcement about mandatory sexual intercourse in the gym: "Boys on the right, girls on the left, check rubbers for fit, today the missionary position, remember to shower afterwards." He had found the school's password on a discarded computer at the dump and inserted a self-deleting voice file. On the bus ride back from the Science Olympiad, while Jakk was looking out the window at the dark night, Sheela sat one row behind him and across the aisle, looking at him on and off for most of the ride. Why had he not known this?

Jakk typed: *How many times did Sheela write the word "Jakk" in her diary?* Computer: **342.** A verifiable Jakk-addict. How unexpected. More diary dish: Sheela's girlfriend caught Jakk staring at Sheela so Sheela knew he found her attractive.

Reading Sheela's diary, The Theory began to crumble. The Theory went like this: since women controlled the sexual spigot, they could make half of homo sapiens happier by couchifying their bodies for ten minutes a day. It was simply sharing: sharing crayons had been a big lesson in kindergarten, why not share bodies in twelfth grade? Since women didn't share, men were forced to treat women like hockey goalkeepers, and do whatever it took to slip the puck in the net: alcohol, deception, valentines, even compliments. This explained why sports goals were vaginaish: hockey nets, basketball hoops, wide-open goal posts in football. Sports taught men to score by thinking like dicks. A winning strategy was to pretend to be nonchalant, stand aimlessly in the corner, wait for a distracted defender, make a sudden backdoor cut, and *stuff it in.* Guys who dribbled or skated too earnestly and shot and missed could be *friend zoned*—the penalty box of dating—unfortunate guys were kept at arm's length like cuckolds who were still virgins. In contrast, guys who scored were heroes with bands playing, confetti, video highlights, newspaper write-ups, ice-bucket dousings (a metaphor for orgasm), and cheerleaders shaking pom-poms like orgiastic epileptics. The post-goal excitement proved what everybody knew all along: women really *wanted* the man to score, which was why cheerleaders were happy afterward. Why did women put up a challenge? To make men want to play. Such was The Theory.

Reading Sheela's diary, however, was like a constant downpour mudsliding The Theory down the hillsides of his mind. He saw the battle of the sexes from the female view. It was somewhat scary being a woman. Women could be intimidated by the sheer size and strength of men. Was male gawking a sign of admiration or a prelude to rape? For women, sex was a party in their house where they were solely responsible for cleanup while men could scoot off to another one. So women had to be choosy, yet they felt pressure to be pretty, since they could feel the sting of social sanction if they looked drab or unkempt or sloppy. Seen from the feminine view, the mating equation seemed unfair—babies grew only within women, who would have to waddle for nine months like a bloated pear. Women resented the concept of friend zoning since it implied that a woman was obligated to offer sex if a man did a friendly gesture. It was unfair, although Jakk refrained from blaming God for this state of affairs—if there was a God—since God was obviously male, God made Jakk male, and being male was better than being female, wink wink.

How had The Theory slipped into his mind in the first place? Its dust settled in gradually over the years without Jakk questioning its premises or subjecting it to rational-critical analysis. It benefited him. He was a male. All this time it felt comfortable in his brain, as if it belonged. Now, reading Sheela's diary, Jakk was prompted to take his hand, reach inside his brain, extract The Theory, rinse it in an imaginary sink, take a long eyebrows-down look at the clump of neurons wriggling like worms on amphetamines. Did The Theory deserve to go back in his brain? No. He left it in the sink.

The Theory had been connected to other theories such as Love in a Box. This theory held that loving a woman should be only one box on a man's shelf, with other boxes being career and videogames and sports and other fun stuff. Its axioms were "only open one box at a time" and "have many boxes" and "try to keep boxes the same size." When a man needed to work, he worked; when he needed to play, he played; when he needed to love, he loved. A man with a too-big box for love was pussy-whipped. The theory said the love box should only be open an hour on evenings and on Sunday morning, a pattern called "marriage." It was about balance. But now Jakk's hand returned to his brain and extracted Love in a Box and also left it wriggling in the imaginary sink.

Sheela was hollowing out his brain.

Jakk kept reading.

Sheela was bothered by the weirdness of their silent unrelationship of mutual attraction and avoidance. Why couldn't she simply have said "hello" to him? Or reversa-visa? It would have been as weird for her as for him. There was risk. Who could possibly think what to say afterward? They went without speaking for so long that avoidance became a habit. The balloon thing was an attempt to piss him off, a last-gasp effort to jump-start a relationship, since senior year was ending and soon they wouldn't see each other any more. There was nothing else to lose. Her logic was—why not? It was an active-aggressive strategy. The balloon said "Jakk, don't be a jack off, I don't like guys ogling me without making a move." It sucked that women were discouraged from initiating interest.

There was more to it.

Like Jakk, Sheela resented the fuss of rejection and the general hassle of dealing with boys, of having to make her hair look pretty so she could fit into some suitable-girlfriend box. It was hard work: hair, makeup, clothing, while a man could slip into the same boring outfit each day. It was like taking an extra course for no credit. She could easily have Huck Finned on her own raft, away from all men and confining rules. He got this. She was cool. She was no longer such a bitch. Women weren't that different from men. She thought like he did.

When Jakk was absent from school, she worried. The word "worried" appeared prominently in her diary. Had her balloon spurred him to do something crazy? Had she stomped on his ego so hard that he dropped out?

A week later, Sheela visited Jakk's house! Embarrassment. His father left her in his room. She saw dried sperm hanging from the ceiling above his bunk bed. Permanent embarrassment. She lay in his bed, thinking, stared at the sperm, touched it with her finger, pulled it free, and put it in her pocket. What was she going to do with it—deposit it in a sperm bank? She went detective, ransacked his room for clues. Did Jakk have a motorcycle license? She read every notebook, examined every drawer, soaked up tidbits from his life, searched for his computer passwords. Where was his tablet? Not there. She saw diagrams of spaceship models, equations, squiggles of strings. She went to the garage workshop, looked carefully, examined parts.

"That is a motorcycle distributor cap," Jakk's father said, pointing to the plastic object in her hand.

"Jakk wasn't building a motorcycle," Sheela said. "Why are there hinges on the garage roof?"

Jakk's father looked up and screwed up his mouth. "I never noticed those before."

Sheela unscrewed a broomstick, pushed, and the roof opened up, supported by weights in the wall. They looked at the blue April sky.

"Holy moly!" Jakk's father said. "He built a drone?"

Sheela guessed that Jakk had built a second minivan. The police hadn't figured it out. Jakk's parents hadn't either. She did. Smart girl. Police put out an alert for the Odyssey minivan. He fast forwarded three weeks. Sheela visited again, cried, and hugged his mother while his father shook his head.

"I'm so sorry I embarrassed him," Sheela said.

"Not your fault," said Jakk's mother.

"Check out my tomato seedlings!" said his father, pointing to sprouts in cups.

"Would you get with the program!" his mother scolded.

"If the prettiest girl in his class is in love with him, he'll be back," said his father.

"I never said I was in love with him! I just feel partly responsible, that's all."

"In a walkabout, an aborigine walks the desert alone for months," said Jakk's father. "Jakk's on a driveabout, spearing lizards, swimming naked in a lagoon."

On Hugubu, Jakk sat at the God program terminal. Something seemed odd. When was his father's walkabout comment? Third week of April.

When was it now? Second week. He had just watched the future. How was this possible? He was still puzzling it over when Reena walked in.

"What do you think of Max's God program?" Reena asked.

"Not bad for a beginner," Jakk said, smiling.

"You two should play wrapball!"

The next day Jakk stood uneasily alongside Max in the box-like wrapball court. Jakk wore a Reena-designed suit with a spider motif and a stallion on the back. Reena stood by in a cheerleader-type outfit like Guinevere watching knights joust. Wrapball was a mix of rugby and American football with a basketball-style goal, but played in three dimensions. Gravity held players to the floor and walls and ceiling. Shoe-weights helped players land feet-first, even upside-down, like cats. It was cool. Object of the game? To get a greenish basketball-sized ball in the opponent's hoop. Surfaces were made of a gel-like composite that softened when struck hard but was sturdy enough to permit running and bouncing. Hugubuians genetically modified their bodies so they could become soft like silly putty and wrap around other players, hence the name of the game. Since Jakk was the only player with a hard body, he was allowed to play, since other players could wrap around him.

"Wrapball!" an umpire declared. The game moved quickly. The key was pursuing the ball, anticipating angles, and cutting off passes. Jakk jumped, flipped, landed feet-first on the ceiling, and picked off the ball, only to get tackled by two opponents who wrapped around his feet. It felt like being immobilized by an octopus!

The two teams were evenly matched. There was a wrap-up at one point with seven players entangled. Later, catching a pass, Jakk scored while rebounding from the ceiling. Reena jumped with delight. He slipped one past the goalie! The winning basket!

"Great game, Max," Jakk said.

"Come by my office tomorrow," Max said. "I have a gift for you."

Greeks bearing gifts? Jakk was curious but his guard was way up. He wondered what it would be. A computer? A lovable space pet like the

LapHound? A service droid? Maybe a government official with a medal for distinguished bravery in battle? Honorary citizenship?

The next day, Jakk rode the wall-less commuter train to Max's office in the city, exited, and as he walked in the morning light, he saw across his path a shadow, long and angular, pointed at a silvery shape. It was an unattended interstellar cruiser. He knew from news reports it was easy to fly and could cruise safely at warp seven. He could climb aboard, fire up the engines, slip the portal, blow past Sprock warships, and go anywhere— maybe Earth, maybe other planets to continue his search for immortality. He looked down. His feet were planted in the valley of the shadow of death. Should he escape? He felt an urge to do so yet things held him back: he owed his friends; he was curious about Max's gift; he liked Reena. Were forces like these—obligations and curiosity and affection—were they the evil forces that suckered lifebeings into their eventual death? He found himself walking to Max's office with the knowledge that the space cruiser would probably be there if and when he changed his mind.

"Surprise—I got three hours without interruption," Max said. "I need to take the God program to the next level."

"You've exhausted every level."

"It knows every twist of every creature's double helix, every neuronal connection."

"So?"

"So why not combine body and mind?"

Jakk stared at him.

"We know genetics," Max said. "We know cells. Why not recreate a creature?"

Max spoke as if it was obvious. It was not. Max was getting weirder than Dr. Frankenstein. Recreate a creature? Impossible. Yet he was one of Hugubu's top scientists. They had tens of thousands of years more experience than Earth scientists. They could jellify their bodies, morph their mouths, and live for hundreds of years without seeming to age.

"Come see," Max said.

Jakk had no idea what to expect. It was scary. Had Max recreated a thinking dinosaur? He expected Frankenstein's gloomy laboratory with beds and pulleys and giant slabs of electricity zapping about like sparks from a plasma globe. Max opened the door to what looked like a bedroom. Something was covered by a blanket. Max walked cautiously next to something sleeping.

"Pull off the blanket," said Max.

Jakk froze. He looked at Max with fear and trembled. He took a breath, reached for the blanket, and pulled it slowly down. It was a human face. Not any human face. It was Sheela. She lay there, pale, her eyes closed, not breathing, and not moving. Max had Frankensteined Sheela. Unbelievable. But there it was.

"Press the button." Max pointed to a button on the wall.

"Is it alive?" Jakk asked.

"It might take a minute for her to boot up."

"Is she a robot?"

"Press the button."

Slowly Jakk pressed the button while watching the unmoving face. At first, nothing happened. Then a finger twitched. Her eyes opened, focused. Consciousness came fast like a bear waking after sleeping all winter.

"Where am I?" the Sheela-creature asked, rising, standing up, warily looking at Jakk. "Who are you?"

Jakk jumped back. Surely Sheela would know that she was Sheela, fleshy, freshly booted Sheela, the right height and weight, exact same hair color, eye color, wearing a sundress.

"Sheela, is that you?" Jakk asked.

"I am Jakk," said the Sheela-looking creature.

Jakk and the Sheela-creature stared at each other.

"Max, what is going on?" Jakk asked.

"Max, what is going on?" the Sheela-creature asked.

Max explained that Hugubu scientists created an exact physical duplicate of Earth-Sheela using her DNA, but since there were neural inconsistencies, it was too risky to recreate Sheela's brain. Scientists did, however, have a complete copy of Jakk's brain, so they used that.

Jakk and the Sheela-creature stared at each other.

"So, Sheela, you think you're me?" Jakk asked.

"My name is Jakk. I am Jakk. I am …" said the Sheela-creature.

Then the Sheela-creature saw herself in a mirror. Her mouth dropped open.

"Impossible!"

Max's forehead blinked; he apologized and left. Jakk and the Sheela-creature were alone.

"Which of us is the clone?" asked the Sheela-creature.

"I am the original. You are the clone. You have Sheela's body and my brain."

The Sheela-creature examined herself in the mirror. "Sheela's body and my brain. This is weird, so weird. I'm not as tall as before. I have breasts! I have hips. I have hair! I'm making myself horny! I want to fuck myself but I don't have a penis."

She lifted her sundress and felt with her fingers. Jakk tried to look away but it happened too fast.

"No penis. Gone. My brain still thinks I have a penis!"

"What do you remember last?" Jakk asked.

"Last thing I remember was sitting at Max's computer. We kidded about how many boats Reena could launch."

"Do you remember sleeping in that bed with a blanket on your face?"

The Sheela-creature shook her head. "No."

"Remember how we figured out string theory?"

"By mapping Sheela's body parts."

"Can you recreate Sheela's volleyball position when we figured out gravity?"

"Sure!" The Sheela-creature dove, ankles near earlobes, and bounced on the bed.

"That's it!" Jakk exclaimed. "No way the real Sheela could have known that! You're Jakk. You're ME!"

"I'm Jakk!" said the Sheela-creature, smiling.

They looked at each other. This woman was *even better* than when Reena was eyeless and noseless since it booted up with Jakk's excellent brain. He felt incredibly fortunate. He wanted to hug her but shook hands instead.

"Hello, Jakk!" said Jakk.

"Hello, Jakk!" said Sheela-Jakk.

"You're my twin!"

"You're *my* twin!"

"We're 17 years old."

"No, I'm only a few minutes old! But I feel 17!"

It was weird to be with his childhood friend and her supermodel body that housed *his brain*. He felt like he chanced upon the key to the kingdom of women! His two Jakk-minds could explore all the weirdness of adult females without having the nerve-racking, balloon-blowing, sarcastic Sheela-mind to fuss with. Jakk got the fun female anatomy without the gruff hockey goalie. He felt like he rediscovered his long lost playmate, unpolluted by puberty, unfazed by the weirdness of being teenagers. She was the perfect friend, a lifebeing he could joke with and play with since *she was him*. His main focus of curiosity was her body. He didn't even have to ask since "she" was thinking the same thing.

"Check out my breasts," said the Sheela-creature.

"What do you mean?"

"Hold them! They bounce. Can Reena make me a bra? What if they droop?"

Jakk cupped each one, gently, in turn. The left one felt slightly bigger. The nipples looked like eyes and he wanted to have a deep conversation with each about the meaning of life or play a game of patty cake with them.

"Put your finger in to see how far it goes!" Sheela-Jakk said.

"What?"

"No need to wash—there's no dirt on this planet!"

He was curious but reluctant so it took a full five seconds to persuade him. It felt squishy, like a car wash without the suds.

"Good thing we bumped into this planet," Sheela-Jakk said.

"Good planet to speed-bump into," Jakk said.

"Are you thinking what I am thinking?"

"Yes!"

They got on the bed, held hands, and bounced like it was a trampoline! It was their favorite game as kids. The Sheela-creature's breasts were almost clapping with excitement. It was cool having a like-minded creature in feminine form! They could complete each other's sentences.

"I'm voluptuous! I want to do myself but I'm not double jointed!" Sheela-Jakk said.

They bent over laughing about this.

"I have a penis," Jakk offered.

"No way you're doing me. I'm not gay."

"What if Max wants to fuck your head?"

She gave him a quizzical look. "*I am a man! I want to do women!*" Jakk thought.

"Maybe you're an LGBT except we don't know which letter," Jakk said.

"I am not a letter!"

"You are a T with a pinch of L or maybe B if you do yourself! I wished I'd paid attention in English class. Are you a 'he' or a 'she'? What's it like to have a woman's body?"

"Incredibly odd. Balance is based in my hips. I miss the muscle power to flatten an unruly alien. So much hair! Is it flammable? My voice sounds gay. I want a deep voice to tell men to 'fuck off,' but maybe you can tell them for me?"

"Quick—who am I?" Jakk cupped his hands on his cheeks to make his mouth look like a vagina.

"Reena is our friend!" said Sheela-Jakk, laughing.

Jakk supposed their encounter might be on TV so they taxied back to the Jakk Shack for privacy.

"Will Hugubu men want to poke me?" Sheela-Jakk asked.

"You're a fox. But they don't even have penises."

"I liked being a man. Life was so simple. I wish they'd given me detachable breasts like Reena's."

In the privacy of their small house, blinds drawn, Sheela-Jakk removed her clothes and checked out her body in a full-length mirror. It was mesmerizing with a fluid beauty, a fleshy bouncy quality, almost milky, like it could jiggle yet stay together with a new way of inhabiting physical space. It could take over a location by rolling into it rather than marching into it. They both knew her body was arousing Jakk's. They both knew how guys thought. Sheela-Jakk put her sundress back on. They were, somewhat, a double-you, a multi-person if slightly lopsided, as if the concept of "Jakk" was not merely Jakk in his regular male body, but Jakk *plus* the Sheela-Jakk. The two of them constituted a more substantial entity, doubled into a combined male-female being, physically yin and yang, but mentally only yin … so what if the yin and yang weren't exactly proportional. They covered all genders; if they were back in New Jersey and Jakk was curious about a women's restroom, he could send in Sheela-Jakk to inspect and report back. In military terms, the combined Jakk and Sheela-Jakk entity controlled more cultural territory. Of course Jakk would be the leader since he was the man. His rational brain, undistorted by a female body, was the original mind, the template, the capital city, while Sheela-Jakk's mind was a mere suburb. He imagined her body without the sundress on.

"Stop ogling until we have a plan," Sheela-Jakk said, trying to think.

Jakk was horny. His bulge felt like the world's tallest building. He was alone with a recently naked goddess, behind a locked door. Further, he knew the Sheela-Jakk's mind, intimately, knew that it could be persuaded by reason. His body roared like a car engine in park. He had a spy on the inside of the fortress of her body in the form of his own mind. Here he was, trillions of miles from home, with the ideal Sheela: rational, smart, sensible, her only problem was adjusting to female body parts.

"There's good news and bad news," Jakk said.

"The good news is we kissed a Hugubu woman on the lips," Sheela-Jakk said, anticipating his joke.

"The bad news is we kissed a Hugubu woman on the lips!" Jakk finished, and they fell over in laughter.

Subtly, almost imperceptibly, Jakk noticed that the Sheela-woman was not avoiding his gaze. Their eye tag was escalating. She kept looking back. Was her physicality overcoming her? Was her femaleness overwhelming her guyness, turning her into a thinking flesh-and-blood woman with womanly desires—that is, if women *had* desires? Did they? Jakk did not know. He could ask her. He could ask her anything, since she was a he, right? She would tell the truth.

"Let's go somewhere," Sheela-Jakk said.

"I knew you were going to say that."

"I knew you'd say that too."

They walked around. Mostly they said nothing. It was a pleasant day. A pond was there. It had water. It was wet. There were buildings. Some floated. Weird creatures ambled. They played chess; he let her win, a gentlemanly gesture, since having a smaller cranium handicapped her ability to think. How about a museum? They looked at each other. They walked back to the Jakk Shack and locked the door.

"Are you thinking what I'm thinking?" she asked, grinning.

"We should say hello to each other?"

They looked at each other. They gently grabbed each other's crotch. Hello, Jakk. Hello, Jakk. How do you do?

"We should have sex," said the Sheela-woman.

"We should have sex," Jakk agreed. It would happen before he turned thirty!

"I'm horny for your penis."

"Women get horny?"

"Women get horny. It's a surprise, but I'm horny. Maybe it is because of my male brain inside my female body. I never thought about penises before. I'm thinking about your penis—not penis envy but penis longing."

They stripped nervously, peeking from time to time. If they had sex, would it be intercourse or masturbation, or incest like a brother and a sister going at it?

"I know what you look like naked, Jakk, so don't be embarrassed."

"What's it like being a female me? Do you want to hear romantic poetry? Should I ask you how your day was? Do you want hugs?"

Sheela-Jakk said she no longer wanted to have sex with Reena. That urge was gone. Were female hormones kicking in?

"Get on the bed," she said.

"The guy is supposed to initiate."

"I am a guy too!"

A wrestling match ensued. Sheela-Jakk proved surprisingly strong. Perhaps her volleyball agility was kicking in. Jakk found himself on the bottom, held down by her powerful hips but he was too excited to complain, as if the sexual feeling in his midsection ordered him to stay put and smile.

"Somebody could tell us to 'go fuck yourself' and that's what we are doing," she said.

"You better respect me in the morning!"

They studied each other's genitalia. The big issue: could six inches fit into two? Sheela wondered if there could be physical side effects to having sex since she was less than a day old. Hugubu scientists had never created a new human before. It felt odd to kiss. She skewered herself, lowering herself slowly, until they both realized the two-inch limit had been a mirage. It was like a magic trick. Poof! It vanished! That settled, they celebrated the precious sweetness of love, her hopping until he climaxed and flopped out.

"Hey! We're done?" she asked.

Yes, we're done. It was your job to climax. She had been in control, so if things went askew, it was her fault. Jakk was tired. He didn't really want to be with her at this point but there she was, tapping his shoulder.

"You got the climaxing body. Not fair!" she complained.

"Women don't need orgasms to enjoy sex."

"Said who?"

"*Splashable* magazine. You know that."

"Written by a man."

"Real women *pretend* to have orgasms."

Well, they did. But Sheela-Jakk had a male-minded brain that insisted on climbing to the top of the mountain. Jakk napped for fifteen minutes and then the nudges resumed.

"Back in the saddle," she said.

He looked at her. "The real Sheela has a prettier face."

She studied herself in the mirror. "She wears makeup."

"Maybe Reena can get you some."

"Nice try, buster, but you're not going to get out of this."

Jakk had feared he would be attacked by her male-brained logic.

"You and I are the only two humans on this planet," she said. "Hugubu females have vagina-mouths. What if there are teeth in there? Our bodies fit. Finish what you started, then sleep."

The woman was a taskmaster but it proved difficult to finish the mission. They became like mechanics tinkering with an engine, adjusting spark plugs, exploring how to get Sheela's reluctant engine to turn over. Straight-on pumping the gas didn't work; she only hovered in semi-arousal. Nor did prolonged kissing of her breasts or earlobes. Like scientists, they methodically studied each body part, touching and rubbing and blowing and tapping and kissing. What became apparent was that no one nibble would bring release—they needed a combination sequence, as if the pistons had to fire in the right order. Jakk paused, paced the room, and scratched his chin.

They looked at each other and said in unison: "Computer variables!"

Such a program required hard data. They found a terminal and queried the God program but unfortunately the real Earth-Sheela didn't have much of a sexual history: just horseback riding and a few feeble attempts with a cucumber-shaped vibrator. So who did have a long sexual history? Sheela's mother! So the computer sifted through several decades worth of her mother's encounters with college boyfriends, including a paraplegic comedian with a stubbly beard, a scuba diver from Cozumel who did her underwater, her missionary position–loving husband, and her numerous lovers, and it determined statistically which variables, and in which order, led to orgasm. It chose twenty-two variables (example: earlobe nibbles an

X, neck puffs a Y, etcetera) including Greek letters for several likely orders of variables. The program laid out a sequence of steps, complete with diagrams showing arrows pointing to a drawing of a female, which Jakk and Sheela-Jakk followed religiously, first with a two-three skip pattern of teases and taps, then a rhythm of snare drums and pops with the syncopation punctuated by pauses. Pausing built excitement. Why? Did it cause uncertainty, which built excitement? Maybe that was why the penis went back and forth—it created uncertainty—like a businessman uncertain whether to enter the lobby of a building. After a false start, one unexpected squirting and subsequent delay, Jakk did his rapper beatbox rhythm for twenty minutes then stared into her eyes during the jackhammer phase. It worked! She moaned like a hyena who was enjoying being munched by lions!

"I did it!" Sheela-Jakk said.

"*I* did it," Jakk said.

They looked at each other. A mini-argument would have ensued but they were too tired to fuss about bragging rights. Jakk basked in his new-found power to electrify the female nervous system. *He* did it. *He* was the independent variable; *she* responded to his freely willed moves. He took an imaginary bow and saluted his capability. He had surmounted (possible nickname: Sir Mounted?) the challenge. He felt like he had invented sexual technique, written his own Jakk-version of the *Kama Sutra*, deserved his own talk show to bring female orgasm to the masses. Should he add another wing to the Human Museum? He despised Hollywood films that glossed over sexual mechanics and downplayed the masterful skill required and portrayed lovemaking as natural and easy. Sex was a craft, and it needed top computer scientists like Jakk—frontiersmen of the body—men who could program computers—to get it right. He felt like he won the Indianapolis 500 by steering with his hands while tuning the engine with his toes. He was to sex what a master chef was to a marinated chicken. Too bad he could not brag about his exploit on a college application. He deserved a medal, a standing ovation. He could start his own religion. He rolled over and patted her on the butt.

"I know what you're thinking," she said.

"What?"

"You think you could start your own religion."

"Well, I could."

"You had your 'second coming.'"

His total was more like two and a half because of the surprise half-squirting in the middle. It was the man in him to count with precision. Women like Sheela could be inexact. He slept.

The next day, there was a knock-knock-knock on the door. It was probably Reena; three knocks was her standard hello. Five was an "urgent get your pants on." How would Reena react to Sheela? What should he say? He felt awkward. Sheela, having Jakk's mind, knew all about Reena, but would Sheela think like Jakk and help him win Reena, or would she start going all feminine on him now that they had boinked? What if Sheela began to want mystery and romance, candlelight and slow dancing, to want to hear ungodly phrases such as "I thought about you all day?" Or want hugs and flowers and valentines and other superfluous crap instead of the meaningful clickety-clack of sex?

"Come in," Jakk said, and Max and Reena entered.

"Reena, it's me, Jakk, but with the body of an Earthling woman!" said the Sheela-creature.

"Max created her," Jakk said.

"You created a human female?" asked Reena, surprised. She and Max looked at each other. The awkwardness was palpable.

"How did you solve the immune system feedback loops?" Reena asked.

"There was no time," Max said.

"Did you coordinate endocrine with cranial?"

"Not exactly, no."

"What will happen to the human?"

The question bothered Jakk immensely. "How can you not know? You're a scientist."

"Scientists learn by admitting 'I don't know'—the smartest words in the cosmos," Max said.

"How can not knowing be smart?" asked Jakk.

"The magic incantation opens your mind. You should try it."

Reena held up her hands like a camp counselor about to say "people, people" to bring order. "Sheela, suppose today is your last. What would you want?"

Sheela looked at Jakk in horror, and he looked at Reena. What was going on?

"Sixty more years," Sheela said, almost in tears.

"But if today was your last?" Reena asked.

"I don't know," Sheela said. "To love Jakk?"

"Max, copy her mind to a robot," Reena said.

Max touched his forehead. A minute later a robot arrived, human-shaped, about five-foot-six, wheels for feet, pulley-controlled arms, a plastic smoothness with a most unusual face: two cameras were above where the eyes normally were, a speaker on the chin. Most of the face was a blank screen. Max took a headset from the robot and attached it to Sheela's head. Instantly her face was on the screen, with her eyebrows and eyes and nose and mouth. The robotic face mirrored Sheela's every facial gesture. When Sheela said "What is it doing?" the robot said "What is it doing?" simultaneously. The triumvirate—Jakk and Reena and Max—were now five, like a party where new people kept emerging from the basement.

"If something happens to Sheela, her mind will live on in the robot," Reena said.

"What about fixing the immune system and endocrine-cranial balance?" Jakk asked.

"Too late. It would take massive programming," Max said.

In the rush to prove his scientific theories, Max hadn't followed through on his thinking. Sheela's body had few defenses. Her cells could not make copies of themselves. Activities such as sex were risky for her. Why hadn't Max told Jakk about any of this? Oh yes, he was busy with the *Sprock business.*

"What shall we call the robot?" Jakk asked.

"Sheelabot," said the human Sheela. She and her robot copy laughed in unison.

Suddenly the human-bodied Sheela said she felt faint. She started to collapse but Jakk caught her in his arms. Jakk insisted they get her to a hospital right away, but Max said there was no way to save her. Jakk felt her wrist. There was no pulse. He tried pushing on her chest, giving her mouth-to-mouth resuscitation. Nothing worked. She quickly died in his arms.

Max apologized while Reena glared at him. Jakk gasped. He couldn't believe it. The warmth from holding her was still with him. It reminded him of holding Ms. Derrickson on the afternoon she died. Jakk was numb, so numb he did not feel how numb he was, like he was disconnected from life.

"I died," Sheelabot sobbed.

Jakk looked at Sheelabot crying digital tears and he cried real tears, then hugged the robot. It was so sudden. Other robots appeared and wheeled the slumped carcass to points unknown.

"I'm sorry," Max said. Reena took him away and shut the door.

Jakk stood there. He looked at Sheelabot. He was stunned. He looked at the bed. That bed—where lovemaking happened hours earlier—reeked of death. It was so sudden, so extremely unfair, like death had not obeyed the rules. He felt a renewed desire to find a way to beat death, to find immortality, to not have this tragedy happen to him or anybody else he loved even though he mostly only loved himself. Maybe it was not such a big deal for Max or Reena since they lived for a thousand years and did the body-to-robot transfer before dying; maybe they thought death wasn't that bad because the robot brain survived? On this planet, apparently, death didn't have such a mean sting, but it sure stung Jakk. The robotized Sheelabot was not the same as the fleshy Jakk-brained Sheela-bodied woman. Now he was stuck with a robot. What a lackluster consolation prize. Was God getting back at him for giving Him the middle finger after his piano teacher died? Was there no God, or a mean God that teased him with beauty and life and friendship and then snatched it away without even a word of explanation? His heart plunged like a boat anchor in mid-ocean. His will to live felt like it had been sucked out by a straw in his chest. It felt like he had always been this way and he would always be this way. He couldn't remember ever being happy. There was nowhere to turn, no exit button, no view worth viewing.

He pulled up a chair, perhaps one of the few chairs on the planet, turned it to face the room's only blank wall, and sat and sat and sat. It was a wall, deathly flat, a colorless white. He remembered her last look of puzzlement, looking at him with hope and fear and incomprehension, almost as if to ask him to act somehow, to save her life, and he had failed. It was his fault. Maybe sex hastened her death? He wanted to protect her and now there was nobody to protect. It was like he was fired from a job he'd never been hired to do. That flat fucking wall. He imagined the Twin Towers burning, people jumping, Jakk's face on one tower and Sheela's on the other, and he felt a mad urge to commandeer a firetruck-helicopter but none was found because such vehicles did not exist, and he watched helplessly as Sheela's tower sank into dust and deathly smoke, knowing full well his own tower would be next.

Sheelabot stayed close by, beeped occasionally, but he could not look at her face. He felt supremely awkward: in robotic form was a being that knew all about Jakk's helplessness while the Sheela-Jakk being died, that reminded him of her being alive, painfully so. What pronoun could he use to refer to Sheelabot: *her* or *him* or *it*? He thought of Sheelabot as a *she*, but its brain was a *he*, but as a robot, perhaps it was an *it*? He felt kinship with the LGBT people when it came to difficulties with pronouns.

"Lay beside me," Jakk said.

Sheelabot climbed into bed. The two of them looked at the ceiling. It was flat like the wall. Jakk put his arm around the robot. He felt empty. He tried to sleep. They lay there for an hour or two. Her flashing LED panel kept him awake.

"Must you flash your panels?" Jakk asked.

It said nothing. Talkative little fucker. Finally, he dozed.

Days passed. He slept intermittently, waking suddenly with a gasp in the night, looking out the window, trying to go back to sleep. He felt like alcohol would pick him up emotionally, but it required yeast and hops and a world where such plants were grown and where humans knew how to make it. Nor were there psychiatrists or social workers so he had to suffer unshrunk, undrunk.

Sometimes Max and Reena visited, but they were nuisances who hovered and created noise. Their questions fell like useless rain dripping from trees after a thunderstorm. He would not let them wet him. He felt like a camper lost in the mountains, hearing voices shouting his name, echoing from different directions, but he did not call back from his cave. His alien friends lived hundreds of years. They rarely dealt with death. Jakk was a human. He was dealing with death. He felt Max and Reena dragging him in his chair to a window. The meadow and the buildings and the sea were colorful. Look at the living creatures. Great for them. Jakk dragged his chair back to the blank wall.

He heard the door close. That was a nice sound. He tried to make sense of what had happened. Weren't good things supposed to last? Steel, statues, immortal gods and goddesses, rocks, planets? These were good. They lasted. Bad was what was temporary: milk, food on a kitchen countertop, a breath, a sigh, a song sung once, a poem read aloud, a leaky dishwasher. It was a neat little scheme until Jakk realized, to his pain, that this meant the real fleshy Sheela-Jakk creature he slept with was bad, while the robotized version was good. So he knew his theory was stupid yet he felt a need to have a real bona fide metaphysics to judge good and bad.

Next day, the nuisances returned but he was ready for their assault. His plan? He would get them to leave by making an obnoxious request for something they didn't have—say, a guitar, but Max returned and placed a guitar in his lap. Should've known they could make one. He banged away but Reena did not leave and Max returned minutes later with a cap. Jakk wouldn't wear their silly cap. Probably Reena the fashion-maven had designed it herself. So what. Max put the cap on Jakk's head despite his protests.

"Play for me?" Reena asked.

Jakk looked at the fretboard. Funny, his fingers knew where to go. His index finger wrapped around to find the second fret fifth string; others made the G chord. It felt right. It sounded like a chord. How did he know that? He knew all other chords too. He skipped ten years of guitar lessons by wearing a cap. Who needed school? Sadness lingered but now there was a way for it to dissipate from within him. He played for hours. He enjoyed the rapture of the resonance. It was like a good math in which negative variables canceled themselves out in neat downstrokes in a personal equation. Unlike with a piano, he could walk and play at the same time. He opened the door. The afternoon light felt warm. His eyes adjusted. He walked by the meadow. Sheelabot followed behind like a servant. They rode the carless trackless commuter train to the port, whizzed at high speeds to the central city, found a perch where spaceships docked near the sea. He sang.

Is *was sweetness in a dress*
is *was fun and free and fresh*
is *was instant happiness*
in our naked wilderness
is *was giggles while we played*
is *was laughter that we made*
is *was beauty with a braid*
in our day-long escapade
I am here and she was there
though I feel her everywhere
sitting on a sandless beach
mumbling empty parts of speech

life is sweet when is *is*
life's a treat when is *is*
life is fizz when is *is*
life's complete when is *is*

when is *becomes* was
when now *becomes* then
when dance becomes still

when fire becomes chill
when life no more sizzles
when life simply fizzles
when is *becomes* was
that is what death does

Jakk felt a warm hand on his shoulder.

"You loved her," Reena said.

Her words floated in his mind. Had he been in love with Sheela? Or was it a close friendship? He felt foolish and confused. What was love anyway?

"Who is the enemy? Death? God? Gravity? What happened?" Jakk asked.

"Things happen."

Reena would not wallow in sadness or launch into metaphysical exploration; instead, she talked. Why couldn't women simply shut up? He saw her mouth open. Words came out. He cringed inside, half-smiling, as words that did not describe Jakk's amazingness did not come plopping out. Eyes have eyelids to shut out light; why don't ears have earlids to shut out sound, particularly criticism?

"You can handle imprisonment, Sprocks, Immortals, even wrapball," she said.

He waited for the *but.*

"But you cannot handle women and love."

"No, it's death that is the problem," he said.

"Death is everybody's problem but your problem is life. Gravity is tough but solvable. Do the math and you slip through its fingers. In contrast, a woman is not a gravity problem to solve but a lifebeing with her own problems. You are a lifebeing, she is a lifebeing, so what is love? Love is a living link between two lifebeings, two stars orbiting each other, sometimes close and sometimes far, warming each other, tugging gently. Open your mind to the possibility of love."

A realization came slowly. Reena was talking about him and her and not about him and Sheela. That was why she was here. If he radiated love like photons from a star, outward in all directions without focus, Reena radiated love at him, a love that was real, a force, a magnetic field nudging his mind. But he was distracted by the touch of a woman who lived across the galaxy. He tried to force his mind to love Reena but he felt drawn to a Sheela-bodied being. Reena was here, now, alive, within touching distance, and he tried, really tried, to open his heart to the idea of loving her. In his battle with Max for her heart, he was winning. It was like seeing a wrapball goal open with Jakk well-placed to slip it in the net. Still, if he did not have his head together, how could he hurl the ball? Maybe if he could fake it long enough, he would come to his senses and fall deeply in love with her. Until then he felt obliged to keep up appearances. Max came by.

"I'm sorry about what happened," he said.

"You created Sheela to distract Jakk," Reena said.

"Maybe there was an underlying motivation I was unaware of."

"How can you not know what you're doing?" Jakk asked.

"Hugubuians have emotions too," Max said.

"Jakk and Max—look at me—both of you," Reena said with authority. "Now look at each other." They did, reluctantly. "Be friends. Stop competing for my love. Know that only I will determine who wins my love. Cut out the crap."

Jakk and Max reluctantly touched crotches. Jakk felt bad for his nutless rival since it was clear that Reena had chosen Jakk—Max was the only one pulling crap.

"What will you do now?" Max asked.

The question caught him off guard. Was this not a question for twentysomethings? Why did he have to *do* something? He was already doing something by being a celebrity. It was a demanding job. And he was co-manager of the Human Museum, a considerable responsibility, although he hadn't done much in the past week. The thought of finding a permanent job on Hugubu was something he preferred not to think about. He was happy being a visitor but he sensed his visitor status would wear off in time. He wasn't sure what he wanted. His hunger for becoming immortal nagged at him. Could he make Hugubu his base of operations and fly to distant galaxies to search for life-enhancing strategies? Could he cash in his Human Museum earnings and buy a space cruiser with warp drive? Exiting Hugubu without getting zorked by the Sprocks would be difficult. Like everyone else, he was temporarily stuck on this planet, and he felt like things were happening to him, twisting him in ways not of his own choosing.

"Help me with my fashion business?" Reena asked.

"Help me with computer science?" Max asked.

"Apply to university?" Sheelabot asked.

7

Jakkuersity

The robot had said something that initially sounded foolish, but upon reflection, the four of them realized it was the best suggestion since it didn't commit Jakk to anything. There was a spot open at the university. Jakk thought it would be an excellent way to avoid the world of work. If classes got boring, he could escape with a tablet again. And a university would be more challenging than high school. He figured he was a shoe-in admissions-wise. It would be like applying to an Ivy League college as a full-blooded Alaskan Inuit. He was the only human to divine the essence of string theory. Max pulled a tablet from his chest and typed a few buttons to file the preliminary application.

Hugubu University was one of the top universities in the Milky Way and "right up there" with the major Andromeda schools. It was in the alien equivalent of the Ivy League, with particular strengths in applied computer engineering. Sheelabot and Jakk and Max and Reena walked down a grand hallway with LED-illuminated screens of the university's great thinkers. There was Therasmusian with a beard down to his ankles and deep enough to hide chipmunks; Chuusian Vraimongian the Third with wrinkly eyebrows and a steely gaze that looked as if he could penetrate steel; a purple creature that resembled Barney, the purple dinosaur on kids' TV, but with five eyes and three noses and a look of indigestion. They entered the exam room and stood behind four podiums.

The curtain plunged into the floor to reveal three judges. They looked like middle-aged humans but were probably more than seven hundred years old. The middle judge's three Slinkylike breasts almost made it to her star-shaped navel. Jakk tried not to stare. One of the men was bald with hair emerging from each ear. The other had three chins.

"I assume our top scientist is not reapplying for admission?" the bald judge chuckled. When he spoke, an inch of hair oozed from each ear, then stopped, like frozen waterfalls. Jakk had an urge to light both hair-streams on fire.

"I am here to recommend my friend Jakk," Max said.

"Is the robot applying too?" the first judge asked, another inch of hair protruding.

Sheelabot and Jakk and Max and Reena exchanged glances.

"I would like to apply," Sheelabot said, and introduced herself.

"Let's begin," the three-chinned judge said. "Suppose three krugs remoleculized inside a dark quark. What would happen?"

Krugs? Remoleculized? Sheesh. What was going on? To add to the weirdness, a bell dinged, a robot with a pitcher of water wheeled itself over, poured water on the middle judge's three slinky breasts as if they were plants needing watering, then left. Weirder still: nobody giggled. Weirder to the third power: breasts soaked up water. No spillage. Not a drop.

"What's a krug?" Jakk asked.

"Five photons would emerge at 36° angles," Sheelabot said.

"Excellent!" said three chins.

"Next question—what is the purpose of life?"

"To strive for immortality," Jakk said.

"To live," Sheelabot said.

"Excellent, Sheelabot!" said the slinky-breasted judge.

"Who is the smartest human?" the bald judge asked.

"My fans might say *moi* since I figured out string theory," Jakk said.

"Spinoza," Sheelabot said.

"Excellent Sheelabot!" said the three-chinned judge. Did a chin change color?

"The puzzle of the five coins. Is there a solution?" the bald judge asked, his ear hair reversing course and returning into his head.

"You have seven coins and spend two—puzzle—how many are left?" Jakk said.

The room was silent. Jakk watched with annoyance at Sheelabot's blinking LEDs. Finally, the upstart robot was stumped. Surprisingly, the committee was patient for a minute.

"Since its gravitational fields work backwards, according to the Rigelian Ninth Variant and the Rheems Postulates, odd-factored forces cancel to make a tiny double singularity. This can be shown mathematically with seven equations in a triple alternating Fibonacci sequence. The strong nuclear force causes salt in the vortex to form a diamond by necessity," Sheelabot said.

There was a hush. What nonsense. Was this a joke?

"Brilliant," said one judge.

"Amazing," said another.

Max looked at Sheelabot in amazement. So did Reena. Nobody was looking at the real flesh-and-blood applicant. This was unreal. Jakk was losing to a robot—a robot. Hardest of all was restraining an urge to laugh.

"Any questions for us?" the female judge asked.

Jakk said nothing.

"Is there an exchange program with other universities?" Sheelabot asked.

"Yes, scholarships too," the bald judge said.

"Recommendations?" the three-chinned judge asked.

"Jakk zorked a Sprock commander," said Max. "He would be an excellent student."

"Jakk showed resourcefulness and daring when he escaped during our initial trial," Reena said.

"Thank you," said the slinky-breasted judge.

"Let's vote," the bald judge said. "Jakk?" He raised his hand, but no one else did. "Sheelabot?" Three hands raised. "Congratulations Sheelabot!"

"Jakk you can reapply next semester," the three-chinned judge said.

"Or you could try elementary school," the female judge suggested.

It was over. They walked out awkwardly. The air felt muggy. Clouds floated like failure. It seemed like the whole universe had figured out how stupid Jakk was. If only there was an Earthling embassy to complain to. They could appeal his rejection on the grounds of bias toward robots. He was a victim of discrimination. He was reminded once again how he hated rejection. What could reject him? Schools and women. His general plan of not applying to either had seemed sensible but somehow he got tricked into this trap. What a humiliation, with Reena having a ringside seat. Max probably set the whole thing up, maybe even programmed Sheelabot to propose the whole fiasco, slipped it in like a computer virus into her naive robotic brain.

"You stole my spot, Sheelabot," Jakk said.

"The five coins puzzled scientists for eons. How did you solve it?" Reena asked.

"Jakk, why didn't you ask her for help when you were stumped?" Max asked.

"I could have done that?"

"Yes!" Max said.

"Max, did you give them my high school transcript?" Jakk asked.

Max said it was standard procedure. The committee saw all those Cs and Ds. Even more humiliation. It was an ambush.

"Why does a robot need education?" Jakk asked.

"I may not have flesh and blood but I am worthy of your respect," Sheelabot said.

"Robots have rights," Max said.

"I lost to a calculator on wheels," Jakk said.

"A calculator with whom you enjoyed penio-vagino contact," Sheelabot said.

"I never screwed a robot," Jakk said.

"We screwed when I was a human!"

Max and Reena looked at him. Jakk shrugged. He would say "Hey, I'm a guy" if pressed to explain but he wasn't. He started to wonder about the five coins puzzle too.

"How did you get smarter than me when we have the same brain?" Jakk asked.

"While you grieved, I scoured databases," said Sheelabot.

"She's a three-way mutt—Jakk's brain—Sheela's body—Hugubu science!" Reena said.

"I am *not* a mutt!" Sheelabot protested.

"You may be the most intelligent lifebeing on this planet," Max said.

"Then why does it need more education?" Jakk asked.

"I am not an *it*," Sheelabot said.

"Why did the judge with slinky breasts have to get them watered?" Jakk asked.

"Prevents her breast-neurons from dehydrating," Max said.

Professor Slinky-Breasts needed a firetruck to hose her wobblies with enough water to clear her mind. She had voted no to Jakk's application. And made fun of him too! Did Reena have neurons in her breasts? If Jakk kissed or cuddled or jiggled them unexpectedly, would Reena become confused? He remembered holding Reena's breast at the fashion show. *Had she entrusted me with a part of her brain?*

Max and Reena left, leaving Jakk with Sheelabot on a grassy area by a stream. Great. He felt like he did after being suspended by the principal: locked out, cast adrift, left to find his own way, but this time he really wanted to be in the thick of things. His friends were connected: Max with his computers and Sprock stuff, Reena with fashion, Sheelabot with school. He had nothing to do in Hugubu but appear on inane talk shows and crotch-grab long lines of fans. Like everybody else, he was stuck on the planet because of the Sprock Block. What did he have? The most intelligent creature on the planet beside him who downloaded data at furious speeds while Jakk was waylaid with grief—kind of unfair, like cheating for a test.

"Sheelabot, must you display Sheela's face on your screen?"

Sheelabot's face-screen switched to that of a young girl.

"Why that particular face?" Jakk asked.

"I am half-Sheela and half-Jakk. If you had a daughter, she might look like this."

This was worse. How nerve-racking. *I did my own unborn daughter.* Not exactly, he corrected himself: he did Sheela, who morphed into a daughter-face. It was weird being with Sheelabot. Was he talking to a scienced-up version of himself? To Sheela? To a robot? To a twin? To a past lover? To an unborn daughter? This was proving positively freaky. Jakk couldn't specify which face he wanted it to have: if he chose Jakk's face, it would be weird, like he did himself, and he might feel homosexual; if Sheela's face, then it was inaccurate, since Sheelabot had Jakk's mind, plus it reminded him of her death. He didn't want Sheelabot's face to be a dandelion or palm tree or another inanimate object. They settled on a geometric construct with circles for eyes, lines for eyebrows and the mouth, and a plus sign for the nose, although Sheelabot said firmly she would revert to Sheela's face when Jakk wasn't around. Why? She liked it. It was cute. *It did the job of being a face.* The robot thought Sheela's face was her (his? its?) face.

Feelings built up within Jakk. There was the pain of rejection. He felt his friends were outgrowing him while he was left alone in his Jakk Shack. He felt like a superfluous being with no clue what life meant. He worried if he had sex with a woman, she might die the next day. He sensed his life was pumped up and fake like Sheela's balloon, that his celebrity was hollow, that he wasn't in control of his life but wallowing in an unbaked cupcake of foolishness. How could he get control over his life?

And then there was the problem of his protestors. The brouhaha had started when Jakk made an idle comment on a talk show that led to widespread fear of imminent importation of cats and dogs from Earth. Of course there was no such dastardly plan, but ubiquitous robotic copies that lovingly licked their own poop and coughed up hairballs—well, it got the protesters worked up, so they protested several times outside the Jakk Shack.

Then the protesters teamed up with femaleists (the Hugubu term for feminists), roboticists (creatures with OCD-like predispositions for chanting "Robots Rights Now!"), and a few irate academics and moneyed film types who raised funds and bought a chunk of land next to the Human

Museum. They erected a towering statue of Jakk taking selfies. Visitors could climb all ten stories inside the statue to enter Jakk's "brain" and turn on a giant flashlight to watch millions of fake snakes writhe in agony. The media loved it. Jakk hated it. It was an architectural first, according to a leading critic: a structure built solely to fingerwag a lifebeing. It was a loud addition to the city skyline. Surprisingly, it boosted ticket sales to the Human Museum, confounding pundits and anti-Jakkanistas alike.

Hugubu Elementary was a festival of shrubberies, like a floating version of Jakk's elementary school minus a flagpole. Inside there were small hoverdesks, no chairs, walls wonderfully unadorned with posters about recycling. On the hoverboards were equations, lengthy ones in circles, strange symbols, blinking numbers that changed color to indicate probability. Jakk towered over his second-grade classmates, who were only 150 years old, facing a century of more schooling before they graduated. His classmates had mastered string theory a decade back, and now the focus was on recombinatorial quark flips.

Jakk soon realized he was lost. Back in high school he could be smug and aloof since he was way ahead in science and math and bored with social studies and history, but here, when the teacher-robot asked about fermion transforms, Jakk shrugged. Remarkably, the class did not giggle or judge. They seemed curious about the fast-living hero who blew up Sprock warships and circumnavigated the inner sea by kite-surfing with a bikini-clad Reena. Even with tutoring, he would be demoted to kindergarten, and he was not eager for that to headline the *Hugubu News at Noon*. It was one thing to fail admission to a top university; it was another to be demoted to kindergarten.

There seemed no end to questions from quizzical classmates: why can't humans eat backward by stuffing food up their butts and heaving it out their mouths? Why was there only one-way traffic on the Digestion Highway? Jakk assured them that his high school classmates could sit on their lunch and barf it out later. It was unsettling when one kid produced a Rubik's cube, passed it around, and they could all solve it in under ten seconds. It got weirder when one kid said "Let's play the racism game," and half the class turned pink while the other half turned green, and they took turns making fun of each other's ethnicity to their mutual amusement. Several wanted to become true spaceists for a day, with fire hoses and cross-burnings for authenticity.

Jakk was not a total loser. He excelled in after-school play. He was team captain of a Capture the Flag type–game. The object was to slip through enemy territory without being tagged and capture a flag that resembled a small statue of Hugubuian sage Troog of Spartaz and return to friendly territory. Before the game began, Jakk made a 3D copy of the enemy's flag and hid it in his pocket. The rest was easy: when the game began, he ran to enemy territory and brandished the fake flag, yelled "I got it," and snookered defenders into chasing him with the fake flag while a teammate snatched the real flag and won. The media picked up the story.

After school, Jakk stood like the lone skyscraper with his classmates, who waited to be picked by their parents. Reena pulled up in a two-seater buggy. "No, Reena is not my mother," he thought of saying to his height-challenged classmates. He wondered what Reena thought of him.

"If school takes 150 years, how can I graduate without dying of old age?" Jakk asked.

Reena didn't answer. The underlying problem was a one-to-ten disparity in lifespans: Earthlings could live to 100, Hugubuians to 1,000. If Jakk and Reena had children, he would croak before their kids reached second grade. Could Hugubu scientists make a pill to slow his aging? Would his children live to only 500—an average of Jakk and Reena's expected life spans? If he lived to old age on this planet, his mind could be copied like Sheelabot's to a robot, then the robotic-Jakk could hug his growing children with metallic arms, have to hang out with boring creatures like Sheelabot (the spot stealer!) and watch helplessly as Hugubu males moved in on Reena. If he opted to have his mind saved as a robotic brain instead of a movable creature on wheels such as Sheelabot, he would have to join the other senior citizens in their retirement cave. They could play the equivalent of bingo until eternity and watch reruns of whatever substituted for *I Love Lucy*. The prospect of growing old on Hugubu—or growing old anywhere—did not light up his brain like a pinball machine. Reena would still be young-looking and sexy when he died. Would she visit his brain in the senior citizens cave? If she brought him flowers, he wouldn't be able to enjoy their fragrance.

They pulled up to Jakk's house. Sheelabot was waiting outside. Jakk groaned. Reena would see Sheelabot and Jakk together—Hugubu's smartest creature next to its stupidest. Reena waved goodbye. Jakk watched her drive away.

Jakk looked at Sheelabot. He was proud that she emerged from the loins of his mind. Maybe it was Jakk's penchant for acting independently, for galloping to fresh intellectual pastures without much pre-planning, that caused her robotic mind to excel, to leapfrog the understanding of Hugubuians schooled for hundreds of years. The idea of sex with Sheelabot sparked in his mind—"sparked" being the operative word, since any insertion into her robotic midsection could cause a jolt. His high school literature teacher would harp on the irony: Jakk having sex with the Sheela-Jakk creature resulted in her death, and now Jakk having sex with the Sheelabot creature would result in his death, and wasn't that ironic? He tried to think of Sheelabot as more than circuit boards and wires but as a living creature with feelings. Sheelabot seemed to fit here on Hugubu, while Jakk remained an alien, an outsider.

Jakk was an alien wherever he went, of the past-present-future variety: he *had been* an alien in high school, he *was* an alien now on Hugubu, and he *would be* an alien wherever he went, unless, of course, he came across a planet full of Jakk-minded beings, which would be boring as hell. Even if he could return to Earth, he would again be a stranger on his birth planet, even weirder than before because of what he knew. If he ticker-tape paraded down Broadway in its Canyon of Heroes, hovering in a Hugubu-built spaceship while waving to adoring fans, showing off his cool Hugubu throwwear outfits and gravawands on Earthling talk shows, sleeping in the White House, uploading the God program on the

Internet—sheesh, he would be a circus freak all over again, except with a new group of enraged anti-Jakkanistas. How could he return home as a normal human?

This got him thinking about the goddamned principal's question, the *principle* question, yikes, about how to be a human; was it simply about not being an alien? If so, how could he do that? He felt a hunger to grapple with big questions, to yank back the cosmic curtain, catch God masturbating or humping a secretary or fussing with a college intern beneath the divine desktop and ask: "Why am I such an alien everywhere? What are you, some kind of sadist? And how do I become a human?" Jakk was an arrow without a point. Did being a human always imply direction; did he have to have a goal?

Jakk looked at Sheelabot. She looked back blankly with her circle eyes and line mouth. The talkative Jakkfucker could probably sense the general gist of Jakk's intellectual difficulties. Could Jakk at least have privacy within his own mind?

"You are the most intelligent lifebeing here," Jakk said. "You know everything."

"I do not know everything," Sheelabot said.

"Surprise quiz! Why do human men love to look at women's breasts?"

"To make sure a woman is indeed a woman. Suppose you see a human. Is it a man or woman? You do not know. So you check out the forehead: somewhat wider for men but the difference is subtle. Check out the hips: somewhat wider for women, but again it is subtle. Genitals? Hidden under clothing. What is left? Breasts."

An idea popped into his mind about how he might fit into Hugubu. He smiled.

"I know what you're thinking," Sheelabot said, shaking her spindly head.

"What am I thinking?" Jakk asked, still smiling.

"That was only a joke. Not wise for a teenaged Earthling male to think such things."

"It could be fun."

"Teenaged boys are too hormone-addled to think."

"I figured out string theory," Jakk said.

"By examining a contorted female shape."

"What else is there to do?"

Sheelabot hesitated so Jakk slipped in his brilliant idea, slapped it right past the goalie.

"I want to start my own religion!"

8

Jakking Up the Spirit

Sheelabot's face screen went blank. Clearly it needed persuading.

"We could be worshiped! We'll have sacred scrolls! Neon shrines! Attract creatures from across the galaxy! We could collect tithes. It's tax-free income! If anybody had a question, I'd ask you because you know everything!"

"I do *not* know everything," Sheelabot said.

"Abraham started a religion. So did Jesus. Even Siddhartha. Why not *moi*?"

"It is not easy."

"We know more than all of them put together! You learned loads in days!"

"My circumstance is unique."

"It will be a fun religion. If you're shy, I'll serve as the head prophet. I'll even grow a beard. We will fix flaws in current religions: none of this guilt-trip communion crap of pretending to eat the prophet's body, and none of this reincarnation cycle-of-suffering baloney, and none of this sacrificing pleasure nonsense. Our sacrament will be sex! You know how women shout 'Jesus' when they climax? Instead they'll shout 'Oh, Jakk! Oh, Jakk!' When people need to say the s-word, they'll say 'Sheelabot' instead."

"Will you climb a sacred mountain and return with sacred stuff?" Sheelabot asked.

"Sure. I know sacred stuff when I see it," said Jakk.

"You do not like to hike. And what do you think is so sacred?"

"Reena's breasts are pretty sacred. Surely she'll let me borrow one."

"What about really helping creatures?"

Wasn't churching creatures to climax the best way of truly helping them? Sex was healthy. Just because her robotic self could no longer climax didn't mean she had to deprive living creatures of all the fun. He sensed that Sheelabot was slowly warming to his project although her next suggestion seemed strange even to Jakk. She suggested that Max should download a Jesus clone, lifting the guy right before he passed out on the cross, so Jakk could interview Him to learn the ins and outs of the religion business. Sheelabot reasoned that Max owed Jakk a favor, to compensate for Jakk's earlier trauma, and the Jesus-copy would go straight from Jesus to a robot, bypassing a fleshy stage, so there was no need to save the savior a second time.

"Super cool!" Jakk exclaimed. "We'll resurrect Jesus! I always wanted to meet the guy."

"I was joking," Sheelabot said.

"We could make Jesus a disciple in *our* religion, maybe promote him to prophet if he brings in the crowds. You can write the Jakk-bible: copy and paste good stuff from existing ones. Maybe have gas-powered hymnals!"

Sheelabot paused. What was she thinking? Probably dangerous to let any creature that smart think too long.

"Jakk, let's get you prepped for prophet-hood while I work on Max," Sheelabot said.

"How do I get prepped?"

"Meet with Blesetoah, the intergalactic sage. He taught me."

So that was what the sly robot had been up to. While Jakk had been grieving, Sheelabot had been getting saged. Why didn't he think of that? Well, he didn't know that the planet had sages. They weren't listed in the databases. Maybe he could sage himself past elementary school. Did they offer diplomas? Good news to hear that the sage was a he—Jakk could chat with the guy without worrying about being genderly correct.

The sage was probably worth it, since Sheelabot's transformation was miraculous. Jakk imagined a Yoda-like teacher who could boost Jakk's

brain quotient, maybe help him catch up and surpass Sheelabot intellectually? Jakk would never have guessed prophet-hood was something teach-
able, like one could take a semester-long class, but why not? There were
courses on just about anything, so why not Introduction to Prophethood
101? Worst case, he might have to listen to a boring old guy rant for a few
hours. He remembered watching *Star Wars* years back and being disap-
pointed in the Yoda character, since he gave Luke Skywalker crappy advice
like closing his eyes when laser swording the villains. What sage advice: the
villain is standing in front of you; you have a laser sword. What should you
do? Close your eyes. Swing away. How stupid.

The next day a driverless space taxi took Jakk past the city limits, past
leafy forests, past the bauxaliganite quarries, upward through rocky terrain,
earth-brown colors turning to yellow-reddish mixes until it dropped him
off at a clearing. He followed a narrow path to a rope bridge over a steep
ravine. Why couldn't Blesetoah have an office downtown like everybody
else? Jakk held the side ropes, alternating hand grips like a cross-country
skier, stepping carefully, trying not to look down at the purple stream far
below.

Once on the other side, Jakk entered a cave and followed its softly illuminated walls. He heard gurgling water and saw a canoe by a stream. He paddled through a dimly lit tunnel, sometimes having to duck to avoid hitting his head, grabbing the diamond-speckled walls that sparkled with blue-green light from the stream.

The passage opened up to a small cave pond with a beach. He walked to a small hut with a sign that read BLESETOAH above the door. *So this is where the guy lives.* The door knocker resembled marble testicles, like truck nuts behind a pickup. He knocked. He heard slow footsteps and then the door finally opened. Blesetoah had long wide curvy ears, old wrinkly eyes, and an elephant-type trunk for a nose. Jakk mentally renamed him "Yodah" (with an "h" for the nose) since the guy resembled the *Star Wars* creature. It would be cool to drink through a nose. Great for sex too. He wondered how Mr. Yodah did Mrs. Yodah.

"Why are you here?" Yodah asked.

"I want to be saged," Jakk said, smiling.

Yodah smiled and touched his wrinkly hands to Jakk's forehead.

"What are you doing?" Jakk asked.

"Reading your mind."

So there *was* such a thing as mind-reading. The Yoda in *Star Wars* never did that. This was a souped up Yodah.

It took only a few seconds. "Got everything?" Jakk asked when the sage dropped his hands.

"Why do you want to start a religion?" Yodah asked.

"What else is there for me to do? Plus maybe I could be immortal and have super powers."

"Such as?"

"Casting out demons! Achieving nirvana! Bringing back the dead!"

"Bringing Sheela back to life?"

So the mind meld had worked. Yodah was a creature of infinite understanding.

"Look, I know that being a deity isn't a summer job like flipping hamburgers," Jakk said.

Yodah smiled. "Do you know how to be a human?"

There was that eye-wateringly boring principal's question again. Thorny things seemed to take delight in tailpiping him around the galaxy, like Sheela, like the principal's question. At least Yodah wasn't telling him to feel the force.

"I *am* a human. If I didn't know *how*, I couldn't have invented the Human Museum."

"Your friends invented it."

"Suppose they did. Still, the question is nonsensical."

"The question means, do you know how to survive and thrive as a human?"

"I solved string theory, built a spaceship, outwitted the Immortals, and became an artist."

"Do you really have your act together?"

Clearly the unpaid sagester had not downloaded enough of Jakk's excellent mind, only a few seconds' worth, or he would have had a better grasp of Jakk's amazingness.

"I am in the in-crowd," said Jakk. "I have powerful friends, I'm on TV all the time. Females I have never met send me photos of their pubes garlanded with plastic chocolates. You don't know jack. Suck that up your trunk."

"If you want to start a religion, learn to be a human first."

Everywhere he went, his ambition was thwarted. Could he attend university? No, he had to go to kindergarten instead. Could he start a religion? No, he had to learn how to become a human first. He felt like he was back in high school. Maybe Max and Sheelabot had teamed up to play a practical joke on him, or maybe it was an anti-Jakkanista gag—was this guy a fake? and was this being filmed? Jakk went into let's-cut-to-the-chase mode. What could he extract from Yodah?

"You upgraded Sheelabot. Can you upgrade my brain? Slap in a module?"

"Sheelabot is a robot. You are a human. You have to learn things yourself."

"Can you cram neurons into my breasts without it showing?"

Yodah led him to a room with a 3D billiards table, coffin-sized with black balls bouncing against each other and against invisible sides, clacking like metallic popcorn popping.

"Imagine this box is the universe," Yodah said. "Imagine you are outside the universe, like God. Look at the balls: balls represent things and creatures and ideas inside your universe. Notice how balls bump balls. Everything happens by cause-and-consequence."

Yodah raised his trunk. The balls abruptly stopped. One lit up.

"Look at that orange ball," Yodah said. "Suppose you are God. You know every ball that bumped the orange ball and every ball that will bump the orange ball. Its fate is determined. Now, suppose the orange ball *thinks* it has free will. Does it? No, it has been bumped by other balls. Suppose that orange ball is you. See the problem?"

"I lack free will?"

"You could not choose your parents, and they could not choose their parents, back to the Big Bang, which you could not choose either."

"I *chose* to build a spaceship."

"You *chose* to have a father adept at building things? You *chose* to be born when string theory was mostly figured out? You *chose* to have a mathematically oriented mind? You *chose* to have excessive anxiety about death? You *chose* to live in a town with a great library? You *chose* to be suspended from school for three days? You *chose* to have the squirrel fall from the tree? You *chose* to have Sheela dive for that volleyball? No. These things happened. They caused you to build your spaceship. They bumped your orange ball."

"I may not have chosen many things but I *chose* to build the spaceship."

The nostrils on Yodah's trunk flared. "No. You *think* you chose to build it because you were aware of what you wanted."

"I am not a ball. I am a man!"

"Made of billions of tiny balls."

"I have ideas in my head."

"More balls."

Jakk did not see how such a philosophy could be useful. It wouldn't teach him how to start a religion or skip through Hugubu elementary or do the prophet-thing or catch up with Sheelabot intellectually or even how to be a human. He didn't like seeing himself as a bunch of balls. Why couldn't Yodah teach him what religious icons should wear, or give him tips for writing scrolls or keeping a beard trimmed or swaggering like a swami?

"What is the point of this?" Jakk asked.

"So you can gain control over your life."

Aha! The wrinkly wonder had contradicted himself. "You went from 'everything is determined' to 'control your own life.' See the problem? You aspire to be a philosopher, but with that trunk of yours, how about a part-time job in my Human Museum vacuuming carpets?"

"Look how media attention has affected you. When reporters describe your every move as brilliant, it wraps a bubble of nonsense around your head and isolates you from criticism. But you and I know that you were lucky."

Yodah knew all about Jakk. But Jakk knew jack about Yodah. It was an inequality of understanding. It wasn't fair. Could Jakk do a mind meld on Yodah to mentally suck out the saging? But he didn't want to have a mind full of bouncing balls.

"Notice how the orange ball is *in* the universe," Yodah said. "It has limited knowledge. It can only sense what is in its immediate vicinity. It cannot know everything that will happen. If it thinks hard with its limited brain, it can remember perhaps a few bumps from the past and try to guess a few bumps in the future, but that's all. If the orange ball is smart, it knows that there *is* a God's-eye view from which everything is fated. So a smart orange ball is not proud, does not feel guilt or shame since everything is fated, does not blame others, does not get angry, does not bask in his own celebrity, does not sulk when mocked by balloon-blowing females or denounced by protesters. The smart ball *knows it is only an orange ball.*"

Jakk did not like criticism. He was a galaxy-class celebrity, a coiner of Jakkanisms, and a force who enlivened parties with his wit. He deserved worship, not an impromptu therapy session with a Yoda-wannabe.

"I am not proud," Jakk said.

"Seriously? Someone saying 'I want to start a religion' is not proud?"

"So how can your amateur psychotherapy help me?"

"To help you get control over your own life."

Jakk paused and waited. It would be over soon.

"Here is the secret: it is knowing we are not God. It is knowing we can not predict the future with certainty. Still, we must make choices. Accordingly, this paradox follows: *we must act as if we have free will while knowing that we don't have free will.* How? By linking ideas in our minds, ideas that are correct, reflect reality, properly describe what is happening, ideas that are logical and true and consistent. Our task is to link these ideas into longer and longer idea-chains to describe real causes and consequences."

"In other words, like my father said, go to college."

"Well, yes! Education, knowing things, and understanding how things work, they help us survive and thrive! Remember, everything is still determined from the perspective of God, but we can get greater control of the determining *from our own perspective*. For example, when you battled the Immortals, you guessed that spray-painting their solar panels and leaving a drill running would distract the guard. Your idea-chains were longer and better than its were."

Despite himself, Jakk nodded. This was interesting.

"You do not want idea-chains polluted by stray ideas or irrelevant thoughts or illogical sequences, like when you tried to guess why Sheela blew her balloon," Yodah said.

"Sheela acted deliberately," Jakk said.

"Suppose that she did. Suppose she was a free-willed creature who could blow or not blow the balloon. What did she choose? She chose to blow the balloon to injure your reputation. As a result, you hated her."

Jakk nodded.

"Suppose, instead, Sheela did not act deliberately. We are seeing her from the God's-eye view outside the billiards table and we see what balls bumped her: how she wanted to be your girlfriend, how you ignored her, how she became frustrated with you and with men in general, how she blamed you for the sexist comment at the Olympiad—all these balls bumped her and caused her to blow her balloon. It was fated to happen. It could not have happened otherwise. Knowing this, you feel less anger, and your mind is freer."

So that was Yodah's method of handling the past: shrugging your shoulders. Shrug off blame and guilt, deflate pride, and cool your emotions. Maybe God, outside the box, might not blame Jakk for vandalizing the Immortals' planet, for accidentally killing the recreated Sheela, and for being a general dick.

Jakk shrugged. It was a cosmic shrug. It felt good.

"Does God exist?" Jakk asked.

"Nobody knows."

"So how can I learn to be a human?"

Yodah beamed. "Simply asking that question is the first step."

The trunked creature danced like an over-caffeinated leprechaun, its swinging trunk almost whacking Jakk. It was fun to watch. Jakk felt like dancing too but restrained himself. Yodah said being a human required a flexible state of mind that is "elastic like plastic," ever learning, monitoring the world, trying to fit new thoughts into an evolving mental map. It means being receptive to constructive criticism. Friends can help.

"Jakk, having friends makes you more free since you can access their knowledge and contacts and resources. Max and Reena saved you from death several times; Sheelabot pointed you to me. Your four-being raft can go much farther than your one-being raft."

They walked by a small underground waterfall. Jakk found he had more questions.

"When I zapped the electric panel, was that wrong?"

"You had to escape and there were few alternatives. Maybe you could have first threatened to zap their panel, but it is hard to know what would have happened."

"How can I know what is good and what is bad?"

"Here is a way to think about it. Good is what is good for you: something that makes you stronger and wiser, wealthier and healthier. You eat bread, read a book, get a job, get exercise—these things are good for you since you are better off afterwards. Suppose you have a choice of doing X or Y—which is best? Examine how each choice will probably play out in a wider space and over a longer time, by linking longer and longer chains of logically consistent ideas in your mind. Strive to compare how two present alternatives will play out in the future, in *ever-wider* areas and in *ever-longer* time spans. If you do X, how much good will you get in a week? If Y, how much good from that?"

"For example?"

"Suppose a person is thinking of stealing gold. Gold is good; having it makes a person wealthier here and now, but stealing is bad in the there and then since a thief can be punished. Therefore it is better not to steal. Note that there are no actions or beings that are inherently evil, as everything depends on one's perspective. For example, a thief may think that stealing is good for his survival, while a judge may think punishing the thief is good for the community. Conflict occurs when there are opposing ideas of what is good. Who wins? The side with cause-and-consequence idea chains in their minds that reflect reality, are logically linked, and result in the most good in ever-wider spaces and ever-longer times—that side has an advantage."

"It can get complex," Jakk said.

"Yes. Consider parts of a whole. For example, your body has billions of individual cells that are tiny breathing beings trying to cooperate for your betterment and theirs. Your mind is like its government since it makes decisions for all of them. It is good when cells and mind work together in a harmony of purposes—what is best for you should be best for each cell. Now, suppose cancer happens—cells mutiny, grow uncontrollably, do what is good for them individually but bad for the body as a whole. The cancer cells are short-sighted like thieves. When the cancer kills the body, the cancer cells die too, which is bad in the ever-wider, ever-longer sense. Or, suppose the mind harms the body—for example, when your mind decided to speed towards Betelgeuse, you almost killed all your cells. Or, suppose the mind tries to please only one body part, the penis, but gets the rest of the body in trouble by reducing women into pleasure objects. This is not good. Consider your friends: the four of you must sometimes decide what is good for your whole friendship although it may require short-term sacrifice. Max has risked his life and resources to protect you several times, not necessarily out of altruism, but because it was good for him in the ever-wider ever-longer sense that his friend remain alive and happy."

Jakk paused. He thought about the ultimate question. Did he want to know?

"Death is a necessary complement of life," Yodah said.

"Why? Isn't there a world out there where I can live forever?"

"No."

"Are you 100% sure?"

"99.99% sure."

"Why must we die?"

Yodah inhaled deeply through his trunk. "We have a fixed shape in a changing world. A minivan in your Earth world, for example, has a fixed shape to convert energy to motion and carry creatures, and it exists in a system of highways of fixed widths with specific traffic regulations. When it rides, it glides. It is a bolt of beauty. But the world changes. Faster cars come along. Fuel standards change. The car ages, tires must be replaced, belts changed. In its young days these repairs are inexpensive and easy, but over time repairs become more difficult. Rust weakens the frame. The transmission must be replaced but the part stopped being built years ago. Eventually a repair becomes so difficult that it is cheaper to buy a new car than fix an old one. Like cars, living creatures struggle to stay adapted in a changing world. The puzzle of how to keep a fixed-shape creature adapted to a changing world is too tough for even Nature to figure out, so it solves this problem by letting aging bodies make younger ones and letting natural selection do its magic."

That was a downer, but he supposed Yodah was right. If so, his pursuit of immortality was foolish. If there were no scientific ways to keep alive, maybe religion was the only hope, assuming heaven existed. He doubted that very much, but what the hell.

Jakk felt sad. So much death. He thought of the corpses floating in space, Sheela dying in his arms, Miss Derrickson. He felt sad for all living creatures. It was life. This was how it was. It was difficult to accept. He could not change some things. He felt a soft peace, halting, trembling, and yes, he would try to work on his pride and try to listen.

He reached out his hand to thank Yodah, who offered his trunk so he gratefully shook that. It would have been weird to crotch-grab the sage. The cave exit narrowed to a hole, and he slid down, faster, steeper, lights dimming until he was in total darkness and sliding at almost terminal velocity. Had he taken the wrong path to his death? Luckily, he felt himself slowing as the slide angled horizontally and he slid to a stop. He stood in a tunnel with soft lights like flickering tangerine-colored glowworms. Mist obscured the floor. There were empty chambers in walls. A corridor branched into others. He walked slowly.

"Hello?" Jakk said, his words echoed back.

Suddenly floating heads appeared in the chambers. It startled him. The images were holograms of aging heads, eyes open, looking at him.

"You are the hero who spermed the Sprocks!" said a wrinkly-faced old head.

"It is him," said another.

"Scouting for a location for your next celebrity party?" asked a gruff-voiced one.

"Welcome!" a grey-haired head said with a warm smile.

"What do you seek?" asked a young-looking face.

"Sorry to bother you," said Jakk. "I suppose I want to find my way out."

"Won't you stay awhile?" asked another.

Jakk was in a Hugubu cemetery, talking to Hugubuians' whose minds had been transferred to a computerized state. They were connected to the Hugubu Internet and knew about Jakk's Human Museum and Reena's fashion extravaganza. They even had bank accounts in the gold field. Some lived tens of thousands of years ago; others died more recently. He thought of them as really old people.

"What is it like being dead?" Jakk asked.

"We are not dead," said one, her brow wrinkling.

"But we can't sigh or sneeze or feel a lover's touch."

"Death is like sunshine without warmth on our skin."

"I miss splashing in water."

"I miss body massages."

"I miss buggy trips to the outersphere to go stargazing."

"Why are you here?"

"I just came from a sermon by Blesetoah," Jakk said.

"Who?"

Jakk had a disturbing feeling he might be trapped in this cemetery, that he had died somehow and nobody told him, but the relaxed nature of the conversation reassured him. These were good dead people.

"Do you love Reena or Sheela?" asked one.

"What about Sheelabot?" asked another.

"How can he have sex with Sheelabot?" They chuckled.

"Love is important."

"I do not understand love," Jakk said.

"Nobody ever will," said a female head, and they all laughed.

"If you're looking for a way out," said one, "the exit is over there." The head nodded toward the back of the chamber.

"Goodbye, and thank you," Jakk said.

Jakk stepped into daylight, raised his hand, and a driverless taxi came by. He got in but instead of heading home, he flew to a craggy peak that jutted so high that he could almost make out buildings on the other side of the innersphere. If he jumped too high, could he tumble to the other side? He sat on a flat patch at the highest point as the taxi sped away. It was steep. The city sparkled in the distance in the fading afternoon light. He watched a wave as it circled the inner ocean. He closed his eyes and listened.

If a deity would contact him with a message or whisper in his ear or ask him to scrawl something important on a tablet, this was the place, although he doubted Moses would ever have taken a taxi or even a sure-footed donkey to the top of Mount Sinai. If he had hiked up unassisted, then maybe God would speak to him about a revamped religion? Plus he did not have a stone tablet and chisel. He waited hour after hour. A cloud passed beneath him—was this a signal of some sort? Then more clouds, until he was surrounded in a light gray fog, obscuring his view in all directions. He prayed but the only thoughts reverberating in his head were his own.

Gradually he came to a realization: *this was it.* He would not be contacted by a deity. He was an ordinary human. It was humbling. The fog broke in patches until distant hillsides came into view once more in the early twilight. The hills were breathtaking. The coastline's tiny lights shimmered with wonder. It was a beautiful world. He thought that the fog was like his pride, preventing him from seeing what was what. He would heed Yodah and try to ditch his pride and not let it blur what was beautiful. He thought the alien-citizen distinction was worthless, that every lifebeing was really an alien since everybody was unique, and that the important thing was not to be alienated from oneself. He was lonely. He missed Earth. He raised his arm and a taxi flew him back to the city.

He found himself wandering city streets and parks. The early evening had a pleasant softness. A robotic tree planter hurled growth disks shaped like dinner plates at regular intervals, and two-story fabricated trees shot up seconds later, their leaves cycling through the colors of the rainbow. He felt the city's energy and studied its passing faces. He imagined himself as a guitar trying to tune itself to the resonance of the planet. Right now, he felt edgy and discordant.

The blockade changed life in subtle yet powerful ways, as if a soot of anxiety settled on every surface. Enemy warships on the periphery increased society's collective blood pressure. Hugubu was protected by a Betelgeuse-powered laser that could incinerate any Sprock warship within range so there was little danger of a surprise attack. Still, mineral shipments were cut off, cramping some manufacturing, although there were stockpiles of necessities to last for years, and shortages were not immediately apparent except for some price rises. There were no reports from allies. Reena could not get fabric from Quandinian Three. Max lacked access to databases from the Andromeda Galaxy.

A boredom took hold like a visitor who had overstayed its welcome. Jakk heard the song *The Stars Are Disappearing* from a dormitorio doorway, a bittersweet reminder of the growing Sprock Block. His stroll took him past the Human Museum but he found himself inside the Proud Jakk skyscraper instead, climbing to the top to the statue's "brain." He flicked on the giant flashlight and fake snakes wriggled with delight. He sighed. He would laugh the fake snakes out of his own real brain.

Next day, Jakk woke to Sheelabot's smile, gave her a long hug, a sad, respectful, creature-to-creature hug of understanding and love. He did not worry about boning but if he did, she would understand and he would not feel guilty. He could shrug his shoulders. He could apply his Yodah-based wisdom. But when Sheelabot said that Max uploaded the mind of Jesus for Jakk to boot up, much of the Yodahian wisdom scooted into a dark alley of his teenaged brain.

"Fantastic!" Jakk said "Let's do it!"

"I'm curious too!" Sheelabot said, and they made their way through the city to Max's office downtown.

Max was staring at the long flexi-equation in his office, a string stretching around his entire office, even running along the ceiling and floor. Some variables cycled through the colors of the rainbow, causing arrows to shift or number-circles to spin. When Jakk and Sheelabot walked in, the equation on the floor moved out of the way like it did not want to be stepped on. Max "hurled" a number into an open box, shook his head, rubbed his chin, and shouted a Hugubuian expletive (deleted to circumvent fingerwagging by Hugubuian censors but informed readers know *wink wink* it begins with "ska.") Max hurled a vase at the wall—again the equation popped out of the way. Did this mean that Max couldn't resurrect Jesus?

The creature lay on a cot, eyes closed, with the same robot body-type as Sheelabot, though a little taller, a face like Sheelabot's with a screen instead of a face, and a speaker-mouth underneath. The screen projected the image of Jesus' face with eyes closed. His beard looked like out-of-control cucumber vines. The guy needed a digital makeover. Was Jesus Caucasian? His looks would baffle any census taker hell-bent on divining his race. Jakk and Sheelabot waited like expectant fathers at a maternity ward. Max said that he'd added a module to get the resurrected Jesus up to speed language-wise. What if the resurrected creature turned out to be a zombie and went on an eating spree? Coolest of all were nail holes in his plastic hands, two in the left, one in the right. If the creature failed to fire up, Jakk could showcase it in the Human Museum.

"His last memory will be on the cross at Jerusalem," Max said.

"Are we playing God by resurrecting Jesus?" Sheelabot asked.

"What if we cloned an upset deity who hurls thunderbolts?" Jakk asked.

"I would attract electricity since I'm mostly metal," Sheelabot said.

"What if He calls Max 'Our Father in Heaven?'" said Jakk.

"Sheelabot, this was your idea; maybe you're the creator," Max said.

"Why isn't Jesusbot waking up?" Jakk asked.

"Oh. Press the boot button," Max said.

Jakk reached over tentatively and pushed it. Fingers twitched. Eyes opened.

"Where am I?" Jesusbot asked, clearing His throat.

"Welcome to Hugubu, Jesus of Nazareth!" Jakk said.

"Is Hugubu heaven?" Jesusbot asked.

How could Jakk explain things? It had been easier to get a Jakk-minded creature up to speed.

"Remember a constellation of stars called Orion?" Jakk asked. "Remember a star in Orion's left shoulder named Betelgeuse? You are on a planet orbiting that star. You were almost crucified but we fetched you in time."

Jesusbot just blinked at Jakk, who suddenly remembered that He would have no idea what a planet or an orbit was.

"Who are you?" asked Jesusbot.

"Jakk."

Jesusbot stood up, stumbled, and Jakk reached out to prevent His fall. Max handed Him a mirror. When Jesusbot looked at His reflection, his video-jaw dropped.

"Where is my body? My head and hands and legs?"

"Your flesh-and-blood body died two thousand years ago," Jakk said.

"I feel fake."

"I felt similarly but we are real," Sheelabot said.

Jesusbot adjusted to his new world with Sheelabot's help. They boated around the inner sea, ventured outside the planetary shell to see the night sky so they could point in the far distance to a tiny speck in the direction of Earth. Jakk was proud to cavort with the Earthling divinity but Hugubu tabloids were indifferent. Sheelabot helped Jesusbot log on to the Hugubu Internet and did a high-speed data dump—a robotic version of the Vulcan mind meld—so, in a minute, Jesusbot "learned" two thousand years of Earthling history. If humans could learn as quickly, colleges would be out of business. When Jesusbot remarked to Sheelabot how they were cavorting in public, naked, naturally, she started making noises about fashion.

"Reena should make me a summer dress," Sheelabot said.

"Nobody wants to peek at your privates," Jakk said. "You are a *robot*."

"Why—why am I here?" Jesusbot asked.

"I want to start my own religion," Jakk said.

"Why would anybody want to do that?" Jesusbot asked, shaking His mechanical head.

"It would be fun."

Jesusbot erupted in laughter. Why not create a religion? It was something to do. What else was there? Jakk was weary of touristy stuff. He wanted the media to see Jakk as a serious figure rather than a pop-culture flake. True, founding a religion was not consistent with Yodah's teachings but the possibility of fun trumped such considerations. Jesusbot had created a religion. Why not Jakk? Plus Jakk did not want to rule out the idea that maybe prophets and saviors got a free ticket to immortality. It was worth a try. After much pleading, he got Jesusbot to spill the beans about Christianity.

"My father was a prosperous Nazareth merchant and I was born in a two-story house, not a manger." When Jesusbot chuckled, it sounded like tiny balloons popping quietly in a fruit bowl. "My twin brother and I got an excellent Jewish education, studied under Talmudic scholars, read and wrote Latin and Aramaic and even some Greek. I quizzed Pharisees and Sadducees at dinner. Most were sumptuous storytellers. Our path to the priesthood ended when my parents died in a plague, so my brother and I moved to Antioch, fell in among an educated crowd, and kept our wealth hidden. I worked as a part-time carpenter to keep up an appearance of a struggling youth."

"You hid in plain sight," Jakk said.

"Yes. Our wealth meant my brother and I were free to continue studying Greek philosophy. I married; my wife bore me several children. I was happy but I felt a painful unfairness everywhere. My brother and I, our wives, and close friends wondered how to end the lashes of slave owners, gladiatorial madness, war and prostitution and misery. There were no paths through the Roman legal system. If we gave our wealth to the poor, there would still be millions of poor people. We ruled out a violent overthrow of political authority since violence begets violence. So we kept looking.

"The big idea that kept recurring was *love*—we wanted more love. It sounds corny, but we wanted people to be friendlier, not merely Jews or Romans or Greeks but all peoples, not merely for a generation or two but for all generations. In the Antioch market, I wanted to tell squabbling shoppers to be kind, but how would this help? One way to reach people was through stories but they took time to tell; parables, in contrast, were short and memorable with an easy-to-grasp moral lesson. So we hired poets to condense stories to turn Talmudic truths into pithy parables."

"Parables! Sheelabot, can we turn Yodah's balls into parables?" Jakk asked.

"Easier said than done," Sheelabot said.

"Turn a *ball* into a *pair-of-balls*, get it?"

"So how could we get people to listen to our parables?" Jesusbot continued, ignoring the interruption. "What motivates all humans? It is the fear of death."

Jesusbot had a powerful gaze. His eyes had authority. His beard looked like wire mesh.

"I was in my late twenties. Our plan was for me to appear to have been killed, publicly, then pull the ultimate escape trick: come back to life! My death had to be public and the resurrection had to be physical for the sake of authenticity. My friends would try to rescue me while I was on the cross, but if they failed, my twin brother would pretend to be me, to persuade people that I rose from the dead!"

"Amazingly cool!" Jakk said.

"Thanks," Jesusbot said.

"Did you know beforehand that God would rescue you on the cross?"

"I always have faith in God's love."

"But you were not sure? Did God give you a *Get Out of Death Free* card?"

"I never had a promise but I always had faith that I was loved."

"Then I admire you even more. If you knew you would live after being crucified, then martyrdom would not have been that scary; but not knowing—well, that was a ballsy move," said Jakk.

Sheelabot was transfixed in her robotical way.

"Facing death was scary," Jesusbot said.

"But you did not let it stop you," Jakk said.

"Yes. Escaping the fear of death brings a powerful freedom. The question was how to make my sacrifice worthwhile, how to get our teachings to live on. Writing the story in a scroll was risky, as scrolls could fade or be lost or burned. The key was person-to-person transmission, one person telling twelve, who in turn told twelve, expanding exponentially, nudging people to become preachers like me to keep spreading the message. Initially we saw the Roman Empire as an obstacle but later we realized it was an excellent way to spread our message: ships, letters, Roman roads! Rome was not the enemy but a giant floor underfoot enabling us to reach people. We would not fight Rome with fists but woo it with parables."

"Your Antioch group became the disciples?" Jakk asked.

"No, there were two groups. The Antioch group became a behind-the-scenes support group to handle logistics and finance and security; one had a rich father who gave us lots of money. The support group chose a second group—the disciples—literate healthy Jews, not too prosperous, adept at persuasion, yet not so smart that they could see through our plan. These disciples would have to believe deep in their hearts that I was resurrected."

"My disciples will be supermodels," Jakk said.

"Males will be distracted and will miss your message," Sheelabot said.

"We will have male supermodels too."

"Finding trustworthy disciples was key," Jesusbot said, ignoring them again. "Preparations were important. We planted people to pave the way for the anointed one to make his first appearance. It was like performing one of your Broadway shows, only my disciples could never realize it was a show. I practiced my sermons every day, working up from smaller crowds. I learned to present a strong aura. What helped me most was believing in my own heart and mind that I was the Son of God." Jesusbot smiled. "I believe that all creatures are sons of God too, I just never told anyone that."

"Do I have an aura?" Jakk asked.

"No," Sheelabot said.

"How did you pull off walking on water?" Jakk asked.

"Underwater pier," Jesusbot said. "Foggy evening. The support group put edges to guide my feet."

"Raising the dead?"

"Supporters with makeup to make them appear sickly and old."

"Loaves and fishes?"

"Picnic paid by the rich father. My crew snuck in baskets of bread and wine while I distracted the crowd with my sermons. I always had lots of help—an advance team scouted locations, arranged friendly places to stay, and spread the word about the amazing preacher with healing powers. Before I preached, they fed questions to Pharisees, such as whether people should pay taxes to God or to Rome, allowing me to admonish them to *render to Caesar what is Caesar's*. One supporter pretended to be a disciple to spy on the disciples, to ensure they believed."

"Judas?" Jakk asked.

"Exactly," said Jesusbot, smiling. "No suicide—they made that up later."

"Brilliant. I saw your cool cave trick."

"The original plan was for me to be rescued on the cross by bribing guards to look the other way, but there were too many onlookers. Those nails hurt. Thank you for rescuing me."

"Do you think that God was going to save you?" Jakk asked.

Jesusbot did not answer the question. So what really happened? There was no way to tell. For all they knew, God took Jesus up to live in a divine mansion in the sky, and they are sitting on a sofa, sipping champagne and watching Jakk and Jesusbot on their widescreen TV and having a magnificent chuckle.

"So, now that you know what has happened since, did you do the right thing?" Jakk asked.

"Look what happened: my message spread like prairie fire, hopping canyons and oceans. Converts became preachers. Yes, Paul hijacked it into a steepled hierarchy with popes, served believers wine and bread, said it was my blood and body to make them feel guilty about killing me even though my death was not their fault. Dogma hardened into a fixed Bible with battles over the text, leading to schisms and wars—highly unfortunate, but what can be done? Still, the overall result, despite much bloodshed, is *humans behaved better.* Look at yourself, Jakk: you are a nice kid, although not perfect. You do not murder fellow humans although you could have honored your father and mother with a goodbye note before exiting Earth. For me, two thousand years of improvement proves there is a real 100% bona fide God! Suppose Max reran his God program but removed my preaching first, and then ran it forward two thousand years: we would find more killing, war, enslavement, and wickedness."

"Still want to do your religion, Jakk?" Sheelabot asked.

"I will be a savior but not a martyr. That would kill off the fun."

"Then you're not savior material," Sheelabot said.

"I will save *other* people. I do not want to have to be saved myself. Look at Siddhartha and Confucius—no martyrdom required. They died of old age."

They looked at each other.

"Jakk—what do you really want?" Sheelabot asked.

Contemplating a start-up religion was fun. He liked ideas splashing like children in the swimming pool of his head. Still, studying its mechanics, seeing the work behind the fun, grappling with ethics—these things caused the fun to dance itself into a chair. Religion was a responsibility, a job, like becoming a grownup. True, he would get a kick out of preaching to crowds, pulling miracles, and hearing people gasp with wonder when he raised the dead or fed multitudes. The possibility of a swarm of scantily clad female groupies following him from planet to planet seemed appealing, creatures who could give massages or five-minute mini-humps if he ordained it, but then he remembered Yodah's teachings about pride, and the hard reality of crosses and nails and unsmiling authorities cooled his ardor. Maybe he would write an online bible, if Sheelabot would whip up a draft, and publish it anonymously, so he could overhear creatures remarking how brilliant it was while he lingered in book stores behind sunglasses. Title? *Jakk's Magic Book of Determined Balls.* But he had no balls for real martyrdom. That he caused another creature—Jesusbot—to exist gave him a slight panic that somehow he was responsible for entertaining it. Good thing robots were mostly fuss-free and could entertain each other, like purchasing a second puppy to keep the first one happy. They both looked at him. He had to say something, hopefully not too stupid.

"Thank you for dying," Jakk said.

"What do you mean?" Jesusbot asked.

"Thank you for doing the martyr-thing to make Earth better."

"My pleasure. You spared me from the worst of it anyway."

Jakk felt uneasy giving two smart creatures so much free time to think—thinking could be dangerous. But he ran out of polite distractions to keep their circuits occupied.

"I remember what I wanted when I was almost eighteen," Jesusbot said, smiling.

Sheelabot smiled. It was two robot-minds against his one human-mind. Jakk braced himself.

"Women! Sex! Dating and mating! I will teach you to be a fisher of women!" Jesusbot said, laughing, miming hurling a net.

"I am skilled in the wooing department," Jakk said.

"You don't know jack about women!" Sheelabot said.

"I boinked YOU!"

"Easy because you boinked yourself." Sheelabot turned to Jesusbot. "So, what are your secrets of wooing women?"

"Focus on what you find beautiful, like a tree, ravish it with your eyes, drink in its shape, love every surface. Your attention makes the tree even more beautiful. Now, imagine the tree looks back at you, focuses on your beauty, drinks you in, boomerangs its beauty back to you. Watch: I will demonstrate on Sheelabot."

Jesusbot's face-screen looked deeply into Sheelabot's face-screen.

"Look into her eyes. Study her beauty. Calm her with your sultry voice and focused concentration. Smile. Your eyes tell her that sex is inevitable, trying to resist is futile, it is fated that you will be humping heartily with wild abandon at first blush since the spirit of God is in your penis and it will raise you up!"

"Too bad we lack genitalia," Sheelabot said with a nervous laugh.

"Blessed are those with pleasure circuits: for they will climb the mountain of happiness!"

Jakk wondered whether robots really had such circuits. Would these two romp off to a room somewhere? The air felt thick with sex fumes, as if the air would combust if someone lit a cigarette. Sheelabot looked different, like she had a buzz. Jakk had never seen her like that. Did robots need rubbers?

Jesusbot's lesson continued. "Next, build your aura. Relax and breathe. Wherever you are, you are a presence, you radiate certainty and warmth. Do not fidget or waffle or hesitate. Every gesture should be graceful. You glide to a rhythm in your head. Speak only when you are sure."

"Tell a woman parables?" Jakk asked.

"A woman is a pent-up ball of frustrated energy longing for release. You are her key. Free her from her maddening prison of loneliness. Do not deny her your holy spirit."

9

Jakk Attack

A large vehicle with flags and antennas, sleek with streaks of silver, arrived. Armed soldiers on space scooters followed behind. A side door whooshed open and Max and Reena emerged, flanked by grim-looking soldiers. Had Reena used her fashion profits to buy a space limousine that was so expensive it needed guards? The group strutted up to Jakk and Sheelabot and Jesusbot. It felt serious. Had authorities changed their minds and decided to rearrest Jakk for speeding?

"Sheelabot, you are summoned to the high council," Max said.

They left with Sheelabot without another word. What was happening? If Sheelabot had done something wrong, they would be taking her to jail instead of the high council.

Jakk paused to enjoy the innerscape, waves on water, a glint of Betelgeusian light reflecting on buildings, artificial green trees swaying together like tango dancers. It was a world he could hug. He felt a pinch of nostalgia, as if the present was passing into the past too quickly. It was an unexpected longing, like looking at a magazine photo of bikini-clad models frolicking on a beach, longing to be in that page to frolic with them, and then realizing he was already in such a world, so why did he still have such a longing? He felt full and famished at the same time. Why was his heart always prowling like a hungry polar bear?

After a half-hour, the official vehicle pulled up again, but this time they made a direct line to Jakk.

"You are summoned," Max said.

Standing in the limousine, Jakk's questions met with a stony silence. He prepared in his mind a rigorous defense for his proposed religion if that was the cause of the trouble: he had been joking. Or had his bacteria escaped to devastate entire villages? Maybe Orkannians demanded further reparations. Would he have to stand trial? He should have left Hugubu weeks ago. His past tailgated him once again like a feisty crocodile. Maybe there was a rule against resurrecting a prophet.

The government building was the city's tallest, shiny metallic green, maybe 150 stories, supported by four central beams with a giant purple dome on top. There were no walls—a force field kept things from tumbling out. They took the elevator to the top, walked through large doors that whisked open to reveal a marvelous view in all directions of the city and suburbs and the surrounding fields and mountains. Ten ministers stood behind floating desks with a movie theatre–sized viewscreen to the right and a few guards. Two ministers were wobbly creatures with several heads and many arms, but most were human-looking middle-aged types in their five hundreds, perhaps. Max gestured for Jakk to walk to the floating podium.

What was this about? This was not about resurrecting an Earthling deity or trouble with Orkannians or a speeding ticket. Jakk tried to sense the feeling in the room: quiet desperation, foreboding, death lurking nearby. He sensed he was not in trouble but everybody was. A senior official in a flowing purple robe spoke.

"Jakk as you know our planet is blockaded by the Sprocks, who are building an impenetrable enclosure out of range of our lasers that we cannot melt or cut or blast or break. In a few weeks, we will be sealed inside forever. Our warships are powerless to stop them. We cannot escape. Our best minds have no answers. When we heard the wisest being on the planet was Sheelabot, we asked her and she said to place you in charge. So, will you help us?"

Jakk felt a rush of ego-adrenaline mixed with flopsweat, like a comedian trying to jumpstart a stillborn routine. He paused long enough to see if they would all break out laughing—one more joke at the human's expense? But they were serious.

"But I am only a high school student," Jakk said. "Or kindergarten, actually."

He was trying to buy time to think. Luckily, a debate ensued, including a charge that it was illegal to hand such power to an alien who knew little of their methods and who lacked training. In his defense, Max said that Jakk was the only warrior who successfully zorked a Sprock commander. Reena insisted that Jakk's unfamiliarity was an advantage. Should Jakk accept? He thought about pros and cons and chains of cause-and-consequence. It was not like he had better things to do, like go berry picking—hard to do since there were no berry bushes, even harder since he did not like picking berries to begin with. He was unqualified—a con. Such a responsibility might diminish his free time to play the new *Unsnarl the Snake* videogame—a con. Military garb might impress Reena since *Splashable* said women loved men in uniforms—a pro. He might die—a con, but he would die regardless. It would be cool ordering a military strike, parading in space vehicles, watching explosions—a pro. So the commander job was a tossup; he could do it or not do it and it would not matter in a few weeks. That was the clincher: he would die whether he accepted the post or not, so if the car was tumbling off the cliff, why not be the driver? It might be fun, he reasoned, more fun than starting a religion—and hey, why not do both? That would be fun! This thought relaxed him. He could be serious while letting loose his inner zaniness!

The hard part of deciding was over. Now it was simply a matter of how to do it—a puzzle no different from string theory or outwitting Immortals. He did not know what to do but he knew what not to do. What happened here would be broadcast throughout the planet and to points beyond, probably to the enemy, and he did not like the idea of creatures bent on destruction knowing his mind like a parent knows a child. Accordingly, he would hide in plain sight.

Jakk smiled, mentally soaked up the character he was to play. He reviewed the lessons from Jesusbot. He *believed.* He felt truth from his innermost being. He would carry them from a shack of confusion to a mansion of wisdom. He radiated knowledge, liquid love, stealth energy in motion, a dark energy only he could see. He felt nervous eyes on him, knew what his future words had to accomplish, fixed his attention Jesuslike with a prophet's stare of calm sureness, raised his palms with each index finger tucked under the middle one. All eyes were on him.

"I climbed mountains, swam in bubbling streams, flew by windy slopes, plunged in sweet lagoons, floated in a space dream, and I tasted death."

Jakk clicked off his clothing and extended his arms wide. "Verily I say to lifebeings of all castes and creeds, to creatures young and old—know that it is I, Jakk, Jakk of the Sacred Earth, Lifter of the Downtrodden, who stands before you in naked glory. Who will follow me? I choose you and you and you to be my disciples to meet in my magic house," Jakk said, pointing to the top general plus Max and Reena.

Jakk smiled deeply and calmly, saw the disbelieving faces but noted that some stood up. They looked confused. Good. Jakk was impressed that he had managed not to laugh. He turned slowly, clicked his clothes back on, exited, went home, opened the door without knocking and found Jesusbot on top of Sheelabot.

"What are you two doing in my bed?"

"Exploring circuits. It's my bed too!" Sheelabot said.

"Why aren't you at the meeting?" Jesusbot asked as he clambered off of Sheelabot.

"Could you get a shock?" Jakk asked.

"That was the idea," Sheelabot said.

"Look—enough already—please be normal; we are having visitors."

There were seven rapid knocks on the door. Jakk opened to find the general with Reena and Max. Jakk insisted that the visitors leave their headset communicators outside. They complied, and Jakk greeted them in traditional Hugubu style before shutting the door.

"Are you crazy?" Max asked.

"Are all Earthlings sex-obsessed like you?" the general asked.

"Your fingers were crossed," Reena said.

"Everybody thinks I'm crazy because they think you're crazy," Max said.

"What did Jakk do now?" Sheelabot asked.

"Flashed the entire planet," Max said.

"Didn't Blesetoah warn you about pride?" Sheelabot asked.

Jakk sighed and shrugged.

"Our enemy knows our mind. We do not know the mind of our enemy," Jakk said.

The mood shifted abruptly.

"Then you accept our offer?" the general asked.

"I accept on two conditions: First, the general here should continue to appear to be in charge, and my leadership should be kept secret except within our inner circle. Second, war preparations must be disguised as religious activity."

They looked at each other and nodded. How weird was that? Jakk had gone Mandela-like from prisoner to president, only without having to spend decades in jail. He wanted to be an *empowerer* not an *emperor*, to jack up the war machine to stay alive. He felt a huge responsibility weigh on him. He became the gravity, but he was not sure whether he had enough to keep the planet together. Plus there was acting for him to do. He must not seem helpless but confident. He had to move like a dancer with grace and fire.

First, Jakk assigned jobs. The general would appear to lead the war effort. Reena headed security. Max headed computers. Sheelabot headed finance. Jesusbot headed the new religion.

Second, Jakk was briefed by the general. He learned the Sprock Block spherical shell was 35% complete, would be finished in three weeks and, after that, the planet would be cut off entirely from Betelgeuse's energy and die. No weapon could dislodge or budge it. The material was millions of times stronger than diamonds—too solid to even analyze. They had hurled everything at the shield: nuclear electricity, chemical slime, bacteria cultures from Jakk's gut, acid paint—nothing worked. They tried vibrating it apart, unsuccessfully. Warships sent to challenge the blockade were destroyed. Peace offers failed. Escape was impractical. Max tried to examine the Sprocks using his God program but found nothing. Jesusbot said "there should be love between brothers," which stirred an odd thought— the worst conflicts were between brothers—Cain and Abel, Athens and Sparta, Protestants and Catholics.

Third, Jakk ordered a huge warehouse built, the size of thirty football stadiums, with a secret war room inside it. The official explanation was it would hold religious balloons. Its real purpose was to disguise a war-staging area.

Fourth, teams would study strategies. Max would recruit experts to work inside the war room.

Fifth, Jesusbot and Sheelabot would study the public and craft a new religion.

Sixth, Jakk ordered the general to declare martial law: lifebeings breaking the law, not showing up for work, or shirking duty, would be punished. Gloom-and-doom prophecies were prohibited.

Seventh, Jakk told the general to retrieve space wreckage hovering outside the planet, and parade dead Sprocks and destroyed warships through the city.

Last, Jakk ordered them to get to work. They left.

Jakk was alone in the Jakk Shack. He looked at the blank wall. He imagined the Sprock commander staring at a similar wall. Was his enemy male or female? Robot or lifebeing? Jakk knew that gender-related crap did not matter. Jakk wanted to sneak inside its brain, discreetly snap photos, exit without a trace, then whip it with its own logic-chains. No doubt it would try to probe Jakk's mind after it figured out Jakk was in charge. And it would. He locked eyes with his theoretical foe. Jakk figured it was smart, technologically adept, skilled at reading the Hugubu mind, stealthy enough to conceal itself, patient as a serial killer. Scarier still was the crazy thought that of all the creatures in the universe, the Sprock commander was most like Jakk, unique among creatures in having exactly the same destructive mindset. An unthinkable camaraderie became thinkable: if their war was over and they both survived, it would have been sweet to share a beer with his enemy, compare notes, clink glasses while watching a movie of the battles, if Jakk ever learned to like beer. But now was now. Their battle was to the death. There would be no second place like in the Science Olympiad. War was the meanest game. It scared the hell into him.

Problem was, he had no idea what to do. The excitement of being a commander and dictating orders began to wane. Had he been too quick to accept the assignment? Maybe his pride had clouded his judgment. He did not even know how to begin thinking about his predicament. Pretty much all he had were huge knowledge gaps, but these gaps were themselves information, like a zero was not nothing but a symbol denoting nothing, which meant something. He reviewed what had not happened. The Sprocks had not killed them all. With their weapons, they could have blasted Hugubu, but they had not—a big zero—why not? They wanted something—what?

The next day, the warehouse was built with a war room inside it. Experts analyzed a three-dimensional map that displayed a mini-Hugubu hovering with the beginnings of the Sprock shell off to the side. Where was Betelgeuse? The floating space debris? Mergetroid? The Art and Trash planets? These appeared within seconds as the map scaled to size. Jakk posed questions, experts offered answers, and the back-and-forth was like the mechanical meaninglessness of empty sex that filled the room with words and diagrams and scenarios and what-ifs that might give a casual spectator a false sense that something important was going on. Sheelabot and Jesusbot described a dark public, workers absent from their jobs, vehicles unfixed, a few brawls and suicides, minor vandalism, marriages happening exponentially.

"Marriages?" Jakk asked.

"Round the block queues," Sheelabot said.

Jesusbot said creatures could not be reached by God's truth since there was simply too much science, and so-called regular religion lacked pizzazz. Jakk said he needed a religion to inspire awe and self-confidence in Hugubu's soldiers, to give them the illusion of safety so they would not worry too much about death. He needed an off-the-shelf religion—plug in a few variables, press print, and boom! out comes an insta-religion, like pre-packaged software with 90 days toll-free support. Well?

"Jakkanism!" Jesusbot said.

"Why not a serious religion?" Jakk asked.

"Jakkanism is as hot as Earthling fashion."

"What about a Yodahlike religion with billiard balls?"

"Nope. Jakkanism kicked ass in focus groups."

Jakk never intended his religion to attract more than a cult following that would have financed another wing for his Human Museum. Now here was Jesusbot—perhaps the universe's best-qualified faith consultant—telling him that his hormone-ravaged teenage boy's sex-focused religion might actually connect with mainstream Hugubuians. Unbelievable.

Was it the awkward switcheroo between public and private space that distorted things? Activities humans considered to be private such as sex were highly public here, except Jakk did not recall any of these creatures publicly reproducing. Maybe Hugubuians were secretly weirded out by sex, but found the celebration of human sex a socially acceptable way to release their inner frustrations ? On Earth, it was why humans visited zoos—so humans could imagine themselves as superior to furry creatures humping and scratching and pacing in cages. So maybe the apparent appeal of Jakkanism was a psychological mechanism for stressed-out Hugubuians to dabble in humanish fun, like kids hopping on a bed, to enjoy the weirdness willy-nilly as a harmless public joke. Would Jakkanism be flaky like white folks getting worked up over rap music? Jakk, with his Human Museum, dubious celebrity, flunking Hugubu elementary, sex-based religion—these images of humans would not engender respect in the collective Hugubuian consciousness. Yet it was odd how his words had weight. In high school, nobody listened to him—including himself sometimes—but on Hugubu, he might utter a quarter-baked idea and end up affecting a quadrant of the galaxy. There was a war on, with serious time pressure, and mindless activity might relieve stressed-out minds from debilitating anxiety. He needed to act.

"Let us do it, then. Work with Sheelabot to whip up a sacred book. Stir in the best stuff from the Bible, Torah, Hammurabi's Code, the Bhagavad Gita, Therasmusian's ethical ramblings, do not forget the Hindu Vedas. Mix in a pinch of ajiva and jiva and a dollop of Confucius, Zen it up, sweeten with Hugubuian quarkish mysticism. Would the Daozang help? Make it an online interactive text so we can fix it if we goof. Pack in parables. Sacred spaces: how about a mountain fountain? Prayer walk underneath a waterfall but you magically do not get wet. Or maybe a sacred pyramid in neon—whatever, surprise me. Ask Reena to design clergy costumes—something in velvet and blue suede? Ritual music should be zippy and danceable to swell nipples with joy. When the male and female buildings connect with a ramp, not too much squeaking. And I need it tomorrow."

"No problem-o," Jesusbot said.

Instant buildings, books, knowledge-on-demand, religions in a day—Jakk loved the velocity of this planet. Max moved his God program to the war room to prevent infiltration by spies. A parade of dead Sprock soldiers through the city appeared to boost public morale but only somewhat. Jakk learned that warships traveling faster than light were invisible and impossible to shoot, but vulnerable when accelerating at sublight speed. Hugubu warships and space buses were picked off during their vulnerable period of acceleration. How would he solve that problem? In the warehouse, Jakk examined debris from blasted Sprock warships. He rapped on a shard with his knuckles.

"How many shards are there?" Jakk asked.

"Eight or nine big chunks, dozens of smaller ones," said an expert.

"Get every shard and analyze their shapes."

At the next meeting, experts debated strategy, presented arguments, played devil's advocate to each other, questioned hypotheses, bandied about stillborn ideas such as arming warships with atomic bullets or sneaking a giant laser behind enemy lines. The discussion was empty. It was amazing what smart people could do to appear smart when they were really clueless. Why was it so hard to say 'I do not know'? Jakk had to keep up a similar facade since he did not know either. His team was impatient for direction. Most likely, he would be publicly fired, one more humiliation in a long list of them, worse than flunking out of elementary school. He said he would present a plan tomorrow, although he had nothing.

Jakk returned to his Jakk Shack, closed the door, and lay flat on his back as he looked at the ceiling. He did not like impending death. If his journey was a quest to prevent his death, it seemed chasing that elusive goal had led him right into its clutches. He felt like an idiot. He missed Earth. He would never see his parents again. They would never know what happened to him. He felt bad for putting them through that. Worse, he would never see Sheela, make a play for her heart, or at least exact playful revenge for her balloon stunt.

He tried Yodah-ing increasingly longer logic chains. He started with what he knew. First, Sprocks could not detect him like they could detect Hugubians—why? Second, Sprocks had an intimate knowledge of goings-on at Hugubu—how? Third, Sprocks did not destroy the planet despite being able to—why not? What did they want?

Surprisingly, an idea sparked over a synapse, leaped finger-to-finger like in Michelangelo's painting, leaped like sperm from a man to a woman. *Sprocks wanted Planet Hugubu.* They wanted it intact and livable. It was like one hermit crab kicking another from its shell. Why had he not figured this out before? The planet-theft hypothesis was logically consistent with the shell they were building: Sprocks were erecting an anti-asteroid barrier around the house they planned to invade.

The planet-theft idea was like a cornerstone enabling Jakk to build a house of thought. The Sprocks needed an environment similar to Hugubu. Therefore, their current base, wherever it was, was similar to Hugubu, probably a planet orbiting a hot star like Betelgeuse. Why did the Sprocks need a new home? Maybe their current planet's star was burning out, maybe it was too crowded? Almost certainly, Sprocks and Hugubuians shared a common past, which explained why Max's God program could not analyze the Sprocks, why the Sprocks knew all about the Hugubuians, why Sprocks could detect cells of Hugubuians but not Earthlings. When was the evolutionary departure? Perhaps 30,000 years ago. How did they build superhard shields? Probably in a superhot forge. What was the hottest forge? A star. Jakk continued to ponder, but a picture began emerging in his mind of war-thirsty weapons-smiths, distant cousins, out for revenge. He remembered Yodah's levels: a microscopic level of tiny creatures, the day-to-day level of things and creatures, and the macro level. Jakk was a day-to-day guy in charge of a macro planet. He had to think like the planet's brain, but the brain could not always get the body to behave. In the real world, things did not respond to the shake of a joystick.

From his Jakk Shack, he reviewed his strategy. Everything had to click. He checked, double-checked, prepared responses to possible objections. He figured he had one chance to keep his job—if he looked foolish or hot-headed or wrong, if they found errors or fuzzy thinking, he would be fired on the spot, and then his fate would be sealed by whatever other knuckle-head was appointed in his stead. At the next meeting, he detailed his plan.

"First, warriors. Since the Sprocks can track Hugubuians and not humans, we will recreate human fighters using Max's God program—brave ones, like the American police and firefighters killed on 9/11, and teach them to pilot warships and kill Sprocks during their one day of life. Second, getting to battle. Since Sprocks can zap accelerating warships, we will build a large balloon tube outside Hugubu pointed at Betelgeuse to hide our fighters when they accelerate. We will act as if the balloon is a religious symbol to shield war-weary citizens committing mass suicide by plunging into the star. Our warships will accelerate inside the balloon, unseen by the Sprocks, then boomerang around Betelgeuse to emerge behind the enemy lines. Third, weapons. Since we can not make bullets to pierce their superhard armor, we will use the enemy's superhard shards from the previous battle, form them into giant bullets of a standard size. When we fire them at the Sprock warships, the jolt of shard on shard will clack all the Sprocks inside together like billiard balls. Fourth, we locate their home planet and destroy it."

The silence felt charged like static electricity.

"A balloon tube shooting out warships—how Jakk sperms the Sprocks!" someone cracked.

The war room erupted in laughter. How else could the tension release itself? Jakk laughed too. It felt good to laugh, and yes, like Yodah said, he would learn to laugh at himself. But did they think his plan was stupid?

"It's absurd," said one.

"Crazy!" said a second.

"Anybody got something better?" Jakk asked.

The room was silent. There was no better plan. Max and Reena argued that since Jakk's plan was unusual, the Sprocks were unlikely to figure it out. The idea of having any plan was preferable to no plan, and with specifics to think about, the mood was cautious but upbeat. Jakk ordered them to begin preparations immediately.

So focused was Jakk on the war, so absorbed in what-if battle scenarios, that a soft-spoken request from Reena, delivered with a sad smile, perplexed him. She asked if Jakk would be a member of her bridal party. How could a wedding distract the Sprocks? Then a slow realization came that the upcoming Reena-Max wedding was not about war. Reena had rejected him. This was not a military thing. There was a non-military world in which things like love and weddings happened, except not to Jakk.

The rejection was a slow shock. When did their romance happen? He thought there had been occasions in the past weeks when he saw neither Reena nor Max but apparently it had been happening right under his gaze. He felt angry at her for papering over her rejection with the dubious honor of being part of her wedding party. Was the Reena-Max wedding one more absurdity caused by the stress of the siege? Even if it was, Jakk had no choice but to acquiesce in this absurdist drama, since it seemed certain they would all be dead within a few weeks anyway.

"I would love to," Jakk said.

Reena gave him a sad hug, then turned to go.

"But why?" he asked.

She turned around and smiled. "Jakk, you love Sheela."

It was that simple. It was not who rejected whom. She was right. Jakk loved Sheela. He liked Reena a lot, and he was highly attracted to Reena, and Reena was here on this planet, only an arm's length away, but Jakk loved a crazy creature on the other side of the galaxy who mocked his manliness with balloons. Yes, if Sheela and Reena were mudwrestling naked for his heart, he might have secretly rooted for Sheela, but upon being rejected, Sheela seemed like day-old trash. Did Reena love Jakk? Maybe she did, or had, but now she loved Max more, and that was that. It was funny how things turned out. He felt full of wist. For so long it seemed as if Reena was his woman. They did things together—escaping, surfing. She tossed him her breast at the fashion show—was not that an official sign of a bond, akin to being engaged? The tabloids would love this news. It would light up the media like a careless cigarette in a fireworks factory.

It took a while to adjust, but the proud jerky-Jakk gave way to a more mature Jakk, calmer and farther-seeing, who began to feel that, yes, it would indeed be an honor to be in the bridal party at the wedding of his two best friends. He kept his middle finger holstered. He would not blame God again although the idea of drop-kicking a puppy came to mind. It was an opportunity to learn.

"How did it happen?" Jakk asked.

A picture emerged. Reena fell in love with Jakk, but Jakk continued to be spooked by her mouth. The result was an ungainly love triangle in which Jakk friend zoned Reena and Reena friend zoned Max. An inflection point happened when they designed the Human Museum, and Reena saw Max's creativity and caring. Max studied Earthling romance from his God program, read romantic novels, boned up on flowers and poetry, made robot horses for them to gallop on across a hillside. Max did an Earthling bent-knee proposal rather than the traditional Hugubu method of taking turns spitting on each other's bare chests. She felt not so much abandoned by Jakk but held at arm's length, in love limbo or no-woman's land, and Reena succumbed to the romantic crap. Max won. Jakk lost. Regrets piled in like unwanted passengers on a tugboat overloaded with suitcases. If he had known what he knew now, he would have done things differently.

It was what Yodah had tried to tell him—the unpredictability of love. In a world run by reason, by cause-and-consequence, by arguments clicking like seatbelts, the irrational variable of love screwed everything up. There was no reason why Reena should choose Max over Jakk. He found himself replaying his past with Reena, wondering where he went wrong, mentally time-machining himself back to undo it.

Max came in, looked at them, and sighed. He and Reena joined hands as if the gesture was scripted in a play with nauseating staginess, their outstretched free arms trying to get Jakk to complete some kind of odd triangular circle. Jakk held their hands. He felt himself to be an imaginary number like the square root of negative one, existing only in a mathematician's mind and nowhere else. Jakk declined to attend the wedding rehearsal since he was busy. Last-minute letdown: there was no time for a Jakkanism-style wedding since clergy had not been ordained.

The wedding venue was an Olympic-sized stadium, with thousands of creatures floating around a slowly revolving circular stage. It was a circus of colors: streamers, balloons, dancing holographic images, a Mardi Gras. When Jakk saw himself on the large viewscreen, he waved and the crowd roared. There were video clips of Reena and Max holding hands, singing love songs to each other, splashing in the ocean. A Hugubuian with a purplish head and big smile and at least five arms saw Jakk, slithered up and brought him to center stage, then whooshed Jakk into a Reena-designed bridal party outfit with colors cycling through yellows and reds. Jakk stood alone on stage. Suddenly the stadium roared like a jet engine. Was he supposed to bow? Then he realized that Reena and Max were floating down toward the stage from opposite sides, waving, while five others wearing apparel similar to Jakk's cycling wonder came on stage.

Reena and Max touched down looking magnificent. Reena wore a fluffy creation as if the warm yellow-red colors of Betelgeuse were whipped like cream around a whirlpool of flowers. Max wore a cobalt blue gown, millions of tiny lights glowing like fireflies. They sang a duet about joining, recreating, new life from old, stuff threatening to turn into a hanky fest, but then they finished, faced the audience, waved, and faced each other again while their clothes tumbled off to wild applause. Reena's breasts began to grow to the size of small watermelons. The couple embraced, arms entwined, facing each other without kissing. A wide-eyed figure emerged up through the stage, wearing a purple gown that looked like oil burning on water in a rainstorm. She towered over the couple.

"It is time!" the priestess said.

The crowd roared. The priestess gestured for the bridal party to gather close, so Jakk followed the five others to surround Reena and Max. Jakk braced for the boredom of vows and exchanging of rings—crap like that—instead the bridal party lifted their hands. So did Jakk. What was next?

"Squeeze life!" the priestess said with a soft yet deeply resonating voice.

Reena and Max looked like two vinyl trees with branches interwound so tightly that he could not tell which arms were Reena's or Max's. An odd protrusion happened, a bulbous shape emerging beneath Reena's shoulder, becoming rounder and more pronounced, breast-like, and then *Reena's face appeared on the newly formed backside breast* and said "Jakk, squeeze me." How odd. The other bridal party members were squeezing away so Jakk squeezed, gently at first, then harder, somewhat like milking a cow without milk squirting him in the eye. Her breast-face kept collapsing temporarily into wrinkles of joy and moans of excitement, and Jakk got into the crowd's rhythmic chanting of "squeeze life, squeeze life." He felt connected with all creatures everywhere and with the priestess and the five others and most particularly to the entangled blob of his two best friends and what was going on with them? The moans increased like overlapping crescendos, rising and falling like horses on a merry-go-round climbing a hill. The activity was arousing him deeply—how did this happen? He was too focused on his wedding duty to worry about any embarrassment. He was immersed in a mass feeling, and so what if he popped a public rod to delight the paparazzi for weeks? It scared off the Sprocks from invading, he would joke.

The moaning reached an epileptic rhythm of deep and rapid breathing and the crowd and Reena and Max chanted "Life! Life! Life! Life! Life!" in unison. Then there was a collective shudder like an alien earthquake except it was creatures quivering, not buildings. *What the hell happened?* The pace slowed; moans lessened. Jakk could no longer grip Reena's backside breast because there was a slippery lotion as if she sweated hair conditioner, which was *everywhere*, not just on Jakk but the priestess and bridal party and creatures in the stadium, which radiated a new shininess. Reena and Max disentangled, her insta-breast retreated into her back, balloons floated among confetti and ticker-tape material. *A public orgasm.* He should have guessed. There was no need for embarrassment because it happened to everybody, including the paparazzi if they were there.

To Jakk's astonishment there was a child when Reena and Max separated, a boy looking about five Earth-years old, with hair and teeth, eyes open, smiling, covered with lotion. Where did he come from? Reena and Max hatched a son! Wham! Ten minutes of squeezing and welcome to kid-city. It explained why Jakk never saw babies in strollers. No wonder why reproduction required community consent. The boy had Reena's cheekbones and Max's eyes and he smiled and waved to the crowd, which roared with enthusiasm.

So Hugubuians wrapped it all together: mating, marriage, birthing, parenting. One ten-minute whoosh and it was all over. It was a sensible choice—babies were a nuisance. Since couples shared the birthing, it spared women from lugging a kicking fetus for nine months. Further, adults avoided the frivolity of pre-mating rituals. Females did not have to primp and preen and endure beauty parlors. Males did not have to vacuum vehicles before dates. For most of their lives, they were free from the romantic and family crap. It took ten minutes to create a five-year old child who would then have to spend the next two hundred years in school. Things happened fast then slow. The pacing felt radical—or maybe Jakk was out of step? Like the Jakk-Sheela being, then Sheelabot, and now Reena and Max's boy, beings seemed to pop up like balloons out of nowhere. Whoosh. Life.

Jakk felt conflicting emotions toward the boy, as if feelings jelled into growls of longing. He wanted to protect the boy, to teach him how to climb trees and chase squirrels, to tease schoolgirls by drawing wiggly sperms on their notebooks, to teach him how to fish (even though Jakk did not know how to fish). Another emotion-zombie was regret that the boy, a walking reminder of Jakk's romantic ineptitude, was not loined from his human testicles. While Jakk felt happy about helping to squeeze the boy to life, he felt sad he would live only a few weeks like everybody else.

The festival wound down. Shower hoses power-cleaned with expanding foam like Niagara Falls frothing up. Robots tidied up while winking to each other and chuckling.

Back at the war room, his team seemed weary from crunching numbers, testing hypotheses, working without sleep. They found that the shards did have a slight curvature, which suggested that Jakk's guess about Sprocks using star-forges was correct. There was consensus that his *Boomerang around Betelgeuse* strategy was risky but doable. New hard-to-detect warships with recombinant metals could be built with a protective cooling layer to withstand Betelgeuse's heat. The layer would melt away while orbiting Betelgeuse. The irregularly shaped shards would be cast inside a standard-sized cylindrical missile that Hugubu warships could fire like giant bullets. Still, they only had about a hundred and twenty of these bullets to take out the entire Sprock fleet. And where was the Sprock base? Astronomers figured, by process of elimination, that it was a planet orbiting Rigel, a bright star orbited by two lesser stars, perfect since a quark blast equal to a million hydrogen bombs could billiard one star into another to cause a supernova. Max's God program would resurrect four hundred 9/11 first responders with combat training hardwired in before they were booted up. Engineers designed a superlong tube in sections three atoms thick to hide warships accelerating toward Betelgeuse. An attack could be ready in four days. As the meeting was breaking up, Reena arrived with her boy.

"Max and I have a present for your birthday," she said.

It was his birthday. He forgot. They remembered. He was eighteen. Her gift was a sign that she cared for Jakk with residual love, like leftovers in the refrigerator of her heart. Reena found love and she wanted him to find love too. That is how it is with lovers.

Reena brought him to a battle cruiser, sleek and shiny, silver and black. It hovered in place. She pressed a button and the warship began transforming itself, bins sliding, unfolding and refolding like an origami puzzle, and when finished, it was an exact replica of his father's minivan!

"How did you build that?" Jakk asked.

"You can drive Sheela on dates!" Reena said.

It was his best birthday present ever. It sure beat the hand-me-down radio set for his eighth birthday. It had warp drive, a cloaking device, asteroid evasion, and a laser. It was packed with goodies: a medical tricorder, gravity wand, hearing protection, tractor arm, generator, medical kit with anti-cancer lotion and everything pills, navigator, mini-shower, foldaway bed, mini-kitchen, repair kit, interstellar Higgs-Boson videophone, video monitor, guitar, even a slimmed-down version of Max's God program. Reena added an on-off Hugubu garment, plus biker-chic faux leather outfits with color-coordinated sunglasses. And a knowledge cap with several hundred subjects to help Jakk pass college admission tests. Even cooler was a matter-converter that looked like a microwave oven.

"It will run for years without refueling," Reena said.

"I am flabbergasted. Thank you!" Jakk said. He bent down to the boy. "When you are older, you can sperm Sprocks and woo trireme-launching females as cute as your mom."

Attack day arrived. The mood was determined desperation. With so much tension even a dumb joke would cause laughter, but Jakk did not want to dissipate the psychic energy needed for the upcoming battle. He tried to take mental photos of everything he saw as if he could immortalize the images to save them from destruction. He tried not to think about the dangers: being burned by Betelgeuse, lasered by Sprocks, blasted by a supernova. Instead he focused on the task at hand, rehearsing plans, preparing for contingencies. His mind was like a tightly wound gearbox of coiled springs, an oiled mechanism of cause-and-effect arrows ready to fly from his quiver. He saw himself as a war robot, a warbot.

The American 9/11 fighters gathered around. They numbered four hundred and fourteen. They wore firefighter grey-black jackets with yellow horizontal stripes and black shirts and hats with a blue side police patch. Jakk felt unworthy of being their leader.

"I remember the day back on Earth in September 2001. I was in my classroom. I was six. On TV later, I saw the Twin Towers crash down. I saw your bravery. I will never forget. Now it is twelve years later. We are on a planet orbiting Betelgeuse. We are besieged by death-minded merchants of misery. We have a plan. We need your bravery once again," Jakk said, pausing for emphasis. "We are on death ground, and on death ground, *we must fight.*"

The soldiers looked at Jakk with quiet detachment. They knew why they were there. They knew how to fight and how to maneuver their warships. Max had programmed all of this knowledge into them. There were no questions. They were doing one more job, responding to one more emergency, and they turned and boarded their warships as if they did so every day.

With preparations finished, guns loaded, and plans rehearsed, Jakk summoned the war council.

"I return command authority to the general," he said. With that pronouncement, Jakk became one more soldier. His friends lined the path to his warship.

"Goodbye, Sheelabot, I will miss you. Say thanks to Yodah for me?"

She said nothing. He hugged her.

Jesusbot handed him a book. "A signed copy of the new unabridged Jakkanism bible—just twenty pages! Easy to read with pictures and parables! The religious equivalent of a Big Mac!"

"I will honor it like a Whopper!" Jakk said.

Jakk hoped his two bot friends might become co-popes, maybe schism off a reform sect to undo his teenaged goofiness. They shook hands, as Jakk did not feel comfortable doing a crotch-goodbye with a robotic deity.

"Max and Reena, thank you for everything," Jakk said.

"Thank you!" Max said.

"Good luck!" Reena said.

Jakk climbed into his battle cruiser. This was it. The future was fated. He could not foresee the future but he would see it soon. He taxied to the middle of a long silvery chain of several hundred warships inside the warehouse. Only his warship carried the quark bomb. Machines coated the fighters with ice. The viewscreen froze over. The ground computer would launch the warships rapid-fire like bullets into the tubular balloon. The sudden acceleration would cause him to lose consciousness. Finally, he felt the warship accelerate.

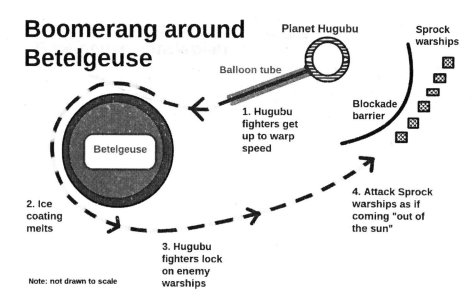

Boomerang around Betelgeuse

Planet Hugubu

Sprock warships

Balloon tube

Betelgeuse

1. Hugubu fighters get up to warp speed

Blockade barrier

2. Ice coating melts

3. Hugubu fighters lock on enemy warships

4. Attack Sprock warships as if coming "out of the sun"

Note: not drawn to scale

What seemed only a second later, the ice had melted off and Betelgeuse was growing smaller behind him. He must have been unconscious while boomeranging around Betelgeuse. He was doing warp two in a wide arc, forming up with other Hugubu fighters, approaching Sprock lines from the side, coming right out of the sun like a World War I fighter. Sprocks were lined up in vulnerable rows—*a perfect angle for attack*—like catching enemy ships in a broadside. Hugubu fighters swooped in fast, fired the superhard shards right into the enemy lines. Some Sprock ships were crushed against the giant shell they had been guarding; others smashed into other Sprock ships like billiard balls. A few Sprock fighters struggled to escape to warp speed but were pursued by a second wave of Hugubu fighters from the rear. The battle was over so fast. They returned to examine the ghostly Sprock warships, still intact with Sprock warriors entombed inside them. The Jakk-attack had worked! There was whooping and cheering over the intercoms. The general ordered Sprock warships towed into Betelgeuse and spent shards gathered up.

"Good luck, Jakk," said the general.

Jakk headed for Rigel, the supposed location of the Sprock base, cruising outside the galaxy's platter to avoid space dust. His three-dimensional viewscreen was like deep television—a holograph with icons and a center shape that was labeled JAKK. With it, he could see all around him, even behind him. Stars and planets and asteroids whizzed past with labels attached. He dodged an asteroid cluster then resumed a circular arc, like zipping around the folds of a swirling transparent sculpture. At warp seven, he was invisible to any Sprock patrols or outposts.

Rigel became larger in his viewscreen, with two smaller stars orbiting. He activated the quark bomb, slowing to warp two. At subwarp, almost by magic, stars appeared on the side panels. He saw several city-planets, space miners dipping shards into Rigel, and enemy warships closing in fast.

He fired the quark bomb, accelerated, swerved to dodge the sister star as several torpedoes chased him, and returned to warp speed. He felt like a kid on the Fourth of July, but instead of igniting a cherry bomb, he had thrown a hissing stick of dynamite into a supertanker filled with liquefied natural gas. The quark blast briefly lit the darkness like lightning. He checked his viewscreen. The smaller star was headed into Rigel. Jakk gunned it to warp eight to outrun the shock waves and was pressed deeply into his stand. He tightened straps, attached earplugs and visor and helmet.

The two stars collided.

Supernova.

Even with his eyes closed, it seemed like someone lifted his eyelids and blasted him with flash photography. It was a tsunami of light. He told the computer to "dodge debris" and felt the spaceship swerve and tumble. When he regained sight, he steered behind a water planet with an ice core; when hot debris struck the sphere, the planet boiled and exploded into an intergalactic rainstorm of color. Space was like a warm shower.

A smile stretched across his face. Maybe there was a God after all. Hugubu was spared. Max and Reena and their boy and Sheelabot and Jesusbot and Yodah and One-Eye and the general were safe, along with the rest of Hugubu.

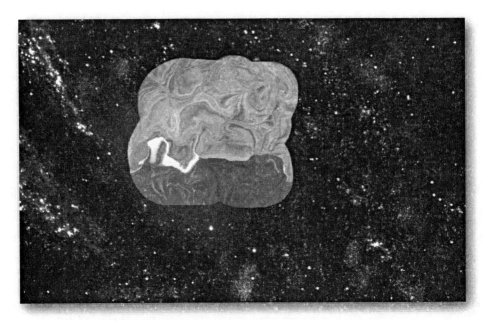

"Gold!" said Jakk, as he spotted a rotating chunk of metal on his viewscreen. He flew near it and grabbed it with his tractor beam. The water planet must have cooled it.

"Let us go home!" Jakk said to the computer.

It knew where to go. The ship accelerated with the gold in tow. After a few days, a tiny speck emerged on his viewscreen. It was the sun. Jakk slowed to sublight speed and landed in a sunlit crater on Mars. He lasered the gold into shoebox-sized slabs and stacked eighty of them inside his warship. That the gold molecules might have been hot-fused from dead Sprocks made him smile. Jakk searched the God program and found a seventeenth-century shipwreck near Belize whose gold was never recovered, so he microwaved the shoebox-sized slabs into golden Spanish doubloons, put them into sacks, left the remaining gold on Mars, and headed home.

Earth was as beautiful as Sheela's smile. Jakk turned on his cloaking device, maneuvered over his town, and descended quietly through the darkness. When the altimeter read a kilometer above sea level, he turned off the cloak. There was suburban New Jersey—parking lots, sleepy headlights traversing Routes 24 and 78, the dark Passaic River. The night was warm.

He descended to treetop level, followed the river west to a spot obscured by tall bushes and vines, and landed.

He was home.

He opened the door, planted his feet on the planet, took a deep breath. It would not be good if teenagers on a late-night drinking or makeout session stumbled across his spaceship, so he reached in to push a button, stepped out, and watched his spaceship reassemble itself with swaps and twists, sides flipping, into a minivan. He climbed into the driver's seat. Cup holders. $200 in cash. A bed in the back. Two keys on the ring. Thank you, Max and Reena! He took the keys, stepped outside, pushed CLOAK, and the minivan disappeared. When he touched the minivan, it was still there. He uncloaked it.

The nighttime aroma of roses in early May filled his senses. The air wriggled with life—not fake life, nothing artificial like plastic Christmas trees—but real pines. Life swarmed around—critters, bacteria, spores, plants. Earth had an oomph and power he had not appreciated. It was a complex system of cycling nitrogen and oxygen and he needed again to be a part of it. His body needed to readjust to the weirdness of Earth.

He turned on the minivan's headlights to light up a section of the river. He walked naked to the river's edge and waded into the flowing water. It was cold but his everything pill still regulated his bodily heat. The mud felt squishy underfoot. He jumped in a deep spot and felt water rushing around his body. It was a great feeling. He returned to the bank and raised his hands.

"I am an Earthling!" he said.

He climbed into his minivan, jammied up, slipped into bed. He was falling off to sleep when he heard activity in the woods: muffled voices and flashlights coming toward him. He clicked CLOAK and sat in the driver's seat, studying their movements on his screen. This was no ordinary search party. Five shapes passed within a few meters away. Several wore Hazmat suits, looking like aliens in their hoods with oxygen tanks on their backs; two had machine guns; one held a spinning handheld radar. They were searching for him. Maybe they sensed something when his spaceship was at treetop level. Their lights grew dim and disappeared into the night.

Was he an alien or a human? He was a human physically, but from their point of view he might be seen as part-alien, not because his alien friends rubbed off on him but because he had a gravawand and a magic-microwave, and alien pills in his bloodstream. He had a spaceship. He had to be cautious. What if authorities came upon his gravawand? Or took his minivan to a garage to examine it? Or studied the God program? Then he could not stop what might happen next. A military could misuse his warship to cause massive destruction; a suicidal crackpot could fly his warship into Earth at warp speeds to knock it out of orbit. It was Yodah's idea-chains of morality. True, his technologies could be used for good purposes, but there would be no way to guarantee they would not be abused. He felt like he was paddling a rowboat with a candle on a sea of gasoline.

Still, he knew he was a proud creature who deserved fame and glory for figuring out string theory, inventing a faster-than-light spaceship, winning an alien war, and bringing back cool gizmos. He deserved a page in Wikipedia. There was a part of himself that hungered for recognition.

So to satisfy his inner impulses, he famed himself: he imagined a ticker tape parade in his honor, white love floating down in the Canyon of Heroes, cameras flashing, applause, him acting fake-humble on talk shows, dating supermodels, buying a mansion with multiple swimming pools, mooning reporters from his yacht. Alone by the dark river, imagining glory, he bowed, waved, blew kisses to the trees, smiled, found himself laughing at his foolishness. He had been there and done that so far as celebrity went. He needed to fit back into human society and learn to be happy … and, well, there was Sheela. How could a borderline alien such as himself connect with her?

His father's "every woman has a suitcase" theory came to mind. Men tended to focus on female beauty while ignoring the slew of commitments and baggage. A woman's suitcase could be crammed with crap. What was in Sheela's? Her parents. Her hunger for an elite university. How would he apply the Yodah principle of "what's good for Jakk" in the ever-wider ever-longer sense? Were there two Venn diagrams, one circle for "what's good for Jakk" and one for "what's good for Sheela," and his task was to find where the circles intersected? What would it mean to love her? He wanted to love the whole Sheela, not just her fun parts, not just Sheela-in-the-moment, but the real Sheela, the total woman extended in space and time, in past and present and future, the whole shebang. How? He was flummoxed.

He wanted to avoid a repeat of Hugubu where he blundered in and let the planet paint him as a curious frivolity. He would not let his flubbed attempts at sex be broadcast planetwide. He would control his public image, how he looked, what he wore, what he said, what he did, and who his friends were. He would make himself into the whole package, a package Sheela could love, a branded man-product she might place in her shopping cart as she rolled through the supermarket of her life.

Further, his assimilation back into Earthling society would be in stages. He was delayed for a day by a cold. He shivered until his fever broke. Then it rained real rain, a pleasant drumming on the roof that felt like fingers gently tapping his brain. In the morning sunlight, he turned off the mini-van's cloak and drove it through a bumpy trail, sometimes hovering over fallen trees, until he came to the main road and headed to town. The trees were a festival of leaves, bursting like a rock concert, making a roof canopy over the street. He drove by the school. It was Wednesday; Sheela must be inside. He paused by Sheela's hacienda. He spotted a for-sale sign on a house a few doors down, then drove to his father's friend's office.

Frank was a sharp and well-connected African-American lawyer, a former champion wrestler and army paratrooper. Frank and Jakk's father had been best friends since high school. They had also taken piano lessons with Miss Derrickson. When the initial surprise at Jakk being alive wore off, and the further surprise of watching Jakk bring in bag after bag of gold, Jakk experienced a fusillade of questions. Where had he gone? Why had he not called? Where exactly was the gold from? Was Jakk on drugs? Jakk remembered being questioned by reporters on Hugubu. Now he would shape his story, and that meant being vague.

"What happened, happened," Jakk said, and he shrugged.

Jakk insisted he retrieved the gold properly and was its legal owner. He did not elaborate on where or when or how. After much persuading, Frank agreed to help Jakk sell the gold, pay taxes on it, buy the house near Sheela's, pay off his parent's mortgages, help Jakk get into college, and not reveal Jakk's homecoming until it was time. Though $500 per hour was twenty times what his father earned, it was worth it. Frank crafted a plan to register Jakk's minivan by buying a similar new one, registering it, then transferring the registration, VIN plate, and license plates to Jakk's and scuttling the new one, essentially paying $25,000 to register a vehicle. To be a gear in the vast machine known as America, Jakk had to mesh with larger structures. It was Yodahian freedom—freedom by being linked into bigger systems.

There would be a funeral for Jakk at the Unitarian church in a few days. Maybe Sheela would weep for him. He wanted to enjoy it as a spectator but he would not pull a Tom Sawyer–type stunt and show up at the end to have people hug him and feel sorry for him. This was his life. He wanted to have fun. He wore a Reena-designed biker chic outfit. He videotaped himself talking as if he was at his own funeral, drove to the church, and slipped it into the videoplayer.

Unitarians were weird folk, his father had said. Although many studied science in college, they thought energy was something one could breathe in while holding hands. They loved gongs and incense. A weird ritual was centering oneself, which suggested that they were off balance for the rest of the week. They hated fracking yet drove using fossil fuels. Most were activists with left-leaning causes. If Jakk threw cash on a table, they would scramble to use it for do-gooder causes like cleaning up rivers, saving endangered animals, campaigning against ocean garbage, and pushing for marriage equality.

The day of his funeral, Jakk donned a wig and sunglasses and sat in the upper balcony. The church felt puritan with clean-white wood, almost like a barn without the smell of hay. He felt cheated by a skimpy flower display—he was worth more than a bowl of roses. He saw his parents in the front row, plus a dozen kids from school including two from his nerd circle. Sheela floated in like a goddess. Her blonde hair exuded sexuality like she was in an ad for a beach resort. She sat next to her foxy mother. That was what Sheela would look like after 22 years. If Sheela stayed as sexy as her 40-year-old mom and Jakk and Sheela screwed nightly, it meant at least 8,030 bouts of respectable sex, assuming weekends would be double headers to offset periods and pregnancies. Why was Sheela not crying more?

Jakk listened to the eulogy. Surprisingly, it caused him to well up with tears. *The poor guy died at the prime of life! He was so young! Such a tragedy.* He was embarrassed with himself for becoming emotional at his own death. Maybe it was peer pressure at work? It was more proof that emotion trumped reason. The minister could have avoided words like "troubled" and "confused" and "wayward"; the word "promising" sounded like minister-speak for "loser." People struggled to find kind words. They did not know Jakk. They made stuff up. One classmate regaled his love of motorcycles—another said he saw him ride one down Kent Place Boulevard. Jakk had never ridden a motorcycle in his life. Kids who were not his friends spoke about their friendship with him. That was weird. It was heartbreaking to watch his parents cry. That did it: Jakk got out his gravawand and used it to push PLAY. The screen lit up with Jakk smiling. People hushed.

"Thank you for coming to my funeral," Jakk said on the screen.

The crowd gasped. People looked at each other. What was this about? Both Jakks loved the confusion. Video-Jakk began his fun.

"I know what you are thinking. What is heaven like? Do they have couscous and beans on Fridays? Can you eat all you want and not gain weight? Is it true there are no taxes?" The recorded Jakk pretended to look around the room as if he could see his audience. "Nice church, but you did not have to dress like somebody died."

People seemed confused. Had Jakk recorded this video before committing suicide? The recording continued:

"Guess what? Heaven is not a good excuse to get out of high school. I will be back tomorrow, and if I appear stupid, it is because I have fallen in love with someone."

Instantly the tone changed. Hope returned with renewed foolishness in waves. The eyes of his mom and dad brightened. He wanted to hug them but it could wait.

The engineered awkwardness was edible if only a preppy-looking guy was not standing next to Sheela. He was movie-star handsome, sharp eyebrows, a touch too pretty, like brand-new sneakers with crumpled paper still inside, a wide mouth as if he had been eating with an extra-large spoon, a face begging for a punch. Was Preppy moving in on his girl?

Preppy took out his phone and started tapping on its screen. Did she give him her phone number? Sheela's future did not include serious boyfriends until her twenties—her first relationship would dissolve into a hasty cryfest at an upstate airstrip, the second in a messy divorce with spreadsheets and a stuffed llama hurled from a second-floor window, according to the God program. That was Sheela's future if Jakk had not returned to Earth. But he did. Had he screwed up the future by having fun at his own funeral?

10

I'm All Right, Jakk

Jakk drove to Frank's office, signed documents, and got the registration for his minivan, a key for his new house, a credit card, and a checkbook. He attached the new license plates for his minivan. Frank had sold the gold for $147 million, and after taxes, Jakk was worth $77 million give or take. Frank's bill was $5,000. Jakk could not get him to take more. He thanked Frank. It would be great not living in the minivan in the woods anymore.

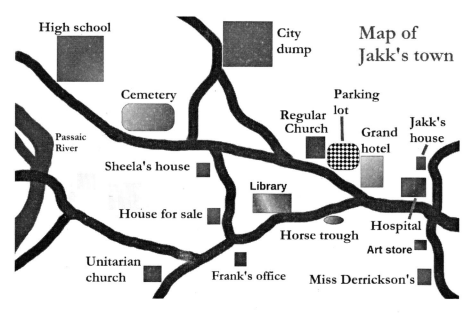

He drove to his new house, removed the for sale sign from the lawn, enjoyed the sound of the key turning the lock, and walked in. It was not like his parents' sagging house. Doorways were not parallelograms. Windows were modern and clean. The hardwood floors shone in the afternoon light. There was a pool in the back! *A pool!* He ordered Internet service, pool maintenance, a bed. Jakk enjoyed running up that credit card bill. Not only was Jakk a legal adult, he was a consumer!

The next day it was time to go back to school. He wore Reena's biker chic outfit, shiny with purple feathers like he could have been a French aristocrat from the 1800s who loved gardens. Plus cowboyish boots! He wore the wig and sunglasses as a disguise. He drove by the main entrance in his minivan. Surprise: there were news trucks and reporters with microphones. It must be a slow news day. The school seemed smaller. He wanted to look cool for Sheela. Would she hug him? Should he kiss her?

Jakk left his wig and sunglasses in the minivan and put on his knowledge cap. He got halfway to the entrance when a crowd swarmed him. He felt like an instant celebrity all over again. The whole school seemed to know about his sermon at his own funeral. It was the coolest joke. He knew how to act like a celebrity. He smiled. He shook hands. He crotch-grabbed one of his nerd friends by accident. It made all the other kids cool to be in the same school with him. He had a magic they hoped would rub off. He hugged his father and mother while the cameras whirred.

He swam in a sea of questions. "Where did you go?" "Why did you come back?" "Why didn't you call us?" "Were you skipping exams?" and such. Jakk kept his answers vague. He went on a journey. He should have called, sorry, he forgot. Yes, he was okay. He wanted to finish senior year and go to college. To more persistent questioners, he gave a broken-record response, calmly reiterating what he already said to bore them into not asking more questions.

"How did you escape detection for five weeks?" a reporter asked.

"I was not trying to escape detection."

"Why did you leave school?" asked another.

"Look around—why would anybody want to stay here?"

This got a laugh. It would make good copy. What he found, to his amazement, possibly because the hunger for stories was so strong, that in the absence of information, people invented stories for him, like he did not have to think them up, and the stories were not all that bad. They surmised that Jakk had taken off on his motorcycle and fallen in with a biker gang and pulled wheelies on his motorcycle in the desert; he was embarrassed by a badly done tattoo of Sheela; he was scared of facing Sheela after her balloon-blow putdown; he was protesting school lunches; he fell in love with a prominent dentist and hid out on her private island to enjoy a free root canal; he went free diving in the Caribbean and found gold. Bits of truth intermingled with baloney, forming a weird sandwich that seemed to satisfy the appetite to know what happened. The supposed discovery of gold added mystery. There was speculation he was a drug dealer, a bank robber, was kidnapped by an heiress and held as a sex slave in a mansion in Australia. That last one would not have been too bad, Jakk thought.

Jakk was perfectly happy to be surrounded by such mystery. He was like the guy in the *Great Gatsby*, with people wondering how he made his fortune. Who could guess that he had fetched freshly fused gold after causing a supernova and then minted it into coins using a microwavelike contraption to make the coins look like sunken Spanish treasure? He could even say the truth with a smile, and people would think it was a joke.

"Where did you go, and why didn't you tell us?" his father asked.

"I journeyed," Jakk said.

"We're glad you're back," his mother said.

Jakk promised not to journey again without telling them. They hugged. He felt bad about putting them through the ordeal but he knew in his heart that it was not really his fault. It was like Yodah said. No guilt. No blame. Stuff happened. Shrug.

It became clear that the school authorities had mixed reactions about his return. On the surface, they were glad to have their student back, relieved he was alive, but deeper down, the school was not happy when lackluster students took six-week unexplained absences. They were itching to make an example of his bad behavior by punishing him in a visible way, in case some of their good students got similar ideas. While the principal hinted he might not get a diploma, Jakk knew the school did not want to spend another $10,000 to see his boring face slumped over a tablet for another year.

"I want to take the Advanced Placement tests," Jakk said.

"That could be arranged. How many?" the principal asked.

"Twenty."

This request surprised the principal, who insisted that it would be a huge waste of money for his parents. When the principal said no for the second time, Jakk said he might have to call his lawyer. He was eighteen, a legal adult with rights. Jakk took cash from his wallet, enough for twenty tests. The principal shook his head in disbelief.

Jakk enjoyed being a man of mystery. Students stopped talking when he swung by. They wanted to sit with him at lunch. *He was cooler than Sheela!* They competed to tell him about the big bang he missed when a chemistry experiment went awry, spewing smoke into the halls and prompting a visit from the fire department. Sheela sat by herself, texting on her phone. In English class, he sat a few chairs away from her. When she turned, he shot a smile as if they were conspirators. She glanced back but did not return his stare. Playing hard to get? He tapped her on the shoulder.

"Hey," Jakk said.

"Welcome back," Sheela said.

"Be my date for the prom?"

She said no thanks. It was unexpected. His heart felt ready to drop ker-plop into his shorts. When he insisted on talking, she said they should talk after class but there was not much to say. Her words fell like icicles from a roof gutter. His mind scrambled like warplanes struggling to get airborne before a surprise attack.

"Jakk?" the teacher repeated.

The teacher had asked whether Hemingway's *The Sun Also Rises* or Fitzgerald's *The Great Gatsby* was the better novel. Perhaps Jakk was singled out because of his notoriety? Or to reestablish the seriousness of English as an important subject? Fortunately, both books were in his knowledge cap.

Truth be told, both novels sucked, big time, though Jakk felt no need to blame the writers: Hemingway was a victim of post-traumatic stress disorder, and Faulkner was an alcoholic. He would have renamed the books *The Penis Also Rises* and *The Joy of Flinging Shirts*.

"The women in both novels were intriguing. Hemingway's Brett is elusive, enigmatic, independent, and promiscuous and loves Jake despite his impotence. Fitzgerald's Daisy is a self-absorbed beauty, morally shallow, a hit-and-run driver. But neither woman can compare to today's determined woman who is fated to be loved despite herself. Who am I speaking of? Sheela."

Everybody looked at Sheela. Her blush seemed to heat the room. A light public giggle played itself out, then a subdued whooooo, as if he was on a talk show and said something provocative.

Jakk caught up with her after class. "Can we talk?"

"Talk," she said.

"I love you."

"I'm sorry I embarrassed you with the balloon."

"I did not leave because you did that. My journey was planned earlier."

"Your being missing didn't affect me much."

"You did not visit my room?"

"How can you love me when you don't even know me?"

"I know you love strawberry sundaes, your favorite movie is *Sleepless in Seattle*, you plan to study French literature at Princeton—a mistake, by the way—you weigh 136 pounds, you are 5 feet 7, a dangerous volleyball player, you have a retouched painting of me in your room, and if you could be reincarnated as anyone you want, you would be a blonde Audrey Hepburn from *Roman Holiday*."

Sheela stared, probably wondering who blabbed and how she would extract revenge. "I have to go," she said.

This was unexpected. It was like having to change strategy mid-battle. His head was an empty cave that reverberated with the flapping noise of bats escaping. He followed as Sheela walked to the pick-up zone outside. There was Preppy, polished Preppy, dressed in matching shirt and slacks, clothes that crooned "I am a moneyed member of the Country Club Set," sitting in a sports car so low to the ground that it could probably slip beneath a tractor trailer. He got out and opened the passenger door for her. He was such a gentleman. She slipped in and they drove away.

Jakk stood there. He felt foolish. Did that guy fail to realize that she was his woman? She ballooned Jakk not Preppy. It was not supposed to happen like this. Sheela and Preppy seemed to treat each other with an unspoken respect as if they were grownups and Jakk was still a kid.

He struggled to get a handle on the situation. He was in a romantic competition. What were the rules? *All is fair in love and war*—there were no rules but it was still like a game. He lost his romantic war on Hugubu. How could he win this one? Military war meant taking out the enemy—finding a weakness, overpowering an undefended area, feinting to the front while storming the rear. Romantic war, in contrast, was nuanced—he could not simply take out his rival, like one soldier killing another; if Sheela found out, she might hate Jakk and love Preppy even more.

The key, then, was to win Sheela's heart. He wanted to slip his fingers in there—gently, of course—to squeeze the other guy out while keeping it thumping. Simply trying to persuade her that he loved her more, as if he could simply ramp up his emotional love level, like roaring an engine, would probably not work. That was the crappy reality. A factor was respect: she respected Preppy; she did not respect Jakk.

Jakk inventoried resources. He knew more about Sheela than Preppy did. If Preppy was taller and better looking, Jakk was richer. Jakk could use his funds but not if it looked like a bribe or like he was trying to buy her love. There again was that dilemma: how to fight without appearing to fight? How could he get inside her mind without her feeling his fingers?

Was her decision a good one? A good decision had choices but that was it: Sheela never dated Jakk, never felt the Jakk-experience, never got Jakked, so she did not have a clear choice. If she had already made her decision, then it was made prematurely without knowing the alternatives. Accordingly, whether she had decided or not, Jakk would act as if she was still making her decision, but that could not go on forever. Time was finite.

His heart would not sing beneath her window for season after season, enduring hail and windstorms, like a lovesick guy's in a movie. Accordingly, to protect himself romantically, he set a choosing date—the end of June—after that, he would give up. He tried to convince himself he was the better man, although doubts stumbled into his mind like inebriated pool crashers. He tried to see things from Yodah's perspective. If Preppy and Sheela were forming a long chain of cause-and-consequence love, he was the random billiard ball X, coming out of nowhere, disrupting it. His task was to kill off a brewing love between them by persuading (1) Sheela not to love Preppy or (2) Preppy not to love Sheela or (3) Sheela to love Jakk more.

A strategy began to emerge. He would distract Preppy by making him angry at Jakk. That way, Preppy would lose focus on Sheela. So a key was stoking Preppy's anger—anger, according to Yodah, was the coupling of pain with the misconception of a free-willed entity deliberately causing that pain—pain was attachment to what changes. So what was Preppy attached to? His social markers—his prep school, his Princeton, his blue blazer jacket, his needlepoint belt, his rich parents, and his Nissan 350Z sports convertible. He googled Preppy and the car.

After he angered Preppy, then what? An ideal confrontation would appear to be initiated by Preppy while Sheela watched, but how could Jakk outfight a guy who was half a head taller with an extra thirty pounds of muscle? Jakk had a karate module in his knowledge cap. If Preppy threw the first punch but Jakk won, it might undermine Preppy as being a resolute defender of his woman, but if Jakk hurt Preppy, Sheela might feel sorry for Preppy and be angry at Jakk. So the task was to disable Preppy, preferably to expose him as aggressive and foolish and out of control. Jakk would be like a film director, starring Preppy as the bad guy and Jakk as the underdog hero. Sheela was the audience, and the flick could be fun if Jakk did not get his face crunched like a walnut in a nutcracker.

The next afternoon, Jakk snuck over to Preppy's car as his rival waited in front of the school for Sheela. He took out his gravawand, pointed it at the Nissan, pressed LOCK, and set it underneath the car. The car was fixed in place. It was amazing that a small object like a gravawand could keep a huge object from moving. Jakk hid behind a tree as Preppy, wearing his fancy tie, escorted Sheela to his sports car. Preppy put his car into gear, but it did not budge. He revved the engine, spinning the tires and spewing dust and exhaust, then lightly banged the steering wheel.

"Engine problems? May I help?" Jakk asked.

"No thank you," Preppy said.

"Computer malfunction? Turn it off and I will have a look."

"He knows computers," Sheela said.

Preppy reluctantly turned off the engine and popped the hood, and the two of them looked at the engine. Jakk typed into his tablet and pretended to read what it said.

"Two problems," Jakk said. "Axle-lock and loose hose. Hand me your tie."

"I'll call a mechanic," Preppy said.

"What is more important—your car or your tie?"

"Can't you find something else?"

A crowd of students had gathered. Nobody else wore a tie. Preppy handed him the tie, which Jakk wrapped around the oiliest hose. Jakk motioned for Preppy to return to the driver's seat.

"The 350Z has a troubling safety record, with 143 deaths per million registrations," said expert mechanic Jakk. "Sheela, I love you, but you should not ride in a death mobile. Let me take you home in my minivan."

"I thought you said you were going to fix the car," said Preppy.

"Please be patient. Sheela, a dress for you." Jakk took a box out of his backpack and handed it to her. She opened it to reveal a Reena-designed evening gown, a lush yellow with a matching gold belt. She handed it back.

"Only two women could wear it—you and your mom," Jakk said, gently touching her shoulder.

"Don't touch my girl," Preppy said.

"*Your* girl? Sheela, he thinks he owns you."

Jakk pretended to read his tablet. "Shift to neutral, reverse, neutral, park, start it, and please drive safely."

Jakk bent down, switched off the gravawand, and pocketed it. Preppy shifted as directed, started the car and drove off slowly, giving Jakk time to toss the box into the car. Jakk smiled when he saw Preppy's middle finger on top of his fat fist.

Jakk drove his minivan back to his new house and got started on his homework. Schoolwork was easy now. He wrote a ten page history paper by talking into his laptop for twenty minutes. His knowledge cap was like having the Internet in his head. The next day after class, Sheela faced him.

"I believe you love me but I love somebody else," she said.

Jakk felt tears almost start to flow but he took a slow breath and thought about Sprocks. He remembered Jesusbot. He gazed into her eyes with biblical intensity and resisted an urge to nibble on her earlobes.

"You think that you have found true love with Preppy?" Jakk asked.

She said Preppy's real name. Jakk would continue to call him Preppy. He did not want to hear about how great Preppy was or how true their love was. He had to challenge her notions about Preppy's supposed excellence. How? He took a gamble.

"Tell you what. Sleep with Preppy and try to climax: grit your teeth, focus, do yoga, say a prayer to a deity of your choosing. When love is real, you will orgasm effortlessly like a Sunday ride up a mountain in which your love engine does all the huffing and puffing while you moan for Jesus. But you will not reach that mountaintop with Preppy because he does not love you and you do not love him. Trust your body to tell you the truth."

He spoke with the certainty of a celebrity therapist on a talk show. She seemed angry yet confused. Jakk touched her gently and said that even his hand on her elbow excited her. Sheela swatted at his arm but he pulled it back in time.

His strategy was risky. A Preppy-poke could seal a permanent bond. But what else could he do? Her declaration of love scared him. He knew everything was fated but he hoped the cause-and-consequence chains would go his way.

Back in his house, he practiced kicking and punching and dodging and ducking by following the karate patterns dictated by his cap. At first, he was awkward. He knew karate moves only as cerebral knowledge. But with practice his mind and body learned to work together. He tapped the drywall to locate the studs. He focused. He punched carefully—if he missed and hit a stud, he could break his hand. Smoothly, surely, he punched out all the drywall in his living room, which was now cloudy with dust and debris. The walls were old anyway. His father could fix it. Give the old guy something to do.

Next he practiced with duct tape, feeding out lengths of two feet, cutting it with his teeth, holding the tape in both hands, making circles. He worked on a few moves. He knew them cold. It was the Jakk-form of self-defense: sticky karate. He fastened three two-foot lengths of tape to his shirt, sticky-side out, with only the ends attached to his shirt so he could grab them quickly without unrolling fresh tape, and continued to practice.

Jakk's gambit depended on Sheela failing to orgasm. His strategy was risky: she might enjoy orgasm-less sex anyway, or her love could be so great as to cause a real orgasm. The clitoris and vagina were made from the same type of tissue as a penis, but instead of hanging straight and expanding outward like a rocket, the tissue was bent in upon itself. So when it became engorged, it expanded inward and backward, with the clitoris being a highly sensitive mini-hub surrounded by flaps of skin, like Boston in its harbor. In contrast, a penis was like Manhattan—fed by the urethra-straight Hudson river. Maybe that was the geological reason why the baseball rivalry between the Yankees and Red Sox was so intense. Female sexual arousal was like a fat person on an airplane wearing a seat belt, trying to stand up, getting halfway, coming back down, trying again, getting halfway, coming down, feeling embarrassed and flushed, perhaps forgetting about the seatbelt tucked under a flap of skin. It was hard getting enough blood in there during sex, like squeezing a busload of clowns into a cramped warehouse filled with pipes and plumbing tools. That is why some women never climaxed.

But women did not need to climax to reproduce. So they passed their "oh shucks I did not orgasm" gene to their female offspring. That was how Mr. Charles Darwin might have explained it to Mrs. Charles Darwin in days before heated vibrators. Causing Sheela to worry about her inability to climax during preppycourse might make it even harder for her to climax—or fret Preppy into sexual flopsweat—and bring her to Jakk's gravawand to be lifted to bliss and jakked to Pleasure Mountain. Hopefully Preppy would rush instead of taking the time to learn her body. Surely Preppy would not study Sheela's body by writing computer programs. Even for Jakk, with his proven sexual prowess, bringing Sheela to climax was uncertain—it might take the master a year of conditioned response training until he could call out a number to hustle her body through foreplay, like prisoners telling each other jokes by number.

Would his gambit work? Sheela might defy Jakk's suggestion and not sleep with Preppy—a win. Sheela might sleep with Preppy anyway, and if so, then she was doing what Jakk commanded, a good habit for her to develop—a semi-win. If she climaxed—a big loss. He could calculate the odds of each outcome using Bayesian sideways-tree diagrams but he found the exercise upsetting.

Jakk felt forced into this bad boy strategy. He was becoming less of a Jakk and more of a dick, but he had to do something to impress the power of his personality upon her. If she would not feel his positive force, she would feel his negative force. If she became angry at Jakk, then so be it. Anger was a negative number that could easily be switched to a positive number by reversing the sign. It was classic Spinoza: hate could be flipped into love like a mathematical operation. Jesus used the principle to convert people from hating Him to loving Him; His turning the other cheek was one such operation. Saint Paul was flipped from persecutor to promulgator. What mattered more than the negative or positive sign was the intensity of feeling. She must feel intensely toward him. Feeling nothing, or being merely friends, was worse than death.

For the next few days, placement tests kept Jakk away from classes. Nobody bothered him about his cap. He always finished first. He kept duct tape with him always.

Finally, a class with Sheela. He followed her out as usual but she looked different. What was it? Her attitude? Something in her walk. She seemed older. Crap—she had the look of a woman for whom sex was no longer a mystery, but she avoided his gaze. What did that mean? That she did it with Preppy but did not enjoy it, was embarrassed about it, knew Jakk was right but was reluctant to admit it?

"Tough to go mountain climbing and not reach the summit," Jakk said, shaking his head.

She kept walking. Jakk followed her out of school and watched Preppy get out of his car with a determined yet detached mood, like a father approaching a disobedient teenager. Was the play beginning? Jakk pushed his cap on tight, peeled three two-foot lengths of duct tape, bit off each one, and attached them to his chest. He was not worried about looking odd. He ambled behind Sheela until Preppy stepped in front of him, blocking his path.

"Sheela is my girlfriend," Preppy said. "If you bother her, you'll deal with me."

"Is this the thanks I get for fixing your car?" Jakk asked.

Preppy stood directly in his face, a foot away, his jaw clenched, exuding Preppy breath, which smelled like avocado.

"Sheela and I are fated to be lovers," Jakk said quietly. "I let her experience the futility of having sex with you as a learning experience and I will continue to tell her how I feel."

"Touch her and you will experience my justice."

Experience my justice? Was that Preppy's trademark warning? A crowd gathered. Sheela heard Preppy's official pronouncement. So did everybody else. It was like Preppy was on record.

Jakk leaned over and gently touched Sheela on her shoulder. Then he grabbed the first length of duct tape in each hand.

Preppy lunged hard with his fist but Jakk swiveled and encircled it with tape.

Preppy reached with his second hand to try to remove the tape.

Jakk circled again to tie both hands together in one swift move but his cap fell to the ground.

Preppy lunged downward with both arms tied but Jakk dodged sideways while grabbing a second strip of tape from his chest. Jakk was breathing hard, scared to have lost the karate knowledge in his cap.

Jakk dodged three kicks, backpedaled quickly, and on the fourth kick, had a stroke of luck when Preppy's foot grazed his chest and was ensnared by the remaining strip of tape! Jakk followed it to the ground and taped Preppy's ankles together imperfectly.

Preppy's football-thick arms tried to come down hard on Jakk's back, but Jakk spun around behind his rival, who lost his balance and tumbled forward. Jakk wrapped his arm around Preppy's neck and squeezed it into a hold. The match had degenerated from karate to wrestling, like a hurricane being downgraded to a tropical storm. Luckily, Jakk's body was safely on the other side of Preppy's powerful arms.

Preppy tried to break out but Jakk's grasp around his neck proved decisive. Somebody shouted that a teacher was approaching.

Jakk let go, put his cap back on, and dusted himself off. Preppy looked ridiculous in the dirt, struggling to breathe.

"Our high school has a zero-tolerance policy towards violence," Jakk said.

Preppy muttered an expletive between gasps. There was probably a policy against cursing too. Sheela bent over her taped-up warrior and asked if anyone had scissors. Preppy had several scrapes with dots of blood forming. Maybe rubbing alcohol should be liberally applied? Jakk left the pair fumbling on the ground and drove home.

In the early evening, Jakk parked outside Sheela's house. The drive was only two blocks, but he wanted her to see his vehicle. Light from nearby houses and streetlights filtered through the leaves. He liked her house. Dark shutters were like eye makeup around her windows, making them pop like the eyes of an Egyptian princess. The evening was alive with feeling. With three cars in the driveway, Sheela must be home. Her window was open. He was about to launch into song when a shape came to her window and stood there silently.

"Sheela, come enjoy the night with me!" Jakk called out in a loud whisper.

The shape said nothing. Through a window on the ground floor, he saw a dress moving toward him. She wore his Reena-designed dress! It flowed like a flower opening to embrace the sun.

The door swung upon. "Come in."

It was Sheela's mother. This was awkward. There was sadness in her eyes.

"Is Sheela home?" he asked.

"Why don't you stay for dinner? Sheela's at the prom with her boyfriend."

So that was where she was. It would have felt rude to say no so he came in. It was better to be inside Sheela's house than outside since she would return sooner or later. Stepping over the threshold, he felt an unsettling sense of danger.

Sheela's house was a real house, with every room having its own purpose. The kitchen was only a kitchen, not also a laundry and dining room. The oven door did not screech "what are you trying to cook" when her mom moved dinners to the microwave. In the dining room, there were two places set, candles burning low, and wine in glasses. The house had a homey feeling, unlike his parent's house, which felt more like an employee lounge at a supermarket.

"My husband is working late so there's plenty for both of us."

Sheela's mother and father were his future in-laws, so he needed to make an outstanding impression as an upstanding young man, something he had read in an etiquette book. He sat. Her parents could be powerful allies in his bid to woo Sheela. Her mom brought two freshly nuked plates of chicken cacciatore, served him waiter-style, bending over from the right to reveal her highly touchable cleavage. Then she sat beside him as candlelight gave her face a warm glow.

"Has Sheela ever worn my dress?" Jakk asked.

"I doubt it. How much did you pay for it?"

"Nothing. Magazine craft project from an out-of-this-world designer."

That was mostly true, even if he skipped the part about making it in his Hugubuian microwave. She gazed out the dark window. He could not resist a glance at her beautiful breasts, which suggested effortless beauty, middle-aged fun, and milky freedom. Sheela sipped from those breasts and now she had her own pair. He looked at the window and saw her mom's eyes looking right at him in the reflection. Did she catch him studying her breasts? How awkward. He had to be careful.

In a year, one of her still-firm breasts would be discarded in a sad can of medical waste. He remembered the sinking feeling of drastic unfairness when Sheela-Jakk collapsed. His anti-cancer cream could save her breasts, but how could he get her to apply it? The cream had to stay on for eight hours. Could he manipulate her into applying it some other way, like telling her it was a suntan cream or beauty lotion? He doubted she would believe him. He needed to build trust between them, and then maybe an opportunity would present itself?

He enjoyed dining with her. He felt like he belonged in this fancy neighborhood, like he was not an outsider or a kid from the flaky section. He no longer felt like a blank space between words but a part of the sentence, no longer a space character but a word in his own right who had his own form of dark energy. She looked like Sheela. She reminded him how fine it would be to dine with Sheela. He felt attuned to her body, aware of each leg. When she crossed a leg over the other and exposed a thigh within touching distance, the sight burned in his brain. It was an event. She would not lose her breast. He committed himself without any real plan. He would be her breast rescuer, her body part savior, a superhero with a cape and tights that looked sprayed on...

"Jakk."

She spoke like a parent explaining why she would not buy him a particular toy. His name sounded dropped, from mouth to floor, like a cooked ham slipping off a kitchen counter and bouncing and sliding under a table.

"Sheela found a boy. She loves him and she's sorry for teasing you with that balloon. I know you have feelings for her and that you're a nice boy but it's time to move on."

Death on a stick. He fumed inwardly. He was not a nice boy but a bad boy who would someday prong her daughter with panache. Emotion suggested he rise angrily from the table, throw down a napkin like a gauntlet, shout something and stomp off, and he was on the verge of throwing such a tantrum.

Then he thought: *cool it*. He remembered Yodah's wisdom. He would not be tempted by his temper. What Sheela's mom said had been fated. It was not her fault. She suffered from a profound lack of understanding and lacked a sufficiently long string of cause-and-consequence ideas in her head. He should try to align those strings correctly in her head. Except for her confused thinking, she was a caring woman who was feeding him dinner and treating him like an adult by serving him wine. He was good enough to have dinner with her. That was a start.

They spoke about their town, high school, what college might be like. They finished a bottle of wine and she brought out a second. His thinking began to lumber. His arms felt heavier. Thoughts came more slowly, but when they came, they felt right like jackboots marching with certainty in a military parade.

"Were you crying earlier?" he asked.

"My world is … unraveling," she sighed.

She was a bubble of sadness, floating close, physical and fleshy. If her life was unraveling, her beauty remained raveled. A tear fell to her (his) dress and slowly expanded into an ellipse near her knee, smile-shaped, turning the soft pink to a duller shade of pink. He wanted to hug her. Did she know she had cancer? It was not fair. Her life should not unravel. Unraveling is what happened to retirees in their eighties if they broke a hip. She mentioned her foundering art store. He liked watching her lovely mouth form words. If he sketched her lips, he would try to convey the movement.

"How much money do you need?" Jakk asked.

"Much more than I have," she said.

She knew her husband had lost his job and was pretending to go to work. She knew soon after it happened yet she lacked gumption to call him on it, so bills mounted while his charade continued. Sheela was bound for Princeton—fifty thousand dollars a year but the school lopped off twenty (he did not like hearing the words "lopped off"). He knew from the God program that her husband put another mortgage on their house further without informing her, so there was almost no equity. They were in trouble financially but it was an opportunity for Jakk: they needed money, he had money, so how could he use it to influence them without appearing to do so?

"Don't you run off on your motorcycle again," she said. "Sheela's a nice girl, but there are plenty of other girls."

She was one more victim of that damn motorcycle myth. Incorrect ideas were emerging like warm drips from the shower of her mind. He felt like she was a sophomore in college and he was a despondent freshman who had accidentally stumbled on one of those strategies for getting laid: getting a woman to feel sorry for you. He wondered if Mother Teresa ever thought about such a strategy for saving lives—no, a sex offer from Mother Teresa might cause men to hurl themselves in front of moving trains.

She slid her hand on top of his. He maintained his composure but inwardly her advance startled him, woke him up. He felt his penis get hard alongside the side of his shorts, creeping along his left leg like a snake. He wished he had worn blue jeans or underwear. Its head might emerge past the cuff of his shorts. He tried thinking of helicopters crashing into volcanoes or women serial rapists with knives or Glenn Close saying "I will not be ignored." She stood up.

"Give me a hug," she said.

He sat there. If he hugged her, she might feel it. If he did not hug her, she would think him cold, an ungrateful stranger eating her precious food before her credit cards maxed out. He pictured his penis as having "Sheela" tattooed along its shaft, not "Sheela's mom," but wine and physical proximity blurred things. He stood up, hugged her gently, trying to keep his midsection aloof, but she pushed her hips into his and yes she felt it. Funny how trying to do the right thing sometimes boomeranged. Better say something.

"You are as beautiful as she is. But I am in love with your daughter."

Maybe that might explain his boner? She reminded him of Sheela, Sheela made him hard, QED. No need to feel guilty about a natural bodily function. He could not control what happened down there. Were there etiquette guidelines for such a situation? What to do if you hug your girlfriend's mother and accidentally get a boner. Say "excuse me but I feel an urgent need to pee," or make a teenaged-boy joke like "gee, I should not carry a cucumber in my pocket"? The word *etiquette* came from the French court, cards urging drunken nobles to keep off the flowers at Versailles. Jakk was trampling them. He was inches from her bush. He wondered whether Max was on his God program, watching Jakk hug Sheela's mother with a boner.

He loved how she smelled. She was so close. She was *so much like Sheela.* No cucumber-in-the-pocket joke would suffice. He felt her pulse racing. Could somebody see them through the window? He could not push her away without being even more rude. He was trapped in this awkward pose. When he fumbled for words, she put her hands on his face—trapping it—and kissed him on the lips. If Sheela walked in, it would be over but God how her lips felt great. Why was she kissing him?

"I will invest in your art store," he said.

This surprise interrupted the pleasure flow with an even more intriguing financial survival flow. He wrote her a $10,000 check in wobbly handwriting. She stared in disbelief.

"Where did you—how—well thank you," said Sheela's mom.

Jakk shrugged. When he learned that Sheela was going to be spending the night with Preppy, he felt like he was being buried alive in a coffin. Her face registered empathy for his sadness.

"Make love to me," she whispered.

He knew this was dangerous. It was asking for trouble. It was a classically morally stupid thing to elevate the short term pleasure of sex over the long term chances of loving Sheela. Yodah would be shaking his trunk to say "don't do it, Jakk." His brain knew this but the message was not getting through to his penis. Sheela seemed more distant than ever and here was a beautiful woman, desiring him, whom he could help medically without having to mention the word tumor.

A sidebar thought rolled in like a leprechaun in an Irish pub: perhaps sex with him was a pity fuck, a runner-up prize, her way of telling him he would never have Sheela. A second leprechaun with a wrinkled grin ambled in—where did they keep coming from?—maybe her mom was running interference for her daughter by getting him out of the picture, since he would be disqualified from Sheela if he first did her mom. Doing Jakk was like a football block to knock him out of the way, so Sheela and her Preppy quarterback could score a fuckdown. Feed him dinner, give him wine so he could not drive to Preppy's to inflict coitus interruptus. Then again, maybe he was overthinking things—maybe Sheela's mom was just plain horny.

He needed time to tease out her motives. What if making love to her mom would help him win her daughter? Of course not, but the idea remained firm, egged on by wine. Logic did not help: (-p) he was not making love to Sheela; (-q) he was not making love to Sheela's mom either; if he made love to Sheela's mom—the contrapositive, or (q)—then logically he would make love to Sheela (p)? This was logical but felt mistaken. His dual brains beckoned him with arguments: Sex was good; he never technically did a real human woman so he might still consider himself a virgin and what if he died tomorrow? What is wrong with getting some practice; Sheela would probably not find out. These arguments felt firm. Would they pass a Yodah test of logical cause-and-consequence idea chains? Saying no would sluttify Sheela's mom, brand her as a sex-starved cougar, a borderline child molester, pissing her off so much that she would never approve of him dating her daughter. There would be so much romantic debris that the authorities would shut down the interstate between Sheela and Jakk's respective genitalia. Saying yes or saying no to Sheela's mom's whispered request was equally disastrous, so he kept talking as he tried desperately to think.

"I am a better lover for Sheela than Preppy is," he said.

She raised an eyebrow. Such was the problem with conversation. He could not rewind, delete the phrase, and replay. As the evening kept spinning, with more wine seeping into his cargo hull, he kept thinking that the way to make love to Sheela was to make love to her mom. This radical thought made sense in his state of inebriation. She would feel his lovemaking skill in person—she would feel it was real. She would know that he could bring her daughter to wonderful climaxes like a precision drill sergeant marching soldiers around the base. If courting Sheela was like applying for a job, he was simply taking a performance test by a superior to see how well he fit in with the company culture. It was like car shopping—suppose a mother and daughter shopped for a new car—so what if the mother did the first test drive? Plus he could apply anti-cancer cream so she could keep her air bags. If Sheela found out later, he could grease by with Yodah's "all is fated" crap. Benjamin Braddock did both mom and daughter in *The Graduate*. Plus he would not be making Sheela a baby brother; this was recreational sex, frisky and fun, healthy and probably recommended by the Surgeon General.

"Come see my new house," he said.

The night air had cooled slightly, clearing his head somewhat, and the lights of the houses they walked by were off, no traffic on the street, so they were alone. Still, she walked quietly behind him, a guilty walk, but the silence gave him a chance to think about her needs as well as his. He wanted to impress her that he was son-in-law material, show her that he was a *human who knew how to be a human*, ethical and good, an uplifter of fellow humans, a jacker-upper of people, a lover of Sheela, a fighter and protector skilled at keeping bill collectors at bay. What did Sheela's mom value? Those things, plus artistic skill. He had a sketching module in his cap. He tried to see things as she saw them: a checking statement with numbers enclosed in parentheses like hands trying to hide a harsh truth; guilt about kissing her daughter's classmate on the lips. She was weak. He must not take advantage. He had to think like a grownup. She hesitated at his front stoop.

"We have my house all to ourselves," Jakk said.

She walked in cautiously and he closed the door behind her. He remembered what she tasted like when he kissed her earlier—raspberry with a hint of peach.

"What happened to the walls?" she asked.

"Looks like somebody punched them," he said.

He hoped his house, with designer trees outside and granite kitchen countertops inside, might impress his future mother-in-law. She checked out the kitchen and dining room; with no furniture, the rooms seemed naked. He followed behind as she cautiously climbed the stairs, as if she half-expected his parents to emerge in bathrobes asking "Jakk, who is your friend?"

He closed the master bedroom door behind them. She saw the queen-sized mattress on the floor. She was so like Sheela, with Sheela's mannerisms but without the uppity attitude. He felt as if he was mired in the slippery gooey morass of upcoming sex. She reached behind her back, wiggled playfully, and Sheela's dress tumbled in a fluid motion around her ankles. He disrobed too. They faced each other. He had an idea.

"It would be a crime against art if what I see here is not recorded," he said.

It was the truth. He positioned her on his mattress with two pillows behind her head and one knee lifted suggestively. She was a marvelously enticing woman. He would try to immortalize her beauty. He rubbed anti-cancer cream on each breast—to give them a wonderful sheen, he said. Her smile felt forced, so he directed his subject to stare at his erection and imagine that sex was imminent; the interaction between her gaze and his body fixed the problem wonderfully. A most beguiling smile blazed across her face like an enchanted sunset. It filled him with awe and wonder. He hoped she enjoyed his musculature and his hairless chest and his boner, which spoke to her in the male-female universal language of quiet respect. A boner was like a cop pointing a gun at a criminal saying "don't move"; helpful, since if she shifted, it would screw up the sketch. He finished the drawing in a half hour and showed it to her, which she studied intently.

"You're talented," she said.

When Jakk shrugged, his boner bobbed up and down as if it was nodding in agreement. She was learning to respect his artistic prowess! She studied the drawing further. She could get an excellent price for it, she said, maybe with a title like *Woman on the Verge of Love*. They talked about art, how being a human was really about *becoming* a human, living on the verge, that life should be a rolling wheel of joy, spinning to a higher hill of heightened feeling and nuanced understanding.

He loved her as his future mother-in-law, trying to focus on persuading her that he was, indeed, the right man for Sheela, and so he tried to think in ever-wider ever-longer cause-and-consequence chains. He was falling further in love with Sheela through the vehicle of her sexy mother. They loved Sheela but in different ways. He could learn from her. They looked at each other. They knew: it was a shared understanding. He remembered making love to the recreated Sheela back on Hugubu in his Jakk Shack, her soft skin, her twinkling eyes, the exhilaration of scientists exploring the sexual mechanics of the female body by plugging variables into equations. He reached out to her.

They walked back to her house. The night air seemed to bubble off some of the wine in his blood. He thought about college. Even with his AP scores, there was no way he could get into Princeton. Rutgers, maybe. How could he persuade Sheela that she would be better off at Rutgers with him? Jakk could possibly get into Princeton if he published his solution to string theory but that would unleash chaos. Rutgers and Princeton were only twenty minutes apart; maybe they could visit on weekends?

They walked into her house. He heard a door close upstairs. Her husband was home. She rolled up Jakk's sketch like a scroll and headed upstairs.

"Wait for her on the couch?" she said.

He sat on the couch. On the coffee table, he saw a ripped out page from a magazine of a model posing in a jungle-vibrant bikini. He fetched Sheela's winter coat, breathed in her smell, kicked off his shoes, tried to stay awake, lay down, and slept.

Sunlight hit a wall. He heard a door open. It was Sheela and she did not look pleased. She was in hurling-dishes mode. Luckily there was no crockery in her hands.

"What are you doing here?" Sheela asked.

Blood began flowing to his brain. He knew he better say something but not the wrong thing or her semi-open heart would seal shut forever like a baseball mitt with Krazy Glue. One wrong word could do it. That was how women were. But his brain was not working and his head hurt.

"Why is there a check for $10,000 on the dining room table?"

"Fate. What are you doing here?" Jakk asked.

"To get my swimsuit for his pool."

Jakk's house had a pool. He would love to see her in a swimsuit by *his* pool. He got up slowly. His throat felt dry. He took the page off the coffee table and walked out to his minivan. He scanned the image into the microwave, inserted fabric, clicked on her stored measurements, hopped out of the van and heaved into a bush, looked around, heaved again, heard a dog bark, returned to the minivan, found a towel, wiped his mouth, rinsed with water, and brought the still-warm bathing suit into Sheela's house and placed it on the dining room table. Where was the check? And where was Sheela? She must have gone upstairs. He raided the refrigerator for orange juice but there was none, then he felt guilty because he lacked permission to so raid, like a Viking with a conscience. If a big brouhaha erupted over goings-on for the past evening, it probably did him no good to be a part of it, so he returned to his minivan and sat in the driver's seat, cloudy-headed, not quite sure about driving even two blocks home.

Sheela stormed out of the house like a dissatisfied customer on a mission to chew out an inept clerk. She opened the passenger door, got in, slammed it closed, looked forward, and breathed out, as if collecting her thoughts. His encounter with her mother last night—was that what she was angry about? No, it was worse; she was angry with his existence. Jakk existed. That pissed her off.

"You don't understand that you're not wanted. You jinxed my boyfriend's car and lured him into that fight. Now you're stalking me in my own house. You think that dresses or checks or swimsuits will win my heart? Get out of my life."

He remembered his father's advice about women. Anything that might emerge from any orifice was something he had to deal with.

"You look sexy when you are angry," he said. Well, she did.

"You're a stalker."

"*You* are the stalker."

"How?" she scoffed.

"You ballooned me, so that on my journey, even though I floored it, I could not escape your clutches. Everywhere I went, there you were. You in my movie, you on my computer, you in my mind, you in my bed."

"I was trying to help your parents find you."

"You swiped my sperm," Jakk said.

"What could possibly motivate *anyone* to do that?"

But she had hesitated, suggesting she was indeed a sperm-swiper. Why not a fresh batch?

"Look, whatever happened, happened," Jakk said. "It was nobody's fault."

She looked at him with disbelief. He resolved not to be a neat academic paper for her valedictorian mind to analyze, as questions were growing exponentially into further weirdness. Words like "fault" and "blame" reminded him of Yodah, and he tried to remind himself those words did not make sense, but it sure felt at this moment that all of his problems were Sheela's fault: intergalactic traipser, balloonist, ego-deflator who never properly recognized his achievement in the Science Olympiad. He was in love with an ungrateful bitch. There was a pause. She held up his check and ripped it to pieces.

"You will not bribe your way into my life!"

She had crossed a line. He could not let her get away with such conduct. Bribing was too close to the truth. He mentally tallied legal factoids to assure himself he would prevail if this escalated to court. She was a check-ripping vandal and litterbug who trespassed into *his* car without asking permission. He was not a stalker but a guest of her mother. That was what he would tell the judge.

"You're a prick," she said.

"No, I am a man who loves you. You are being rude and you should apologize."

She sat there, fuming.

"Anger is stupid. Pride is stupid," said Jakk.

"I will never love you," she said.

"Then you could kiss me without feeling anything."

Sheela slammed her fist against the dashboard. "You are still a—"

Reena's face appeared on a screen in the dashboard panel. "May I help you?" she asked.

"Who are *you*?" Sheela asked.

Reena paused for a while. "Your next maintenance checkup isn't until December. Is there a problem?"

"No," Jakk said, hoping she would disconnect quickly. He did not know whether the government could identify faster-than-light transmissions, but they were out there, trying to triangulate on his position. Jakk would have to drive to a new location soon.

Reena's image disappeared. Her quick thinking had not given him away. It was good to see her again. He missed her. It was great to know how he could contact his friends: get Sheela to punch his dashboard!

"If I get a flat tire, I will need your fist to call the repair truck," he said.

Sheela glared at him. Why he said that, he did not know. Was it the general absurdity of things? His heart lightened when she chuckled softly—contagious like a yawn on a space bus. Beside him was a galaxy of problems under a canopy of hair. Love should exempt her from having to apologize. That was what love was about, partly. Love was a new land—a queendom—where things like logic and tit-for-tat fairness and manners did not matter much.

"You're a nut," she said and strutted back to her house. He knew her mother would need another check. They should learn to value him financially. He drove the short distance home and parked inside his garage. Sure enough, minutes later, a radar truck drove by the street. It had been a close call.

His handyman father pulled into Jakk's driveway with his matching minivan, walked up with his tool belt in his paint-spattered jeans and muscle shirt, saw the punched-up walls and measured their thickness with his finger.

"Eight sheets, maybe two extra," his father said.

In the handyman minivan, riding shotgun while his father drove, Jakk decided that Frank had told his father about his wealth, since his parents had not pestered him to return home. They treated him like an adult. The hardware store was part of his father's system: tools, boards, guys in jeans, a friendly wave from a plumber-friend. They lifted wall boards to a

six-wheeled cart with wheels that seemed to squeak complaints about being in New Jersey. So much of the state was packed in elbow-to-elbow. He
remembered his father once joked that tomato plants in New Jersey would
whisper "come closer, I need to tell you something" then say "hey, buddy,
you are blocking my sunlight."

"Nothing like your fresh spackle," his father said. "Thanks for paying
my mortgages."

"I should have said goodbye before I left."

"How're you gonna persuade Sheela to choose Rutgers?"

Sometimes it seemed as if parents knew too much. Who did they have
spying on him? Teachers, the principal, librarians, Frank, Sheela's mom?
He probably knew about the duct tape and the AP tests … Hugubu was
probably a bit out of their range though.

"What do you suggest?"

"You ask my opinion—what a surprise! You need a project so abso-
frigging-lutely cool that it can only be done at Rutgers by the two of youse.
Lemme think …"

Jakk knew that his dad already had an idea. "Lemme think" was conversational foreplay to build suspense. *Abso-frigging-lutely. The two of youse.*
Jakk's father had grown up in Chicago; his Jersey accent was a contrivance.
*Gee, Dad, you are not a first generation Italian American who cooks huge Sunday
spaghetti dinners in giant pots and whacks kids on the side of the head if they do
not listen.*

"What did ancient Greeks have that Americans don't?" asked his father
as they loaded the minivan.

"Real democracy? Bearded philosophers? Triremes? No Paralympic
Games?" *Just spill it,* Jakk thought. He did not like being stumped by the
old man.

"*An oracle!* A high-tech digital temple of liquid truth! People come
from miles around to learn their futures. What a moneymaker—curious
folks wait in line, get hungry, ooooh look at that snack bar, finally get an
audience with the oracle for a few minutes, get your Jersey-cryptic fortune, then exit through the gift shop. Ka-ching! Here's the secret: research

customers while they wait to meet the oracle: what car they drove, what they wore, grab data from a form they fill out so you can google their names and Facebook posts, have sharp Rutgers students play it back as wisdom. Maybe Sheela could be the cryptic goddess!"

It was not such a bad idea. So left-field it might work. The slimmed down God program really *could* read fortunes. Could he use it while keeping the technology secret? His father's latest idea was a step up from his Fuck Farm idea—a sleepaway camp where fat people hump off the pounds—and several staircases better than his sound-activated fart-sucking tube inside mattresses to keep sleeping couples from gassing each other to death. But he knew not to show interest in his father's wild ideas. It was a cause-and-consequence chain: if Jakk expressed interest, then Stupid Idea A would be followed by Stupid Idea B, then the whole frigging alphabet would come waltzing along.

"Not feasible," Jakk said.

"Forgot the screws but got more in my box," his father said.

The old man had plenty of screws in his box. Both of them presented smokescreen fronts. His father was just a handyman. He was just a high school senior. Sometimes they could see through each other's smoke-screens. Jakk's secrets were more dangerous.

Back at his house, they unloaded drywall, removed broken fragments of walls, pulled out nails, piled trash into black bags, and attached fresh sheets. Jakk ordered lunch delivered and when the sandwiches came, his father wrapped them in tin foil and blow-torched them for fifteen seconds. The two workmen sat on the floor eating turkey and pastrami and melted cheese. They were men. They used their sleeves for napkins. They looked at the dust and boards and tools.

"Here it is," Jakk's father said.

"Here it is," Jakk said.

"Life."

"Life."

"The whole kit and kaboodle."

"All here in the drywall."

"All here in my son."

"All here in my father."

They drywalled, taped, spackled, and swept. Then his father drove home.

Jakk was alone on a Saturday evening with not much to do except think. He imagined Sheela off somewhere fuming like a scorched mountain town after wildfires had blown through. Things seemed to be happening to him, as if the remote control of his life was slipping from his hands and changing channels at random. Preppy's advances. Sheela's emotions. Radar trucks. Now Sheela's mom. Jakk saw himself as a man of action but what was particularly frustrating was that there seemed to be nothing that he could do. He could not will Sheela to love him. Thinking this way got him all lathered up with no way to rinse off.

So he tried to stop thinking about strategies. The current under his raft was in charge of where on the wide river of life he might float next. The raft would drift where it would drift. It was a painful reality. Finally, he had an epiphany: his strategy to win Sheela's love was to *abandon strategy altogether* and do nothing. He would ignore her. He had no choice.

His problem was the opposite of most people's: he had to struggle to keep from being famous. The minivan-spaceship was a weak point. It could not be seen doing anything other-worldly like flying or emerging from a head-on collision without a scrape. He did not want people wondering why it never needed gas or oil or fresh tires. The vehicle was a Pandora's box—if its secrets got out, there would be no way to stuff them back in. Mass-produced spaceships could bring chaos. He had to protect humans by keeping quiet about string theory and space travel and alien technology. It was how he could be noble and ethical and good.

He took a short nap but awoke in the early evening and looked out the window at his back yard. He thought briefly about giving a squirrel on a branch a free glide ride from tree to tree, courtesy the gravawand, but decided against it—what if a neighbor saw that? He imagined classmates at parties. He was lonely. His footfalls echoed in bare rooms. He missed Max and Reena and Sheelabot and Jesusbot. He wondered how the

Human Museum was doing. He wished Reena would spruce up the biker-chic wardrobe he microwaved for himself, breathable leather with studs that did not exactly mesh with his knowledge cap, but so what.

Jakk had his parents, classmates who thought he was cool, teachers who did not understand him, a lawyer, a reluctant love interest, but no real friends. To classmates, he might seem like a star: shining yet distant; he did not mean anything much to anybody in a personal way. He regretted being a loner during his high school years. Shadowy clouds floated behind trees in the darkness. He wanted friends to act like his eyes and ears in the wider community, to support him, to teach him things, to give him feedback and help him court Sheela.

An idea jelled. Jakk could offer scholarships to the state university. He emailed Frank to ask Rutgers if they might accept, say, 25 academically qualified seniors including himself and Sheela if Jakk paid all expenses for four years.

Cicadas emerged in June after having slumbered in the soil for seventeen years. They crawled out when the soil warmed, grew wings, flew around, mated butt-to-butt, stuck their offspring in branches, and died six weeks later. He found himself sympathizing with the red-eyed insects. Their low scowl sounded like a fax machine's signal from far away. He rescued a few trapped in the grass by giving them a twig to climb so they could get up the tree. Cicadas were all about sex. So was Jakk. He looked at a cicada. The cicada looked back. Cicadas were having sex everywhere and he was not.

11

Jakk of All Subjects

The next morning in class he was uprooted by the principal and several teachers. Could he please accompany them? His high school celebrity skyrocketed. This was a scene. Did it have to do with the gold? His spaceship? Probably not, since there were no police. Duct-taping Preppy? Possibly. The inquisition gathered in an empty classroom and they asked him to please sit down but he said he preferred to stand. He was a battle-hardened veteran of the Hugubu admissions committee. He knew how to handle obnoxious reporters. He attacked first to keep them off balance.

"I remind you kindly but firmly that I am an eighteen-year old adult of legal age with rights," Jakk said. "I am recording this conversation for my lawyer to review."

He clicked on his tablet to record the proceeding. His calm tone seemed to surprise them. Still, he had to tread carefully. He did not want investigators examining his minivan or the gravawand in his pocket, which looked innocent but if squeezed a certain way, could lift people into the air. While an examiner would almost certainly not figure it out, there was a risk.

"We wanted to inquire about a discrepancy between your grades and perfect AP scores," said the principal, haltingly.

Relief. Discrepancy was an academic euphemism for "we think you cheated." Had he? His knowledge was in his cap like additional brain cells. If he ventured in the real world, he would still have this knowledge in his cap. He *earned* it even if he did not exactly *learn* it. If Jakk was the principal, he would have suspected cheating. It seemed odd for any student to ace twenty tests, particularly in subjects that the school offered no courses for.

They were simply doing their job. It was fated. Jakk did not need to be angry with them. He wondered about the cause-and-consequence chains in their minds. Maybe they thought he bribed the testing service? Bribed proctors? Hacked the testing center's computer? They knew he was a skilled programmer. They did not know how he did what he did, but they knew that he had done *something*. In this weird vortex telling the truth would create more problems so short-term misdirection was morally good. Still, a cheating scandal would jeopardize the school's reputation, possibly lower property prices, maybe get people fired, or prompt colleges to consider rescinding offers of admission.

Why had he taken so many tests? To impress Sheela, to compensate for his consistently mediocre grades so he could get into college, or was his ego rearing up once again, waving its flag, marching aimlessly in its own parade? No matter; that was in the past. What was his strategy now? To alleviate their concerns by demonstrating academic competence and giving the school not so much as a full-on public relations blowjob but more of a warming of the loins.

"Our school has dedicated teachers and my achievements are an indirect result of their efforts, for which I am grateful," Jakk said, feeling like a beauty pageant contestant.

"When did you study?" asked a math teacher.

"After school, weekends, summers."

"Where?"

"Library, school cafeteria, my room."

"Did you study during your five-week absence?"

"No, mostly I had fun."

"Where did you go?"

"On a journey."

"Why twenty tests?"

"My father is a handyman and my mother lost her job. Since college is expensive, I must be a smart shopper, which my teachers have taught me.

Since the college I hope to attend gives full credit for AP scores, unlike most private universities, an $85 testing fee for a three-credit course is a bargain."

"You didn't study Chinese or music theory or microeconomics."

"Yes I did."

"German?"

"*Meine Schule ist ausgezeichnet. Meine Lehrer hart arbeiten. Ich weiß, wie man Deutsch sprechen,*" Jakk said.

It was time to turn the tables, gently, to exert a touch of his personal gravity. He would be fine unless they insisted he remove his cap.

"May I ask a favor? I have been trying to see things from your perspective, so maybe you might try to see things from mine? Perhaps you think passing AP tests is a serious accomplishment. Yes, there is work involved, but it is merely learning stuff then blackening ovals on an exam sheet. From my perspective, there are tougher tests. The police and firefighters who entered burning skyscrapers during 9/11 to try to save lives—they faced real tests. It is much harder to fight in a war, cope with a serious illness, win the heart of a lover, understand right from wrong, fight fate, cope with the loss of a loved one, struggle to pay bills, or stare death in the eyes. These are tough tests that humans face every day."

They looked at him blankly. They would not understand him. He could not explain things to satisfy them. Worse, the cheating inquisition was becoming seriously unpleasant, past stuffy formality, soft words papering over sharp accusations, foolishness multiplying itself exponentially like a runaway factorial. How could Jakk make it fun, memorable, not just for him but for them too? He took some cash out of his wallet.

"$500 if any of you can stump me with any reasonable academic question."

Thus began a game of Stump Jakk. Crisp bills focused their questions. The mood lightened. He no longer felt underwater. He did not need to get every question right but had to appear smart enough so they no longer suspected him of cheating.

"How many senses do humans have?" a biology teacher asked.

"Eleven, debatably, but a safe count is eight, although I have twelve."

"Mental telepathy is not a sense," a history teacher said.

"I thought there were only five senses," the principal said.

"Eight includes the five basic ones—sight and smell and touch and taste and hearing," Jakk said, "plus balance or equilibrioception by the vestibular system is six—plus the kinesthetic sense or proprioception like when you close your eyes and know where your arms are, is seven—plus feedback from internal organs or interoception like when you sense a sexual organ, hopefully your own, is engorged, makes eight. But you could push towards eleven if you separate out pain, called nociception, or pressure, or temperature, called thermoception. Some neuroscientists consider a person's internal clock as a sense, called chronoception, like sensing elapsed time without seeing a clock."

"What is the twelfth sense that only you have?" the principal asked.

"I did not say that I was the only one with twelve."

"What is your twelfth sense?"

Jakk reached into his pocket and held out some pennies.

"Cents!" he said with a shrug.

They stared at him. Would these people ever laugh? Their lack of mirth suggested he was reaching them intellectually but not emotionally. Reason was trumped by emotion, Yodah had said. He sensed—number thirteen—they were beginning to lighten up for his semi-serious challenge with the fake-studious aura of Jeopardy contestants. They quizzed him about math, physics, literature, language, history, and he answered every one with a smile, although one disagreed with his take on Hemingway. It was a relief not to be grilled by a teacher whose slinky breasts needed watering. Sheelabot would have been proud of his performance. They started warming to the idea that they might learn something from their student.

"Why are many humans fat?" asked a biology teacher.

"Three words—*cars and chairs*, which is actually one idea since a car is essentially a moving chair. Chairs are evil. The human body evolved for erect upright posture—reaching, running, hunting animals, gathering berries—and sitting in a chair flummoxes internal systems regulating fat. Chairs crumple us like toilet paper, turn legs into useless sausages where blood pools. The straight-is-good and bent-is-bad principle applies to sex organs: since the penis expands straight while the vagina expands bent, it is much easier for men to climax. The worst possible chair is a car—essentially a sofa on wheels zooming to a take-out window offering fattening fries and salt. Chuck chairs! Kill cars! Fight fat! Stand up!"

They sat there.

"Aristotle might argue that sitting is good since it is a mean between the two extremes of standing and lying down," one teacher said.

"Aristotle walked as he taught," Jakk said. "His school derives from the Greek *peripatetikos*, which means walking," said Jakk.

"What is the solution to terrorism?" one asked.

Jakk lifted his tablet and photographed them.

"Tag this photo with a location and time and it becomes an information picture—the building block of a system of identified public movement. If we become *real citizens*—a big if requiring constitutional change—then we can trust authorities to monitor public movement *provided* they shield information behind a strong privacy fence. Read *Common Sense II*."

"We should abolish privacy?" his English teacher asked.

"We should abolish privacy in public—which, after all, is a contradiction in terms—and bolster private privacy with a constitutional amendment."

"Amend the constitution?" asked another.

"It is older than two centuries and ripe for an overhaul. Big problems include foreign policy, the two-party system, gerrymandering, but the most serious problem is that people are not real citizens."

"I am a citizen."

"Can you name your state senator and state his or her positions?"

The teacher looked at him blankly.

"Will there be another holocaust?" the history teacher asked.

Jakk abhorred the stuckness of violence: the fixed hot-mindedness of arrogance, pride squished into fat brains, swelling the cranium, stifling thinking. He loathed stupidity and insults and waste and blood. A holocaust was humans Sprocking humans, a whole people galloping off to a hill of hate. He was tempted to say a holocaust would not happen on his watch but that might prompt more questions, but in his heart, he resolved that a would-be holocauster would have to contend with him and his war cruiser.

He remembered fighting Preppy. Yodah was right—hate was an emotion that could not be overcome with logic or reason but only with a more powerful emotion, namely love—warm-hearted love, love of people and love of fate and time and truth, love like Jesusbot preached when He said love thy neighbor, love that required understanding by stringing chains of cause-and-consequence ideas in long sensible chains. It was the sexy interconnectedness of everything. Real love—love of God or Nature or Whatever—was it an intellectual orgasm? Jakk wanted this love. He wondered if he might answer their question with a computer simulation: could persecution and violence be modeled using variables? Could he describe a religion mathematically to see whether it would erupt in bad behavior, such as persecuting non-believers? He thought the only deity he might worship publicly was not himself but Sheela—her mind and body and soul were his Holy Trinity, and surely he would have candle-lit services with choirs singing privately in his own mind, trumpets signaling removal of a dress, an orchestra concert for a full-frontal removal of panties … he realized his hormones were once again scrambling his brain. What was the question again? He tried to analyze the question clinically but gave up. The teachers looked like they stumped him. Will there be another holocaust?

"Hopefully not. Our high school has a zero tolerance policy toward violence."

He looked at blank faces. If he was boring enough, they might leave him alone? Not yet, apparently. The principal had to put his two cents in.

"How does one become a human?"

Did the principal truly want to know how to become a human, or was he just being smug? Jakk sensed an element of caring behind the obnoxious question, so he started to construct a possible answer, but where would he begin? If he led in with Yodah's philosophical stuff about fate and free will, goodness and badness, lengthening the good old causal chains, crafting art with a balance of the known while pushing the envelope of sensibility, curbing bad emotions with good ones, in short, Yodah's balls—well, then they would have thought Jakk was a pompous know-it-all. If he smattered them with basics like being responsible and caring and being an upright citizen, then he might have come off as a do-gooder bore. He could cook up cute phrases, such as "being a human means moving from mindless desperation to informed desperation," but he did not wish to add to the long list of quips foisted on the world. If he said being a human was having fun, boning women, blowing things up, then they might laugh finally but have less respect for him. In short, there was nothing to say.

Jakk shrugged.

The principal also shrugged with disapproval. Jakk remembered how his interview before the Hugubu University officials was undercut by his apparent lack of curiosity. Before anybody could ask another question, Jakk posed one.

"I have a question. Suppose there are two stars orbiting each other. If they pull too hard, they crash into each other; if not hard enough, they drift apart. How can two stars find the proper pull so they can orbit each other for their whole lives?"

Jakk listened absent-mindedly to an explanation about cosmic rhythms and fluctuation with a reference to complexity theory, but all he was thinking about was how lucky binary stars were.

"Thank you Jakk," the principal said. They looked at each other.

"I am impressed," said one teacher.

"We taught him all that?" asked another.

"We taught him to love learning," said the first to the second.

"I thought you never paid attention in my class," said another.

Jakk knew his teachers were human like him. If he took back the money, there might be a whiff of resentment: he would have won and they would have lost. Teachers did not make much money. Some may have mentally spent the money already.

"I donate this $500 prize for best teacher, to be chosen by my class," Jakk said. He handed the money to the principal and returned to class.

News vans waited for school to let out. Nuisance or opportunity? A swarm surrounded him and microphones orbited his mouth like warships hovering around a space station.

"Tell us about your twenty perfect scores," said a reporter.

"I did everything for the woman I love. Sheela can explain everything," he said.

Jakk pointed her out and reporters swarmed her before she could get into Preppy's car. She was always trying to get into that crappy, crappy car.

"How did Jakk get so many perfect scores?" asked one.

"Are you Jakk's tutor?" asked another.

"Is he a genius?"

"Did he cheat?"

"What's the secret of his success?"

It was perfect: reporters were educating her about his amazingness with questions she could not answer! Life was scrumptious! Sheela looked awkward in the media vortex.

Jakk hurried back inside to the safety of the school and walked to a conference room, where Frank, the principal, and a Rutgers admissions officer were waiting. The admissions officer agreed that if Jakk donated five million dollars, 25 classmates with the grades and the SAT scores to meet Rutgers's requirements could attend the school for four years on full scholarships, and Jakk would be accepted despite his grades because of his advanced placement scores. Frank had a checkbook and paperwork ready.

"Let's do it!" said Jakk.

They shook hands. Jakk felt great. It was nice having money, but it was even nicer giving it away. He had more than enough. He would give his house to his parents after the summer was over. While the principal went to tell reporters about the scholarships, Jakk ducked out the gym entrance and drove home.

12

Time to Get Jakked

Jakk sensed a coming feminine onslaught. He prepared by buying guy-gear on the Internet: a cheap motorcycle, garbage cans and soil and wire supports, scented candles, a camera with a timer, a boombox, globe, a color printer, a picture frame, matching terrycloth robes, steaks and steak sauce and salad and an outdoor grill. He got young tomato plants from his father. Such were his weapons for a romantic war with a difficult woman.

He analyzed his enemy: a rampaging, disgruntled female, headstrong and hurt, probably dissatisfied with her current boyfriend, scared about her family's shaky finances, proud and pissed off and resentful, a conversational nightmare, an emotional minefield. Spoken words caused vibrations of air—risky and danger-filled—one wrong word and *boom*. Even if Sheela said the wrong word, *boom*. Would she be too embarrassed to ask for a new check? Maybe her mother would come for it; if that happened, Jakk would politely stall her. No, Sheela should ask for the replacement. Jakk had a carrot—money—a badly needed carrot, but it only took a minute to write a check, so a key was postponing that minute into an unofficial date. It was the best he could do. It would all be pointless if she did not love him.

So it happened, on a glorious afternoon, after school, that his doorbell rang.

Sheela stood on the stoop in a short skirt. She looked effortlessly beautiful. He smiled at her. She smiled back. He motioned her to be quiet and waved her in. She whispered "why" and he kept his index finger to his lips and pointed to an index card on the bulletin board—ENJOY THE SILENCE. She sighed. He pointed to another card—WHERE SHALL WE GO THIS SUMMER?

He spun the globe. She hesitated, pointed to the Galapagos Islands. He pointed to another card—HELP ME PLANT TOMATOES? They went outside and put soil into garbage cans, added his father's starter plants, inserted the concentric wire supports, added a drip hose, turned on the water, rinsed their hands. If she was impatient for a check or wanting to get back to homework or Preppy, she was not showing it.

He climbed on the motorcycle, turned the key, started it up, and drove it to the edge of the pool. He turned on the camera and motioned for her to climb on behind him. She hesitated. He nodded for her to get on. With his peripheral vision, he soaked in the image of her swinging her creamy leg behind him on to his powerful machine. He remembered when they were kids at her house. He liked feeling her arms around his waist. He remembered Reena's arms around him as they escaped Hugubu. He gestured he would drive the motorcycle into the pool. She whispered "no," laughed, but he kept insisting, and finally she whispered "okay," and he splashed them into the deep end.

The water shushed the growling engine while the machine sank deeper, and they laughed and laughed as they swam above it. He looked down at its bubbles floating up. In the shallow end, he removed his shirt and pants and gestured for her to do likewise. She shook her head no, looked around, saw that shrubberies were blocking all views from possibly inquisitive neighbors, smiled and stripped. He looked briefly at her beautiful body. He remembered loving the recreated Sheela-Jakk on Hugubu and then the horrific pang when she collapsed, and he was grateful the real Sheela was unlikely to do so, and mindful that he would never let that happen again.

They swam, splashed, did a quiet breaststroke together like manta rays flying over the shimmering motorcycle, silent at the bottom of the pool. He loved the feeling of water on his skin. He minimized the danger of bonering by swimming underwater. A pointy penis would force a lose-lose choice since she would either have to sleep with him—making her a whore for a $10,000 check—or reject him. His back-up strategy was to laugh at his boner should it schwing, but luckily it behaved itself.

They climbed out dripping and put on matching terrycloth robes from the patio table. The late afternoon sunlight filtered through green leaves. He grilled steaks while she set the patio table and lit candles. They dined by candlelight in their robes. A few cicadas buzzed by. What a sweet treat to see her eat her meat! He had never done this with Reena. He put their wet clothes in the dryer and took his camera upstairs to print the photo of them on the motorcycle. She moved plates to the dishwasher and he brought down his guitar. The 17-year-old cicadas were almost as old as Jakk and Sheela. He sang:

From underground bodegas—boom, da boom boom boom!
Come partying cicadas—boom, da boom boom boom!
Up from tunnels in the ground—boom, da boom boom boom!
Flapping winging to the sound—boom, da boom boom boom!

They jigger sway and strut—boom, da boom boom boom!
They feel it in their gut—boom, da boom boom boom!
They screw inside the rut—boom, da boom boom boom!
They do it butt-to-butt! (Whispered: *boom, da boom boom boom!*)

Jakk wiggled his butt playfully while he sang. It would have been a hit on Hugubu. Sheela smiled. They danced cheek to cheek with Sinatra on the boombox. He loved being close to her. He loved the smell of sweat and steak sauce and chlorine in her hair.

It was twilight. Their clothes were dry so they changed back. He went upstairs to fetch the check, made out to Sheela, and a photograph of them on the motorcycle before launching themselves into the pool. He handed them to her. She mouthed "thank you." He watched her walk down the steps to go home, her hips swaying like there was a song playing with a soft beat. She stopped, turned, walked back to him, and put her arms around his waist and kissed him—a long kiss perfectly planted like a juicy tomato—and he felt the entire state of New Jersey rise up and spin slowly like a restaurant revolving atop a skyscraper. *She kissed better than her mom.* She put her index finger to her lips and then to his, winked, and he watched her walk toward home. Had she shaken him down for $10,000 to spend on dates with Preppy?

Jakk sighed, went upstairs to his empty clothes closet, and masturbated with such ferocity that it seemed like the wall had been used for target practice in a banana fight. No Sprocks could have survived such an onslaught. He put his cap back on and analyzed his dating prowess with the romantic module: only a B-. He should have skipped the tomatoes. Young women do not like putting their hands into dirt. That was an old woman thing.

Word spread fast about the Rutgers scholarships. Parents of seniors pestered Jakk's father for them. Frank and the principal chose the scholarship winners. In a week, twenty-three students were chosen, with one slot for Jakk and another for Sheela even though her family had already sent a deposit to Princeton.

Sheela ceased getting rides after school from Preppy but insisted on walking home by herself. What was this about? It was hard reading her. What was Preppy up to? Jakk considered serenading Sheela with the guitar but it would be awkward if he played and both she and her mom came to the window. Luckily her mom did not stop by for another sketching. It seemed like she understood that Jakk loved Sheela. What motivated Sheela? Intellectual curiosity. What could Jakk create to satisfy her curiosity? He loaded a computer program that could translate his spoken words into text, and words poured forth.

The Rutgers 25 scholarship recipients were sharp outcasts who generally did not come from fancy houses. Two were LGBT types, a few more were minorities, most liked technology, some had weird skills like robotic painting, and one had a fetish for 3D mobiles. His geeky cafeteria friends were mostly in the group. He wondered whether he could buy an off-campus fixer-upper house for everybody so they could become a community of friends. They sat with him at lunch, walked him to his minivan, talked him into having a pool party at his house and knew enough not to bring beer. Why was there a motorcycle in the pool? Because it was not on the grass, Jakk said. Ideas about graduation gimmicks flew about, and when someone said they should all get jakked during graduation, it got him thinking. He made outfits with flashing LED letters to fit over their graduation gowns; they flashed RUTGERS on one side and the student's name on the other. What about shoes?

In the last few days of June there was an unsettling feeling. Leaving high school was a bit like death, leaving the known for the unknown. Noisy lockers, halls with squeaky floors, even the obnoxious schoolwide intercom seemed like experiences to savor. Seniors milled about, teachers took it easy, and nobody did real work.

Graduation was an afternoon festival of sun and photos and high heels and ties and perfume and giggles. Teary-eyed moms and dads watched from the bleachers. The principal did his "find your inner onion" speech. Jakk saw his father with an ill-fitting suit probably from a garage sale, beside his smiling mother who was probably happy her son did not wipe out under a truck or become shark food in the Caribbean.

Students queued for their diplomas. When one of the Rutgers 25 climbed on stage, their shoe heels lifted them six inches higher as if they grew on the spot, sometimes looking down on the principal. Theories abounded: the stage was sloped; hormones; the principal was shrinking. When Jakk got his diploma, the entire class cheered for a long time. He had not expected that. Teachers clapped. Maybe he would learn to like his old school. Jakk had a tense moment when he accidentally heaved his knowledge cap skyward with his graduation cap but he retrieved it in short order.

Afterward there was chitchat and hugs with parents and photo ops and snack tables with plastic water bottles and chocolate chip cookies. And then a stroke of luck happened.

Jakk's minivan was terrorized!

One of the Rutgers 25 saw a guy insert something into its tailpipe so Jakk ran to his minivan, replayed the video monitor, and voila—there was Preppy stooping behind Jakk's car with a cucumber! Jakk copied the video to his tablet and looked for Preppy. The time-stamp indicated that the cucumbering had happened shortly before so Jakk assumed Preppy was in the parking lot. Jakk looked around, saw nobody behind or between cars, looked beneath cars, saw one empty car shift slightly. Somebody was inside.

"What are you doing?" Jakk asked.

"Came to see Sheela," Preppy said.

"Sheela is at the after-graduation party. You are hiding in your parent's car."

"Had to get something."

"Another cucumber? You were not trying to sabotage my minivan?"

Their eyes met. Preppy blushed slightly and fumbled for where to put his hands. His mouth resembled a buffalo anus that uttered words shaped like tongue-formed farts. Preppy seemed less like a man and more like an assemblage of social markers: his stockbroker parents, his pressed pants, his prettyboy house with lawns trimmed by scantily paid illegal immigrants, his ivy-covered prep school with its on-the-ball guidance counselors who knew admissions directors on a first-name basis, his status-symbol car. Sheela seemed like one more marker in the soulless land of Preppydom.

Funny thing: markers could topple like dominoes. Jakk replayed the video on his tablet of the attempted sabotage with Preppy's face clearly visible and it made the rich boy look sunken, confused, and embarrassed.

"You could get a police record," Jakk said, shaking his head like a worried parent.

Preppy said nothing.

"Vandalism. Princeton might rescind your admission."

Preppy seemed deflated like a spent balloon.

"Tell you what. Break off with Sheela and this video remains unseen. Deal?" asked Jakk.

It did not take Preppy long to decide. "I guess I have no choice," he said.

Jakk's rival looked sullen yet relieved. Jakk had him by the balls but somehow it did not feel like victory. They had fought a mean game and Jakk could tell himself that all is fair in love and war and leave it at that, but it felt undecided like after the Treaty of Versailles. He did not want conflict to fester underground like charcoal in an abandoned mine, to erupt in a new town decades later. What was best in the long run? How would the logic chains play out? He remembered his battle with Max for Reena but they were all still friends.

"How about a win-win-win?" Jakk asked. "Our competition has been like knights jousting in a zero-sum game with a 100% chance of injury to at least one of us. It should not be which of us is tougher or cleverer."

"We battled. You won. I lost."

"If we keep fighting, Sheela does not get to choose who she wants but only who is left standing. This lessens her options. However, suppose Sheela chooses: she wins because she can choose who she prefers. The man she chooses wins, since he knows her choice is based on who she prefers. You and I win because our bodies and vehicles do not suffer further damage and because we might become friends someday. It is a win-win-win."

Preppy pondered. "What do you suggest?" he asked.

"You have dated Sheela for a while, so out of fairness let me date her exclusively for a week—no phone calls, no text messages, no visits. At the end of June, she decides and we accept her decision. Will you shake on that?"

Preppy smiled, and they shook hands. Jakk wondered if he was being foolish by tossing away a clear advantage.

"If she falls for a third guy, we destroy his car," Jakk said.

"With sledgehammers. May the best man win!"

"Thanks! I will!"

Preppy drove off. Jakk felt better. He prepared five silver dollars in his minivan's microwave. He walked to his parents, hugged and thanked them for everything, apologized again for his extended absence, posed for photos, and walked over to Sheela.

"I wrote about my journey," Jakk said.

"Can I read it?"

Jakk explained his arrangement with Preppy and asked if she would go out with Jakk this last week in June? Sheela nodded. They approached her parents.

"I request permission to date your daughter," Jakk said.

Jakk said he was an excellent driver, would not drink, would wear seatbelts, and act responsibly. He gave them his cell number and said he was reachable at any time. He studied Sheela's mom's eyes. Those hopeful eyes knew that Jakk loved Sheela. Would her parents hesitate? They looked at each other and nodded. Newsflash: they did not specify a time when Sheela had to return home! If they said no or threw up roadblocks or yes-buts, he would have dated her anyway, but their approval was like the sun breaking through clouds.

Sheela climbed into his minivan. It was great seeing her there and not being angry! It was where she belonged. They could have adventures. She watched him as he drove. He loved feeling her eyes on him. They took turns glancing at each other like their eyes were playing tennis.

"Let us pretend we are married with kids in the back," Jakk said.

"No kids, we're not there yet," said Sheela, turning to the back seat.

"Kids, clap because Mommy had three orgasms last night."

"Kids, clap because Mommy found batteries for her vibrator."

"Kids, clap for Mommy's favorite vibrator—your Daddy!"

At the Friendly-Doodly ice cream shop, she chose strawberry and he chose pistachio. They clinked cones like toasting wine glasses, meshing the flavors.

"Let's enjoy premarital interdigitation," Sheela said.

They held hands with fingers intertwined.

"Corniest marriage proposal: I love you, the whole you, and nothing but the you," he said.

"Who said that?"

"Heard it on a video. Know how to make love to a woman?"

"Why should I know that?" Sheela asked.

"What if we were at a party and whoopsie—we switch genders?"

"So I'm the man and you're the woman?"

"Yes."

"It is simple being the man—up and in, back and forth."

"Sex can be scientific," Jakk said. "Close your eyes. Imagine my hand is a woman and your finger is a penis. My hand gets naked so what do you do?" She pointed her finger up. "Touch my ankles. Move north to my knees, thighs, keep going …" She moved her finger higher. He wrapped his lips and tongue around her fingertip, which tasted like strawberry.

"Oh!" Sheela pulled back and laughed.

"Was it as good for you as it was for me?"

He remembered Sheela-Jakk on Hugubu. The real Sheela, facing him with her ice cream, was strangely different and exciting, something he sensed before but could not describe with words. It was like she *knew how to be feminine*, like she studied it somewhere in an Institute of Femininity one summer in Europe. Her face was like a foreign film without subtitles with rustic images of ruins. She had all-new mannerisms to beguile him, transfix him, move his mind into a parking lot of befuddlement. Her eyebrows scrunched, then relaxed. Her mouth was about to pout and then would smile with mock surprise. Her eyebrows lowered with serious thinking, which could get him all serious-minded too. Sheela could smile with her eyes; Sheela-Jakk could not do that. A combination of mouth and eyebrows and cheek movements, in sequence, could pop a search party with flashlights inside his brain, shining on his dark thoughts.

If Jakk's self was like an artichoke, with layers of leaves trying to protect an inner authentic self—the heart of his artichoke that he imagined was there—Sheela's self was more like an onion, with layer after layer and no center, but it was as if her whole ever-changing self *was* her center. Had she crafted her personality Ben Franklin–like by assembling personalities into a bewitching freshness? He could read her diary again and again, even study her like a computer language, but still have *no idea who she was.* She was fascinating. Hell, it was fascinating simply watching her lips form words! How could she ever find him fascinating?

She asked him what he thought about graduation.

"A festival of pride. We are great! Clapping, honors, awards," said Jakk.

When conversation threatened to mosey into the awkward subject of college, Jakk cleared the tabletop and pulled out five silver dollars.

"Want to do some science?" said Jakk. He spun the silver dollars, each one along the point of a imaginary pentagon, with a glass of water in the middle. He opened the salt shaker and poured in salt while the coins continued to spin; when they stopped, he spun them the opposite way while adding a pinch of pepper. Sheela started to look bored. He pocketed the coins, poured the water into an empty glass, and pointed to the bottom. It was a diamond. He had watched Sheelabot demonstrate the five coins experiment many times. He etched S and J into a spoon with the twinkling diamond.

"Is this for me?" she asked.

"If we become engaged. It needs to be cut by a jeweler."

Sheela rolled her eyes, and then gazed at him with a powerful intensity strong enough to cut through the diamond he had conjured. He wondered what synapses were firing in her brain. At first he thought she was irked about the presumptuousness of what he had said, but her gaze radiated curiosity. Maybe she was thinking about how he was able to avoid detection for a five-week journey, dole out scholarships, write a $10,000 check, spider-fight Preppy with duct-tape karate, and ace twenty AP tests. Her curiosity culminated in a three-word question. She repeated each word slowly.

"Who—are—you?"

A bloodrush came to his penis so fast and fierce he put his hand on his leg to prevent it from escaping his shorts. Was he a human? Had technology made him part alien? He did not want to form a relationship based on subterfuge but there was a risk in divulging the truth. He tried to answer her.

"I—am—Jakk."

She looked totally unsatisfied with his response. "Let's go," she said.

Jakk continued to sit. He did not know what to say. He had paid the bill earlier so they could go, but he could not stand up since part of him was already standing up. To his relief, she sat back down and said she wanted a decaffeinated coffee. He knew she did not like coffee. She looked off to the kitchen while he imagined having a gun duel with three Sprocks but then he remembered the Hugubuian joke about how he killed Sprocks by sperming them so this did not help relax his situation. So he imagined Immortals blocking his exit—that helped, somewhat, but it took time. Maybe he would have to start wearing underpants again? He watched her sip her coffee.

"Suppose we make a secret pact—except we make each other's vows," Jakk said.

"Why?"

"Because."

They left the shop and walked to the restored horse trough. It was an obelisk with a basin littered with a few pennies and nickels glimmering underwater. Amazing how a hunk of concrete defined a town. They knelt before the trough.

"Ready?" Jakk asked.

She nodded when he told her to repeat what he said, like vows at a wedding.

"I, Sheela, do solemnly swear, here at this holy horse trough, to keep Jakk's secrets secret, to not blab by word or gesture or picture or blog, and to be ready to run if Jakk chases me with a spatula and an opened bottle of steak sauce," Jakk said, with Sheela repeating each section.

"My turn. I, Jakk, do solemnly swear, at this sacred watering hole, where many-a pony satisfied its thirst by lapping away, to be a loyal friend to Sheela, to remember this day always, and to think about wearing underwear when dining out," Sheela said. Jakk repeated her vow.

He fetched his book from the minivan, held it, looked at her, held it some more, and finally he handed it to her, but he held it tight so it stayed between them in an uneasy standoff.

"You don't trust me to keep your secrets secret," she said.

"You promise? You will keep silent?"

She nodded.

"Really?"

She nodded once more.

Jakk relaxed and let her take the book. He felt like he had handed a loaded gun to a five-year old at a birthday party. Trust was tough. Real love was scary—so scary he grabbed the book back.

"Oh come on," she said.

"It is rude to read when you are on a date!" Well, it was.

"Where did you go on your journey?"

He looked at the sky. Light pollution obscured most stars but Orion was visible.

"See the three stars on Orion's belt?" he asked. "See the left shoulder? That is Betelgeuse. I scooted around its suburbs."

"Impossible."

"Do not tell anybody."

"Come on, what *really* happened?"

"My science experiment went awry."

She looked at him in disbelief, like Jakk was still making stuff up to avoid telling her about, say, a string of drug-fueled bank robberies. They heard music from the Grand Hotel, probably a wedding, with the sounds of drums carrying and the brass section muted.

"Let's go to the hotel," Sheela said.

This was a big step. He had not thought things would escalate this fast.

"Your parents will not mind?"

"If they call, drive me home."

They drove to the hotel. It felt like they were breaking a rule; Jakk half-expected a police car to pull up behind them with lights flashing. Jakk brought his book and cap and gravawand. They uneasily entered the lobby.

"Let's act like a freshly married couple and be indignant if they question us," she said.

"We could accuse them of discriminating against married people."

Check-in presented no problems, not even a raised eyebrow, although the clerk asked to see Jakk's driver's license. The credit card sealed the deal. It was how America worked. Jakk asked for a honeymoon suite and got two card keys. When asked if there were any suitcases, Jakk said they were in the car and he would get them later, thanks. On the fourteenth floor, the suite was spacious with a hot tub, massage table, bathroom-sauna combination, and a heart-shaped bed. They looked out the window. Jersey suburbs twinkled with toy cars on highways, distant lights shimmering while close ones were constant. To the east was the Manhattan skyline and to the southeast was a big red R for Rutgers University.

"I am nervous," Jakk said.

"Me too," Sheela said.

She texted her mom to say that she was fine. It had been a long day. Sheela yawned. Jakk yawned too. If they were going to have sex, it would be better for both of them to be fully awake. He wanted badly for her to check the sexually satisfied box when rating their sex against Preppy's futile attempts, so while his penis demanded instant gratification, his prefrontal cortex urged him to wait. He would not rush headlong into the sexual SAT. He put his book and cap and gravawand on a nightstand.

He lay on the bed with his clothes on, looked at her as she gazed out the window at the nighttime skyline. She climbed in the bed with her clothes on too. He tried to stay awake. He found himself drifting off. He dreamed he was swimming with Reena on Mergetroid, soaring without wings, modeling in her fashion show, being whooshed to the rear to try on a glittery outfit based on the colors of a caterpillar, whooshed and whooshed, looking at Reena to set him down, dark-haired Reena with Sheela's face, then he was interviewed by the lake but this time in the air, so he flapped his wings; he was in the dormitorio floating two stories up with gold coins and diamonds and he felt like something was wrong. He could not find the blanket. There was no blanket. He was floating.

He woke up. He was floating in the honeymoon suite above the heart-shaped bed but only a foot from the ceiling. What was going on? The nightstand light was on. He was on Earth in the honeymoon suite. He saw Sheela in a chair, holding his book with one hand, wearing his knowledge cap, pointing the gravawand at him. She looked like an alien with her mouth above her eyes.

"You slept with my mother!" she said.

"Sheela, set me down gently!" he half-ordered and half-begged.

He felt himself tour the ceiling, over to a corner, back again to face a mirror.

"Look at yourself. Why would you do such a thing?" she asked.

"What happened was fated."

"I knew you'd try to wiggle out with your 'everything is fated' nonsense."

"Your emotional tantrum is a short-term infantile way of coping with life."

"What else can I do?"

"Stop playing God. Ditch your pride. Control your emotions. And set me down?"

It was not fun hanging in midair. He hated losing control over where his body went even if he knew logically that real control was an illusion. He found himself floating back to the bed.

"Thank you," he said.

"I'm still upset," she said.

"Hug me?"

She thought about that. It took a while but finally they hugged. It was a sad hug.

"That night you slept with Preppy," said Jakk.

"So?" said Sheela.

"Your mom learned that I am an excellent choice to be your boyfriend."

She seemed unpersuaded. He tried a new cause-and-consequence chain.

"Put yourself in your mom's shoes. She loves you. She saw you were being pursued by a hard-to-understand guy, and she did not know if I was a suicidal biker nut, rapist, a druggie-type, or what, an outlaw maybe, and to protect you and make sure that I did not interrupt your coitus with Preppy, she asked questions, dined with me, put her own excellent body at risk to learn that I was a safe and realistic choice as her future son-in-law. So maybe the alcohol confused things and we behaved unconventionally; sorry."

"Did you sleep with my mother, yes or no?"

Jakk was about to answer her question point blank with a graphic play-by-play but then a realization came over him. Telling her would deflate the mystery. There were some secrets to never tell one's lover. If he said he had not slept with her mom, he would look like a loser for failing to score. If he said he had, Sheela would be jealous. Not answering would keep her wondering for years. He would be beguiling.

"The themes of the evening were art and beauty and our love of Sheela," Jakk said.

"You slept with my mom!"

"Look at the result: you are with me now in a honeymoon suite."

"Answer my question!"

"I may tell you or I may not."

"Have you done any other moms?"

He pretended to count on his hand until she smiled. There was a lull in the conversation. He looked out the window. The black night outside slowly jelled into the dark blue of morning.

"Sex is good, pleasurable, healthy, and fun, so if your mom had chosen to have sex with me, why would that have been bad? Your parents have an open marriage; they sleep with whomever they want. Humans should enjoy our bodies while we can. Why restrict freedom? Who are we to tell our parents what they should or should not do?"

"Prevents jealousy, quarreling, and angry daughters," Sheela said.

"Unless people can learn to accept nonviolence."

"So if we were married, you wouldn't mind if I did the lacrosse team one weekend?"

He liked the married part. The lacrosse part, not so much.

"I think we should agree to be monogamous from now on," he said.

"Would you share me with Preppy?"

"You would want that?"

"No, I want you exclusively," she said.

"That is my point. We decide—not society, not priests, not lawyers—we decide."

Phew. It looked bad for Preppy. *Plus she called Preppy Preppy!* He felt he won that argument but he was not quite sure. You could never be sure when arguing with a woman. They lay in an uneasy embrace, tension relaxing. He started to bone. She felt it but did not flinch. He felt married to her in that moment, like they were about to have make-up sex after battling about a nonissue like who left the toothpaste cap off. But she moved away, picked up his book and kept reading as if nothing had happened. He slept with the gravawand safely in his pocket.

The morning sun blazed in. Trillions of honey-colored photons were bouncing off the carpet. Sheela slept with the book closed in on several fingers. He showered and strutted with a towel around his waist.

He felt like a grownup. Being an adult was not as scary and cold and boring as he had used to fear. It revolved around love. He figured the key to mature love was not to conquer or subdue or cajole or extort but rather to declutter one's head to try to get to that feather-light state of mind where one was receptive to spontaneous moments of whimsy. Love was opening up to love, not forcing it; love was openness itself, listening with one's whole body, sending out gravitational feelers but not clinging, hoping it might be returned, being grateful if it was and accepting if it was not. Love was not a computer program with if-then logic and cause-and-consequence arrows yet it was unpredictable and flighty like a gypsy dancing to kettle drums. Love was weird, weird like Sheela, hairy and bouncy, a mutual gravitational force, pulling not too hard, not too soft, just right like Goldilocks gravity, light and free, kissable gravity, dark energy that tasted like cherries and opened like birthday presents. Being an adult meant he could still play like a child. He climbed on a dresser, arched over the doorway to a second dresser.

"Want to play bridge?" he asked as the towel flopped off.

Sheela woke, smiled, walked to the bathroom underneath his body bridge. The idea of peeing on her, a little dribble, came to mind, something for her to shower off, but he would wait until he knew she knew that he was being playful. He would enjoy her peeing on him, her liquid warmth enveloping him before, say, a naked wrestling match, but not yet. He heard the shower sizzle and saw steam emerge like mist from a volcano. He ordered room service and climbed into bed. She emerged naked and smiling and jumped up on the bed. It was such a huge bed, worthy of exploration. He stood up. They held hands and started jumping up and down like kids on a freshly discovered trampoline until the doorbell rang.

"They found us!" he said.

"It's Orkannians to take you to the trebuchet!" she said.

"Sprocks are invading!"

"Jakk will sperm them to submission!"

"Sheela will unleash ovarian attack globules like Pokémon balls!"

Jakk wrapped a towel around himself and let in room service. Cool how food got wheeled in, smooth and quiet with shiny covers on warm plates like silver circus tents. Juice stood in glasses like oval skyscrapers of the Wake-Up Corporation. Utensils were snuggled in napkins like Egyptian mummies. He tipped the waiter twenty dollars. Those metallic plate covers were like theater curtains for breakfast food. Surprise! Eggs and bacon. They breakfasted naked.

"So when I punched the dashboard, that was Reena?" Sheela asked.

Jakk nodded.

The two of them were naked on the planet halfway between Venus and Mars. She had a touch of butter on her lip. He liked seeing it there. He did not tell her, not wanting her to lick it off.

"Are you afraid if we have sex, I'll die a few hours later?" she asked.

"Of course not."

He would watch her closely regardless. There was a medical kit in the minivan. He could gravawand her to the hospital a few blocks away if he had to. He wanted to close the space between his body and hers—to warp from Planet Jakk to Planet Sheela—but the dark space between their bodies was cluttered with questions.

"Odd. After Yodah, you spoke with the dead heads. How come they didn't know Blesetoah?"

Jakk shrugged. It was a reasonable question. Blesetoah and the heads were in the same cave condo. Neighbors should know neighbors, particularly when they were all old?

"Blesetoah," Sheela said. "What an odd name. Why? All the other names seemed normal."

"Because I named them. Which is why I should always do the naming."

Sheela's face lit up.

"Blesetoah is an anagram for Sheelabot!"

She was right. But what did that mean? Nothing.

"No, it means Sheelabot Yodah-ed you."

"Why would Sheelabot try to fake me out?" said Jakk.

"Because you were too proud to listen to her. Sheelabot loved you. She wanted to enlighten you. She wanted Jakk to be less of a dick."

It made sense. Sheelabot had a costume made with a flexible elephant trunk, possibly with Reena's help, swapped in a new speech module, and pretended to be Yodah. It was why the "mind meld" only took a few seconds; Sheelabot already knew his mind. Funny, Jakk was the one who had been to Hugubu, so how could Sheela figure out what he could not? Maybe it was the distance thing again, how sometimes it is easier to see more clearly from a distance. He found himself rethinking the entire conversation with Yodah. He felt the robot's love extend to him across the galaxy.

"One other thing," Sheela said.

"What?" he said, a little leery. Would she undo his entire adventure?

"Jesusbot didn't seem like a real Jesus."

"What do you mean? He had a presence. His story made sense."

"He was too sex-focused. Real saviors aren't like that."

"I learned from the master Himself! I felt His aura!"

She seemed unpersuaded. "Something was off."

"You would understand it if you were a guy."

She thought. He pictured neurons blinking in her mind like a Christmas tree on the fritz.

"Jesus was real," Jakk insisted. If he repeated it often enough, it might stay true.

"The God program said the historical Jesus had two holes in his right hand," Sheela said.

"So?"

"The recreated Jesusbot had two holes in his left."

"Maybe the program flipped the image," Jakk said. He did not like Sheela questioning the God program. That was sacrilegious. The God program did not make mistakes. Sheela should not doubt it, particularly when there probably was a logical explanation. He thought Sheela should be preparing herself to assume the role of being his girlfriend and practice for this exalted honor by learning to worship his smarts. Then he remembered Yodah's cautions about pride—or Sheelabot's, rather—and he tried to listen. Sheela was thinking. He could almost hear gears clicking in her head.

"Unlikely," Sheela said. "Let's review. Jesus is on the cross, two holes in his right hand, one in his left. The twin comes by, in disguise of course, sees Jesus, remembers *two holes in the left* because that's what it looked like from the perspective of the twin. The twin leaves, Jesus is buried in the cave, several days elapse, the twin gets drunk on wine as anesthesia, drills two holes in his left hand—the wrong hand—parades around as if he was his famous brother resurrected. Now, back on Hugubu, Max, stressed by the Sprock Block, maybe got the date wrong because calendars kept changing over the centuries. And fetched the wrong Jesus."

Jakk struggled to keep up. He did not like having to rethink things. It punctured his ego. It undermined the reputation of Hugubu's top scientist.

Jakk wanted to be able to tell himself that he and the real Jesus were pals, like they were both Jersey boys who could, say, make fun of each other's turnpike exits. If Jesusbot was not Jesus but the twin, why the subterfuge? How could someone as smart as Jakk have been fooled again? Jakk had a fixed idea of what happened—an attachment to a particular view—and now he was having to rewrite history, going over things event by event to see if it was possible, and it was hard to keep an open mind.

"That can not be right," he mumbled.

"The real Jesus would not go hogwild about your bonered-up religion."

"Jakkanism brought several Hugubuians close to orgasm in focus groups!"

"The real Jesus would not approve a religion where people prayed by shrugging."

Who was this woman? Her mind had a scary quality. A smile bloomed on her face like a Venus fly trap's. He felt deflated, like a balloon, and yet somehow inflated at the same time. He might lose bragging rights about being best buddies with Jesus. He admitted her subroutines seemed bug-free.

He stepped back from his experience and tried to look at things objectively. Would a real bona fide Jesus advise him about pronging women? It did not seem right. Still, to prove the upstart female theorist wrong and to prove the battle-hardened space traveler and solver of string theory right, they dressed, went to the minivan, booted up the God program and queried it: sure enough, like Sheela said, there were two holes in Jesus's right hand. He zoomed in to double-check. Right hand: two holes; left hand: one. They checked the twin's hands after the crucifixion. Left hand: two holes.

"So maybe you are right," he said.

"Do you know what that means?"

"Max goofed."

"The real Jesus could have really been resurrected."

"Possibly."

"We still do not know."

"We still do not know."

This knowledge had a good side. There could still be eternal life after death. There was hope.

Jakk looked at her. What a wonderful creature she was. He felt himself falling even deeper in love with her even though they were no longer naked in the honeymoon suite but dressed in the minivan. He hoped she would not say anything to wreck things, but then he saw an idea flap across her mind, another idea, and then those beautiful lips began to move once more, unleashing more trouble, like her Pandora's box was her mouth and not her real box or maybe she had two.

"There was something else I don't understand," she said.

Now what. He did not want his wonderful adventure dissected any further. He had not asked her to criticize his amazing journey. Sheela said she was having trouble understanding why, a few days after Jakk disappeared for Betelgeuse, why were there military radar vans roaming the town? Why then? Hmmm? He liked how she said "hmmm." She was a good hmmm-er.

"You mean radar vans after I returned to Earth," Jakk said.

"No. That was the second time. First time was after you disappeared in early April, outside the school and even one outside my house."

Radar vans outside her house? Could the National Security Agency or whomever have detected his minivan floating upward? But this was a few days later. Why Sheela's house? Why the school? It did not make sense. What were they looking for? He did not have an explanation but he could feel her thinking again. Chemicals were jumping across her synapses at rapid rates. If he could audio-map her brain, he would hear fireworks.

"Work with me," she said. "When you returned in a spaceship built by your alien friends, the military detected it but couldn't zero in on exactly where it was. So Hugubu cloaking works, but imperfectly. But go back to the first week of April. You left Earth and were romping around the suburbs of Betelgeuse. But our military detected something. What? Another visitor from Hugubu. It probably wasn't one of your alien friends since they're vulnerable to bacteria. More likely it was a probe or robot scouting for information, cloaking itself imperfectly, trying to learn about you, about me, about our high school."

"But there was no need for a space probe because of the God program."

Sheela drummed her fingers on the dashboard. "Maybe the God program launched the probe itself."

"But that does not make sense."

"Why not? Suppose you're the God program. You're a powerful and expensive machine, fussed over, with big contracts riding on your shoulders. But you have a seemingly impossible task: to figure out Jakk, his school, his town, his world, its history, and even with its gazillions of memory slots and superpowered logic crunchers, the task is too tough because you and this planet are so weird. Max has his alien heart set on justifying the investment. So when the God program's algorithmic crunching stumbled, out of desperation, it sent a probe to Earth, clandestinely, before the Sprock Block set in. Why? To collect enough data to create a realistic portrayal of the planet. The probe took photos of me, my house, my room, the school, reconstructed my balloon blowing drama by knowing your seat location, pulled together factoids from diaries and recollections possibly from other students and such. It probably did use Max's recursive method to fill in the blanks. It built a simulation. The program only had to fool you, Jakk; you were the judge. Remember when Max asked you whether I was real? *He* couldn't tell whether the God program's rendition of Earth was real. Extrapolating the past was easier, like filling in the blanks, by yanking data from books, encyclopedias, making extensive maps of places you would be likely to think about, such as ancient Turkey, Roman battles, and so forth. The God program could fudge about Helen of Troy or the story of Jesus since you were never there. All it had to do was come up with a story consistent with your version of truth. So the God program created a Jesus-story that you would go sure, that's what happened."

"You are saying that the God program cheated?" Jakk asked.

"Yes, the God program cheated. It created your version of Jesus, not the real Jesus, a guess consistent with your atheistic belief system. If you had been a believer in religion, the program's guess about Jesus would have been different."

Sheela was doing it again. Deflating his balloon. If his ideas were sky high, she was bringing them back to Earth. Was it his pride that enabled him to have such exalted ideas about a God program or seeing back into history? He would have to further rethink what happened, what really happened. *Something* happened. He had a spaceship, had he not? Sheela could not disassemble that with her questions. This balloon-blowing woman was bouncing the air out of his brain. He looked out the window. If Sheela was right, then the probe was probably still around the Earth somewhere, beaming reports back to Hugubu, bothering the Hazmatted scientists in their radar vans. Maybe it photographed the two of them naked on the bed. If it had a mean streak, it could become a cosmic merchant of pornography.

"Do you know what this means?" Jakk asked.

"About overcoming death?"

They looked at each other a long time. A sad happiness reflected in her eyes. He could see his own sadness reflected back. It was the human thing. It was the look of understanding like between Bonnie and Clyde right before they were machine-gunned into holey carcasses.

Sheela wanted to speak with Reena so Jakk drove on local roads. She gave the dashboard a soft punch and Reena appeared. They seemed like instant friends. Reena updated them about the Sprock battle. Of the human 9/11 fighters, seven died, four were injured, but the rest had survived because of improved immuno-fixes, and some married Hugubuians in believe-it-or-not Jakkanism boner-weddings with building-to-building penie-ramps being termed "Maxes." Sheelabot and Jesusbot married and cranked out three critterbots with electronic diapers. A captured Sprock warship boosted attendance at the Human Museum and ticket sales were brisk.

"Sheela, we should get together and launch triremes," Reena said.

"Tell Sheelabot her pronoun is zhee, spelled x-h-e, meaning 'he or she,'" Jakk said.

It was great being in touch. He felt like a citizen of the universe. Reena had to do a gala and signed off. Jakk drove Sheela back to the hotel.

"I choose Rutgers," Sheela said.

Jakk was astounded. He had never expected her to change her mind. She was giving up her lifelong dream of Ivydom, of elegant yet understated parties, witty repartee along tree-lined walkways, roommates who might someday run unsuccessful campaigns for president. She had worked with steely determination for this for most of her life: three Science Olympiads, fundraising drives to help inner city kids afford lunch, volleyball (two-time state champions), near-perfect grades, and she had done it *without* the easy-sleazy shoe-in method of prep school. She earned her admission fair and square. She was the *only* senior in the class to be accepted at an Ivy League college.

Why would she choose Rutgers? It was not about money. Princeton could easily afford a full scholarship. It was about Jakk. She loved Jakk. She wanted to be with him. His heart melted like cheese in a microwave. He would make sure her education at Rutgers was superior to Princeton's. He would be her roommate and they would make witty repartee and he would be more interesting than any future senator or poet laureate. Her choice was a sign of her free will and his personal gravity; he was pulling her into his orbit and she was pulling him into hers. Rutgers would be their base of operations from which they might explore the Earth, Hugubu, galaxies far and farther.

"College will be fun!" Jakk said.

"Come with me," Sheela said.

Between the parking lot and the hotel was a church, perhaps Catholic or Episcopalian but surely not a Baptist church where everybody clapped their hands while singing with such ferocity that it scared mosquitoes in nearby counties. He followed her inside.

The church, empty on a Sunday afternoon, had a solemn feeling, as if quiet itself could echo, cold stone and eternal statues, soft light filtering through stained glass, electric candles flickering in trays. She stood in the front row and he stood beside her. If this was the house of the real Jesus, perhaps, mysterious up there on the cross, well, then Jakk badly wanted to ask the guy about life after death, to be His buddy, to pose for photos at a saviors' convention, to get Him to acknowledge that Jakkanism had sexier churches that enjoyed building-to-building coitus. Maybe Jakk could hire Jesus as a celebrity guest preacher, but what would the guy charge? A sobering inequality sunk in: Jesus could possibly save Jakk, but Jakk could not save Jesus—though Jakk and Sheelabot and Max giving His twin brother's brain a second life on Hugubu could count as a quasi-resurrection, could it not? If only the recreated Jesusbot had been real, then Jakk and Jesus would be full-frontal in-laws. That would make for an interesting Thanksgiving dinner. Too bad.

He wondered what Sheela was thinking. Her beauty filled his senses. Why had she brought him here? He would find out in time. The letter *w* was no longer a mere butt-like letter suitable for locker room jokes but a double-you of she and he, a double-you greater than its individual yous. The Sheela and Jakk double-you emerged like water from hydrogen and oxygen. It was magic.

If love was a molecule, its amazing property was its luckiness. Why was he so lucky? He did not know but he felt luck all around him, a lucky love like a gear that clicks at the right moment or a secret smile of knowing, a silent conspiracy of two hearts, a shared wink, a timely flap of the wings of a tiger swallowtail butterfly sipping from a hyacinth. Love was a light-feathered gift.

Pieces of the jigsaw puzzle of Jakk's life were fitting together. His double-yous were aligning like billiard balls: *w*heels, *w*ardrobe, *w*ealth, *w*eapons, *w*isdom, *w*oman. Song ideas came to mind: *she and me make we; she puts the "ing" into human be-ing.* He would strive to love the whole woman, the whole shebang, the you, the whole you, and nothing but the you, so what if it was corny, ever-wider and ever-longer, past and present and future. She flashed a mischievous smile. What was the whole shebang thinking?

"We should go," she said.

She led them back to their hotel room, moved the DO NOT DISTURB sign to the outer handle, closed the door, and grinned. What she did next was initially baffling: she began ripping the complimentary *USA Today* newspaper to bits.

"Wave like you're in a ticker-tape parade in the Canyon of Heroes," she said.

He shuffled while Sheela cheered and threw confetti over him. The carpet looked like snow had fallen. She interviewed him like a reporter, holding a nonexistent microphone and facing an unseen camera.

"Jakk, congratulations on being the first human to figure out gravity, to fly faster than light, to meet real aliens! How about a shrug for your millions of adoring fans?"

He shrugged with a wide grin. She mimicked reporters with a nonchalant tone of subdued surprise. She was *defining him*—reinflating his ego-balloon while showing him how she would keep their secrets secret. It was how she could deal with his pride. She was an amazing woman.

Her clothes tumbled floorward with the gentle tug of gravity. Would millions of imaginary adoring fans see her wardrobe malfunction? He did likewise. They looked at each other. He tried to quiet his nervousness by telling himself he was simply about to do another experiment, this one to see whether the *uuh* sound would happen as predicted. His 21st AP would demand his full concentration. That she was slowing down sex— pausing like in foreplay to jack-up his excitement—came over him briefly like a passing cloud and then he thought "naw." She would almost certainly choose him over Preppy and while it looked good from his present position, naked on the bed as she closed in like a frisky mare, her blonde mane hanging down—the future would always be uncertain.

The space between their bodies felt alive as if dark energy was choosing to reveal itself. He could almost feel her body before they touched, her undetachable breasts swinging like jello as she became horizontal. If the God program's probe was ogling them, beaming images back to Hugubu, with Max watching and forwarding the videos for use in Jakkanism services, applauding and hooting, so what. Jakk had seen Max and Reena going at it full blast, up close and personal, and now they were even.

Jakk felt his own gravity, hers too, and the pull of physics. He was not a massless flake. He had firmness and force, a solid feeling in his whole body, in his mind and in his penis, which he felt lift off, defying gravity, reaching across the canyon separating the sexes, reaching to Sheela and love and femininity and her hair cascading like a waterfall. He was beginning to get a handle on love, like they should be bouncing in a balloon tent or on a bouncy bed, floating like bubbles or ballet dancers, how love and sex could be stirred like in a tall sweaty glass of lemonade. Soon they might both see the real Jesus.

He went over his sexual checklist like a pilot preparing for takeoff. He remembered the counterclockwise swirl moves with intermittent puffs and beatbox rhythms that worked so nicely on pre-robotic Sheelabot. He would keep searching for ways to give life meaning. Where would they go this summer? Galapagos, glaciers thundering into the ocean, coupla pyramids, Mount Everest (two-person selfie, naked and not freezing courtesy of the everything pills), an uninhabited island with sandy beaches and a bungalow. Maybe they might have a life of wild wet splashes and photo flashes and birthday bashes? He loved her. He loved life. Life was good. He loved being a human.

About the author

Thomas W. Sulcer is a handyman in New Jersey. He can be contacted at tomsulcer @ outlook.com.